GW00836267

Praise f(
The Coalition Reb~~ellion~~ Series

First two books in the series recognized as

***Romantic Times* 200 BEST OF ALL TIME!**

***Lord of the Storm*'s Accolades and Honors:**
Romance Writers of America's RITA Award
Romantic Times Reviewer's Choice Award
Romantic Times Career Achievement Award
National Reader's Choice Award
RRA Book Award
BTC Bookstore Network Award

***Skypirate* Accolades and Honors:**
Romantic Times Reviewer's Choice Award
Romantic Times 5-Star review!

Praise and Awards for Justine Dare Davis
Romance Writers of America's RITA
4-time winner, 7-time finalist
Romantic Times Reviewer's Choice Awards
5-time winner, 19-time nominee
Romantic Times Career Achievement Awards
3-time winner, 6-time nominee
Authored 4 books selected for
"*Romantic Times* 200 BEST OF ALL TIME."

Justine Davis Books from Bell Bridge Books:

The Coalition Rebellion Novels

Book 1: *Lord of the Storm*

Book 2: *Skypirate*

The Kingbird

(A Coalition Rebellion Short Story)

Book 3: *Rebel Prince*

Book 4: *Raider*

Book 4: Gambler

Book 6: Renegade

Also by Justine Davis

Wild Hawk

Heart of the Hawk

Fire Hawk

Renegade

The Coalition Rebellion
Book 6

by

Justine Davis

Bell Bridge Books

Bell Bridge Books
PO BOX 300921
Memphis, TN 38130
Print ISBN: 978-1-61194-950-6

Bell Bridge Books is an Imprint of BelleBooks, Inc.

We at BelleBooks enjoy hearing from readers.
Visit our websites
BelleBooks.com
BellBridgeBooks.com
ImaJinnBooks.com

10 9 8 7 6 5 4 3 2 1

Cover design: Debra Dixon
Interior design: Hank Smith
Photo/Art credits:
Man (manipulated) © Starast | Dreamstime.com
Landscape (manipulated) © Mega11 | Dreamstime.com
Ship (manipulated) © Philcold | Dreamstime.com

:Rtgctr:01:

Dedication

This one's for my wonderful editor, Debra Dixon, who let me take this adventure I love further than I had ever hoped.

Chapter 1

COALITION MAJOR Caze Paledan knew he had reached the tipping point. That point at which all the grim warnings from the Coalition doctors back on Lustros did not outweigh this fierce need for physical action. Any action, as long as there was a lot of it, and it exhausted him. Not in the way lack of sleep exhausted a person; he'd been dealing with sleep deprivation for so long he barely felt it anymore. He wanted—no, needed—to be physically exhausted again, in the way he had not been for far too long.

The two were linked, he knew. He'd had no trouble sleeping when he'd been able to work his body to that point of collapse. Several hours of his own unique brand of training, put together from methods distilled from any opponent who had ever bested him or impressed him, had left his body with no choice but to sleep.

But he'd been unable to do so since that day on Darvis over a year ago, when his vehicle had triggered an explosive device left in a roadway by a vanquished enemy, a sort of farewell volley from a defeated force that had put up only a token resistance anyway.

He supposed, were he as honest with himself as he tried to be, that was part of his irritation at his current situation. To suffer the first serious wound of his career at the hands of an already beaten enemy was a bit ignominious. And another part of that honesty would also have to be that he had made an assumption that cost him; he had trusted the local commander when he said they had no such devices. It had been the last inaccurate information the man would ever pass on, for he had died in the same blast.

All of which was the reason for his more intensive, first-hand study of Ziem and the inhabitants; he did not wish to make another mistake of that magnitude. This one had cost him too dearly.

It is too close to the spine, even the automatons cannot guarantee a safe procedure. But one misstep, Major, one wrong combination of movements, or a well-placed blow, and the shrapnel will shift and sever your spinal cord.

For all his strength, for all the fit power of his body, one wrong move and he would crumple like a shipjack subjected to too much weight.

When they had told him he would live, he had been relieved.

When they had told him how he would have to live, he had rebelled.

There was no other option, the doctors had all agreed. Trying to remove the shard of planium was an almost certain death sentence.

Almost.

He had fastened on that word. "Almost" was not a certainty. And better to die trying than to live a half-life, the kind of life they said he must to survive. And he had taken this post only for the time to regain his strength, for he was certain in the end he would choose the operation no matter the risk.

He had never expected to become so fascinated with this distant, mist-shrouded world. Or its unique, surprisingly resilient people.

He had never thought he would regret dying without knowing what the final result of the battle for Ziem would be. That he was even thinking of it that way, that the final result could be at all in question, he well knew was sacrilege. That he even called it a battle for Ziem would be thought so in some quarters.

But in those quarters, they did not know the Raider.

The medical staff had recommended minimal movement, meaning at most being trapped at a desk, as his best course. But he knew he could not live wearing a desk chain.

What he hadn't realized was that living this way would be nearly as bad. Constantly reminded by the ache, and the occasional sharp jab from the shrapnel that his body was no doubt trying to expel as the foreign object it was. Constantly wondering if this movement or that would shift it that last critical fraction, leaving him paralyzed or dead.

Dead. It had better be dead.

He could think of nothing worse than being totally immobilized. What especially haunted him was the thought that he might be left unable to end himself. For most officers, ending up unable to function would be handled, for they would be of no further use, and thus be discarded. But he had often been told his knowledge of battle and tactics were valuable resources. What if the Coalition decided his knowledge, his experience in battle, required him to be kept alive even when he could no longer move, for his mind alone?

He would have to make arrangements for that. There were ways, he knew, that required nothing but the ability to swallow.

A now-familiar need welled up in him. He fought doing what he knew he wanted to do. But he decided after a moment to give in, because for the first time in his life he had more than a glimmer of understanding. Not of her reasons, for that was beyond his ken, but of the idea of reaching the point at which you truly could no longer go on. When the future you saw was more nightmare than the end you sought.

He crossed the office to the storage room. He'd been thankful that the rebel attack on the council building had not taken down his office, mainly because of what was stored in that closet.

He opened the door, reached in, and grasped the edge of the stretched canvas. The simple frame that had once bordered it had been shattered in the bombing of the taproom, but it had done its job and protected the piece itself. He'd removed it to keep any splinters from damaging the canvas.

He pulled it out carefully. He lifted the arm-span-wide painting and propped it on the chair. He denied even to himself he'd placed the chair for that very purpose.

He stared at the woman in the incredible painting. He could barely credit the taproom keeper's claim that it had been done by a mere art student. And the Coalition would refuse to believe a back of beyond place could produce such a talent at all.

But then, they had also found it impossible to believe a lowly taproom keeper was in fact the Raider, who had brought Coalition efforts on this world to a standstill. The bedamned world that had nothing to recommend it but a vast reserve of planium.

And in the end it did not matter to him whether the Coalition would reach their goals here. What mattered was the woman in this portrait—the vivid, blazingly alive woman with the amazing eyes and the fiery hair. That she had been reduced to the act he had just been contemplating seemed as impossible as everything else about this world.

What seemed the most impossible was her reason. He knew who she was, or rather had been. He had known before he had ever arrived on this world that its one-time leader, the man named Torstan Davorin, had been the one to first incite the population to rebellion. First, but not for long. The Coalition had learned from its failure on Trios to nip such insurrection in the bud and had taken out the fiery orator before the revolt had gathered much momentum. And this woman had been pledged to him, a local custom of binding, for life apparently. By all accounts she had been unable to bear her grief and plunged from Halfhead Scarp, that stark, towering half mountain to the west of Zelos.

That was the part that seemed the most impossible to him. Not the plunge itself, not even that she left four children behind—the Ziemite devotion to such primitive bonds was something he was familiar with from other worlds—but that she had loved the man so much she could not go on without him was the impossible concept.

He—and the Coalition—had long ago relegated that kind of love to the realm of folk tales and imagination.

And yet what else could possibly drive the woman in this portrait, so achingly alive, to take that leap to her death? Not fear, not anger . . . for in fear she would stand, in anger she would fight. He was not certain how he knew this, but he did. However, that left him back at the beginning, the tales of a love so great that the loss of it ended a vibrant life, with nothing left but the formality of physical death. The kind of love the Coalition scoffed at, when it wasn't denying its very existence.

This woman had not only been the mate of this world's most powerful man, she was the mother of the man who had nearly brought the Coalition to its knees on this remote planet. How did a woman with that kind of strength give up?

It had once seemed to him the weakest way out, and therefore not worthy of consideration.

Now he was not so sure.

Now, he could only think of how immense that love must have been, to drive this woman to end her own life when she had had four children who, according to the structure of this world, depended upon her.

He, however, had no one who would miss him or help him leave this world if the worst left him immobile. He'd likely be remembered for his victories, but there would be no one weeping over his grave. The Coalition would go on, and he would soon be nothing more than a few lines in the approved histories. Which was as it should be by Coalition tradition. A simple passing, acknowledged but not dwelt upon. Grief was one of the worst of emotions, ungovernable, useless, and among the first to be forbidden by Coalition edict. And after love, that softest of all emotions, grief was the most ridiculed when encountered on the more primitive planets not yet taught the proper way to deal with such things. He himself thought the two defects were entwined, for the one seemed to set the circumstances for the other. For the Coalition, both were oddities to be studied only to find the best way to quash them, nothing more.

Such emotions had been extracted from him in childhood and replaced by Coalition logic. And yet here he was, staring at a painting of a woman he'd never known, feeling an odd sort of ache that was beyond physical. He knew there was a word for it, even though it, too, had been excised from the Coalition lexicon long ago.

Sadness.

Chapter 2

"WHAT ARE YOU doing?"

Iolana turned from the holoprojector to look at her eldest daughter. Eirlys looked merely curious, and there had been no edge in her voice. In fact, there had not been since she and her love, Brander Kalon, had pledged, as if she were now too happy to concern herself with old angers.

Iolana hoped that was the truth, for it would augur well for her hopes to regain her family. She was making progress. She had achieved forgiveness, but she had not reached the kind of love she wanted yet, with any of her children. She felt a pang of sadness at the thought she might never reach it but refused to let it taint this overture.

"Studying," she answered.

"Studying what?"

She gestured at the holoprojector. "Thanks to Brander, many things. His power system is a wonder." Eirlys smiled, as she always did at the mention of her mate. Which made Iolana add, "When I think of what he could do had he the resources and tools he should have . . ."

"Such abundance wouldn't have been nearly enough challenge for him," Eirlys said as she started around the table to where she could see the holoprojector's screen. "I fear he would have become some eccentric inventor, building things of infinite cleverness but very little use."

Iolana laughed. "I think you would keep him from sinking too far into that."

Her daughter's smile widened. "I would certainly try. I think—" She stopped the moment she could see the document projected on the screen, a lengthy list of awards, medals, and commendations. And at the top of the page, a single name. "You study . . . him?"

"Is it not wise to learn all you can about your enemy?" Iolana asked.

"Our enemy is the Coalition, not one man."

"True enough. But this man is the Coalition on Ziem, at least for now."

"Unless that High Command ship that arrived held an executioner," Eirlys said sourly.

"Indeed."

She wasn't certain if it was her daughter's grim familiarity with Coalition cruelty that disturbed her, or the thought that she could well be right. Paledan's masters did not accept failure, and while most of the Sentinels' successes had occurred on former commander Frall's watch, the biggest of them had occurred since Paledan had arrived. And even though it had been a relatively short time, she knew the Coalition was neither reasonable nor discerning when it came to laying blame.

And yet by everything she had found, Paledan was indeed one of their most heroic officers. What that meant in terms of worlds conquered and innocents slaughtered she did not care to think about just now. She was trying to get the measure of the man, even as she was uncertain why it seemed so important.

"What are your thoughts on him?" she asked her daughter.

"I know what we all know. He is one of their most decorated heroes and was posted here after an injury."

"A battle wound?"

Eirlys nodded. "We believe so, but not having access to any details or reporting, we cannot be sure. Brander found out he chose this over a desk chain at High Command."

"What is your personal assessment of him?"

Eirlys shrugged. "I have never dealt with him directly. Drake and Brander have."

"I have their opinions, but I would like yours."

Drake had told her of his mixed feelings, and his wariness about Paledan's explorations of Ziem. As if he were assessing, studying the landscape for battle purposes. He may not be able to conquer the mist, but he will know the ground beneath it. Drake's words rang in her mind, and she knew how concerned he was. I dread the day when he truly rises to fight us.

When Eirlys didn't speak, Iolana said, "You must have heard things, when you were still in Zelos. Formed an opinion."

"He is Coalition," Eirlys said, as if that said everything. As, perhaps, it did. "But I will say that he seems . . . not fair, but less cruel than his predecessor. Although Brander has said that Paledan himself says he only believes in efficient allocation of time, tools, and energy."

"So he does not devote time to being cruel, as some do?"

Eirlys's mouth curled tightly. "Some such as Jakel?"

"That was the fiend I had in mind, yes."

"No, it seems he does not." Eirlys looked thoughtful. "And I know he has had opportunity, time and again, to hurt the twins, and instead he has protected them."

Iolana nodded. She felt the usual jab of pain. Her youngest children yet refused to acknowledge her as their mother, but even more than her wish to resolve that, she lived in constant dread that their foolhardy fearlessness would end in their deaths.

"So I have heard. I don't know if that should be a relief, or cause for more concern."

"As is everything involving the twins," Eirlys said with a roll of her eyes.

Iolana smiled. Decided to take a chance. "Do not think I do not know how much you did to raise them. You were there for them when their mother shirked her responsibility."

To her relief, her words did not spark the old enmity. "But it was Drake who guided them. Their cleverness, their fearlessness, comes from him."

"And their talent for trouble? Where did that come from?"

Eirlys smiled widely then. "I believe that," she said, "can be directly attributed to my mate."

"I suspected as much."

Eirlys's gaze flicked back to the holoprojection. "Do you study him because he is the Coalition commander here? Or because he has your portrait?"

"I can't deny that is disconcerting."

"But as far as we know, he believes you are dead."

"And I am not certain if that makes it better or worse, either." Her mouth quirked. "Although it is likely for the best that all the Coalition believe Iolana Davorin is indeed dead."

"It must feel odd. The people believe Iolana dead, but the Spirit of the mountain, the mysterious seer and healer, alive. What would they think if they learned not only that Iolana Davorin is alive, but she and the Spirit are one and the same?"

"We must hope they do not, at least not yet."

"Why?"

"I think that is a knowledge best saved for when it might do the most good."

Eirlys considered this, then nodded. "The troops on the mountain, when you helped take out the fusion cannon, apparently believe that they encountered the legendary Spirit in a flare of light, and she . . . put a spell upon them."

It wasn't a question, but Iolana answered it anyway; she would do anything to nurture this tentative reconnecting. "It was not a spell. It was merely a calling upon the power of the mountain to hold them fast. It only lasts a minute or two, but it was enough, in that case."

"Like the hum of the Heart of Ziem?" Eirlys asked, referring to the stone from the heart of this very mountain, the stone that, among other things, sent out a hum to all born of Ziem, which they had used to help Drake and Kye find the trapped Brander and Kade after the ambush.

"In a way, yes." She studied her daughter, wondered if she might be pushing her luck a bit, but said it anyway. "You have a form of the same gift. If you have the desire, I could teach you how to harness it. And use it." Eirlys didn't speak for a moment, and Iolana thought she had indeed asked for too much too soon. "Or if you prefer, Grim could begin the lessons. He has less of the gift, but it is there."

"Is that why you keep him with you?"

"I do not keep him. He stays."

"A fine line, considering he does your bidding at all times."

"Not so fine. Would you have Brander bound to you against his will?"

Her eyes widened. "Never. It would be meaningless."

"Exactly. And your creatures, once they are healed, do you not let them go?"

"Of course. Those who stay choose to . . ."

Iolana nodded as Eirlys's words trailed off in understanding. "Grimbald Thrace is his own man. We do not always agree, but there is always respect. And he is also my friend. We have been through much together, and I would remain his friend even without the ability he has."

"Some have speculated that he is more than a friend."

Iolana sighed. "Naturally. Are you among them?"

"I have . . . wondered."

"I will say only that we are dear, close friends, but nothing more. Anything else to be told is up to Grim."

Eirlys nodded. "He seemed to me to be too much in awe of you for those speculations to be accurate. I shall quash them when I hear them, if it is your—and his—wish."

She liked that her daughter included Grim in that offer. "I would appreciate that. Grim you will have to—"

"Ask myself." Eirlys smiled suddenly. "I look forward to it. He is

7

speaking to us more and more. I think we should feel honored."

Iolana smiled. "I believe you mean that."

"I do. Grim is a remarkable man. Different, but remarkable. I am glad you had each other."

This was more than Iolana had ever expected. She, too, was glad she'd had Grim's steady presence, although that had not been the reason she'd helped him when she'd found him injured and in agony all those years ago. A favor he had returned tenfold.

But she was gladder yet—and a little stunned—that Eirlys had just implied that she was also pleased that she herself had not died after all. Her surprise must have shown, for Eirlys gave her a rueful smile.

"Most of my anger was at my situation, being unable to join the fight. And now . . . if I think of losing Brander as you lost father, I . . ."

Her voice trailed off. Iolana smiled gently. "You have walked in another's shoes and learned, my daughter. I am proud of you."

Eirlys smiled back, still somewhat tentatively.

Iolana turned back to the holoprojector. Tapped at it to turn the page. This time an image appeared. And for a moment she forgot to breathe. She simply stared at the picture, caught by eyes that seemed too vividly green not to have been altered in the image.

It looked like an official portrait, a man in a Coalition-crisp uniform, the left chest strewn with medals. His hair was militarily short, and touched with silver, just enough to add gravitas to a face that was nearly too perfectly chiseled and strong.

That man also did not look happy. Whether it was the formal garb or impatience at having to pose, it fairly radiated even from the still image. And she sensed something else, under the surface. Weariness? No . . . pain. From the wound that sent him here?

"That is truly him?" Although the label, Major Caze Paledan, was clear, she couldn't seem to stop herself from voicing the words.

"It is."

"He is . . . compelling."

"He is more so in person."

"Do you know how long ago he was injured?"

"I know only that it was on Darvis, before he came here. And that he was obviously not incapacitated permanently."

But not healed, either. It came to her with that piercing certainty she had learned to never doubt.

When Eirlys had gone, she went back to her perusal of all the files the Sentinels had accumulated. They had more than she'd expected, because her ever-wise son had put the word out to anyone who joined them to bring what they had, even though at the time they had not had the power capability to even look at them. But Brander—also now her son, she thought with a smile—had remedied that as he had so much else. Including her daughter's mood. Which also made her smile. But it faltered a bit as she acknowledged her children hadn't really needed her at all. Their choice of mates proved them quite capable of doing without her advice.

She called up the image once more, of that man in the Coalition uniform. An image she should hate on sight, and yet could not seem to. Instead she studied his features and saw no cruelty—the thick hair cut short, the strong, intelligent look of his forehead and brow, the stern expression softened just slightly by a mouth she could only imagine in a smile, no matter that Brander had told her he did, on occasion, actually laugh. And the eyes. Those vivid green eyes . . . were they common on his world, the norm, as blue eyes were here on misty Ziem?

His home world. Lustros, the spawning ground of the Coalition. The thought made her shudder inwardly. She knew little of the world itself, only that it had become the production center for Coalition officers. And a producer it was, a factory of sorts. A factory producing fighters, not families. This man would never know the feeling of being a part of a family, which held you as nothing else could. Even when the ties were strained unto breaking, as hers had been, they were still there.

And for that, to her own amazement, she felt sorry. Pity, for not just a Coalition officer, but the man in charge of keeping Ziem subjugated.

Weary of sitting, she reached out to turn off the holoprojector. Stopped. Once more looked at the image of a Coalition hero. The man she should hate.

Instead she was curious. And the moment she realized that, she finished the action of hitting the switch. The image vanished.

Would that the Coalition and the man himself were so easy to be rid of.

Chapter 3

"I AM NOT CERTAIN this is wise, my lady."

Iolana laughed at Grim's carefully chosen words. "I," she said, "am fairly certain it is entirely unwise, my tall friend."

"And yet you are determined to do it."

"Fairly," she said.

"Will you at least consult with Drake?"

She studied the man who had been with her from the day he had pulled her from the Racelock, sodden and broken in so many ways. Little had she known years before that she had changed her future, when she'd healed a frightened young man with a viciously broken leg. That he'd not been from Ziem did not matter to her then, and when she learned he'd been abandoned here, she'd felt bound to him as more than just healer.

"Or if you won't consult your son," Grim added, "at least . . . the Raider?"

"There you have a point. I would not wish to interfere with any of his plans."

"He has said he thinks it best the Sentinels stay hidden for a while, in the aftermath, while the Coalition is hunting so fiercely."

"And I agree. But I am not a Sentinel."

"No, you are something even more valuable."

"I think my children might argue that with you, my friend."

"Not so much, anymore."

She smiled at that. "I hope you are right, Grim. I do feel as if I have made progress. I am not where I want to be, but I am beyond where I hoped to be by now."

"Then may I suggest you not endanger that?"

Grim argued so doggedly only if he felt very strongly about his point, and so she said, "I will discuss it with Drake."

"And if he says no?"

"That will depend on whether the no comes from my son, or the Raider."

After a moment, Grim nodded, and she turned back to her preparations. When nearly an hour later she was finished, she called him back for an inspection.

"Will I pass?" she asked.

He looked at her critically. "Away from here I believe you will, my lady, to even the most discerning eye."

She nodded, pleased. Then they set off for Drake's quarters. As she passed through the large cavern, where many were gathered during this respite from the fight, she drew some curious glances. But not one of them held recognition, which both pleased and concerned her. If they thought her a stranger, they should confront her. Then again, she was with Grim, who was familiar to them.

They encountered Drake and Kye coming out, looking as if they'd put this lull in the fight to very pleasant use. She allowed herself a brief moment to hope that one day there would be that grandchild she had asked him for.

"Grim," Drake acknowledged the man, then glanced at her. "Who have you brought us?"

"A visitor," she said, using the inflection of someone from the flats.

Drake frowned. "A dangerous journey for only a visit."

"And if I wished to join your ranks?"

"We take in whoever is willing to lend their skills, whatever they may be. Have you someone here already?"

"Yes," Iolana said. Then she looked up at the man beside her and smiled. Grim sighed in capitulation. Drake frowned. And then Kye gasped.

"Iolana!"

Drake blinked. Looked back at her. Frowned again.

"I see it took an artist's eye," Iolana said, in her normal voice.

Realization dawned on her son's face. "It is you."

"Amazing what some bark dye and enhancers can do, is it not?"

She had darkened her most recognizable feature, her hair, to a brown nearly as deep as Kye's, and pulled it up into a smooth knot at the back of her head. Then she had used what she had in the way of tints and other facial enhancers to recontour her features so that she looked not enhanced but different.

"Amazing indeed," Drake agreed.

"I am more interested in the reason than the results," Kye said.

"As am I. Why have you done this?" Drake asked.

Iolana drew herself up and faced this tall, strong man she was so very proud to call her son. She was not used to asking for permission, but he was also the Raider, and this was his command. "I am going to Zelos. I ask your blessing."

Drake stared at her. She both saw and sensed the rejection surging in him. But she knew it was the Raider, not her son, who responded.

"Why?"

"I am more than willing to do anything you believe necessary while there," she said, "but my reason is my own."

He was still frowning as he studied her. "It is bad enough Brander insists on frequenting the city, even if his reasoning is sound."

She thought about that for a moment then nodded. "True. If Brander has nothing to do with the Raider, then there is no reason for him not to be there, and if he suddenly vanishes, it will all but convict him."

"Exactly. Do you have as valid a reason? This would risk much."

"But not the Sentinels. I am a woman from the flats, unremarkable, ordinary, seeking word of survivors. And I can gather useful information while I am there."

"Assuming," Drake said flatly, "you return alive."

"I might be harder to kill than you think."

For a brief moment, an old anger flashed in her son's eyes. "I think I have a fairly good idea of how hard you are to kill." She didn't flinch, although it took an effort. And after that brief moment, the look faded. "My apologies," Drake said. "I thought that behind me."

"Such pain as I caused is difficult to forget."

His mouth twisted wryly at one corner. "It would be easier to stay angry did you not take the blame so readily."

"What else am I to do? Blame someone else for my own horrible choice?"

"Many would," Kye said quietly. "And for that I admire you."

Iolana shifted her gaze to the woman who had the heart and courage to love both Drake and the Raider. "I assure you, the feeling is mutual."

Drake sighed, and it sounded much as Grim's had, a giving in. "And how can I deny one who so esteems my pledged mate?"

She knew she had won, but Iolana looked back at him and said steadily, "Drake could not, but the Raider could."

"And you would comply?"

He said it dryly, as if he expected her to say no. And so she chose her words and her tone carefully. "His wisdom and leadership has brought us to great success. He has my complete respect. Thus . . . yes, I would."

For a moment Drake looked away, as if embarrassed. But he quickly regained control. "You will find Zelos—what is left of it—much changed."

"I expect as much. If I see no one that I once knew alive, I will not be surprised."

She saw him draw in a breath, and then nod. He glanced at Grim. "You accompany her?"

"It was my wish—"

"But I forbade it. He will fly me to the edge of the high valley, but he will wait there. Grim is too recognizable, his height undisguisable. And there could yet be someone who remembers him, given he is not Ziem born."

"Agreed," Drake said. "I will trust, Spirit, that you will find a way to come back safely."

She knew it was the Raider speaking now, to someone who had been of use. "I am glad that is of concern to you."

"It is." And then, just for a moment, he was her son again. "I would hate to lose my mother again."

Moisture welled up in her eyes. It was enough that she almost reconsidered. But she had been a coward once, abandoning her duty to avoid her own pain. Something this man who had once been the babe she had carried would never do. And for that, she owed him whatever help she could give.

His needs would come first, she thought. And her own mission after. Or not at all, if it came to that.

"Are there things you wish to know from Zelos?" she asked briskly. "Things I should look for or observe? Or try and draw from those I encounter?"

Again it was the Raider who gave her a short list of things; the condition of the council building and the docks they had blown up as diversion to cover their evacuation to this stronghold. And the landing zone she would have to pass, and any sign that the foundation for the fusion cannon they had destroyed was being made ready for a replacement. Plus any rumors that she might hear that could be worth following up.

"And if you come across any collaborators with the enemy that would be good to know," Kye said rather sourly.

"I will see Eirlys before I go," she said. "Perhaps she will loan me one of her birds who knows the way back here, should I come across anything of urgency."

Drake nodded. She left them then and went in search of her gentle yet fierce daughter. She found her, as expected, in the sanctuary Brander had made for her, with the injured and ill animals he had risked—and nearly lost— his life to bring to her.

Eirlys turned when she came in. Gave her a puzzled look, the same that she had seen in the cavern, the look of someone seeing a stranger in an unexpected place.

"Hello," she said, back to using that accent of someone from the flats.

"Hello," Eirlys said, not warily but still hesitant. "I don't believe we've met." A smile then. "Have you brought me a new lodger?"

Iolana realized in that moment that she had just experienced something few mothers had, the novelty of seeing how her children—half of them anyway, she wasn't about to risk showing herself to the twins just now— reacted to strangers. Interestingly, both she and Drake had responded in an almost identical fashion, cautious yet welcoming. Drake perhaps more wary, but that was to be expected.

They did not react like a populace at war. At least not here in their stronghold, and she felt a burst of satisfaction that this, at least, she had given them, this place to be as they had once been, a kind, welcoming people.

"It appears you are nearly full, so it is as well I have not found you another creature in need of your special aid."

Eirlys smiled. Her daughter was truly a lovely woman, she thought proudly. But then her expression changed; the smile remained, but her brow furrowed anew.

"I do know you," she said, her tone that of one who is not quite convinced yet.

Iolana decided more harm than good would be done keeping up the pretense, and her relationship with Eirlys was not so strong that she wished to risk any further damage. She spoke in her natural voice.

"We are acquainted, Eirlys. But if even you are not certain, then my disguise is effective."

"Mother!"

Just hearing the appellation, even in such a shocked tone, warmed her.

"Your hair," Eirlys exclaimed. "You've masked it. And your face . . . it is changed as well. What is this for?"

"I am going into Zelos."

Eirlys stared at her. "But you have not been to Zelos since . . ." Her voice trailed off, and a doubt that struck pain deep into Iolana's heart came into her voice as she finished in a whisper, "Have you?"

She recognized the source of the pain immediately. "I have not," she said quickly, firmly. "I dared not risk it, to be so close to you, and not come to you? I could not have borne it."

The look of doubt faded; in this, at least, her daughter believed her. "The price of your vision is high," Eirlys said, her voice soft now.

"Higher than I ever wished to pay," Iolana admitted. While it had been her heart that had driven her to try to end the life she could no longer bear, it had been her vision, that blessed, cursed ability to See, that had kept her away after she had survived. Knowing it had been necessary, for her son to become the man he must for Ziem, had made it no easier. "But to have you understand this is a great relief."

Eirlys smiled. "I have understood much, since we worked together to save Brander. And more since he pledged to me. But why go to Zelos?" Eirlys asked. "And why now?"

She chose the second question to answer. "We are in a quiet time just now, while your brother determines our course from here." She smiled. "I think he did not expect the trap he set to work quite as well as it did."

"I think," Eirlys said rather grimly, "he half expected to die."

"And yet he did it anyway."

"Because he is the Raider."

"The first son of Ziem."

"And that," Eirlys said with a small sigh of understanding, "is why you left him alone, to become what he had to become. And now that we're in such sweet agreement, will you answer the first question? Why go to Zelos?"

"Drake wishes information on the state of things," she said.

"Mmm. And for that he could ask Brander. Or any number of scouts. With more experience at going unnoticed, and more awareness of what is needed."

Iolana didn't take offense, for she knew it was true. "But perhaps not . . . certain abilities to deduce things others might be hiding."

"Does that not require physical contact, that skill of yours?"

"Yes," she admitted, "but only the merest brush."

"You 'brush' the wrong trooper and you will need that freeze-them-in-their-own-footprints skill," Eirlys said with a grimace.

"It is well that I have it then," Iolana said lightly.

Her daughter studied her for a silent moment. And then she said, softly, "I know your real reason."

Something in those eyes so like her father's warned Iolana, but she kept silent.

"You go to learn more of him. Paledan."

And so. Her daughter was as clever as she was beautiful. Or her inherited gift was expanding, now that she knew it existed. Iolana knew it would do more harm than good to deny the accuracy of her guess.

"If the commander of all Coalition forces on Ziem kept a portrait of you in his office, would you not wish to know if you should be . . . concerned?"

Eirlys's mouth quirked. "I cannot imagine not being concerned, in such a case."

"Then you understand."

Eirlys sighed. "I should go with you. Two unarmed women of Ziem would seem no threat."

"Unarmed?"

"Visibly," Eirlys amended, to Iolana's great amusement.

"I cannot tell you how my heart rejoices to hear your offer. But you are too recognizable, having so recently lived among them."

She knew her point was valid, and before Eirlys could suggest she take on the same sort of disguise, she asked her favor.

"I did wish to ask something of you, however."

"What?"

"One of your birds as messenger, should I happen across something urgent."

Eirlys looked thoughtful. "Runner is the swiftest."

Iolana shook her head. "I do not want the responsibility of Brander's darling. One of the others who has learned to return here will do."

Eirlys's smile then was almost a grin. "She has good judgment, that bird. Although it took him a while to realize it."

"All in its own time," Iolana said, her own smile showing she meant much more than Brander's acceptance of a tiny creature's adoration.

Eirlys selected a bird, lighter in color than Runner, yet still a rich gray. "He is the next best," she said. "And with his color he nearly vanishes in the mist."

"I can see he would." She took the tiny cage. The bird had settled in without complaint, for it was lined with soft cloth and he had several seeds to work on.

"He will be happy in the pocket of your cloak," Eirlys said. "Have you the message paper needed to fit in his case?"

Iolana nodded; she'd picked that up from the table in Drake's quarters. "I hope that I will not need him to fly."

"As do I." Eirlys gave her mother a steady look. "I have a wish for a long period of quiet before the battle begins again."

"As does your mate, I'm sure. Make the most of it, my girl," Iolana said softly.

She slipped the bird and cage into her pocket. As she made her way to the cave that served as a hangar for the air rovers, she was smiling. Hope filled her, that one day she would again be part of the family she had never stopped loving.

Chapter 4

PALEDAN DECIDED he would walk the distance to the landing zone. It would be more fitting of his rank to order a conveyance with a driver, but he didn't even think of that. He needed all the exercise he could manage, to regain his full strength after his injury. He also needed the time, the distance, and the exertion to get his mind back under control. So he could stop thinking of peculiar things like the idea that if he ordered the crews repairing the landing pads to work around the clock, it might occur to them to wonder how, exactly, their lot was any different from the enslaved miners ordered to do the same.

As he walked, he found himself looking at the destruction of what had once been a busy, if not Coalition-level efficient, city thriving on the success they'd gained by utilizing their resources. He knew life had been good here—despite the bedamned mist—by how easily they had fallen. They had, as many before them had, been lulled into thinking that what they had needed no maintenance, no defense. The peace they had found had lulled them into ignoring the basic law of the universe, that those who were strong took from those who were not.

And yet this place, this soft, unprepared place, grown lazy by feeding on its own success, had somehow produced one of the most magnificent fighters he'd ever come across. And that man's success had emboldened even those he passed on the ruined streets to look him in the eye rather than show the usual cowed diffidence of a conquered people.

This, he thought, was the difference. In all the victories to his credit, he had been at the head of the invading force, leading the battle, deciding, moving the troops like men on a game board. A much larger, more complex and risky game of chaser, played out with lives and land, the outcome of the gamble depending on the skill of the adversaries. Such as Brander Kalon, his one-time chaser opponent, another man from this shrouded world who had surprised him.

Here, unlike the battles of his past where he was above it all, victorious and then moving on to the next, he was down among the people, not simply maneuvering troops indicated by markers on a map. They were not simply targets anymore, but living, breathing people.

He was charged with keeping control while at the same time keeping the miners, the only ones who knew how to safely extract pure, usable planium, working. He had had to deal directly with the people of Ziem.

He could not deny it was different. He refused to think this was a softening in him; it was merely that, different. And now that he'd realized it, it was only a matter of adjusting his thinking. That had ever been his way, and it had never failed him.

And yet you cannot seem to stop yourself from staring at the portrait of a woman you never knew, a woman long dead. A portrait of no use, trumpeting no glory to the Coalition, and thus not allowed to exist in that world.

He gave an inward shake of his head. It was only because he was now on the bridge over the river they called the Racelock, the river that had carried her away after her death plunge, that he thought of her.

If he looked to the northwest he could see the Halfhead Scarp, where it had happened.

Where she had done it, to herself.

It still seemed impossible to him, that the life so vivid in that artist's rendering could have been snuffed out of her own will. But then, neither could he conceive of an emotion as powerful as that thing some called love. How could a person allow another to become so important to them that they could not go on when the person was taken from them? It was, as the Coalition taught, illogical, irresponsible, and unlawful to value any one person above the whole.

Perhaps it was that which truly fascinated him. It was a matter of study only, an analyzing of the oddity that had him so captivated by that image.

It was a comforting thought, but Caze Paledan had never been one to lie to himself, and he knew it was more than that. What it was, he could not put a name to. He only knew that destroying the portrait would not cure him of it, for it was committed to his memory now, and he would ever be able to call it up in every detail, just as he could call up the map of a battlefield.

Which is where you need to return. Much better to risk death by old wound or new than to languish here acting as no more than an administrator.

He realized he had stopped at the bridge railing, with the rapidly flowing river below and the towering cliff of Halfhead in the distance. A sharp jab of inwardly directed anger made him turn on his heel and continue his crossing at a more rapid pace. One citizen stumbled on the uneven surface—the bridge had taken some hits as well, and would need repair—and brushed against him. The woman, dark-haired and wearing a long cloak, stepped back with a small gasp, lowering her head.

Her reaction somehow jabbed him again. "Be at ease, woman. I do not condemn people for a stumble," he snapped.

It was only after they had both continued on that he realized he was rubbing at his arm, as if the contact had been somehow charged. He stopped, turned, and looked back. Had the woman done something? Jabbed him with some poison-laden needle? It had been known to happen.

She was nowhere in sight. Suspicion spiked, and he wondered if in a few more steps he would feel the burn of some lethal toxin.

He wondered if he would care.

But he felt nothing, and after another moment of fruitlessly scanning for the woman in the cloak, he went on.

DEAR EOS!

Iolana leaned against the one still-standing wall of the bell tower, drawing in deep breaths. She closed her eyes for a moment, willing her heartbeat to slow.

Never in all the years she'd been privy to this reading of people had she felt such a thing. True, she had opened the channel and intended to take all she could discern, but the merest brush against that man and it was as if a flooding conduit had opened. It was the sign of a very powerful mind, and it would take her a long, quiet time to sort it all out. Then would come the assigning of meaning, and with someone she did not know interpretation of what she'd received was a tricky matter.

But one thing she'd plucked from his mind had earned that label of urgent, and when she could move again she darted into the ruin of the bell tower. She carefully lifted the small cage from the pocket of her cloak. The bird cooed at her, giving her a bright-eyed look as if he knew he was about to be released. She drew out the paper she had taken, pre-sized to fit into the tiny tube. She wrote quickly, rolled the message as tightly as she could, and with an inward smile for the daughter who had revived this ancient method, she lifted the bird out of the cage and slipped the furled paper into the small cylinder attached to his leg. Then she walked to the gaping hole where the north wall had once stood.

"To Eirlys, my sweet," she whispered, and gently tossed him to the air. In an instant the graybird's wings unfolded and he took flight. And an instant later he was indiscernible from the mist.

The most crucial thing done, she turned back into the cover of the ruin. There was so much, more than she'd ever expected to gain from such a brief, brushing touch. Neither had she ever experienced the kind of snap and crackle that had come with the rush. Both Drake and Brander were warily admiring of the man, and it seemed they were correct.

She would need Drake's help with this, for amid the rush had been military matters, plans, protocols, and while she was certain they would be of use, her knowledge of that kind of detail was limited. Her son, she was sure, would be better able to interpret these. But she'd gotten enough to know that, insanely, this man was the only thing standing between Ziem and the Coalition's worst. And that he had stood down even some of his superiors, who wished to destroy them and deal with the aftermath. What she didn't know was why. It might be there, amid the rush, but she would need time to discover it.

And Brander would need to know that he was in the Major's mind, that there was suspicion there. He must take great care now. Thankfully, there wasn't a trace of Eirlys in what she'd gotten, and she would tell him this as well.

Not so the twins, however. They had been there, near the surface. But not in a suspicious way, more in the nature of a question he had not resolved, which in itself was irksome to him. But there were shadings to that as well, something she sensed was personal to the man. She stored that away to be examined when she was back at the stronghold and could retreat to a place of calm where she could analyze the flood she'd gotten bit by bit.

But one thing she could not store away for future study, and it took her breath away. It had been so powerfully, clearly uppermost, so strong she knew it occupied a large, active part of Major Caze Paledan's thoughts. And as clearly as if it were before her and she were staring at it herself, she could see it.

The portrait.

Her portrait.

She had thought to spend more time, perhaps gather more information that might be of use, but she knew her capacity well, and she had reached it. Likely overflowed it, with that unexpectedly huge burst from Paledan.

In one way she was glad that she had all this now flooding her mind, for it left her little time to dwell upon or mourn the state of the city she loved.

Chapter 5

"USE THE RUBBLE from the council building," Paledan ordered.

The lieutenant in charge of the repair crew blinked. "Sir?"

"Was I not clear?"

"No, sir. It is only that the distance to transport the material will slow the process."

He marked the lieutenant—Stron according to his uniform—as another who perhaps had a functioning brain. "It will. Especially when you take the time to be sure most of Zelos sees that we are repairing our landing zone with pieces of their most revered building."

The lieutenant's expression changed to one of understanding. "Understood, sir. I will see to it, by route and noise."

And a quick brain, Paledan thought. He would remember the name.

He made his way to the hanger on the edge of the zone. Snapped an order for an air rover and pilot to head for the mines. The nearest, a man who had flown him satisfactorily before, threw a salute as he volunteered and headed quickly to the closest craft. Several other men stopped what they were doing, and the sergeant among them spoke diffidently.

"I have only a half-dozen men to act as guards, sir. I can have a full platoon within—"

"Not necessary, sergeant." If he couldn't deal with a mining crew with less than a full platoon, he truly had lost his touch. He glanced at the troopers beside the sergeant. Recognized one.

"You were at the council building, the day of the bombing."

"Yes, sir."

"You rescued several of your comrades."

"Many helped, sir."

"Why did you not pursue the perpetrators?"

The man paled, but remained in place. "I had been in the compound, sir. I had no idea who or where they were. I did know where my comrades were."

"The Coalition has little use for such judgment decisions." The man went paler. But he held his ground. And Paledan smiled. "But I do. You're with me. Pick two others to accompany us."

Breathing again, the man gave a sharp—and relieved—"Yes, sir!"

He did not relish what he must do next. That he once would have did not escape him.

Perhaps, he thought, there was something in the mist that befouled this place. Perhaps, for all it seemed more annoying than harmful, there was something in it that affected more than vision. Perhaps breathing it in had some deleterious mental effect that only appeared with time. Perhaps that was the explanation not only for his own mental state, but for why the troops that had survived the assault on the fusion cannon were to this day unable to explain what had really happened, but only to repeat the fantastical tale that they had seen a glowing presence, heard a thunderous command to hold fast, and instantly been unable to move, as if frozen to the very rock itself.

But there were those who had been here longer than he that showed no sign that being here had affected them. But he did not know what they had been like before his arrival, except as evidenced in their records. Which were pitiful enough; the best were not sent to this remote world which had been deemed beaten.

Which explained why Frall had been assigned.

His own sardonic thought nearly made him laugh. And that in itself had him wondering about his state of mind again and the mist's effect on him.

He would ask Brakely when he returned. He, at least, would be honest. And he had been with him so long he would notice a change. Or at least, any outward sign that might have slipped through.

But right now, he must deal with the miners and their—

He broke off his own thoughts when he realized he was rubbing at his arm again. Not because he was still feeling anything; there was no soreness or even a tingle. The woman had not stabbed him, or pricked him with some needle to poison him when she had brushed against him. There truly was no lingering aftereffect. It had been merely a bump between two people in a hurry. It could even have been his fault. He had been preoccupied with a host of things.

It was nothing. And yet he couldn't quite put out of his mind that odd sensation generated when she'd touched him.

"WE ARE—"

"Bored. And—"

"You know—"

"What happens—"

"When we are bored," the twins finished in unison.

Iolana watched Drake as he looked down at his siblings. She had come in just as the pair had approached him. He looked, she thought, much rested. He also was beginning to act a bit restlessly. She had asked him about that yesterday.

We have struck a great blow, but that is all.

You—and the Sentinels as well—have well earned a respite. Let the Coalition expend themselves searching.

But at what point does it turn upon us and make them more likely to destroy all of Ziem's people in their frustration?

She had had no answer to that. She could only tell him that she would sense that turning point, if indeed all of her people were at risk.

But right now, she needed to talk to Drake.

She looked at the twins. They glanced at her, and then Lux looked back again, frowning.

"You have changed yourself," the girl said.

"I had reason."

"To spy?" Nyx asked.

"Clever boy."

"It is a good disguise." Lux said it in the tone of one rendering a final judgment. Iolana nearly smiled.

"I know you can learn nothing from your mother," she said, "but perhaps the Spirit might have more to teach?" She had mentioned she would like to discover if they had any of the skills she had apparently passed on to Eirlys, and they had seemed interested.

As usual, Nyx looked wary, Lux thoughtful. The girl looked at her twin who, after a moment, shrugged. Lux looked back at Iolana.

"Perhaps," the girl said.

"Then give me a moment to speak with your brother, and I will meet you at my home. Do you remember the way?"

She deserved the scornful look she got from them both, but she had intended it so; there was nothing so guaranteed to send them off than an opportunity to prove an adult lacking. They were gone at a run almost instantly.

"You are learning their ways," Drake observed as he watched them go.

"It is that or be forever at their mercy."

"Indeed." He turned to look at her. "I thank you for the warning to the miners."

"You were able to get word to them?"

He nodded. "Pryl and Eirlys got there quickly. They managed to get everything hidden before Paledan arrived."

She nodded, although it was an effort not to wince at the thought of her barely-of-age daughter undertaking such a mission. But Eirlys knew these mountains nearly as well as the old man, and was strong and agile enough for the trip. And it had been crucial that the miners who were doing their best to sabotage the mining process and slow the Coalition's supply of planium, not be caught with their hidden tools and devices.

"I know you do not like the idea—"

"She is a Sentinel," Iolana said.

"Yes."

She studied him for a moment. "I am surprised you did not wish to go yourself. You have been . . . restless of late."

"I did wish," he said wryly. "But having Pryl or even Eirlys seen would be one thing, the Raider quite another."

"You are wise. Although I know it is difficult for you to stand down."

His mouth twisted. "Very. Now, you have something else for me? Was your gambit worth the risk?"

"Yes." *To me, at the least.*

"Shall we go to my quarters?"

She followed him through the cavern.

"A few things, although the trip to search the mines was the only critical one. The rest is more in the nature of . . . illumination."

"Such as?"

"Paledan expected to be recalled and perhaps executed after the ambush."

Drake blinked. "Even at his level?"

She nodded. "And he has stalled them—I do not understand why—but eventually he expects the Coalition order to eliminate all Ziemites."

"I . . . see."

"There is more—plans, protocols—but I cannot interpret them. You will be able to, I'm sure."

"Before we get to that," Drake said, and she recognized the tone that had crept into his voice, "am I to understand you actually made contact with the man? Physical contact, to get such a reading?"

"I merely brushed his arm."

And I felt . . . whatever that was.

Drake's voice dropped to a near whisper. "Are you yet suicidal, then?"

She winced; she could not help it. Nor could she blame him for the thought. But she answered steadily. "I was but a frightened woman from the flats he had never met before. He saw nothing but my cloak."

"He is a very observant man."

"Yes." She moved so that she brushed against her son's arm, a bare moment of touch. "But the contact was no more than that."

"He is a well-trained fighter, a man who expects an attack from any quarter. You think he did not notice?"

"He noticed. And assessed. And in the moment I had to appraise, he deemed me no threat. As I was not." *Be at ease, woman. I do not condemn people for a stumble.*

"Not in the way he is accustomed to, perhaps." He said it rather wryly, and she decided to take it as a compliment.

"He is also," she said, "a very intelligent man. So much so that I marvel he has come as far as he has in the Coalition."

"Only to end up in a mainly administrative post on a backwater planet few not native to it can bear for long? Most in his place would consider this a harsh punishment."

"He has found diversions. He is, as Brander has said, curious, and as you said, learning much, especially about Ziem. I do not know if this bodes well or ill."

"Is one of those diversions the portrait he holds?"

She had not intended to discuss that, for she was still processing the intensity of the burst she had gotten about that. But neither would she lie to her son. "Yes." She left it there. "And it is true that he admires you. A great deal."

"He has always respected the Raider, where Frall did not."

"Yes, he admires the Raider. But he . . . *liked* the taproom keeper. And was surprised by that."

Drake looked oddly disconcerted, as if he were just as surprised.

"And Brander? Did you get anything of him?"

She knew he was concerned about the danger his second might be in if he were to continue his own charade that he was nothing but a wastrel gambler, so she answered carefully, with the caution that, as always, this was her interpretation of what she had sensed.

"I don't believe he has fully formed suspicions yet, but he questions that anyone so clever could be content with the life he presents to have."

"And since when has the Coalition worried about the contentedness of their conquered worlds?" Drake asked rhetorically, sourly.

"Contention valid," she admitted. "But he admires the deception you managed to carry off so well. Admires it in a way that suggests he has some experience with keeping his true self masked."

Drake looked thoughtful, much as Lux did. The likeness made her smile inwardly. "You know Brander and I have both thought there is much beneath his Coalition surface."

"I believe you are right." She drew in a deep breath and went on. "He is also very aggravated that they have been unable to find us." At Drake's smile she said, "Yes, but I got an image, the briefest flash, of his view of Ziem should they not find us. A smoking ruin, as far as the eye can see, only the mines left intact. I believe, if they could mine the planium themselves, it would already be so."

"They will be able to, in time," Drake said. "They will someday find a way to adapt their equipment to the mist, learn to read the mines, learn how to keep the quisalt separate, and whatever else it will take. They are not stupid."

"But when it comes to matters of innovation, they move with the speed of any huge, lumbering thing. Thank Eos."

"We must have warning, when they reach that point. There are places the people can shelter that might save them. And unless they are utter fools, they will not risk taking out this mountain, for fear of damage to the mines and their own facilities."

"Yes. And I still believe I will know when all of Ziem is in imminent danger."

"I hope that you are right. Is there more?"

"I spoke with several of the people who remain in Zelos." Few enough overall that it nearly broke her heart. "They are inspired to continue by the Raider's success. The supplies we have sent also give them hope. They will hang on for a while yet, thanks to you."

"Thanks to the Raider," he said, as if it were someone else. She supposed he must feel that way sometimes.

"Several also told me that Paledan could have taken action against them, even ordered their execution by Coalition standards. And yet, he did not."

Drake's brow furrowed. "By those Coalition standards, that would be seen as a weakness. I do not know what it signifies in this man."

"He does seem to be an exception to many rules," she said neutrally. "Now, let me give you what logistical details I gleaned, before I lose them."

Drake nodded and, as she spoke, began to make notes.

Chapter 6

"SIR?"

"Sit, Brakely," Paledan said, gesturing to the chair opposite his desk. "I must ask you something. And I would like your usual honest answer, please."

"Of course," his aide said, looking puzzled, but not wary. He sat, and Paledan got right to his point.

"Have you noticed . . . a change in me since we've been here?"

Brakely frowned. "I'm not certain what you mean, sir. This is an . . . unusual kind of posting for you, and therefore different in many ways." He looked almost anxious as he asked, "Are you not feeling well? Your wound was grievous and—"

He cut Brakely off with a shake of his head. "It is not that."

"I know it yet . . . troubles you."

"Some days it aches like hades," Paledan said, knowing there was no danger in admitting that to this man who had been of inestimable aid to him during the days after his injury. "But it is more a . . . mental status question."

Brakely blinked. "You are the sanest man I have ever known, even if—" His aide cut himself off this time.

"The door is closed, Brakely," he said, their long-established shorthand for the promise what was being discussed would go no further, nor have repercussions.

Still, Brakely shifted uncomfortably before going on. "I was going to say even if that is little valued of late by the High Command."

Paledan stared, then laughed. "I have ever admired your ability to condense things to the essence."

Looking relieved, Brakely studied him for a moment. "May I ask you something, sir?"

"As you will," he said, curious. That bedamned curiosity that seemed to have only grown since his arrival here. Perhaps it was fed by the noxious mist.

"I have often thought, despite the fact that you are a warrior among warriors—and that is not flattery," he added when Paledan shifted in his chair.

"What skills I have come from good reflexes, long training, and fitness. Your question?"

"I have thought that you . . . in a different time and place, perhaps would have had another calling."

He was truly interested now. "Such as?"

"You . . . think. Deeply. I could picture you as a . . . philosopher, were such people allowed."

You have the mind of a thinker, Paledan. A sage. You had best bury it, if you wish to survive in the Coalition.

The words of his first instructor echoed in his head. He had been but a child, and still the old man had seen it. He had also, rather than take the normal step of tagging him as potentially dangerous, focused on what else he had observed.

You are clever at tactics, you have strength already, and a quickness unlike any I have seen in a long time. I will work with that, you work with suppressing that curiosity of yours, and we will see what we can make of you.

It was barely a week later that he had learned the size of the gift the old man had given him; another student, with a similar tendency to question, to ask, but without Paledan's physical abilities, was pulled from the ranks and his mind blanked, his conscious life ended practically before it had begun. He'd been sent off to one of the slave colonies before night had fallen.

"I am sorry if I have offended, sir," Blakely said, snapping him out of the memory.

"You have not," Paledan said. "But I would thank you not to spread the idea around."

His aide's eyes widened. "Of course not, sir. It's just . . . my grandfather was . . . of the same ilk. And you think in similar ways, sometimes."

"And what became of him?"

Blakely lowered his gaze. Swallowed. "After the Coalition arrived on our planet, he was dragged from his office at the academy and executed, for his questions."

Paledan had expected that answer. It was what the Coalition did. Just as they had so unjustly slaughtered Brakely's uncle for mistakes his commanding officer had made. "I am sorry, Marl," he said quietly, using the man's first name, which he rarely did. Brakely's head snapped up at the sound of it.

"Thank you, sir."

"Life is difficult for those whose worlds allowed blood ties during their lifetime."

"Yes. But that will end, soon. Soon all worlds will be as yours."

I'm afraid you are right.

Paledan blinked, hearing the words so clearly in his head that he feared for an instant that he might have spoken them aloud.

When he was certain by Brakely's lack of reaction that he had not, his mind went to the next logical step.

He should be afraid that he had even thought them.

IOLANA WAS FINALLY alone. The twins had gone, restless after a quiet hour in which she had tried various exercises with them. Her conclusions were still forming, but two things were without doubt. One, they communicated in a way few human beings could, often without a word spoken, so in sync were their thoughts. And two, perhaps since they had to spend so little effort in understanding each other, they were uncannily adept at reading other people and gauging their mood. Which thus far had saved them, although she had little doubt they could end in serious trouble should they push too far.

It was remarkable that they carried even this much intuition, at their age. And she thought that, with time, they might indeed develop some form of the gift that would continue to develop as they grew. Whether it would come to be like the one she and Eirlys shared, or more like their brother's, she did not know.

They had been wary about her touch at first, knowing that was how she read people, but she had explained that it was not automatic, that it required she open a pathway in her mind that she swore not to do when she touched them. They still hesitated, their trust in her limited. It was Lux who finally demanded that she swear not to them but to the Raider who, the girl said firmly, would hold her to account should she violate her word. She was both proud and sad; that they held their brother in such esteem was a testament to his success in raising them, and a poignant proof of her own failure as their mother.

But now that she was alone, she must put that aside. She had much to do. She prepared her sanctuary, the alcove she had designed for the task, the place that isolated her from external sound and sight and let her more easily turn her vision inward. Normally she would ask Grim to be at hand, for he was accustomed to making notes as she spoke the things that surfaced.

But not this time. This time, she needed to sort through much of this alone, for what she'd received and what she'd felt from Paledan were things she was not ready to share.

She sat down, let the quiet seep into her for a few moments. And then she closed her eyes and opened the pathway in her mind, just enough to let the images through in the order they had happened as she had approached the bridge over the Racelock.

There he is.

He walks with certainty, but not pride.

He is even more compelling in person.

The slight silver in his hair adds to the compelling effect.

Despite his wound he is strong, fit, a warrior.

His jaw is strong, his face refined.

His eyes are more vivid than even the picture.

He is . . .

Breathtaking.

She was jolted out of her calm perusal, and her eyes snapped open. She was not certain if she was recalling a thought she had had then, or if it had come just now, watching the images unreel before her mind's eye. And that had never happened to her before; she had ever been able to separate the two. Her mind seized on that, even as another part of her was aware she was grasping that puzzle to avoid thinking of what it meant either way that she thought this man breathtaking.

She had thought herself far, far removed from such feminine reactions. While it was true she was yet young as Ziemites went, she had long been removed from the ebb and flow of normal life, and of even the potential for such things. And she had always assumed her capacity for such had died with the blast from the coil gun that had wiped Torstan from existence.

The familiar ache, which she considered a lifetime companion, sometimes painful, other times welcomed as a reminder of what she had once had, rose within her. Usually she quashed it; she was the Spirit of the mountain, and lived without. But now she sat in shock as she forced herself to recognize that her reaction to Caze Paledan had been nothing less than purely female.

And that reaction had been before she'd risked that brief touch. Before she'd learned that, beyond his immediate goal of searching the mines for any evidence there was sabotage occurring—hence her urgent warning—and his Coalition concerns, the image of her portrait occupied a large part of his mind.

It was the strangest feeling she had ever experienced. She had never used her gift for her own gain, and yet she felt as if she had this time even if it had been by accident. She had meant to do exactly as she had told Drake, learn what she could that might help the Sentinels. She had hoped she might also learn enough of Paledan to guess why he kept her portrait.

She had never expected it to be so uppermost in his mind that she got in a fierce blast how her image gripped him.

Her certainty of this warred with her belief that officers of the Coalition had no such feelings, were focused only on war and conquering and cruelty.

Her breath caught. The rest of what she had gotten in that blast swept through her, despite the fact that the normal pathway had been shut down. And as important as what she'd found was what she had not.

Cruelty.

She'd been right in her interpretation; there was none of it in this man. Harshness, yes. Toughness, as expected. Even a capability for brutality, but measured, only enough to achieve the required goal.

But no cruelty. He got no pleasure out of such ruthlessness. It was a tool, to be used only when necessary, and ended when the desired objective was reached. This surprised her, for she had thought cruelty present in all Coalition officers. Whether it had been trained into them, or it was that only those with that vicious streak who became officers, she had neither known nor cared; but cruelty was always there and all that mattered.

Both Brander and Drake had sensed from the beginning that there was something different about this man. She had trusted their judgment, but she had never expected such a difference.

With a great effort she steadied herself. This time when she opened the pathway she narrowed it, trying to hold back the fierce flow so that she could make sense of it all. And she forced all about the portrait to one side, for she was in no way ready to deal with that part yet.

There is truly no cruelty in him.

There is anger, coupled with an image of the damaged Coalition bomber.

She smiled at that one, pride in her son and all the Sentinels spiking, but she had to tamp it down and continue.

There is curiosity. As Brander had suggested.

A sardonic sort of humor, another surprise.

Of all people, the ones he would most like to talk to at length were the Raider and . . . a dead woman.

Her breath caught again, and she fought it; she would delve into that later. Right now it was enough to realize that he ranked the Raider above most of the Coalition officers he knew.

Except himself. The confidence is there. But well founded, grown of accomplishment, not ego.

He is . . . not uncertain, but unpracticed in the type of work he must do here. A fighter, not an administrator.

And there was a glimpse of a memory, some shadowy figure in a beribboned Coalition uniform, and of Paledan stating he would take the assignment, but only if allowed to do things his own way.

What kind of man did it take to, in effect, make demands of a superior Coalition officer? What kind of courage, self-assurance, and reputation did it take to win that demand?

With an effort—this was all taking more effort than was usual—she set aside the realization that the demand, to be allowed to do things his own way, could well be the only reason the entire population of Ziem had not been erased already. She was nearing the end of what she had received in that rush, and was into the part of the stream that was more broken into bits and pieces that didn't necessarily fit together.

Pain. It was constant, yet he suppressed it, allowed himself no quarter.

The mist both frustrated and fascinated him.

She delved deeper, searching. Found . . .

An ability to separate himself from feelings? No, she sensed something stronger than that. This was no mere walling off. It was a . . . void, where something else should be.

She could not discern what, and so she went on. The bits got smaller, less clear as she reached the end.

An image of a building, tall, towering against a dark sky.

The crossed sabers of Ziem.

Another small jolt to see, although she'd been told he had them on the wall of his office. One of the smaller offices, selected not for import but for its view into the compound. He clearly put duty before prominence.

The stream faded, and then was gone. She opened her eyes. The light from the torches attached to the cave walls danced. Brander had offered to run a power line to her from the main cavern, but aware of how much wiring that would take that could likely be put to other uses more helpful to the rebellion, she had thanked him but declined. She was used to this, and in fact thought it helped her with such processes as this one. If she needed power she would go to it, she'd told him, an option she had not had before his arrival.

She spent much of her time there with the Sentinels anyway. It did her good to see their numbers increase almost daily, all of them ready to fight, or if they could not, to support the fight.

She was, she knew, thinking of such things to give her mind the rest it needed after such intensity. Normally she would take up a piece of handwork, something to be worked on with her fingers, until her mind was clear enough of what she called the debris to function clearly again. It normally only took a few minutes, but she was still feeling the effects of this deluge and did not quite know when it would ease. And until it eased, she did not dare take up what she had shunted aside throughout this torrent of images and impressions.

Until then, she could not deal with the obvious fact that this man, this dangerous Coalition officer, was more than just idly interested in the portrait that had once graced the wall of the man he considered the fiercest enemy he had yet encountered.

Her portrait.

Chapter 7

THE WOMAN HAD been ill.

It was the only explanation he could think of for the odd sensations he had been having ever since she had bumped into him yesterday.

He had inspected his arm carefully that evening, and there was no mark or any other sign that she had somehow injected him with something. Nor was there any rash or other indication that something had gotten through his skin in some other way. He had, since he had left the Coalition medical unit, learned to monitor his own vital signs, although it had seemed pointless to him; if the shrapnel shifted, his rate of respiration and heartbeat would be pointless, for he would be done. His only hope was that if it happened it would either be his death blow, or that he would have the ability left to get to the capsule of swift, deadly poison he had had secreted in the insignia of his rank.

He sat staring out his window into the mist, which was particularly thick today. So thick that he could not even see the ground outside. Everything slowed down on these days, out of sheer necessity. But he was not thinking about productive time lost at the moment. He was trying to determine just how ill he was. This tightness in his chest was new, as was an echoing tightness in his throat. Yet it was not incapacitating, and seemed to recede if he became occupied with something.

He could have ignored it all, except for one thing. When he had succumbed to the temptation to drag out that bedamned painting once more, at his first look at it he'd been swamped with unaccustomed sensations. As if it somehow had been the trigger for the full unleashing for whatever this was, he'd run cold, then hot, then aching, as if he'd gone through every stage of the Lustranian virus in less than a minute. This was . . . worse than worrisome.

For someone who had taken his strength and power and health for granted for so long, this was indeed worse than worrisome.

Had he somehow incurred an infection after the injury that had waited this long to surface? It seemed unlikely—no, impossible—but it made more sense than that a split second of brushing contact with a Ziemite woman had done this to him.

Now if it had been this woman, he thought with a glance at the portrait, he might understand. He had read, somewhere, that on the conquered worlds that had had artists, those commissioned for a portrait often flattered their subjects, painted them as much more attractive, dynamic, fit, or powerful than they were in fact. Had this artist done so? Would this woman, in real life, have been a faint imitation of this vivid image? Was her hair perhaps not so fiery, her eyes not so vivid, her body not so lithe or female? Was her spirit less than what fairly leapt out from the flat canvas?

Without knowing who the artist was, he could not know if they were the sort to curry favor in that way. And while a part of his mind wanted to believe that no one with that kind of talent would compromise it, the stern, Coalition-trained part of his mind quashed the idea immediately. The part that said artists were of little use when building an empire the size of the Coalition, except for propaganda.

He knew he could likely resolve this question. There were still records, many of which he had studied on his way to this posting. But he had not bothered with images of those already dead, other than one of Torstan Davorin in the moment before his death, captured at the height of his seditious speech through the targeting scope of the coil gun that had killed him. He had studied that for a while, noting the fire in those eyes that even the uncolored image from the scope had shown.

But there were other images, and it was quite possible there would be one of this woman who had been the mate to the fiery orator. Yet he resisted. And he was uncertain as to whether that was because he feared she would not be as beautiful and alive as that portrait . . . or that she would be.

He flexed his arm yet again as he stared at the painting. Realized he could think of nothing beyond it when it was there in front of him, and closed his eyes. Tried to remember more about the woman on the bridge. Tall, the top of her head past his shoulder, even bowed as it had been. Dark hair, long but pulled back; he had seen a strand caught on the edge of the hood of her cloak. She had seemed so frightened, had made that little gasp of sound as she jumped back awkwardly. As if she had truly feared he would strike her down for the insult of bumping into him.

There were, he knew, Coalition officers who would do just that. Some, even, who would have blasted her on the spot for such an offense. And he had been told he was too tolerant, an accusation he usually countered with the true tale of the commander on Carelia who had done just that, and had ended up killing the one local healer who could have saved his life when he'd later been bitten by some venomous local creature.

He'd seen little more of the woman than that, she'd been so shrouded by that long, hooded cloak. Intentionally? Had she wanted to hide, not be recognized? That would imply she was recognizable. To him? That seemed unlikely. More likely she simply wanted to pass unnoticed by the conquerors of her world.

He tapped a finger idly on his desk. It was very different, this dealing first hand with the inhabitants of an addition to the Coalition empire. He had expected it to be so, but he hadn't expected to be this consumed by it. In fact, he had expected to be bored and eager to be freed of the drudgery rather quickly. And it was true his job was full of that, and yet . . .

He was fascinated.

This obsession would not, he knew, be approved of at High Command. Conquered planets were mere possessions, and their people to be either pressed into service or disposed of, whichever was most appropriate to Coalition goals. Those who were of use were to be treated like children, and even the most useful of them would quickly be put on the elimination list should they cross their masters by trying to think for themselves.

And of course there was nothing in those conquered cultures worth anything to the Coalition—there was no worthy way of life except that of the Coalition—and so individuality must be stamped out.

He'd always known all this, but usually by the time those things began to happen he was long departed, off to another world to lead another conquering force. This was the first time he'd been involved after the fact, and it was proving much more complex than he'd expected.

The problem was not in the task before him, it was in himself. The problem was his own reactions to the task.

And unlike most things in his life, he did not know what to do about that.

IOLANA LOOKED up as Grim came into the cave. He stopped the moment he saw her face.

"My lady? Are you well?"

"I am," she admitted frankly, "overwhelmed."

The tall man dropped to a cushion on the floor across from her. He studied her for a moment. "This is a result of your contact with the Coalition commander?"

"Yes."

She knew she could be completely honest with Grim. He would not chastise her for the risk she had taken, nor question her reasons for doing so. His preference was to always be there as a protector, but he accepted her word as the final decision.

Diverted for a moment, she asked, "Do you not wish for your own life, Grim, now that our lives have changed, and I have people—and family— around me?"

"You are not yet happy, and that was my vow."

"I am happier," she corrected, for it was true.

His face expressionless as usual—although that seemed to be slowly changing with the more time they spent among the Sentinels, and especially around her family—he asked formally, "Does my lady wish me to withdraw?"

"Of course not. I only wish that you have something for yourself. You have dedicated too many years to me, my dear friend."

"I believe that is mine to decide."

She smiled at him. "I do not merit your devotion, but I cherish it."

"So I may stay?"

"I don't know what I would do without you."

He smiled at that. "Now, will you tell me what you saw in your reading that has you so troubled?"

"It is not what I saw, Grim, but what I did not see. Not what was there, but what was missing."

"Which was?"

"Not a trace of . . . personal history outside the Coalition. No family, no friends, save an amenable connection with his aide."

"This is not unusual, for the Coalition demands all loyalty be to them, do they not?"

"Yes, but to have not a single memory? Even of one's own parents? I don't believe the Coalition has managed to create humans from nothing yet, although I do not deny they are likely trying."

"I believe the androids are as close as they have come."

"Agreed. And those will turn upon them are they not watchful. But that is for another time. What is most . . . disquieting about the man is that lack. I think he is fascinated because he has never known the loving connections of family, or between other people. He understands bonds in an intellectual way, but in his heart? There is nothing of it."

No concept of love.

Chapter 8

"HOW LONG ARE we going to stand for this?"

Paledan looked up at Governor Sorkost. He'd seen little of him recently, and he suspected it was because the man had been hiding in a shelter beneath the large, luxurious residence he'd taken over upon his arrival here. It had once belonged to the most prosperous planium broker on Ziem, a man among the first to be eliminated after the Coalition had declared the planet conquered.

Declaring it does not make it so.

He brushed off the unwanted thought, the latest in that annoying string of them. And he did not rise for this unannounced intrusion. Instead he leaned back in his chair.

"You disagree with the Coalition-approved strategy?"

The portly man flushed. "Of course not. It is just hard to accept what a ragged band of rebels has done."

"Indeed it is."

That the man had bestirred himself to come all the way to Paledan's office—a considerable hike, and within yards of the destroyed east wing of the council building—indicated just how unsettled the appointed governor of Ziem was. He had, no doubt, expected an easy posting here, perhaps to add to his already considerable bulk of both body and wealth before retiring to life on a more pleasant planet.

He wondered if the man would take the single chair available. Wondered if he would even fit into it. If it would hold him if he did, or shatter under the burden.

"Then why do we just accept it? Why do we not wipe them out?"

Paledan lifted a brow. "You should have told me you know where they are hiding."

Flustered, the man shook his head. "I do not. But surely the thermal satellite—"

"Has scanned this entire planet multiple times and found nothing. No sign of an encampment, a base, or for that matter not a single group of more than twenty people gathered, outside of Zelos itself."

"Then where in hades are they?" Sorkost yelped.

"Something I would much like to know," Paledan agreed. "But even more, I would like to know what they are planning next."

Sorkost paled. His hand, the one with the two missing fingers—or without them, Paledan supposed—went to his mouth as if the very thought made him ill.

"You think they will strike again?" the man asked after a moment.

"I would," he said.

Sorkost's eyes widened. "You put this Raider on a level with yourself?"

I am not entirely certain he is not better. "You yourself have acknowledged what he has accomplished."

"But . . . you are the most highly decorated officer—"

He waved the man to silence. "That does not make the Raider any less of a brilliant fighter."

He knew he was skating on the edge of heresy. For the Coalition never lost because the adversary was better. It was always bad luck, sabotage, betrayal, or the like. The document excusing the victory of the rebels on Trios and Arellia had been full of excuses enough to glaze any reader's eyes.

Sorkost seemed at a loss for words for the moment, even his usual bombast failing him. Paledan stayed silent, letting the awkwardness grow. Finally, words broke from the man, and they held an edge of panic.

"What are we to do?"

"I understand your concern," he said, putting on a thoughtful mien. "And I appreciate your willingness to participate. Not many in your position would be willing to actually fight."

Sorkost gasped, paling. "What?"

"You did ask what are *we* to do, did you not?"

As he had expected—and planned—the man suddenly remembered crucially important business elsewhere. Paledan was glad to see him go, but he felt no more settled than he had before the man had come bursting in. After a fruitless effort to focus on the work before him—if he saw one more form to be sent out to every person of rank he thought he might hurl the processing unit through his window—he stood up.

He could not afford one of his longer excursions just now, but he would walk the perimeter again, he decided. He did his best thinking while moving. He told Brakely where he would be, and to use the comm link if he needed him.

The moment he stepped outside into the cool mist, he knew he'd made the right decision. There was something about this stuff, perhaps the way it masked the surroundings—allowing visibility for only the few yards immediately surrounding you—that aided his thinking. The removal of distraction, he supposed.

Yet when he had finished his circuit of the perimeter of the compound, he found he was still restless, and decided to walk through Zelos as well. He looked impassively at the destruction they had rained down upon this quiet place. It had been necessary, but that did not mean he had enjoyed it.

Some thought he must surely take great delight in flexing Coalition power. He could have told them, although he would not, that he took delight in nothing. He felt most things only mildly, and many not at all. Such things had been prohibited in his childhood, for he had been born on the planet that had birthed the Coalition itself. And once he'd been selected for their academy, the Coalition had finished the job of crushing what was left of such emotions out of him. He considered it a benefit; he did not feel the heights as those who had come from other places did, but neither did he plunge into despair.

At least, not until I came here.

That was a foolish thought. His injury, not this place, had weakened him. He kept walking.

He hadn't consciously intended it, and yet he found himself again on the lane that led past what had once been the prosperous taproom run by Drake Davorin. He was not certain why he kept returning, unless it was to remind himself of the strength and abilities of his opponent, who'd been able to lead the double life he had for so long, under the very noses of the Coalition.

And it was not until he stood before the flattened building that he realized he had once more thought of the Raider as his opponent. Not as his enemy.

He became aware of someone's presence and moved his hand to the weapon on his belt in the moment before the voice came out of the mist behind him.

"Still missing the place, too?"

"Brander Kalon," he said, turning. His one-time chaser rival looked as he ever did, strolling nonchalantly, his dark coat swirling the mist with his passage. His eyes held the same cool insouciance, despite the ruins around him. They held something else as well, something new that Paledan couldn't put a name to.

"You've been scarce."

The man shrugged. "You never know what insanity the Raider will attempt next."

"He's done much more than attempt," Paledan pointed out.

"And you are remarkably calm about it."

He thought of Sorkost, and smiled inwardly. "Frenzy accomplishes little."

"True enough," Kalon agreed easily.

"He has also been scarce since his ambush succeeded."

The man lifted a brow at him and asked, "You so easily admit he succeeded?"

"Where it's due."

"You have an . . . interesting code, Major." Kalon was silent for a moment before saying, "Do you often find yourself in conflict with your overlords?"

Paledan took no offense of the characterization of the Coalition. How could he, when he had often thought it himself recently, although he had never voiced it. There was no swifter way to bring their wrath upon you, and his position was tenuous enough already.

And suddenly an impulse he'd buried, because he was not given to them by nature, surfaced. And also uncharacteristically, he acted upon it without further thought.

"You once said you could likely contact the Raider, if you wished."

Kalon raised a brow. "Did I?"

"You did."

"Hmm. Wonder what I was thinking?"

He had to admire the man's casual manner. This was, after all, his lifelong friend they were speaking of. Paledan might have no experience of such bonds, but he knew from his study they existed, and how powerful they could be.

"Can you still?"

The casualness vanished, to be replaced by a considering stare. "And why would you want to know? Aside from perhaps thinking I could discover where he is and would betray him—and Ziem—in that manner?"

Paledan shook his head impatiently "I know you would not, if you did know."

"There is always Jakel to assist you."

"Do not tempt me." His tone was sour, for the invader near his spine had just sharply reminded him of its presence. "And I believe he would have the same luck with you as he had with Davorin."

Something flashed in Kalon's eyes, but was quickly gone. "Drake is much, much tougher than I."

He grimaced. "Apparently he is tougher than is possible."

He still had no reasonable explanation for why the man he had seen in Jakel's soundproofed cellar room, broken and so near death as not to matter, had not only survived but risen to lead his rebels on the attack that had destroyed the fusion cannon such a short time later.

"No more talk of that creature. I need only an answer to my question."

Kalon studied him for a moment. "Perhaps I should ask why you wish to contact the Raider."

"We met once before. I wish it again."

"You wish to meet with the Raider? Why?"

"That is to be between us."

Kalon frowned in obvious puzzlement. "You think he does not know what his head on a spike is worth now?"

"I'm sure he does."

"Yet you expect him to meet with you, the leader of those who would like nothing more than that? Why would he?"

"He did not strike me as an . . . incurious man."

"And you think him curious enough to risk it?"

"I think he knows that if I give my word, it will be kept."

Kalon was silent for a moment, then shrugged. "I will make the effort. On one condition."

"And you think Davorin tougher, when you dare to make conditions to a Coalition commander?"

The man looked almost startled for a moment, then smiled. "I only wished to secure your word that if I am not able to contact him, it will not be my head on that spike."

He smiled back. "You have it."

He watched as Kalon turned and disappeared back into the mist. And realized anew that he had missed sparring with this man.

Chapter 9

"YOU SPOKE WITH him and he wants a meeting?"

Brander nodded at Drake. Iolana felt Eirlys tense beside her at the news her mate had risked himself once more. But she said nothing. Iolana admired her self-control; she was learning quickly what it meant to love a gambler.

They had met before, the Coalition commander and the Raider, and both had walked away. But she, and she was certain Drake, were not foolish enough to think there was a guarantee it would be the same again.

"What does he wish to meet about?" Drake asked.

"He would not say. Not to me, anyway. He wanted only to know if I had a way to contact you."

"Surely you're not considering it, Drake?" Kye's voice held all the tension Iolana had felt in Eirlys. "Not now, after we did such damage? The Coalition will be out for your blood more than ever now."

"She's right," Eirlys agreed.

"Maybe he wants to bargain!" The exclamation came from young Kade, who had followed Brander in when he'd arrived. That Drake let him remain spoke to his belief that the boy had great potential. "Maybe he's afraid of us now."

"It is a glorious thought," Drake said, careful not to smash the boy's enthusiasm, "but I'm not sure Paledan has any fear in him."

"Agreed," Iolana said; there had been nothing of it in the blast she'd gotten. They all knew by now that she'd had direct contact with him, and so she did not have to explain her assessment. In this they trusted her completely. Or they trusted the Spirit, at least.

"So he has another motive," Pryl said from where he was leaning against the cave wall. "Your head, for instance."

Drake looked at the canny old woodsman. "So you think he would use himself as . . . bait, to lure me into a trap?"

"Make you think he wants to bargain, then capture or kill you? Sounds typically Coalition to me."

"Especially after the blow we've struck," Eirlys said.

Drake was silent for a long moment, thinking. And then he looked at Iolana.

"You have offered no opinion."

"As your mother, I would scream no, you must not. I, and the others who love you, cannot lose you."

"Is that what the Spirit Sees? My death?"

She shook her head. "As is too often the case, the Spirit Sees nothing actually helpful in this situation." She had lived her entire life with the capriciousness of that part of her gift, yet it still had the capacity to exasperate her.

"And as a Davorin?" he asked softly.

She drew in a deep breath. "As a Davorin, I would say that, for this moment, you hold the upper hand, for the Coalition believes you have the mightiest weapon on Ziem."

"For the moment," Kye said. "If they figure out it's only a device emitting the cannon signature . . ."

"They did not, on Trios," Iolana said. "They never realized they'd been duped."

"But the Triotians managed to actually build one," Brander pointed out.

"Eventually, yes," Iolana agreed. "But we do not know how long that took."

"Paledan is no fool," Drake said. "Eventually he will conclude we have no way to move a weapon of that size and power in the way the transmitting device suggests. And once he has eliminated the impossible, it is probable he will land on the likely, that it doesn't really exist." He glanced at Brander and added, "Yet."

"The matter at hand?" Brander suggested, then added dryly, "Since I have no idea where to even begin with the matter of actually building a fusion cannon with what tools we have."

Drake looked back at Iolana. "You got no feel that he was planning a trap?"

She shook her head. "None. But that is no guarantee."

Drake nodded.

"If you're going to do this insane thing," Kye said, her voice remarkably even, "it should be a new meeting place, that we've scouted thoroughly. That way Paledan can't prepare an ambush."

Brander nodded. "And if we pick it right, it could throw them off on where we are now."

Kade stirred, looking as if he wanted to speak but wasn't sure he should try again. Drake turned to face him. "You are here because you are clever and quick, Kade. And you, just as Brander, sometimes have a view others miss. What is it?"

The boy, who had begun to practically glow at Drake's words, spoke quickly then. "I just . . . if we chose someplace that will lead them away from the stronghold here, but also away from the old cellar, and away from where you met before, it would make it look as if we can go anywhere we please. Like they don't matter anymore."

For a moment they were all silent. And then, slowly, a grin spread across Drake's face. "And never," he said, reaching out to put a hand on Kade's shoulder, "underestimate the power of that kind of victory."

Kade fairly beamed under the praise. Drake turned back to Pryl. "What say you, old friend? Is there such a place?"

"There may be," Pryl said, clearly thinking. "In the low valley, perhaps."

"Across the Racelock?" Eirlys asked, sounded startled.

"And past their compound?" Brander asked, sounding nearly as startled.

"Which is ever more fiercely guarded now?" Kye reminded him.

Drake, on the other hand, merely waited. And Iolana smiled in spite of the grimness of the subject, to see this vivid demonstration of the leader he had become.

Pryl looked at Brander. "You have said you believe their security perimeter ends on the far side of where the fusion cannon once sat when it guarded Zelos."

Brander in turn looked at Kade, whose face became set as he answered steadily, "That is where my father installed it, fifty yards beyond the emplacement."

"You're certain?" Pryl asked.

"Since that is where they then murdered him, immediately after he threw the switch, yes, I'm certain."

"Then it is well that we will use that against them," Pryl said. After a moment the boy nodded.

"What have you in mind?" Drake asked.

"The foothills of the south range, overlooking that emplacement. That now empty emplacement."

Kye let out an audible breath. "Well, that would surely chap his armor."

"And be a worthy reminder of what he is dealing with," Iolana said.

"As long as it doesn't make him angry enough to take your head before you say a word," Eirlys said, her tone more than a bit sour.

"I do not think that kind of reaction is . . . innate in him," Iolana said. "He does not feel anger, not in that way. Or many other things."

Drake frowned. "In what way?" he asked.

"Personally."

"You mean as Frall did?" Eirlys asked. "Taking everything as an affront to him personally."

"Exactly that," Iolana said with a smile at her daughter.

"So you do not think he will attempt to take my head merely because I chose a location that could be construed as an insult?"

"He is not of that . . . delicate a nature," she said. "But do not think him incapable of taking your head for other reasons," she added warningly.

"I think Paledan capable of whatever he feels necessary."

"Then you are correct."

"How would you get there, without being seen by the troopers?" Kade asked.

Drake smiled. "A practical voice heard from," he said approvingly. Iolana saw the look that glowed in the young man's eyes then, and knew her son had earned the boy's loyalty for life. "Pryl?"

"There is a way, although it is long and somewhat arduous."

"I shudder to think how bad it is if *you* think it's arduous," Brander muttered.

"How?" Eirlys, who knew the terrain surrounding Zelos as well as anyone save Pryl.

"Around the back of Halfhead and the Brother."

Brander let out a low whistle. "Arduous isn't the half of it."

"But what about the guard tower south of the Brother?" Eirlys asked. "Wouldn't that be right under their noses?"

"They are focused on Zelos, not to the south. And you know how the mist accumulates in those hills, intensified by the water in the basin below."

"If we went down the badlands side and then west, we could use the river down to the foothills," Eirlys said, obviously thinking rapidly. "We would have to disembark well before Zelos to avoid the guard tower, but it would make the trek easier and quicker."

"There is the small detail of us not having any boats," Kye pointed out.

Eirlys grinned at her brother's mate. "But the fishers do. And there is not one of them who would not gladly make the loan to the Raider."

"As long as they know they may not be floating as well when they get them back," Brander quipped.

"This would be a different approach," Drake said.

"And might throw even Paledan off," Iolana said. "He is a land fighter, and while I doubt we could fool him completely, it might delay discovery just enough."

"We are agreed, then," the Raider said.

"On all but one thing." Brander's tone was dry now. "Who constitutes 'we'?"

Iolana glanced at them all in turn, realized that every one of them intended to accompany their leader on this risky mission. And she realized both that she had expected no less, and how very proud she was of them all.

Chapter 10

IN THE END, Brander, as the Raider's second and the one who must be kept secret from Paledan, and Kade reluctantly stayed behind. Kye would be flying high cover, as the best pilot save Drake himself, and the best shot with a long gun.

That left Drake, Pryl, Eirlys, and herself as the boating party. She would have preferred more guards, well armed, but saw the wisdom in Drake's decision to keep the party as small as possible.

Paledan had, a bit to their surprise, accepted both the meeting place and the parameters without question. Of course, the Raider had given him little option; he had sent the location and instructions, and left the Coalition major only the option to accept or decline.

The message had been found, as intended, by a young trooper, who had swiftly carried the page emblazoned with the Sentinels' symbol, the curved sabre of Ziem, to Paledan.

The acceptance came in the form of a Coalition battle pennant draped from his office window, to be seen and the information secretly relayed. This, Iolana knew, had a double significance, that Paledan would not be needing the flag for its intended purpose, leading a battle, and a reminder that the Raider's spies were everywhere, even in half-destroyed Zelos.

Drake and Pryl had been givens, and Eirlys logical—if worrisome—for her knowledge of the area. This was the result of letting the child run free, Iolana thought. She had knowledge of immense use, but now it also put her in immense danger. But she was of age now, and nothing would stop her from doing her part in this war.

The biggest resistance had been to her own presence. But she'd been prepared for that. What had surprised her was Eirlys's support.

"She will be of use if someone is hurt," Eirlys had said evenly.

"Unless it is she herself that is hurt," Brander pointed out.

Drake had spoken then. "Yes, but as it stands she is somewhat of a secret weapon, in more than one sense."

"Until now," Iolana said, "I have been content with that. But this man, I believe, will require all the weapons we have."

"She is right," Eirlys agreed. "And now that she has shed her disguise, that might be of use as well."

"In what way?" Drake had asked.

"Again, to throw Paledan off just that bit that might be needed. For how would anyone react if the subject of an image you have had in your possession, a subject you thought long dead, suddenly appeared before you in the flesh?"

"I see the tactical mind is not linked solely to the male," Iolana had said with a smile.

Eirlys looked at her, and smiled back as she answered, "It may well be. That was Brander's idea."

There was such pride and love in her daughter's voice that Iolana felt a pang. They were so well matched, her daughter and her pledged mate. She prayed to Eos that they never suffer as she had, the loss of the person who made you whole.

"YOU'RE CERTAIN you wish to do this?" Brakely asked. "Sir?" he added.

"I think we are beyond formalities at this point, Brakely." Paledan settled his tanned-hide jacket on his shoulders. He had chosen this rather than his formal uniform with all his insignia and decorations. Not because he expected to have to fight, but because he was going as himself, not a Coalition major. And if that was heresy, so be it. "If there is a chance to end this, I must take it."

Brakely nodded in understanding as Paledan settled the small blaster, the only protection he would carry, as agreed. Even the Raider, it seemed, did not want him taken out by a feral slimehog or some other odd creature this planet harbored.

"Perhaps you will garner some clue as to where they are hiding."

"Perhaps. You remember what we discussed?" he asked his long-time aide.

"Of course." Paledan could almost see the man bite off another "Sir."

"Then you know what to do, if I miss the comm check tomorrow."

"Yes." And in that simple answer was the essence of the Coalition mindset—an order would be followed, a patrol sent out, and eventually, if necessary, someone else sent to replace him. A pause, then, "But it will not come to that, will it?"

"I believe the Raider will keep his word."

"And you will keep yours."

"Yes."

Brakely nodded. "Good luck, sir."

When he reached the outer door, the two troopers on watch snapped to attention. He threw them a salute and continued. There was an air rover, as usual, waiting for him but he waved it off.

"I will walk," he told the attendant who had been about to summon the pilot.

"Sir?"

The young—very young—man, who was obviously new, sounded so astounded he nearly laughed. "I am not headed up into the mountains, trooper, merely the foothills," he said with a gesture toward his chosen path.

"Yes, sir," the man said embarrassedly.

Paledan wondered if this was what the Coalition was coming to, stretched so thin they needed to send children out to remote planets such as this. And how long it would take for the young man to learn he must mask such human failings as surprise and embarrassment. More to the point, he wondered if he would learn before he crossed some Coalition officer who decided to teach him the hard way.

He headed west, thinking as he went that the Raider obviously had no qualms about being so close to the Coalition compound. He also wondered what it meant that this meeting place was on the opposite side of Zelos than both their old quarters and the ridge that separated the city from the badlands, their presumed new hideout. Was he trying to throw them off? Or merely show them that the Raider went where he wished, when he wished, and the Coalition be damned?

He would not be surprised if it were the latter. What this warrior lacked in equipment and weapons he more than made up for with skill, brains, and brilliant tactics.

Did you know? Did you know what you had given birth to?

The words were directed at the woman in the painting, who still occupied far too much of his mind. In the guise of researching all of Ziem he had finally made himself pick through what had been left after the destruction of the annals, but had found little. At least, not enough to sate the curiosity about her that seemed ever to grow. The one image he'd found had been at such a distance he'd only been able to see she was tall, slender, and her hair had truly been that fiery shade. In the text, he had been shocked to learn her age when she'd given birth to the boy who would one day rise to lead this rebellion; had she lived, she would be only two years older than he.

But she had not. Somewhere in her there had been a fatal flaw, hidden beneath that perfect, stunning exterior. The strength that seemed to radiate from that portrait apparently had never truly existed, was perhaps a contribution of the nameless artist. Perhaps it was that artist's spirit resonating from the painting, not that of the subject.

He gave a sharp shake of his head; this was not the time to get lost in ruminations better left to the privacy of his office. He focused on the act of walking, now that the ground had begun to rise. He assessed his own movements, waiting for the ache of muscles still unable to move freely because of the invader in their midst, or the sharp, tearing pain that would announce that invader had advanced yet another micro distance.

He did not have many of those small shifts left, he knew.

When he turned to check the trail behind him, seeking the source of that odd tickling at the back of his neck, he stopped in his tracks. Realized the location the Raider had chosen for this meeting looked down on the base for the fusion cannon. The fusion cannon he and his Sentinels had taken out shortly after his own arrival here.

He should have become angry. Perhaps angry enough to break the rules set for this meeting and blast the man out of existence.

Instead, he found himself laughing.

And he continued walking.

Chapter 11

"YOU HAVE BROUGHT support, I presume?" Paledan asked.

"As before and with the same promise. They will not be the first to shoot." Paledan nodded, and the Raider continued. "And you, as before, have not. Is there no one you trust?"

An odd expression crossed the man's face. It was only a flicker, but Iolana could see it clearly from where she was concealed by the low sweeping boughs of a mistbreaker tree.

"To understand what happens here? No."

"It is a hard path you walk."

"This from you?"

"I have the best at my back."

Paledan's mouth—that oddly expressive mouth, Iolana thought—twisted.

"Given what you have accomplished with them, I cannot gainsay that. And that is why I asked for this meeting."

Drake, standing at ease, dressed in the light armor and the gleaming silver helm of the Raider, simply waited. Yet again Iolana felt pride in her son swell within her. As near impossible as it had been for her to keep her distance while he struggled to keep the family together and safe and at the same time lead the Sentinels in the fight for Ziem, she—and Ziem—were reaping the results of forcing him to grow into the leader he had to be.

After a long moment of silence, Paledan nodded, as if in tribute. There was little doubt who held the upper hand at this moment, despite the Coalition at Paledan's back.

"I have come to ask you to stand down."

Iolana drew back; this she had not expected. She doubted Drake had either, for again he did not speak.

And again Paledan let him have the win. "At any moment," Paledan said quietly, "I expect the orders to come. The Coalition has little patience, and Ziem has only avoided annihilation thus far because it has value to them."

"You think we do not know this?"

"I know that you do. I only wished to tell you it is . . . imminent."

"And you believe if the Sentinels stand down, as you say, those orders will not come?"

"I believe that if you stand down, I can contest them. Convince High Command all is now well."

"Trying to save your reputation, Major?"

Something flickered in Paledan's eyes. Those eyes that were so vividly green, even from where Iolana hid in the trees. The knowledge swept over her with the engulfing certainty of her most vivid visions.

No. Trying to use it to save Ziem.

But why? Why would this Coalition officer, however different he might seem in so many ways, wish to save what to him must be a strange, remote world? A world he had come to only because it had been his sole alternative to a desk chair?

He said only, "My posting had many purposes. I am here for the time when that order comes. The Coalition does not doubt my success in that eventuality. Neither should you."

Drake studied him for a long moment, then asked, "And will you take pleasure in executing that order?"

"I take pleasure in nothing."

He means that. He understands the word only by definition, not experience.

Iolana stared at the man she had learned so much about in a brief, brushing contact. And realized that what she had sensed ran even deeper than she had known. Beyond his admiration for the Raider, that sardonic humor and the curiosity, she had seen nothing of what she would call normal emotions in the man. And this was what he credited for his accomplishments with the Coalition. He was so good at what he did because there was nothing to get in the way, no feelings, no messy sentiment. He approached the job at hand methodically, efficiently, and remorselessly.

And yet here he stood, asking Drake to not force his hand.

"Then you live a cold, hard life," Drake said softly.

"It is more of a life than you will have if you are ever captured. You would be collared, Davorin, and your people would likely be destroyed anyway."

Iolana suppressed a shudder at the mention of that most hideous of Coalition techniques of subjugation, that of implanting controllers in the brain to turn the victim into worse than a slave, a willing slave.

"You need the miners," Drake said, seemingly unruffled.

"Yes. But they can be evacuated, if necessary. And brought back to retrieve the planium when the planet is habitable again. Or," he said coldly, "before, for we will only need them a short while longer, until our equipment is adapted."

Iolana's breath caught. Had she thought him different? He was speaking, as if it were nothing, of wiping out the entire population of a world with some deadly weapon, then sending the miners back to work until they died in the poisonous aftermath. That was Coalition thinking at its purest.

And yet . . .

He spoke of "they," "them," "the Coalition." As if they were other. Other than he himself.

"Why?" Drake finally asked. "Why do you give us this warning?"

Again an odd expression flickered, but this one Iolana recognized. Paledan was more than a little bemused at himself, perhaps because he did not have an answer to that question himself. It softened his look for an instant, and he wasn't merely the powerful, imposing, intimidating Coalition officer; he was a man she could imagine smiling, even laughing.

A man who could command the attention of any woman breathing, if he cared to try.

"You are a warrior," Paledan said after a moment. "I would dislike seeing you die in such a way, wiped out from a distance."

"A safe distance," Drake said dryly.

Paledan lifted a brow in what looked almost like a salute. "Indeed. It is a very ugly and painful way to die. And you are strong, so you would live long enough to see others in such agony as you cannot imagine."

Drake lifted a brow in turn. "I can imagine quite a bit."

Paledan's voice went very quiet. "Yes. Yes, I'd forgotten, you had experience with agony." For a moment the major studied his adversary. And Iolana found herself holding her breath. "Before that happens, I would greatly like to know how you did that. You were as near to death as any man I've ever seen on a battlefield. I nearly blasted you myself, down in that cellar, simply to put you out of your misery."

"And that, Major, answers my original question of why."

Paledan looked disconcerted.

Well done, my son, Iolana thought.

The call of a trill came from the trees to the north, where Pryl was hiding. Iolana froze, knowing it for what it was, for the bird with the simple but distinctive call had been extinct on Ziem for an age.

It was a signal.

A warning.

Had Paledan not come alone? Had he betrayed his word?

Was he not who she thought he was?

Everything seemed to freeze, go quiet. And she held her breath, waiting.

PALEDAN HAD BEEN studying the Raider. He'd immediately noticed the metal sweeps of the helmet that had hidden his face before, along with the mock mass of scar tissue, were gone. No longer needed, now that all of Ziem knew that the Raider was exactly who they had once expected him to be.

Then he heard the bird's call, wondered which of the multitude of the creatures this world seemed to have this one was. In the next instant he was aware of the Raider's sudden tension, and his thoughts shifted to wondering what had disturbed the creature. Did the man have even the beasts and birds of this world trained to assist him, to give warning? It would not surprise him in the least. He had heard from townspeople that Davorin's sister, the one he had sacrificed himself to save, had a knack with all living things.

He heard a rustle among the leaves. The thought of Davorin's sacrifice had brought to mind Jakel, so much so that for a moment he thought he'd seen the beast, or at least something his size, moving in the shadows.

And then he knew he had seen it; the hulking shape barreled toward a tall tree with branches that swept the ground. Jakel. The mindless brute had violated orders and followed him.

The Raider reacted as swiftly as he did, drawing his blaster. Paledan gave him no chance, but fired first.

At Jakel.

The huge man screamed and tumbled down the grade to sprawl practically at Paledan's feet. Paledan whirled to face the Raider. He heard the sound of an air rover, closing.

"I did not bring him," he said urgently.

The man's voice was ice. "I am to believe that?"

"You must."

If he did not, it would all be over. Life on Ziem would be eradicated. He was aware that this should not matter to him, yet he could not deny that it did. He held the Raider's gaze as he did what he had never done before. He pled for the life of a world he was here to subjugate.

"Please, do not begin what the Coalition will finish."

Chapter 12

IT WAS A SPLIT second only before the Raider called out, "Hold!"

Paledan did not know how many the man might have nearby in addition to the air cover. He only knew he would do well not to underestimate the number; these Ziemites seemed able to blend into their trees and mist as if they assumed those forms themselves.

He crouched beside Jakel, reluctantly reached out to touch the man.

"You have deprived some Sentinels of a long-awaited pleasure."

Paledan's gaze snapped back to the Raider at the wry observation. And found himself smiling, yet uncertain exactly why. He stood once more. "He is still alive. Take him. A token of my . . . thanks for your trust in my word."

"I simply weighed options and outcomes."

Paledan stared at the man. "You indeed would do well in the Coalition."

"And you would perhaps be better off with the Sentinels." Paledan gave the Raider a sharp, penetrating look. The Raider eyed him back coolly as he added, "You are, at least, a good enough shot."

Paledan did smile then, before he looked back at Jakel, who was stirring now. His left leg was smoking slightly from the blaster's hit. If he'd had it at full power it would have taken the leg off.

"I left strict orders no one was to follow me," he grated out the moment the man opened his eyes. They glinted red even in the misty light as he clutched at his wounded leg.

"I didn't know that."

"How did you know which way to come? You were not close behind me."

Slowly he sat up. "The attendant at the main door told me which way you went."

Paledan's gaze narrowed. "Did you hurt him?"

Jakel laughed. "That boy? I merely had to look at him."

From the corner of his eye Paledan saw the Raider, simply standing, watching, waiting. Amazingly calm, given this was the brute who had tortured him near unto death not so long ago. His opinion of the man went up another notch. It took a serious amount of control to maintain such coolness in such circumstances. And make the kind of decision he had just made, on the fly, based only on trust and his assessment of the situation.

The man wasn't just a warrior and a commander, he was a leader.

"I know I promised him to you," he said with a grimace, "but it tests my limits to leave him alive."

Jakel frowned, clearly not realizing Paledan was referring to him. But the Raider laughed.

"With that kind of thinking, then you are truly on the wrong side, Major. He is just the sort of tool the Coalition favors. His death is no benefit to them."

The Raider lifted his head slightly, looking toward the trees where Jakel had been. Paledan followed his gaze. He saw nothing, but apparently the Raider had, for he nodded.

"I think," the Raider said, "there is someone else who would find it even more difficult to leave him alive."

"You?" Paledan asked.

Something about the warrior's smile then left Paledan feeling odd, an empty sort of sensation that spoke of things never known rather than things missing.

"No," he said. And then, looking past Paledan's shoulder he added softly, "Her."

Paledan whirled. And there behind him, barely two strides away, stood a young woman. In his shock that she had somehow snuck up on him, it took him a moment to place her, the bright-gold hair braided back, the eyes . . . the Davorin eyes.

"You are his sister," he said.

She nodded. "I am Eirlys Davorin, daughter of Torstan and Iolana, and a Sentinel."

She said it proudly, with love and respect for her dead parents. *Iolana.* He fought down the image of the portrait, oddly more difficult now that he was facing her daughter. He searched for resemblance, found it in the eyes, the delicate nose, the chin, the shape of the mouth.

"And the one he"—he gave Jakel a look of loathing—"used to trade for your brother."

Her voice turned cold, icy cold. "Yes."

She walked, with the grace that seemed inherent in the Davorins, over to Jakel. The man squirmed. The girl pulled a dagger with a carved hilt from a sheath on her belt. She crouched beside Jakel, tapping the blade against her palm. Then she turned her head to look at Paledan.

"You meant what you said? You would give him to us?"

He studied her for a moment. "I understand that you have an affinity for . . . beasts."

Her gaze snapped to his face. "You think me weak because of this?"

"I would never call anyone able to shadow me as closely as you did without my knowledge weak."

He thought she almost smiled. "Wise," she said.

"I've found a certain judiciousness useful when dealing with your brother."

She did smile then. And looked at the Raider, who as before stood calmly. Yet Paledan did not mistake his readiness. Should he make one move toward this girl, it would be his last.

"I see why you like him," she said to her brother.

He hid his surprise, but could not resist a glance at the Raider. The man faced him steadily, neither denying nor confirming what his sister had said.

Eirlys looked back at Jakel, who was watching her—and her blade— warily. As well he should, Paledan thought. It would not do to underestimate either Davorin.

And how did the woman who had given up, thrown herself off the escarpment he would be able to see from here if not for the bedamned mist, manage to birth two such children? Was the strength they had inherited from their father so powerful that she hadn't been able to weaken it? How did they possess the planium-strong courage they both had, when she did not?

"If we are speaking of wisdom," he said to Eirlys, "it would be wise of you never to trust this one."

"I would no more turn my back on this beast than on an enraged blazer." She tapped the blade again. "At least, not until he is a eunuch."

Jakel scrambled back as best he could with his mangled leg. But he was glaring at her, fury boiling in his eerily red eyes. Paledan thought that she might well prod one of those mythical, fire-breathing creatures as easily as she poked at Jakel. And he couldn't quite stop himself from smiling,

"You share more than a bit of your brother's reckless courage, little sister, but beware of this mindless fiend. I suspect he knows he has outlived his usefulness as a tool."

Jakel snarled.

"Why did you not put him down yourself, then?" the Raider asked.

"In truth, I was about to, although I had not yet decided." He looked at Jakel. The man was clearly both enraged and yet cowering, a very dangerous combination. "It would appear I left it a bit too long."

"You would have been a bit too long had you killed him," the Raider said dryly, "the day after his birth."

Laughter burst from him then. He could not stop it. And he wondered what the unfettered reaction meant, and why he found such enjoyment in his conversations with this man who should be his mortal enemy.

Should be? Was he not?

"Agreed," he said.

Jakel growled. Somehow he got his good leg under him. Launched. His sheer bulk carried him forward. Paledan spun back. Saw the girl move, deftly flipping the dagger into a striking grasp. He held back, let her do it. She had earned the right. She dug at the already wounded leg. Jakel roared. Fell sideways. Tumbled toward him. Paledan had to leap clear.

The instant he landed he felt the sharp, ripping pain in his back. And then it spread, rippling through him in waves as every muscle contracted in agony. He tried to bite back a scream, succeeded only in muffling it.

His legs did not go weak, they vanished. He hit the ground. It sounded hard, but there was already so much pain he barely felt it. Was vaguely aware he had simply collapsed.

It had finally happened. The shrapnel had shifted that last critical distance, torn its way through flesh to bone and beyond. His legs were gone. His arms moved, but weakly, not as he commanded. And the mist of Ziem seemed to be closing on him. Or he was going blind in addition.

He could barely lift a hand. His worst fear, that he would be unable to end it himself, had come to pass. He wondered how he was still breathing. Would it spread there, too, would he end not in glorious battle but suffocating as those muscles, too, were cut off from the natural signals?

The Raider was there; he could hear his voice. With an effort that seemed impossible for such a simple thing, he opened his eyes. Looked up at the man in the notorious silver helm.

"It is your old wound?" the man asked. Paledan could see that he was touching his arm, but he could not feel it. Nor could he feel the ground beneath him. Nothing.

He thought he might not still have speech, but the words came. "It is the end I've expected." *The worst, most helpless end.*

The Raider looked to his right, gestured to someone Paledan could not see.

"Kill me," he grated out over the pain. How could he still feel pain when he could not even feel a touch? And yet he did, waves of it, rolling through him as if the mist had invaded him, burning him from the inside out. "Blaster, blade, it does not matter."

"Major—"

"You have your enemy at your mercy. End it." He saw something in the man's eyes that made him add, "Please."

"I think you must endure a moment longer," the Raider said.

And then whoever he had summoned was there. The person crouched beside him, reached out, touched him.

He felt it.

His gaze snapped to the newcomer.

Ah.

He understood now. He could not move because he was already dead. So the pain would eventually fade, surely.

He looked at her. She was even more beautiful here, in whatever place this was. More graceful, even more vivid. And her eyes, those eyes . . .

And he decided in that moment that it was worth it, just for this glimpse of the woman in the painting.

He smiled. This was merely some figment, provided by his brain in these final moments, perhaps to make the transition to nothingness easier. But just now it did not matter that it was a mirage; it seemed utterly real, and he would accept and be glad of it.

And then she spoke, and her voice was all that he'd imagined it would be. Soft, low, soothing yet vibrant. Husky with emotion, the kind of emotion he had never felt. The emotion of the truly alive.

"I can ease your path."

It took him a moment to realize he could still speak. And he found his own words an odd choice even as he said them. "Why would you?"

"I would do it for any creature in such pain."

And then the mist closed in. All went dark.

Chapter 13

IOLANA STARED DOWN at the man for a long, silent moment. This was their enemy, was it not? Her instincts warred with her knowledge, and both were overlain by her undue and strange fascination with this man. She touched him, put a hand on each side of his chest. Closed her eyes, even as her mind continued to race. He was here, helpless, and it would take but a stroke to kill him. Left as he was he would die anyway; she could feel the process had started already.

She knew what she wished to do.

She could think of many reasons to do it, but feared too many were her own. And perhaps not the best for Ziem.

Without opening her eyes she whispered, "Drake?"

"He is dying?"

"He will. Unless . . ."

"Assessment?"

She withdrew her hands, unable to focus on both, something that had never happened to her before.

Too much was different about this man.

She looked up at her son.

"It is his spine. I sense something . . . foreign. I cannot yet tell how complete the injury is. It is old and yet . . . new."

She shook her head sharply. She reached down to touch Paledan again, probed deeper. And then she had it. She pulled back and looked up at Drake.

"The old was incurred in a battle. It is a shard of planium. Embedded. The new is the shard shifting. It has damaged his spine. I do not yet know how severely. But he cannot move. If left, he may never again. If he survives. And . . ."

Drake lifted a brow at her. "And?"

"He knows this. He has known it since the original wound."

Drake looked down at the man lying helplessly on the ground. "That is why he begged me to kill him."

"He would not wish to live that way."

"If we were to leave him here, like this . . ."

"He will die. Slowly."

"He is the head of the Coalition on Ziem, and so we should welcome this," Drake said, but Iolana heard in his voice he was not yet convinced.

"There are people alive in Zelos because Paledan refused to order their execution," she reminded him, not certain why she felt she must. "And he has, in his way, protected the twins."

"Yes," Drake said. "And he came here today to warn us of the inevitable order to come from the High Command."

She could almost feel her son thinking, analyzing, weighing. The rush of information she'd gotten during her brief encounter with this man ran through her mind again. She hesitated because the decision was the Raider's to make, but he should have all the information necessary, should he not?

"I have said he is not cruel. It is not in him. He is more . . . unfeeling, although I do not mean that in the usual sense. I mean he does not react emotionally, to anything. It is as if he has not learned how. Or it has been crushed in him. He is utterly rational, and does not believe in killing for the sake of it."

Drake's mouth twisted. "No wonder he and Jakel didn't get along."

She glanced at their downed enemy once more before adding quietly, "You must decide now, Drake. Or he will be beyond my capability to help."

"But you can help him?"

"I believe so."

Her son studied her for a moment. "And you wish to."

It was not a question. It seemed her son was becoming quite adept at reading people as well, albeit in a different way. "Yes."

Eirlys, who had been securing—fiercely—Jakel, approached them and spoke for the first time. "If he had a portrait of me secreted away in his office, I would wish to speak to him, too."

Drake nodded, taking his sister's opinion seriously; he had learned much as well since his charade as the beaten, cowed taproom keeper had finally ended.

"Pryl?" he said, and Iolana gave a small start; the woodsman had appeared as if out of nowhere, so quietly did he move.

The old man gave a one-shouldered shrug. "He's Coalition, but . . . he is different. You've said that from the beginning. And if the Spirit is right about him stalling off High Command, I'm thinking his replacement could be much worse."

That much from the usually taciturn Pryl was tantamount to a declaration. Yet Drake still hesitated. "So the Spirit heals him, and we send him back? The commander of the enemies who will eventually try to wipe us all out?"

"Or we let him die, they bring in someone new, one that will likely do it tomorrow," Pryl answered. "They would not take lightly the death of one of their heroes while we had him."

"Contention valid," Drake agreed. Then, with a smile he clearly could not suppress, he raised his voice. "Come in and join the parlay instead of just listening in, Kye."

Eirlys grinned. "I thought I heard a faint swish a moment ago."

"She's bedamned good with that rover," Pryl said, his grin echoing Eirlys's.

"And now we have the man who designed it," Drake said. Iolana's gaze snapped back to Paledan; she had forgotten that discovery of Brander's.

Kye emerged from the mist. "You're really going to let Iolana save him?"

"He has but a moment or two to decide," Iolana reminded her son; she could sense the man on the ground slipping away.

"They will come looking for him," Kye warned.

"That is true," Drake said.

"Unless we can divert them somehow," Pryl said.

"Surely he told someone he was coming? And when he would be back?" Eirlys asked.

"Perhaps not," Drake said slowly.

"The idea would likely not be met with encouragement from High Command," Iolana said.

"Exactly my thought," Drake agreed.

She felt a sudden inward chill, as if something icy had brushed her heart. "Now, Drake," she said urgently. "You must decide. I can at least stabilize him, give you more time to consider."

He met and held her gaze. Then nodded. "Do what you can."

She swiftly knelt beside the dying man, and reached out to touch him once more.

"CAN'T TRUST YOU alone for a moment, can I?" Brander's tone was joking as he stepped into Iolana's home, but she heard the note of relief beneath. She also heard a distinct lack of surprise at the trouble they had brought with them. "Why here?"

She felt Drake's glance but didn't open her eyes; she was so weary it was all she could do to stay upright on the cushions Grim had brought for her. She needed respite. Yet she could not rest, for she knew this was only temporary.

"She says she can mask this place from him when he wakes." Eirlys's voice came from across the room, and Iolana guessed she was looking down at the unconscious man they had placed on the long bench that served her as seating.

"I know she can," Brander said, his tone dry. "Don't forget I came here searching out the Spirit to save Drake's life, and saw Grim walk right through the rock."

She felt her daughter looking at her now, and this time she opened her eyes. "It is an illusion I can maintain indefinitely where the Stone of Ziem is."

"My lady is very talented," Grim said rather primly. "He will have no idea where he truly is."

Iolana could sense Grim did not approve, but his support was yet unwavering.

"He doesn't look like he'll be running anytime soon," Brander said frankly.

She agreed. "He is paralyzed, and very weak. I have soothed him into sleep, but it will not last for more than a few hours."

"Who shot him?" Brander asked.

"No one," Drake answered.

Brander frowned. But he was nothing if not quick. "The old injury, the one that got him posted here?"

Drake nodded. "He would have died on the spot."

"If not for the Spirit," Eirlys said.

Iolana shifted her gaze back to her daughter. "Who had much-needed help."

Eirlys smiled. She had been hesitant, given who they were trying to save, but she had joined her strength with her mother's, and between them they had beaten back the black tide.

"It was . . . unsettling. It felt as if he were welcoming death."

"He was," Iolana said softly.

Drake nodded. "He is a warrior, not a man who could accept living such a life."

"Not to mention," Kye said wryly, "that the Coalition would likely do away with him anyway, if he were unable to function."

"He knows that, such are the people he serves," Iolana said. "But he feared more that they would keep him alive for his mind, as one would keep a book on a shelf."

Eirlys looked at her. "And yet . . . I got the sense he felt nothing about his own death. No fear, trepidation, reluctance."

Iolana nodded approvingly. Eirlys might be new to this aspect of the skills that had served her so well with her animals, but she was learning swiftly.

"Is this lack of feeling a result of Coalition training or some medical procedure we do not know of?" Drake asked.

"I've read of his home world," Brander said. At Eirlys's glance he grinned. "I had a lot of time to read, when I was making up for lost blood. Although it sickened me to read of the birthplace of this pestilence. But one of the things I found said that there, children are turned over to the Coalition from birth. And those whose minds are too unruly have those minds destroyed. Blanked, they call it."

"That'd chill the emotions out of anyone," Kye said.

"What a horrible way to live," Eirlys said quietly.

Iolana looked at Brander. "You do not seem surprised that we did not simply let him die."

Brander nodded. "I was not surprised. I would not have, either. Not this one."

"Why?"

Brander grinned. "Sheer, raging curiosity?"

Eirlys laughed affectionately. "He cannot resist figuring out why things work the way they do. Apparently that includes people, too."

"I admit to more than a bit of that myself," Drake said. "But before you start trying to figure the man out, remember he does not know your true role. You must stay clear while he is here."

"And while you're doing so, figure out a way to keep the Coalition from tearing the planet apart looking for him?" Kye suggested.

"That as well," Drake agreed, then shifted back to Brander.

"I was thinking," his second said, and Iolana saw every one of them smile, for with those words from Brander, the impossible often began. "I could go down, maybe get someone to mention when he's expected back. So we'll at least know when to expect them to start searching."

"Under what pretext?" Drake asked. "I doubt he told anyone he'd asked you to contact me."

"Maybe I'm just bored to the brink of insanity and looking for a game of chaser. Maybe I can even complain that he postponed our game because he'd be gone. Or something. I'll think of it when I get there."

"And this," Drake said dryly, "is why you drive me to that brink."

"So little faith," Brander chided.

Iolana sat there, realizing with some surprise, that watching these people she loved together, for the moment safe and healthy, was as restorative as actual rest. She was already feeling better, stronger.

"You truly must stay clear of him," Drake told Brander. "If he survives this, we may need you in your current position. You are too valuable if he is yet uncertain about your allegiance."

Brander nodded. "I will, unless it becomes clear he has guessed."

"How long do you plan on keeping him?" Eirlys asked. "Not to mention, what are you going to do with him in the end?"

"He cannot be moved now," Iolana said. "What I have done thus far was only to stabilize him enough to be moved here."

"But you can do more?" Eirlys asked. "You have healed such an injury before?"

"Once, in a woman who had fallen and broken her spine. This is different, obviously, but I can draw out that shard, and once it is gone, heal his spine. However," she cautioned, "I cannot do that and mask myself. Or keep him senseless. He will know who I am."

"And you are willing to risk that?" Drake asked.

"If it will save Ziem from someone worse, yes."

"And wouldn't that just be the way to get a Coalition major indebted to the Sentinels for life?" Kye asked.

"And this," Brander said softly, "is a man of his word."

"Yes," Drake agreed. "Brander, do as you discussed, see if we can learn when he is expected."

"I will try to return before he wakes, or at the least send Runner with word, so you know what we must deal with."

Drake nodded.

"I presume we'll need to mount a guard?" Kye asked. With a glance at Iolana she added, "No matter how weak he is, I wouldn't trust this man not to surprise us all."

"Nor would I," Iolana agreed. And she meant it even more, perhaps, than her son's mate, for she had seen deep into Major Caze Paledan's mind, and knew that this was a man who would never quit as long as he could fight, that only the likes of what had brought him down now could defeat him. "There will be a time, if I am successful with the healing, when he will be able to move again, and even weak, I would not underestimate him."

"Then we give him the choice, if we must," Drake said. "He will hold off the hellhounds and you will heal him, or he will let them come . . . and we will let him die."

Iolana nodded. And let nothing show of the odd, piercing sense of loss that shot through her at her son's pronouncement.

Chapter 14

HE HAD NEVER felt quite this way before. There was little pain, which surprised him in that small part of his mind that seemed to be functioning. He could not move, except for feeble, uncontrolled motions of his hands. This did not surprise him, for he'd felt the moment when the shrapnel had finally reached his spinal cord. And the agony as it sliced into the cable of nerves. It was the last thing he'd felt.

But not the last thing he'd seen.

He couldn't open his eyes; they felt weighted down, sealed, as if they, too, were no longer functional. But that he didn't care about. For as long as they stayed closed, he could cling to the last image he'd seen. That impossible, beautiful vision of a woman who, despite being long dead, had managed to invade too much of his waking day, and take over every moment of his sleeping world. As she had now, although he doubted he was sleeping.

What his state was he wasn't certain. Perhaps dying took longer than he'd thought, or perhaps it just seemed longer; perhaps the process affected the brain in such a way as to distort the concept of time. He was glad there was no longer pain, but his practical, no-nonsense mind was not happy with not knowing. It occurred to him, somewhat vaguely, that the hyper-awareness that had been an asset in battle was no longer necessary. If he was dying—or perhaps already dead in all but this tiny corner of his mind—then perhaps it was for the best that it be this way.

"He is fighting it?"

The voice came from a distance, so great a distance that he should not be able to hear it at all. And yet he could. And not only that, he knew the man's voice. But the name, the face that went with the voice was lost somewhere in the fog that encompassed most of his mind.

And then he heard another voice. Speaking with admiration.

"He is. I don't believe he was ever completely under."

Him. She meant him.

She.

That voice. It was still as he'd imagined it. Even dying, his brain was consistent. That final image rose up in his mind once more. And with it came the memory of the thought he'd had in that moment, that if this was to be the last image of his life, the last thing he would ever see, it would be enough.

And then all faded away again.

"I HAVE NEVER encountered a more disciplined yet brilliant mind," Iolana said.

"Does that speak to him, or to the minds you've encountered?" Eirlys asked lightly. Even Grim, sitting in the corner—where, Iolana knew, he could move swiftly should their guest somehow surprise them—chuckled.

"The two qualities are often in conflict," she said. "As in your mate, for instance. The brilliance is enormous, the discipline selective."

"Selective?" Eirlys was genuinely interested now, but then they were speaking of the man she loved.

"When he is engaged, focused on some intriguing puzzle, he is incredibly disciplined. But when not, that brilliance tends to run wild."

"That," Eirlys said with a loving smile, "I cannot dispute."

"It is one of the many reasons you adore him, is it not?" Iolana asked.

"Talking about me again?"

Both women laughed as the subject of their discussion in fact appeared at the entrance to the cave. He glanced at the man lying motionless beneath the blanket she had put over him, knowing the state she had put him in slowed all processes and becoming too chilled would only make things worse. Eirlys quickly rose and ran to him, and Iolana knew she was suppressing the worry she'd been feeling the entire time he'd been gone.

She watched them embrace, then glanced at the man who had paused behind them, clearly unwilling to interrupt. Drake was smiling, clearly still greatly satisfied that his sister and his best friend had finally done what had seemed inevitable to all those around them, and become one unbreakable unit, just as he and Kye had. It was quite a family unit they were building, Drake pledged to Brander's cousin, and now Brander pledged to Drake's sister.

They've done well, Torstan. Despite it all, they've found what we had.

To keep Brander clear, they stepped outside, leaving Grim to watch over her patient.

"Were you able to learn anything?" Eirlys asked, her tone remarkably even given what Brander had risked.

"I did. I spoke to his aide, Brakely."

"Brakely? Is he connected to—" Iolana began

"Yes," Brander said. "He is Brayton Brakely's nephew."

"Who?" Eirlys asked.

"Brayton Brakely, commander of the Coalition ship *Brightstar,*" Iolana said.

Eirlys mouth twisted. "Sorry, my Coalition history is limited. For too long I liked to pretend they didn't exist."

"He was a Coalition hero on his level," Brander said, nodding toward the cave where Paledan lay. "Until the rebellion on Trios."

"Had fighting that rebellion been up to Brakely, it might have ended differently," Drake said. "But he was under the command of General Corling, and we've learned how that turned out."

"And he was executed along with Corling for his failure," Iolana said.

"I'm surprised the nephew's still alive," Drake said.

"He nearly wasn't," Brander said. "I heard someone say that he was in line to be executed himself, simply for being related to Brakely, when Paledan plucked him out of his cell to act as his aide."

She glanced at Paledan, wondering what kind of Coalition officer would make that kind of decision.

"Yes," Drake said, and she shifted her gaze back to her son. "It is interesting, that this is who he picks as his aide, someone already with such a black mark against him."

"That is so unfair," Eirlys said. Then her mouth curled sourly. "And I cannot believe I just protested unfairness in the Coalition."

Brander hugged her. "It is one of the things I adore about you," he said, clearly playing back on the words he'd heard when he'd come in.

"I think," Iolana said, "it might just be another sign of that brilliance. For who better to have serving you than someone who genuinely owes you his life?"

"Contention very valid," Drake agreed, then looked at Brander. "What feel did you get of the younger Brakely?"

"That if necessary," Brander said without hesitation, "he would die for the man. I think his loyalty is to Paledan, not the Coalition."

"So he has a functioning brain as well," Eirlys said dryly, "not to remain in mindless support of the Coalition machine that wanted to kill him simply because of a relative."

Iolana laughed. She glanced toward the cave, where the man lay unconscious just a few feet away. She did not need to check on him so often, especially with Grim right there. She could sense that he was, for the moment, stable. And both she and Paledan would require their full strength if she was going to make the attempt to heal him. But she could not seem to stop herself from wondering.

"What is it?" Eirlys asked. "You get the strangest expression when you look at him."

"I cannot help but wonder what it must have been like, to have been handed over to that machine you spoke of as a baby, to never have known anything but Coalition cruelty and coldness."

"We have lost much," Brander said, "including many we loved. But at least we had them to lose."

Eirlys looked up at her mate. "Have I mentioned how much I love you?"

He smiled at her. "I'm not sure. Perhaps you could mention it again?"

"Perhaps," Drake said dryly, but with a wide smile, "you could mention first what else you learned? What you went there for?"

"Oh." Brander looked discomfited. "Of course. Brakely mentioned that he"—he nodded at Paledan—"might not be back until tomorrow. I asked, as a joke, when he would call out the troops, and he said only if he misses a scheduled daily contact."

"Scheduled?"

Brander nodded. "I could not push for more without rousing his suspicions. He's not as . . . curious as the major. But from what someone else said, I believe the schedule is every twenty-four hours."

"He would be gone so long without contact?" Eirlys asked.

"He always carries the comm link, should they have need of him." Brander hesitated, then said, "I got the impression he does it often, at will. And given the times and places I've encountered him, that does not surprise me."

"Nor I," Iolana said. "He is very much his own man."

"An oddity in the Coalition," Eirlys said.

"Yes," Brander said. "He said as much once. I said he was a rarity in Coalition uniform, in the way he admired the Raider's tactics and success. He said he was more often called an 'oddity.'"

Drake looked thoughtful, then nodded in turn. "So he is aware he does not . . . fit."

"He is very aware," Iolana said quietly, thinking of those times when what should have been "we" had been "they."

Drake went back to Brander. "Were you able to ascertain when he might have left?"

Brander nodded. "I overheard the boy Jakel frightened near to death saying he had passed him some six hours ago. So that would be just after first light."

"So . . . we would have until that time tomorrow morning before his aide would send out a search patrol."

"Unless the aide breaks the protocol," Eirlys said.

When Drake looked at him, Brander shook his head. "I think he would follow Paledan's orders unto death."

"Agreed," Iolana said. "He is more certain of his aide's loyalty than anyone else in the Coalition."

Drake's mouth twisted wryly. "To be at such a level and yet be unable to trust those around you, of your own people . . ." Then he looked back at her. "Can he be roused by then, by first light?"

"Yes," she said. "Sooner, if necessary."

"Likely," Drake admitted with a grimace, "for we'll have to talk him into making that check-in."

"You think that will be possible?" Eirlys asked.

"I could compel him," Iolana said, "but there is no guarantee he would not say something that would be a warning."

Drake nodded. "I'm sure they must have some procedure in place."

"Not to mention," Brander added, "that if he learned he'd been mentally forced, he is not a man who would take that lightly."

"Why?" Eirlys asked. "Is he not compelled every day by the Coalition?"

"But he believes in them." Brander's expression shifted. "At least, he once did."

"We are not the Coalition," Drake said. "We will not compel him. We offer him healing because he is . . . less cruel and brutal than his replacement would likely be. And with that offer comes the necessity of some subterfuge. He will understand that, I think."

Brander looked at Drake. "You have a plan?"

"I'm hoping that curiosity of his will go along," Drake said. He glanced at Iolana. "But that will also mean you must be absolutely certain this place is completely masked from him. He must have no hint where we really are."

Iolana nodded. "Here, with the help of the stone, I can make it look however you wish to him."

"Ought to make it look like his office, then," Brander said with a grin. "That should befuddle him a bit. Especially with you there. He'll think that portrait has come to life."

Drake's brows rose, then he smiled. "Indeed."

Iolana studiously avoided their gazes, for her feelings about that were something she did not wish to share.

Then Drake spoke briskly, decision clearly made. "Brander, check his comm link. Do what you can mask its location when it is turned back on."

His second nodded, and he and his mate left. Drake stepped back inside as Iolana went to check on the motionless figure under the blanket. Drake glanced at Grim. "Can you give my mother and me a moment, my friend?"

Iolana knew it was a testament to the position her son had gained in

Grim's eyes that he did not look at her for permission before leaving. She braced herself for what she knew was coming.

She decided to save him from having to bring it up by saying briskly, "I will need a decision soon after he wakes, or I will not be able to heal his injury."

He studied her for a long moment. "If it were solely up to you?"

"I would heal him," she answered without hesitation.

"But not simply because it is in your nature to heal, just as it is in Eirlys's."

"No," she admitted. "Also because there is . . . something."

"A vision?"

"No. Nothing so defined as that. Just a feeling that keeping him alive is, or will be, important somehow."

Her son let out a long breath. "All right."

And so, Iolana thought. Paledan would live. For now.

She hoped she did not live to regret it.

Chapter 15

PALEDAN OPENED his eyes to two impossibilities.

One was that he lay in his own office, on some sort of cot that had not been there before.

The second, greater impossibility was the woman sitting beside him. The woman he'd seen in what he'd believed to be his final moments. The woman whose vivid image was merely feet away, behind a single door in that office. The woman he knew to have sprung from his mind, not reality. The woman who had fascinated him beyond sanity.

Beyond sanity because he knew she was dead.

He had so committed that portrait to memory that he could bring it to mind even now, with such clarity that he could compare the features exquisitely rendered by the artist to this, his mind's hallucination. Which he supposed would explain why it was so accurate; his mind had conjured it. Therefore it would, of course, be exactly the image he would expect.

"Welcome back, Major."

Her voice. There had been no recordings of her in the records, only her firebrand mate, so how could he have imagined it so accurately? Or was his brain—or whatever was producing this—simply providing a voice that he'd also imagined, and therefore in his mind, of course fit? Low, soft, but with a resonance that demanded attention for all its quietness.

He closed his eyes for a moment, trying to wade through the muddle. But almost instantly regretted it, for he feared when he opened them again she would be gone.

He nearly laughed at himself. Gone from where? His office? If that wasn't proof enough this was all illusion, what was? There was no reason he could fathom why the Raider would have him brought here. If by some freak of chance he truly was still alive, he would be on that misty hillside where he had fallen, his spine finally victim to the injury that had in fact slain him long ago. It was only that his body had delayed the inevitable until now. It was a shadow he had lived with for a very long time now, and it was no surprise that it had finally fallen.

What was a surprise was . . . this, whatever it was. He had studied beliefs across many worlds, knew that some primitive places believed in a sort of afterlife. He did not, perhaps because he had seen so much of the finality of death. But he could accept that he did not know everything about the process of dying. No one did. The Coalition dealt in death, but it did not study it except in examining how much torture someone could endure before that moment was reached when the body gave up fighting to stay alive.

Perhaps this was no more than a dying brain's way of easing the path, perhaps the perception of time shifted when those last moments were dwindling, perhaps that same brain hung onto those last moments and spun them out so that they seemed much longer than they were. It was an intriguing idea, and one he almost wished he had time to explore. But how would one do such an exploration when the only ones who would know were dead?

It was a puzzle, and—

She would know.

His eyes snapped open almost involuntarily.

She was still there. Smiling at him. And he realized with a little jolt that this was not the woman of the portrait, with her haunted eyes. And yet that woman was there, beneath what he now saw.

It was as if she had been softened somehow, yet the power, the fire remained. Or as if she had been cured of some dread ailment, and the joy of it had overwhelmed the loss that had put that wildness in her vivid eyes.

"So," he said, the differences from her portrait for a moment overtaking his logic, "you found peace, in the end."

She looked startled, then thoughtful, and finally a different kind of smile curved her mouth. "I did. And much more," that perfect voice said. "I found happiness."

He frowned. Happiness was hardly a worthy goal, unless it came from advancing the Coalition. And even then it was more satisfaction than the ebullience most described as happiness. He himself would not know; it was not something he experienced.

Her smile widened, as if she'd heard his thought and found it amusing.

At the same time it was a softer kind of smile that did odd things to his pulse.

Pulse.

His heart still beat.

How was that possible? Or was this, too, a manufacture of his dying brain, which seemed to be taking a damned long time with the process?

"You are not hallucinating nor dreaming, Major," she said. And then that smile turned somehow impish as she added, "Nor are you dead."

He stared at her. His logical mind was trying to register its opinion on the absurdity of this, but his gut was screaming at him to believe. It was rare the two were in conflict, and he did not know what to make of it.

"That is not to say," she went on, her expression serious now, "that you are not hovering very near that death you've been expecting for so long. That is why I immobilized you, so no more damage could be done even accidentally."

He tried to move, to test what she'd said, and could not. He could do no more than turn his head. She merely smiled as if she'd expected him to do exactly that. He was seized with the desire to see that smile every day, an even further sign that this was all some figment concocted by an oxygen-starved brain.

"You see? And it is best for now, I assure you. You must rest, conserve your strength for what is to come."

He wondered why she would think he would believe her when she swore to good intentions. But realized it was irrational to dwell on the details of a discussion with a figment of his dying mind. "To come? What, hades? Damnation? What final stop on this journey of death do you envision for me?"

"I see you are not convinced," she said. "Very well."

She reached toward him. His reflexes overtook all, and he tried to pull away—the last he'd known he'd been in enemy hands, after all—but as she'd said, he could not move. At the same time, an odd sensation welled up in him, a desire to accept her touch, even welcome it. Perhaps it was as he'd heard, that in the end death was welcomed, not dreaded. Yet somehow this seemed more. Because it was her his mind had contrived to present, no doubt because she had absorbed so much of that mind for far too long.

Her fingers touched his arm. Barely, just a brush. An odd yet somehow familiar sensation shot up his arm. The arm he still could not move. So how could he feel anything in it? And then he felt something else, something deep, a faint echo of the pain that had engulfed him in the moment of his collapse. Distant, as if far removed, yet definite and recognizable. As if every nerve in his body was screaming with outrage.

His gaze shot back to her face. That familiar, much-studied face. She looked much the same, albeit a bit older.

But how could she have aged if she was dead?

The absurdity of that question struck him. Because she was dead.

And yet she was here. In some form.

"Did I guess correctly?" she asked. "Is that what it takes for you to believe you are alive, the knowledge of pain?"

He frowned. "It should . . . hurt more."

"I have muffled it, for I could not imagine even you wishing to feel its full impact again."

"Again?"

"I saw you go down, Major."

If he had not already been frozen that would have done it. For it made this all sound real, too real, and he was not ready to accept that it was, even if it meant he was not dying. "You were . . . there?"

She nodded. "And even from where I stood in the trees, I could feel the fierceness of it."

The thought that she somehow could sense—and control—how much pain he felt was too much, and too illogical, to deal with at the moment. So his brain seized on the other words she'd said.

"*Even* me?"

"You are a strong man. I can only imagine how much pain there would have to be for you to even acknowledge it. And you have been living with it for some time now, have you not?"

He was carrying on a conversation with this apparition as if she were real. And in the moment he realized this, she smiled again.

"Tell me, Major, if you are truly dead, then what do you have to lose by talking to me? A vision, a phantom, a . . . spirit?"

"So you can also read minds?" he asked dryly.

She laughed, and it was a marvelous sound that somehow eased his mind. "Not usually, unless I am in physical contact with someone."

He shoved aside the images that had shot through his mind when she'd used the words "physical contact." He was far beyond ever worrying about slaking those needs again. He wasn't certain he hadn't been beyond those needs even before the injury that could now mean losing his life for a moment of physical pleasure.

But she had a point; if he was dead or dying, and she was merely a vision conjured up by his brain, then what did he have to lose?

"I would prefer to die sane," he muttered, as much to himself as to her.

"Your trouble is not sanity. You have a firm grip on it. Your trouble is something you never had."

"Now come the riddles."

"No riddles, Major. Now, shall I mute that pain for you again?"

"Just that easily?"

She touched his arm again, again only the merest of brushings. But this time a memory shot through his mind, of the woman on the bridge, who had touched him in the same way. But she had caused feeling. Not pain, but that strange sort of tingling.

But now, with this woman and this touch, the echo of the pain he'd felt receded.

He stared at her. "How?"

"That is a long story, and likely involves too many of those riddles you do not wish."

"Then here's a riddle for you. If what you say is true, that I am indeed alive, why?"

"That," she said as she rose to her feet in a graceful motion, "you will have to take up with my son."

It all tumbled in on him then. He'd been so enraptured with this image from the portrait he knew so well come to life, that he'd forgotten exactly who she in fact was, that woman.

Iolana Davorin.

Wife of the firebrand who had first inspired the rebellion.

And mother of the Raider.

Chapter 16

SHE REALIZED SHE did not want to send for Drake. She wished more time alone with this man, to perhaps explore the things that made him so different from other Coalition officers. More time to discover what had made him this cool, compartmentalized thinker who brooked—or had—no emotion.

But they were rapidly nearing the moment when his check-in must be made. And Drake would need time to persuade him, if it could be done. This might be her only chance. She wanted to know, down deep, why he'd kept her portrait all this time.

"If you can control pain, what else can you do?" he asked.

"Were you Ziem, you would not have to ask the Spirit about her powers."

"The—" His brows lowered. His eyes, she thought, truly were the vivid green of the new growth on the mistbreaker trees. In this world of varying shades of blue, they were beyond striking. "The Spirit is a local myth," he said.

"Is she?"

He stared at her for a moment. And she realized, with a little shock of surprise, that holding his gaze was an effort. She had thought that holding her composure at her children's cold regard had been hard, but this was a very different kind of difficult. But she did not answer, for the answer was not something he was ready to hear. If ever he would be.

"Where are we, really?" His question was harsh, almost angry. And she could tell by the tension in the tendons of his neck that he was still trying to move, fighting what his body—and she—told him with every bit of strength he could muster.

She made her voice even more relaxed. "It does not look familiar?"

True, it had been a while since she'd been in an office in the council building, and never in his, but Drake had, and had provided a detailed description. Which, she thought with an inward wince, the twins had happily confirmed. The thought of those two brought on a whole new rush of emotions as she remembered that this man could have killed or had them killed many times over. They'd given him many chances, yet he had not done it.

"Very. It is also impossible." He said it flatly, in the tone of one certain of his conclusion.

"Why?"

"For so many reasons."

She merely lifted a brow at him. For a moment she thought he would not speak, but she could almost see the moment when curiosity—that unusual curiosity—won out.

"I was dead upon that hillside. I felt it. Even if I were not, moving me here would have completed the job. And why would the Raider do so in the first place? I am the ranking Coalition officer on Ziem. His enemy. And there's the little matter of getting past the guards."

"You do not think your men would allow safe passage in return for your life?"

"It is against Coalition regulations."

"An answer that is not an answer." She saw a spark of . . . something in his eyes.

"And I still have no answer to where we really are. Or how you have manufactured this illusion."

"Illusions are something I have experience with," she said. "And if I wish it, you will never know."

But he reacted so strongly that she knew something had registered. She did not think she had given anything away but—

"It was you," he breathed. "On the mountain, with the cannon. It was you the troopers saw, who froze them in place, made them believe the mountain held them motionless."

Iolana could not help herself; she laughed in delight. Oh, he was quick! Even when the answers warred with his highly logical mind, he was able to make such a jump.

He was staring at her now, something new in those green depths, something she'd never seen before. She did not know what to make of it. And giving into a sudden urge, she went straight to the heart of what she wanted to know.

"Why have you kept my portrait?"

His mouth tightened slightly. "I see the Raider has an efficient information network."

"He does. And it grows with every atrocity the Coalition commits. But yet again you do not answer the question."

He looked at her steadily for a moment. And she was again surprised by how relatively calm he seemed. But perhaps he was marshalling his strength for a greater effort later. But she would have thought he would try now, if he was going to, since only she was here.

"And what would you say if I told you I kept the portrait as a means of studying the enemy?"

"I would say answering a question with a question is still not an answer."

"Then . . . perhaps we can negotiate, an answer for an answer," he said rather slowly. "Your son keeps his word. Do you?"

"No."

He blinked. His brows lowered. He could, she thought, look quite fierce. Never less than striking, a fine-looking man, but fierce.

"Explain."

It had the ring of an order, but she could sense that curiosity behind it, and so answered anyway. "I promised to look after my children by the simple act of bringing them into the world. I did not keep that promise."

"Why?" Something in his expression had shifted.

"Is this the question you wished answered?"

"Yes."

That made no sense, for why would he care? She wasn't even certain why she answered, but she did. "I thought I could not face life without the man I loved beyond all measure." She smiled, sadly. "I was young."

"You are still," he said.

"In some ways," she agreed. "Now that you have your answer, I would like mine."

"We did not actually agree to this bargain."

"I see." She rose to her feet. "I expected nothing else from the Coalition."

To her surprise, his mouth twitched, almost into a wince. She would have sensed physical pain, so it must be at this assessment.

"If you wish answers," he said, "why do you not simply let the pain return, since you apparently have that ability?"

She looked down at his helpless form. "I cannot imagine the level of pain it would take to break a man like you. You would die first."

"Yes."

It wasn't a boast, it was fact, and she saw that in his eyes. She also saw that he was growing weary, and knew that she had no more time to spend. She walked over to the corner of the illusory room, where one of Eirlys's creatures sat nibbling at a lingberry.

She lifted Ringer, cuddling him for a moment. He had regained some of the weight he had lost while scrounging to survive in the ruins of Zelos, before Brander had found him and brought him home to Eirlys. He patted at her face kindly. She had discovered, to her surprise since she had never tried it before coming here, that the sharing of skills went both ways; Eirlys had some of hers with healing, and she had some of her daughter's with animals.

"Can you find her, my sweet?" she whispered to him. His ring-marked tail twitched. "She will know what to do. Go to Eirlys, now."

She put him down and he trotted away. The illusion of the office did not hold for him, and so it appeared he went straight through the wall.

"You send animals on errands?"

She turned back to him. "I merely told him to seek out my daughter, who will take it from there." She smiled, unable to deny her pride.

"The daughter your son traded himself into hades to save."

She went still at the memory. "Yes," she whispered.

"Speaking of such, where is Jakel?"

"To my regret, he still breathes."

His brows rose. "Feeling murderous?"

"When it comes to those who try to harm my children? Completely."

"Then why am I still alive, if that is what this is?"

"You had an easy chance, once before, to kill the Raider where he stood. Yet you kept your word and did not."

His mouth twisted wryly. "A decision I was worried about living to regret."

She realized in that moment that he still thought himself dead. Or about to be. Whether he yet believed any of what he was seeing now she did not know, but he thought—and accepted—that even if it was real, he was still as good as dead. It was only a matter of time.

She understood, for in a way it was how she had felt, after Torstan's death. That the blast that had reduced him to specks on the wind had taken her just as completely; it had only taken longer for her heart to give up. For she had her children holding her here, but there had come a time when her weakness and her grief had both soared at the same moment, and she was lost.

She could not picture that ever happening to this man. Internal and external, Major Caze Paledan was a man of massive strength. A strength she admired. A strength she wished she herself had had.

And yet, if she had not taken that fateful plunge off Halfhead, she would never have learned the secrets of the mountain, never have gained the skills to pull her son back from the very maw of death. She would have never been able to save the Raider for Ziem, and without him, Ziem would be already lost.

"I kept the portrait in part to remind me of the cost. That the most beautiful woman I had ever seen died because of our objectives."

She stared at him as he not only answered her question without further prompting, but gave her an answer she'd never expected. That it was not the whole answer he had admitted. But for the moment, it was enough.

Shockingly enough.

She turned away from him. For in that moment, she was afraid she had lost all ability to mask her own emotions.

And the major was, besides being clever and strong, a very perceptive man.

Chapter 17

WHEN PALEDAN woke, only then knowing he had slept again, the Raider was there. Not only there but in full gear, including the famous silver helmet he wore. And oddly, it was his appearance in battle attire that made Paledan believe this was actually real, that he was somehow still alive. He wondered if they'd done something, sedated him with something, for he felt unexpectedly calm given he was unable to move beyond breathing. And again he wondered, with a frown, why could he still breathe? Or talk? Or for that matter, even think?

"You have a decision to make, and little time to make it," Davorin said without preamble, cutting off his speculations.

"I was of the impression I held no dice here, Davorin."

"You have one. How you roll it will determine your future."

Paledan studied the man for a moment. In another time, another place, he would have welcomed this man into his ranks. Except that he was too independent, too strong minded . . .

There is no room in the Coalition for independent thought, Caze Paledan. If you continue to let your own mind and thoughts have sway, you will be blanked and relegated to the slave ranks.

His first battle instructor's words echoed in his mind. The threat of having his mind surgically blanked had terrified the child he'd been. He'd made the only choice possible. Which had led to many other choices.

But if he'd known then what he knew now, would he have made the same decisions?

It did not matter. Apparently, to his surprise, he had choices to make now.

"My options?"

"You make contact with Brakely before time runs out and tell him to hold. Or you do not, he sends troopers after you . . . and we let you die."

So. The man knew Brakely's name. And that he had a scheduled check-in. He was not surprised. The man had a network that nearly surpassed the Coalition. In fact it likely did, here on this mist-shrouded planet.

"And what have I to gain by delaying the inevitable destruction?"

"Your life."

He would have shrugged, had he been able. "It is of little import. I would prefer death to what is left to me now."

The Raider smiled, a strangely understanding smile. "And if you could be healed? Completely?"

He let out a sour chuckle. "The best Coalition doctors have made it clear that when this shift happened, it would be permanent, so do not think to fool me with such blather."

For a moment the Raider was silent. He lifted off the silver helm and ran a hand over his hair. Then he crouched beside the cot, looking at his helpless prisoner steadily.

"Have you never wondered, Major, how I went from what you saw in Jakel's den to leading that raid on the fusion cannon in such a short time?"

Paledan's gaze narrowed. "Of course I have. It should have been impossible. You were a breath from death when I saw you there."

"Yes. I was." He said nothing more, just held his gaze.

"You're saying," Paledan said slowly, "that you have some method of healing such grievous injuries? Some advanced medicine beyond even Coalition abilities?"

"Not exactly."

Paledan frowned. His arm, which he could not feel . . . tingled. The woman. The portrait. What she had done with the pain.

"Her?" he whispered in disbelief. "She healed you?"

"She pulled me from the brink of death." Paledan saw his mouth twist slightly. "I am not yet convinced that I had not already gone and she coaxed me back. Such is her power."

"This is . . . your mother you speak of."

"Yes."

"So it is likely . . . some part of the connection between you that allowed her to save you."

The man smiled, again in understanding. "So would I think, in your place. Trying to make logic out of impossibility." Paledan nearly nodded, so close was this to his own earlier thought. "However, I can attest she has healed many who are no connection to her at all. And she is the reason you are still breathing, since you cannot move those muscles on your own."

So that was the answer to what he had wondered himself? He could not deny the truth of it, for he did still breathe, but. . . . "How?"

"She draws something from Ziem herself. I do not pretend to understand it, but I cannot deny her results. This," the Raider said, gesturing at him, "will be a lesser challenge, but perhaps more complicated because of the location of the shard." Paledan blinked. They knew even this? "I presume it shifted when you moved so quickly?"

He discarded for the moment the impossibility that they knew this, for obviously it was not impossible. "And if I am healed, it will only happen again."

The Raider looked at him with open curiosity. "Most would say any precious days of life gained would be worth it."

"If you can call knowing that any wrong step will end it living," he said dryly.

"Contention valid," the Raider said with a nod. "But I was not speaking of merely putting you back to the condition before you fell. When I said your life, I meant it. The shard removed, your spine healed."

Something sharp, bright jabbed through him as if he had regained feeling. He did not know what it was, but it seized him, tightened his throat. Was whatever they—or she—had done wearing off?

"It is not possible." It came out harshly, with a note he didn't recognize, no doubt because of that odd tightness of his throat.

"It is not possible that I am alive, and yet I am here."

Paledan was finding it hard to think, so tangled was his mind. He was not used to such confusion, and he reached for something, anything to slow it all down. Seized upon the Raider's battle attire.

"You are dressed for fighting."

"Actually," the man said casually, "I was merely overseeing some building."

A thought struck him. "A base for your cannon?"

"Not yet. I prefer to keep it mobile for the time being."

"How can you possibly—"

"Please, Major. You know better than to ask such a thing. Would you reveal to me your . . . scheduled visits to High Command?"

The jab about the timing of the cannon raid was precise and delivered with a touch of humor that Paledan admired even as he was forced to admit that this man had outmaneuvered him on more than one front.

"Contention valid," he admitted.

"You are nearly out of time," the Raider said. "I will have your decision, please. I would suggest you placate your aide and buy yourself another day to consider, if nothing else. Although the Spirit tells me the healing process cannot be delayed too much longer, if you wish optimum success."

"The Spirit," he muttered, shaking his head slowly.

"Impossible, is it not? And yet there it is."

It was, of course, absurd. To think that some mystic woman could do what the skill of Coalition doctors could not. And yet . . .

"I would speak to her again first," he said.

The Raider's brows rose. He realized he'd spoken it in his usual tone of command. He closed his eyes and let out a breath. The man before him apparently accepted that as evidence of his realization and left it there.

More than I would do.

"I'm afraid there is no time. You are supposed to check in within the next few minutes, are you not?"

"And how," he snapped, "am I supposed to know what time it is? I don't even know where I am."

The Raider smiled. "True enough. And that is how it will stay. But it is nearly dawn, which is when you left. And I would suggest that if possible, you gain at least two days without contact, for there may be a time in the healing process when you are unable."

He did not like the sound of that. Nor did he like how much the man knew. Someday he would like to learn how he managed it, but this was not the time, nor was he likely to learn from him anyway. The Raider didn't make that kind of mistake.

"Well, Major?"

"I see my choices somewhat differently," he said. "Either hold off my troops, as you said, or let them come and die anyway in the process. Which is what a Coalition officer would be expected to do, so that a new commander can be sent in to destroy anything that's left of you."

"I will not deny that the fact that you have not yet initiated that destruction, while your replacement most likely would, is one of the reasons I offer you this choice."

He hadn't expected that. "One of the reasons? There are others?"

"Yes."

"May I know them?"

"Only if you make the decision that will give me time to relate them." One corner of the man's mouth quirked upward. "And, of course, if I feel it wise to tell you."

His own mouth quirked in the same way. "I still say you would have gone far in the Coalition."

"No. For I have a powerful aversion to having my thinking done for me. And I confess, I am surprised you accept it."

Paledan thought of all the times that very thing had nearly brought him down, the times he had been saved only by his record of successes.

"A decision, Major." This time it was the Raider whose voice held the tone of command, and he had every reason for it. He was utterly, totally in charge at the moment.

With some thought that if he lived, he could learn more of this man he must one day fight, Paledan finally spoke. "You have my comm link?"

The Raider walked over to the shelf on the wall. A place that would have been mere steps away if he had been able to move. He walked back with the comm link in hand. "You should know the locating chip has been disabled. They will have no way to trace where you are."

He was surprised that he was not more . . . surprised.

The Raider crouched beside him. "I'm sure you have duress codes in place. Obviously it is up to you whether to use them. But I assure you it will not help; they will never find us. And we are watching and will know if you did."

"And what makes you think the temptation of you putting an end to what is left of me will not overcome all else?"

"I could not blame you for that. But what makes you think I will not just turn you over to Jakel, to whom you so endeared yourself when you handed him over to us?"

"It is hard to torture a man who has no feeling in his body."

"The Spirit could restore the sensation of pain, as you learned." The Raider lifted a brow. "But I would think the temptation of being healed and whole once more would be greater."

"And then what happens?"

"That remains to be seen. Your time is up, Major. Now. Or not."

One last deep breath, and he nodded.

"Ready?"

"I cannot hold it," he said, fighting the images that tumbled through his mind of a life spent like this, unable to do even such a small thing, and unable to even end it. He would welcome a Coalition decision to terminate him, rather than spend his days like this. And the fear that he would not be granted even that small mercy, that he would be keep alive as this useless thing hovered like a darker, thicker, poisonous version of Ziem's mist.

The Raider held out the comm link and keyed it. Paledan spoke. "Ziem Outpost Leader to base." He knew Brakely had been apprehensive by both the speed with which he answered and the worried note in his voice.

"Base here. Cutting it close, Major."

"Yes."

"All well?"

"Well. There?"

"Nuisances. Nothing of import since you left."

They've been a little busy. Then, slowly, he said, "Call only if such occurs. I will remain out."

Brakely didn't sound surprised. "How long, sir?"

"Uncertain, as yet."

"Have you found some sign of them?"

He found himself having to stifle a sour laugh. And when he glanced at the Raider, the damned brigand was grinning.

"Perhaps. Enough to continue." It was the only thing that would keep Brakely at bay, the thought that he might have found something. The Raider seemed to understand, for he made no move to cut off the connection.

"Excellent, sir." Brakely sounded encouraged then. "Check-ins the same?"

He glanced at the Raider again. Then said, "Double it."

"Yes, sir."

"Paledan out."

"Base out."

He'd done it. Committed himself to an uncertain fate and submitted himself to the will of the man who had the most reason of anyone on this planet to want him dead.

Perhaps his spine had not been the only thing affected.

Chapter 18

PALEDAN WATCHED AS the Raider released the microphone key and shut the device off, without looking, as if he dealt with it often. He rose, walked over and put it on the shelf—it was very disconcerting, this illusion that they were in his office in the half-destroyed council building—then turned back.

"You know much of how our equipment works."

"Necessary knowledge." He gave Paledan an odd look. "Although I would much prefer to know how a man who is not a pilot managed to design such a versatile and agile craft as the air rover."

Paledan stared at him, wondering if he looked as stunned as he felt. "As much as I respect you," he said slowly, "I still underestimated you."

The Raider held his gaze before saying quietly, "I will take that as a compliment. Something I would say to no one else in your uniform."

"And I would say it to no other rebel I've encountered." He frowned. "And perhaps I will answer your question, if you in turn will tell me how you managed to move a fusion cannon with only four of the craft."

"Would you not think the cannon useful in a smaller, more mobile form?" he answered. "But that discussion can—and must wait. We must discuss what happens next."

"Obviously," Paledan said dryly, "I am at your mercy."

"I didn't think the Coalition even knew the word," came a voice from the entrance.

It was the sister. "It is not in the Coalition protocols," he answered.

He studied her as she studied him, although it was an uncomfortable feeling, since he was paralyzed and helpless. When she had first appeared on that hillside, he had remembered her only as the device Jakel had used to entrap Davorin. But now she was clearly much more; that had been proven when she had taken on Jakel with nothing but a small blade. He tried to analyze the change in her, finally decided it was the anger he had noticed the few times he'd seen her in the taproom before. Then, it had flared like wildfire; now it was a fierce but banked burn.

"I see you aren't surprised to see me," she said. "Nor were you at the meeting place."

"I assumed where your brother is, you would be. It is what is customary here, that blood ties hold, is it not?"

The woman's expression changed. "But not customary on your world."

"Not permitted," he corrected.

She shook her head slowly. And when she spoke again, the harshness was gone from her voice. "What a cold, cruel way to live."

And suddenly, uncharacteristically, he spoke before he thought. "The twins."

He managed to stop himself there. Davorin and his sister exchanged a glance. "Concerned, Major?" the sister asked.

"Just . . . curious."

"I understand they also are not . . . permitted on your world," Davorin said.

He decided then that wondering how the man got his information was pointless. Better to focus on avoiding any betrayals of information better kept secret. But he saw no harm in admitting this fact.

"That is correct. And the contributors are forbidden from producing together again."

"Contributors?" Davorin asked.

"I believe you call them parents. On Lustros they have no connection other than being chosen to contribute the child."

"I repeat," the sister said softly, "a cold, cruel way."

He thought of the two beyond-lively children, the boy's inventiveness and the girl's wit and cleverness. The girl who would, on his world, have likely been the one destroyed for being the smaller, weaker.

"In this," he said slowly, "I would have to agree."

The sister looked surprised. Then thoughtful. It made him think of what she had said, out there.

I see why you like him.

Uncertainty was not a feeling he was used to, and yet he was just that about these rebels. From his position as commander he had always operated on the assumption that rebels were at best misguided, at worst fools, for no one could succeed against the might of the Coalition. But now—

There was a stir at the door. In came the woman, the Spirit, if her son was to be believed. She was accompanied by a tall, angular, nearly gaunt man with watchful eyes.

She crossed to where he lay. "I am told you have agreed."

"I have forestalled an attack, yes."

"So you wish to live."

There was an odd note in her voice, and he realized she would have understood if he had chosen otherwise, for she had done so herself once.

"Perhaps I just wish to know if any of what you have said is truth."

The moment he said it he realized it was no doubt foolish to taunt the person who supposedly would heal him, and he wondered if somehow his self-control had been crippled along with his body.

But instead of taking offense, she merely laughed. "And how much trouble has that curiosity gotten you into, Major?"

To his shock this time, he nearly smiled. What *was* this woman doing to him? Or was it merely this place, extending its effect? Or perhaps it was simply being around these people, whose ways were so different from anything he'd known.

He liked either of those ideas better than laying it all at the feet of this woman whose image he had lived with and been drawn to with more intensity than was easily explainable.

"Enough," he replied, his voice gruff with the effort to stifle that smile.

She laughed again, and it was an even lighter, brighter sound that seemed to want to draw out that smile. She looked at . . . her daughter. He was so unused to thinking of family connections in that way it always took him that extra half second to remind himself.

"Will you need me?" the younger woman—although now, seeing them together, he could well see that there were not two full decades between them—asked.

"Not in the beginning," her mother said. "But you will stay close?"

A nod was her answer, and the girl left. She looked then at her son. "We are agreed?"

Davorin drew in a deep breath, the only sign of hesitation he had seen from the man. He did not blame him; if this were all true, he was about to allow his enemy to be healed, when he could more easily let him simply die. That is what he would have done, in his place.

Or would he? A frown creased his brow.

"Second thoughts, Major?" Davorin asked.

"No. Merely wondering what I would do were our positions reversed."

"You do not know?" the woman—he must decide what to call her—asked.

"I know what Coalition protocols would demand."

"And you also know that is not what I asked. So in essence, you have answered," she said.

She reached out then, to touch him. Not his arm this time, but his neck, where one would touch to feel for a pulse. If she found nothing he would not be surprised at this point; this entire interlude would make more sense as a dying brain's delusion than reality.

The moment her fingers touched his skin that odd tingling sensation began. Grew stronger the longer she maintained the contact. His gaze went to her face; her eyes were lowered, as if she were concentrating.

And suddenly, belatedly, it struck him. "It was you." Her gaze lifted. Met his. "On the bridge."

For a moment he thought she would deny it. But she said only, "You sound very certain."

"When you bumped into me . . . it felt the same. A tingling, almost burning. I first thought you had poisoned me."

Something in her gaze shifted then, changed. "Is that what it felt like to you?"

"It felt like nothing ever had."

She stared at him. He held her gaze. He could do nothing else, could not move from the neck down, but he would not cower.

"How did they do it?" she asked, her voice barely above a whisper.

His brow furrowed. "What?"

"How did they crush the emotion, the feelings out of you?"

"I do not think I ever had them. Not as others did."

Her brow furrowed in turn. "Yet you have humor, feel anger."

"Anger is permissible. Even required, for the Coalition's work."

"And the humor?"

His mouth twisted wryly. "I found it required, as well." Then, wondering if the trouble he was having focusing on the subject was a side effect of his injury, he asked, "What did you do to me, at the bridge?"

"What I did, Major, was very simple. I gave you a tiny bit of true feeling, normal emotion. And anything you felt after that was a fraction of what most people feel every day."

He blinked. "That's . . . impossible."

"What will be impossible is healing you, unless we begin quickly. Drake, Grim, turn him please."

His natural instincts rebelled at the thought of turning his back on them, but he quelled them quickly with the silent admission that he would be no more helpless lying face down than he was already.

The two men did the job easily. It was the tall, gaunt one who adjusted his head so that he could see into the room. So he could see her. That surprised him.

He saw the Raider stand, easily, after the task was done. It came back to him again, the memory of what he had seen in Jakel's dungeon room, that bloody cell the man had soundproofed so his victim's screams would not be heard. The very man who moved so easily now, with such strength, had been broken, beaten, and tortured until he was unrecognizable, every harsh, shallow breath seeming likely to be his last. He had thought him already dead at first, held up only by the chains Jakel had used.

If he was to be believed, she had healed him. And if she could heal that, in a matter of days . . .

"I will stay," he heard Davorin say.

"It is not necessary."

Paledan realized it was her safety Davorin was concerned with. As if he could so much as lift a hand to touch her. Even if he wished it. Thoughts such as he had not had for an eon slammed through his mind, all tangled with visions of the portrait, the living subject of which was here now, alive and even more striking than the image he knew so well.

"Grim will be enough, for now, and you have much to do. I will send for you when he is mobile again, but it will be some time."

He heard footsteps as Davorin, the Raider . . . her son left them. Wondered if he had truly gone insane, to even consider that this woman might restore him to where he might someday hear his own footsteps again.

. . . when he is mobile again.

She sounded so sure. So confident. He recognized the tone, for it was regularly in his own voice. So he did not doubt her certainty. It was only what it was claimed she could do he could not accept. It was fantastical, a kind of thinking that wasn't just frowned upon in the Coalition, it was punishable. Severely. High Command did not tolerate variations from their norm.

"This will be difficult for you, Major. For you will have to discard the beliefs of a lifetime." He nearly laughed as she came so close to his thoughts at this very moment. "Major?"

His gaze snapped back to her face. He still found it nearly impossible to believe she was really here, vibrant, alive. Somewhat scarred, yes—he had noticed the scar on her arm, wondered if it had happened in her plunge from Halfhead or after, in some battle against the Coalition troops here. How long had she been with them? All along? Had her children always known she had survived that fall? That did not fit with the legends he'd heard, of the Spirit of the mountain. But then, he had paid scant attention to the tales, for they were . . . fantastical.

"For the moment, you must set aside those thoughts. For this will not work as it should if you do not believe that it will."

His lips tightened. Had he, when face to face with the end, become so obvious? "You ask much."

"I give much," she answered simply.

He could not make the jump. The capacity for such imaginative acts was long gone, if he had indeed ever had it. He understood only logistics, procedure—

"Let me explain the procedure. Perhaps that will help."

Had he been able to move, he would have gone very still at her using the very word he had just thought.

"You must talk, as I work on the healing."

"What has that to do with—"

"I must know that I am not doing further damage. Which also means, I am afraid, that you must feel some of the pain, for the same reason."

"Why would I feel pain at all, if the cord is severed?"

"Because it is not. Not completely."

He frowned. "How can you know this?"

"The same way I can know that long ago, perhaps in childhood, your left leg was broken."

He blinked. Would have drawn back if he could. How could she possibly know this? "I—"

"Perhaps if you think of me as any other physician, it might help?" For an instant, just an instant, a woman with a stern face and in Coalition medical uniform, looked down at him. And then she was Iolana Davorin once more.

A low short laugh escaped him. "You look like no Coalition physician I have ever seen," he said. And realized with a little jolt, as she nodded and reached out to touch him, he had almost added, "Iolana."

Chapter 19

HER CHILDREN WERE stubborn. Drake had the drive and determination of his father; Eirlys had the fire and energy she herself had once had. And the twins had a brand of willfulness all their own.

But this man could give lessons to them all.

He fought down his doubts; she could feel it through the connection between them. And she was more than surprised at the strength he still had to do so, although it was strength of mind that was required, not body.

Kneeling beside him, she pressed her hands against his back, some part of her recognizing how powerful the muscles were. This was no chair-bound Coalition officer; this was a warrior. She'd known that before, but feeling it beneath her fingers, even through his clothing, was much more vivid. As was the ridge of scar tissue she could feel, where the piece that had shifted had originally ripped into him.

It was, she thought, no small wonder that he was still alive at all, let alone functional.

It took her a few moments to set up the channel, in large part because his mind was as powerful as his body, and she had to take extra time to wall it off so she could focus on the healing. In the moment before she successfully isolated the pathway she needed, a single, incredible piece of knowledge hit her, a piece buried so deeply she knew he had never been aware of it. It was well hidden within, in that place where the very basics of a life were stored, things so elemental they were never conscious thought or awareness. It explained something she had sensed only the edges of before, something she had been worried about, but never understood.

She pushed it aside. It could wait. Everything could wait, except what she had to do now.

She heard him make a sound of surprise tinged with that stubborn disbelief. "You feel it," she said; she did not have to ask.

"Something," he admitted.

"Like on the bridge, only stronger?"

She sensed the mental tension as if it were physical, even in a body that could not, at the moment, do such. Never had she had to build such walls to separate the flow from the chaos of thought.

"Yes," he finally said.

She steadied herself. She needed to keep him talking, and he was clearly not inclined. She was spreading herself thin, and might well end torn between asking Grim to join, or sending him for Eirlys, who could give her more strength.

"And . . . different," he said when she had thought he would not.

"Yes. This is focused on your injury." She moved her right hand slightly. She could feel it now, as surely as if it were heated glowmist. The old damaged tissue, and now the new, with the bleeding, the screaming nerves surrounding their brethren that had been severed.

After a moment he said, rather acerbically, "Then what was that moment on the bridge focused on?"

She hesitated, but then gave him at least part of the truth. "The measure of a man. Do you wish to know how this will proceed?"

"Should I not?"

"Some don't. They only wish it over."

"That"—the acerbic tone was back—"I can understand."

"Is the pain too much? As I explained, there must be some so you can tell me if it moves."

"Which will mean?"

"Possibly new damage. And a shift in my focus."

"Is this always so . . . conversational?"

She nearly laughed at his tone this time. Yes, the wry humor was intact, which given his situation was rather remarkable. But then, she already knew this was a remarkable man. And that he was a Coalition major didn't change that, but it did give her pause.

"No," she answered, "for usually those hurt badly enough to need me are either unconscious or must be rendered so to survive. And later, when the pain will be the worst, I can lessen it. But the nature of this injury requires I know immediately of any change. And it is helpful that I know you are still sensible."

"There is nothing about this that is . . . sensible."

She did laugh this time. And the burst from his mind battered the barrier yet again, in a way that unsettled her enough that she almost lost focus. This could not happen, so she hastened to give the explanation he hadn't actually asked for.

"I will seal off the bleeding first. That is the fairly simple part. Healing muscle and bone is more complex, but nerves are the most difficult of all, and take longer. That will be the most painful, too, I'm afraid."

"So am I."

And yet again he took her off stride with an almost acid humor in his voice. "I would not think you afraid of anything. Does the Coalition allow such?"

"If you have no fear, you have no caution and become foolish. Not desirable for Coalition officers of higher rank. They only concern themselves with crushing fear out of those who must ever and always follow orders."

He said it so coolly that it sent an echoing chill through her. She made herself focus. "The shrapnel is planium, I believe?"

"Yes."

"Good. Then I can remove it."

"Our surgeons said—"

"Not with surgery."

"What?"

She knew he would likely not believe it. But she told him anyway. Better now when he was forced to hear it than when he could walk away.

"It is of Ziem."

"As all planium is, yes." He looked toward her, clearly questioning.

"It is of Ziem and therefore I can draw it to me. It will flow, as mist on the breeze," she elaborated.

She saw him blink. Nearly smiled. He said nothing, but she could almost feel him quashing down his natural reaction to a claim that to him must seem utterly preposterous.

When she spoke again, she did so briskly. "I will trust you to advise me about the pain. This is no place for stoicism, Major, I must know of the slightest change of location. And I will speak to you regularly. You must respond, with an answer that shows you understood the words and can form an answer. Is that clear?"

"Quite."

Something about his tone this time made her add, "And have I your word?"

"You would trust it?"

She held his gaze for a moment, a moment that was surprisingly difficult, before she said, "My son says you will keep it. My trust lies with him."

"He is worthy of it." With any other, she might think the words flattery. Not this man. He meant it. And once more she thought of how he had spoken of the Coalition he served. Not *we* but *they*. "I understand I am the prisoner here," he said. "But I would ask one thing of you."

"Healing you is not enough?" she asked, keeping her tone purposely light.

"Are you saying there is no chance anything could go . . . wrong?"

"There is always that chance, in delicate procedures like this," she admitted.

"Then if it does, I ask that you let me die."

"I see." She was not surprised; she already had seen on that hillside that a life so impaired would be unbearable for this man. Even as she thought it, he confirmed it.

"I have not the courage to live as I am now. I must have your promise it will end, even if you must aid that end."

"You want my promise to kill you if I cannot heal you?"

"Not you, if you cannot. I am sure there is someone here who would take pleasure in the death of a Coalition officer. And something more," he added rather abruptly.

"You are used to giving orders, aren't you? What else?"

"If . . . it comes to that, I would suggest you make it look as an accident. A fall, perhaps."

"You think that would be believed? A man with your strength and agility?"

"They will think the shard did what they said it would do."

"But it will be gone."

"I doubt they will bother to check."

"Won't bother? One of their most decorated officers—"

"—is still dispensable."

She shook her head slowly as she looked at him. "And you wonder why we fight?"

"No." She lifted a brow at him. "I only wonder at how well you fight."

"Flattery?"

"I do not flatter."

She set aside the thoughts that wanted to rise up and consume her mind. There was no room for speculation now. She could feel the active bleeding had stopped, so it was time now to begin edging the metal shard back, away from the new damage it had caused.

And it would not do to wonder what would happen if she failed. What would happen if the leader of the Coalition on Ziem died under her hands. But she could not stop herself from wondering how it had come to pass that the best thing she could do for this home she loved was to save the leader of their conquerors.

HE HAD ENDURED pain before. A great deal. But this was different than anything he had ever experienced. It was made doubly difficult by the need to respond to—he truly must think of what to call her—when she spoke to him. Sensibly.

Oddly, he found what helped most was remembering the way she had laughed. It had been a sound unlike anything he'd heard. Or rather, the reaction it caused in him was unlike anything he'd ever felt. He'd lived an expansive life, seen many worlds, done many things, led a conquering force around the galaxy, and yet never had he felt the odd sort of sensations that laugh had caused. Something about the light, silvery quality of it, the genuine mirth, had brushed over him like the feathers of one of those bedamned birds they had so many of on this foggy world.

"What is it you're doing, exactly?"

"First I must establish a barrier around the shard, so it will not slip. Then heal the blood vessels and tissue it damaged, so you will not hemorrhage when it is removed. Once it is gone, then the work of healing the nerves will begin. And that, I promise you, Major, will likely be the most unpleasant experience of your life."

"I will endeavor to focus on the goal."

"I sense you are strong-minded enough to do just that."

He wasn't certain, with her, if that was a compliment or not.

"Tell me, Major, are the children of your world truly taken from their parents as infants?"

The abrupt question startled him, momentarily shoving the pain to the background. Which, he supposed, was the intent, for surely she was not truly interested in such things.

"Yes."

"Cold. And they agree to this?"

He frowned. "Of course. It is expected."

"How did yours feel about it?"

"I do not know. I never knew them."

He heard her breath catch, felt an odd sort of snap, as if whatever it was, this flow she had set up between them, had wavered for a moment. Then it resumed. And only then did he realize he could . . . not feel her touch, but sense a sort of pressure on his back, near where the scar marked the metal's entry.

"Who looks after the children?"

He tried to focus. "Attendants."

"Were they kind?"

His frown deepened. As a distraction, her unexpected questions were working. He had spent little time with anyone who did not already know all this, did not accept it as a matter of course. "That is not their job. They are only to keep the children healthy. Strong."

"Did they not become . . . attached?"

"It was not permitted. And they were rotated regularly, to prevent just such violations."

"Violations." It was said so under her breath he almost didn't hear it, wondered if he'd been intended to. But she had to know he could, the way his head was turned to the side where she knelt. With an effort and the bit of control he had left above the shoulders, he could see her. She said nothing more, and it was a diversion from the pain, so unaccustomed as he was to it, he kept talking.

"They also begin the initial sorting. Pulling out those who are abnormal, physically or mentally."

He quoted it by rote; everyone knew what the process was, and no one thought about it much.

"They watch for—" a sharper pain jabbed through, and he had to make a greater effort to continue "—certain signs, signals of what a child might have an aptitude for, so they can be tested in that area."

"And if they show no specific aptitude at that young age?"

"If they are otherwise normal, they are held in a separate group." He shifted his gaze to her face, and was surprised at the tension he saw there; her voice had sounded normal again. "They are not unaware that some talents are latent, and do not manifest in early childhood."

"So rational. Tell me, Major. Do the children understand what they are missing?"

"They miss nothing. They have food, get exercise, mental stimulation."

"And where do they go in your glorious Coalition to get the love all children need?"

"That is strictly a . . . cultural concept. The Coalition has found it unnecessary."

She moved slightly. He saw it, not felt it. No, wait, he did feel . . . something. A shift in that strange flow he could sense. "So your children are treated as less than animals, who at least have parents to nurture them until they can survive on their own."

"They have what they need."

"And you, Major? As a child, did you never yearn for something more, even if you sadly did not know what it was?"

"No." He said it with an edge he put down to the jabbing increase in pain he suddenly felt.

"Did it move, or just get worse?"

So she had sensed it. "Worse. Same place."

"Odd," she murmured. She moved again.

He suddenly could not breathe. Nor could he speak to tell her.

"Hold on," she said urgently. She moved her hands, not far, perhaps an inch. Nothing changed. His vision began to oddly narrow around the edges.

"Grim! Your blade!"

The tall man moved quickly. Handed her something. Was she going to put him out of his misery? It did not matter, except he would regret the end of this time with her.

And in this moment, with it all slipping away from him, he didn't even think it strange that that was his last thought.

Chapter 20

IOLANA MOVED quickly, using Grim's razor sharp blade to slice through the jacket and shirt Paledan wore. She shoved aside the layers of cloth; she needed direct contact now. Another time she might have admired the sleek skin over solid muscle, but now she focused only on the knotted scar that marked the entryway of the invasive shard. She put her hands over it, pressing down, sending an intense burst, closing her eyes to give it her full effort.

And suddenly she felt him breathe again. He gasped reflexively, sucking in several deep gulps.

"I am sorry, Major," she said as she sat back, shaken. "The shard is larger—longer, to be specific—than I thought. But I have it now. Are you all right?"

"I . . ." He stopped, took a couple more breaths, as if he were making certain he could. "Yes," he finally said.

"Take a moment, then we will resume."

"The treatment, or the conversation?"

He was remarkably calm for someone who had just nearly died under her hands. Had he come so close to death so many times he was inured? He had asked for it, out on that hillside. But that had been when faced with the end of his life, as he knew it anyway.

It struck her then to wonder, for the first time, what Drake would have done had she not been there to offer an alternative. Before the question even formed, she knew the answer; her son would have granted Paledan's request before he would leave him there to die helplessly after possibly days of suffering. Which was, she thought, more than the Coalition would do in turn.

"Both. I find the conversation . . . interesting. Disheartening, yes, but interesting." She hesitated, then thought she would have no better time to ask. He could use another moment to rest, and she was curious. "Tell me, Major, are there any children of your own in that unfeeling nursery?"

She had surprised him. But he answered, rather sharply. "No."

A nerve? "I'm surprised the Coalition hasn't come up with a way to produce the necessary soldiers in a laboratory."

"They're working on it."

She gave a slow shake of her head. "Your masters do not read much history, do they?"

"They write it, not read it."

"And so they have not learned what others have from their mistakes, and must repeat them."

"Mistakes? In some quarters simply implying the Coalition is capable of mistakes would end with your head on a pike."

"I am fortunate, then, not to be in such a quarter."

"Some would say you are. The Coalition has declared Ziem conquered."

"And you, Major? What do you declare?"

Something glinted in those impossibly green eyes. "That they have pronounced that victory too soon."

She laughed, delighted with the answer. He stared at her, and their gazes locked. Something shifted in her, making her feel oddly off balance. He was, she thought, a very different sort of man.

She moved back into position. "I think we will resume now. Both healing and conversation," she added, thinking that she liked his dry humor. More than she ever would have expected.

She let her hands hover over the scar once more, although it took her a moment she found embarrassing to finally focus below the surface, so drawn was she by the skin over taut muscle around the mark. She searched her mind for something to distract her.

"Is it true that Barcon Odom is dead?"

"It is." After a moment he asked, "Does that bother you?"

"Only that in now I will never understand why he betrayed us."

"Betrayed? Some would say he merely accepted the inevitable. Many have welcomed the Coalition, have understood the benefits." He sounded as if he genuinely wanted to understand.

"The benefit of being taken care of, as long as you march in step? The benefit of never having to think for yourself, in exchange for doing exactly what they say? Of never having the freedom to choose your own course, but having it chosen for you?"

"It suits many," he said, and she had the feeling he was keeping his tone purposefully neutral.

"I'm sure it does. For there are those who would never question. I have known both kinds of people, those who would look at such a life with gratitude, and those who would regard it with horror."

"And you are of the latter."

"As is most of Ziem." She grimaced, from her thoughts as much as the effort she was expending. "Except for the likes of Barkhound."

She felt an odd sensation in the moment before he smiled. "Is that what you called him?"

"My youngest children coined that particular name for him."

He went silent. Then, quietly, he said, "The twins."

She went still, although she maintained the flow. She had the feel, the rhythm of it now, and this strong, fit body was responding quickly, more quickly than she'd expected.

"Yes," she finally said.

"They are . . ."

He seemed at a loss for words, and she laughed. "Yes, they are."

There it was again, that jolt of shock, because she was enjoying this conversation he had joked about. She had to remind herself that he was not simply a Coalition officer, but the commander of the conquering forces on Ziem.

. . . they have pronounced that victory too soon.

"REST FOR A WHILE," she said.

"In the enemy camp?" Paledan said. "Not likely."

"But are we not in your office?" she said lightly.

"No, we are not," he said, convinced of that at least. "But I will grant you it is a very accurate representation."

Except for the storeroom in the corner which held—

He cut off his own thoughts. Realized, impossible as it seemed, it was because he was half-afraid she truly could read his mind.

"Then what convinced you it is not?"

She again sounded genuinely curious. "The impossibility," he said.

"And what of the healing we are doing here? Did you not think that impossible?"

"Yes. But I now have first-hand evidence it is not."

"So you are open to . . . changing your mind."

"When not doing so becomes the impossible, yes."

"Utterly logical, yet flexible. A rare combination, Major."

He was feeling neither at the moment, so did not comment. But he did seize the chance to say, "What should I call you?"

She looked at him for a moment, and he thought he saw the corners of her mouth twitch slightly before she said, "Calling me the Spirit does not appeal?"

She was teasing him, he realized. Not in a taunting, malicious way, but genuinely, with humor. And, he realized in succession, she was trusting him to understand that.

"I cannot say that it does," he admitted, not quite sure what this realization meant, for him or for her.

She smiled. "Then Iolana will do. What we do here is a bit too . . . personal for formality, I think."

"And 'Major' is not formal?"

She lifted a brow at him. Something about the way it arched made him aware again that she was indeed the beautiful woman from the portrait.

"Contention valid," she said, smiling in that same way. "What would you prefer?"

He felt the strongest urge to tell her to use his first name. No one did, not even Brakely, who was as close to a friend as he had. He had never thought about it overmuch, because it had never been an issue. But now, with this woman . . .

It filled him again, that strange, unaccustomed tangle of feeling.

I gave you a tiny bit of true feeling, normal emotion. . . .

Was that what this was? Did people who had not been properly trained truly feel this . . . all the time? How could they stand it? It was exhausting.

"Call me what you wish," he said, wearily. "I can hardly stop you."

"But you could," she said quietly, "for I am of Ziem, and we respect the wishes of others."

"I thought to Ziemites, each being had sovereignty."

She laughed, but it was different this time, more amused at him than pleased. He didn't like the change. "You speak as if those ideas are in conflict, when in fact the one creates the other."

He had not thought of it in quite that way.

She stood up. Easily, he noticed, although she had been kneeling beside him for a very long time.

"Now you truly should rest for a while, for the next stage will be worse . . . Caze."

And then she was gone, leaving him stunned at the impact of the simple fact that she had, indeed, used his given name.

Chapter 21

DRAKE AND BRANDER looked up as she approached them in the cavern, beside the water pool.

"You are not finished, are you?" Drake asked.

She shook her head. "The bleeding is stopped, the surrounding tissue healed. He is resting. Next I will remove the object, which will be painful. He will have to rest again before I begin to repair the nerves. He will need all his strength for that stage."

"He is a very strong man," Brander said.

"Yes. And it helps that we began so quickly."

She glanced at Drake, remembering almost against her will those horrible moments when she feared she would be too late to save him. He had been so battered, so broken, barely holding to life, indeed surrendering that hold in the seconds before she had begun to call him back. Her son held her gaze for a moment, and she knew he was thinking of the same thing. That would ever be between them, those moments when she had poured everything she had and was into saving the son she had had to abandon to create the man Ziem needed.

"You will be able to restore him?" Brander asked.

"I believe so, for the most part. Judging by how he responded to what I've done so far, I think he will tolerate removing the shard. But the pain of the final stage, where he must feel every damaged nerve, could drive him to insanity. It has happened."

"I think Paledan's grip on sanity is very fierce," Brander said, his tone half-wry, half-admiring.

"Yes," Drake agreed, then looked back at her. "But I would think having to accept what is happening, what you are doing to and for him, might shake that grip a bit."

"He is more . . . flexible in his thinking than I would have expected," she said.

"Their way, or this way to the chopping block," Brander said sourly.

"Which will contribute to their eventual downfall," Iolana said. Both Brander and Drake went still, and she answered before they asked. "No, this is not something I have foreseen. But I have read much history, and it is as inevitable as the night."

"And Paledan is not a stupid man," Brander said.

"He asked me, if something went wrong, to let—or make—him die."

"I am not surprised," Drake said.

"Nor I," agreed Brander.

"There is more. He said, if that were to happen, that we should . . . disguise it. As an accident."

Drake drew back sharply. "He specifically said that?"

"Yes. His concern seemed to be what the Coalition would do if they thought he had died at our hands."

Drake stared at her for a long moment, then exchanged a glance with his second, who seemed as startled as his leader. She thought she could read what they were thinking.

"You are wondering how he cannot see how wrong they are?"

They both turned to look at her. "In a way, yes," Drake said.

"I think he does, on some level," she said. "But he has had no choice but to accept, in most of his life. The most alive part of that intelligence has been rechanneled by force. Yet even the Coalition has not been able to quash it completely. He is just very, very good at disguising it as something in the Coalition interest."

"Yes," Brander said. "He spoke of that to me once."

Drake looked thoughtful, and Iolana thought she could guess at what he was thinking. And so she risked saying, "There was something else, out there, when you asked if he was trying to save his reputation."

Drake focused on her then. "What?"

"It came to me with a certainty I have only felt with my most vivid visions. He wasn't trying to save his reputation, he was trying to use that reputation to save Ziem."

Both Drake and Brander stared at her.

"Why in hades would he do that?" Drake almost snapped.

"Anything more is only speculation on my part, interpretation, which is always the most questionable thing."

"Have you ever been wrong when it really mattered?" Brander asked, a little less intense than Drake, a bit more of genuine curiosity. He shared that with the man she'd left in her cave.

"Only once," she admitted, "and it was when I did not understand what I was seeing." Her mouth quirked. "It was when I was carrying the twins."

"And that"—Eirlys's voice came from behind her—"would be enough to confuse anyone."

That broke the intensity completely, and Iolana smiled at her daughter who, to her continuing joy, smiled back. "Where does it stand? When will you need me?"

"Not until the last stage. If you can stay close, I will likely need you fairly soon, once I begin on the nerves. It will be very difficult. And," she said, looking at Drake, "I may need you—or rather the Raider—as well."

Drake lifted a brow. "He will be mobile that soon?"

"Doubtful. But the pain will be tremendous, and he will want to give up."

Drake looked puzzled, but Eirlys said, "And he will not, not in front of the Raider."

"Exactly," said Iolana, pleased at Eirlys's quick understanding.

Drake nodded after a moment. "I will be ready. Now, what was your speculation? Why would he risk himself for us?"

"He is . . . fascinated by Ziem. Against his will for the most part. I think . . ." She hesitated, and this time it was the Raider who told her to continue. "I think he has never had to deal with the people he has helped conquer before. Not personally, face to face. He was ever at the head of a conquering force, and able to ignore that those he dominated were, in fact, people."

"I didn't think the Coalition allowed such feelings," Eirlys said.

"They do not. Especially on their home planet, where he was born. They are trained from near infancy to quash or control all emotions. I do not know if he has the capacity left for the kind of feelings we experience, I only know he does not, as a matter of course, experience them now."

Eirlys stared at her mother. "That is even worse. I thought perhaps after generations they had somehow managed to eliminate normal emotions. But that they are still born with them but are forced to crush them . . . I cannot imagine."

Iolana could, she whose emotions had always run high, so high she had had to learn something of quashing them when they interfered with sound thinking.

"When I met him on the bridge, I sensed this. And so I gave him a tiny bit, just a taste of normal emotion. By way of an . . . experiment."

Drake frowned. "Why?"

"I was curious."

"That sounds like our visitor himself," Brander said dryly.

"What happened?" Eirlys asked.

Iolana smiled, almost sadly. "He thought he was ill. That I had given him some fast-acting disease. Or poisoned him."

They all stared. "This, with only a little?" Eirlys asked. She nodded. "That is . . . almost sad."

"Yes," Iolana agreed, hard though it was to include that man and pity in the same thought.

"Well, if we ever need to completely immobilize him again once you've got him on his feet, you can just make him take the whole blast," Brander said with a raised brow.

"It is more a matter of letting him, not making him. I cannot give what he lacks, only unleash what is now blocked by sheer force of will. He would be . . . vulnerable," she said. "Although I could not promise for how long. He is very strong-minded. And," she added, "I find it significant that he chose not to . . . be of the Coalition when he came to meet you."

Drake brow creased. "Significant?"

"When you said to him he might be better off with the Sentinels, there was something," she began, then stopped, shaking her head. "I am not certain. And perhaps I am linking it to something else that it should not be linked to."

"Which is?"

She hesitated. "This is not something I have Seen," she cautioned. Drake nodded. "Have you noticed," she asked, "that he speaks of the Coalition as 'they?' Not 'we'?"

"I have, frequently," Brander said. "And wondered."

"I cannot say with certainty it means anything, but when you said that to him out there, Drake, he reacted. Not in surprise but in . . . recognition."

"Recognition?"

"As if . . . it were not a foreign thought to him." When they all fell into stunned silence, she hastened to repeat, "As I said, I cannot be certain, nor have I Seen anything in the way of a vision, to give me this idea. It is only a feeling."

She caught a flash of movement at the entrance to the cavern, and looked. Grim. When he saw she had seen him, he nodded, then disappeared.

"It is time?" Eirlys asked.

"Yes," she said. "You will be close?"

Eirlys nodded, as did her brother.

As she turned to go, she heard Drake mutter, "I hope I don't regret this decision."

She looked back. "I am glad my son is not so hardened he could leave a man he admires to die in such a way."

"But I may yet wish I had ended it then."

"Or you may be glad you did not."

She left, not even certain of what had made her say it.

Chapter 22

"YOU LOOK," PALEDAN said to the boy he had awakened to see sitting a few feet away, a blaster in his hand, "as if you'd like to use that."

"I would," the boy said, his expression grim.

"Then why don't you?"

"Orders."

That, Paledan understood. "We all must follow our orders."

The boy grimaced. "I am not like you. I do not follow orders because I am part of your machine."

He let that slur pass, in a way he might not have had he been mobile. "Then why?"

"Because they came from the Raider, and I would die before I would have him disappointed in me." The boy's face took on an expression of hatred that seemed harsh in one so young. Even Coalition cadets rarely looked like that, for hatred was an emotion that brought on mistakes, and so was not allowed until they were old enough to channel it. Then he added, "Even if I wish I could blast the entire Coalition to Ossuary."

"You would not be the first to wish that," he said dryly.

For a moment the boy—and he did not miss the statement being made that a mere lad was enough to guard him in his current state—looked surprised. Then the dark expression returned.

"What do you expect? The Coalition killed my father, and your evil beast Jakel brutalized and murdered my mother."

"He is no longer . . . my beast."

"I know. But he was."

"Yes. He was a tool that occasionally was of use. But the kind that always might turn on you."

"Is that why you gave him to us?"

He found, somewhat to his dismay, that he quite missed being able to shrug in answer to a question he did not have or wish to give answers to. But he was saved from having to do it now by the return of the tall, gaunt man they called Grim.

"You may go, Kade," the man said.

The boy sighed. Paledan thought he saw the faintest trace of a smile at the corners of the stern man's mouth. "You might want to see if the Raider's third needs a break from guarding that beast."

The boy brightened. "Jakel? I would give much to see him in that cage!"

The boy darted out, just as Iolana Davorin came in.

Iolana. She had given him leave to use her name, yet he found it difficult to even think it. But the Spirit, that title uttered almost reverently by the boy, was even more impossible.

"Are you feeling better?" she asked.

"That depends on your basis for comparison."

"Perhaps it should be if the boy who just left here had gotten his wish."

"In that case," he said dryly, "there is little question I am feeling better, since he wished me dead."

"Not you, specifically. What you represent."

"And yet he did not do it when he had the chance. That says much about the esteem he has for your son."

"He is but one of many who would follow my son into hades, were he to ask. Which he would not."

He frowned. "Sometimes a commander must ask such of his troops."

"My son would not. He would go himself, and let them decide whether to follow. He rises or falls on his own merits as a leader."

"That," he said slowly, "would be a foolish tactic for anyone less than the Raider."

She laughed, that lovely, silvery sound again. "Now, if you are recovered enough, we will begin the next stage. And again, I still must know, so you must be awake and able to speak."

He looked at her as she fastened the sleeves of her robe out of the way. Noted again the scar on her arm, and the other on her temple. "Did someone do this for you, when you were injured?"

He didn't really expect her to answer, and was a little surprised when she did, and easily. "Grim did what he could, but we had not yet learned everything that could be done. And the physical pain was as nothing next to the anguish in my heart."

"You mean . . . emotions."

"I mean the agony of knowing I had done irreparable damage to my children. That in my own grief I had caused them even more."

She could have been speaking a foreign language he had no knowledge of. In his world, one did what was necessary, and it ended there. Yet he could not deny what echoed in her voice, a pain as real as the physical. It was a weakness, he knew, that had been taught for as long as he could remember. And yet that she felt so much fascinated him.

She fascinated him.

"And even coming to know that it was necessary for Ziem did not ease that anguish," she added.

"Necessary?" he asked as she echoed the word in his thoughts.

"For my son to become the man he must be to do what had to be done, and to keep him alive long enough to do it."

He stared at her. The idea that occurred to him seemed impossible, yet he somehow knew it was true. "Your other children," he said slowly. "Caring for them . . . held him back."

"Long enough," she said. "I think even you would agree to that."

"A boy could not have done what he has done."

He acknowledged it even as he thought what an unusual woman this was, to have been brought up on this world of tight bloodline connections, yet to nearly sever that line between herself and her own children, for the sake of that world.

"You did this . . . purposely?"

"Not in the beginning. Then, my choices were selfish, driven by the loss of half my soul. It was only after that Ziem showed me how to use it for her good."

"You speak of your planet as . . . almost sentient."

"Do I? Clearly it is not, although my world has much to teach."

"And you have learned it?"

She shook her head. "I will never learn everything Ziem has to teach. But is that any reason not to try? Now, if you are ready?"

"What must I do?"

"Endure," she said, and there was an undeniable touch of regret in her voice.

She had, he thought a few minutes later, understated things. He had never, even at the time of the original injury, felt such pain. It had begun as a singeing heat, but now felt like acid eating away at him, and if her intent had been to torture, it could be no worse.

She asked him questions, and it took a great effort to answer them with some kind of reason. And the pain got steadily worse.

"We can pause, give you a slight respite, but it will be as bad when we begin again."

"No."

"As I expected, but I felt I must offer."

"Why," he asked between harsh breaths, "would you care?"

"If for no other reason than I feel an echo of your pain. It is . . . more extreme than I thought it would be."

He did not realize she would feel this. It changed things, somehow. He did not know what to say, doubted he had the breath to spare to say it if he did.

"Is that not what you expected? A selfish reason?"

"Yes. No." He meant them both, but could not get out the words to make it clear.

"I think I am flattered," she said, as if she'd understood he'd meant yes, he would have expected it, but not from her. "But you say you do not."

"Flattery . . . implies . . . falsity."

"That can be true. It is also often the tool of some who wish to cajole something from you."

He had not expected that. "I—"

A particularly sharp, hot pain slashed through him, stealing his next words from his mind as well as his lips. As it faded, she spoke, as if nothing had happened.

"In some, however," she said, and he made himself focus on the words—because they were all that kept him from dwelling on the agony coursing through him in a hot, searing trail down his back, "there is a tendency to interpret any praise as false flattery, when in fact it can sometimes be genuine."

"Rarely." He had to clench his teeth to get it out.

"Do you consider the acknowledgment from your superiors that you are very, very good at what you do flattery?"

She'd again caught him off guard. Not that his guard was particularly high at this moment, when every passing second seemed to bring a new level of pain.

"That," he said, having to pause for a breath, "is different."

"Why?"

"That . . . is . . . verifiable."

"I see. So by the same standard, compliments on your looks or bearing are not flattery, then."

The pain was obviously affecting his hearing. "What?" was all he could manage.

"I meant that you have your reflection to verify your appeal, just as your record in battle confirms your skill."

Appeal? For an instant his pulse leapt, even as he struggled against the pain to process what she had said. He was both out of commission and out of practice on that front, and he was nearly certain he had misheard—or at least misinterpreted—her words.

But she went on as if her words were merely a given. "It is curious, is it not, what fascinates us?"

Was this a change of subject? A guess? Or perhaps . . . an accusation.

"For instance," she said as she moved, seemed to lean in a little harder. Pain blasted all thought out of his head. He had only the power left to endure. And then she finished her sentence, shocking his brain back into functioning. "I would still give much to know the true reason you keep my portrait in that storeroom."

He felt as if his wracked mind was careening wildly, like an air rover with damaged controls. Had this been the goal all along? She wanted that answer and had set this up, this slamming pain, in an effort to get it from him? Was she simply Jakel with a much softer, more alluring approach? Had Davorin known; was this the true reason they had kept him alive?

"And there we have it," she said softly, and the pain eased.

The room's spinning slowed. The swirling of his brain took a few moments longer. But when it slowed enough, he opened his eyes. She was sitting back, now in his line of sight. He stared at her. What he saw answered two of his biggest questions.

It had been a ruse, but not to drag information out of him. It had been an effort at distraction, to pull some part of his mind away from the worst pain yet. That he understood, even as it unsettled him to think that she knew enough to know that particular question would work.

But at this moment, it was that other question, that of whether she could do what she'd said, that rose above all others. And the answer was here, now, in plain sight.

She could.

For she sat beside him now, a jagged shard of planium in her hand.

Chapter 23

BRANDER LET OUT a long, low whistle as he stared at the piece of the familiar metal, the product of a mine not far from here.

"He's been walking around with that in his back?" he asked.

Iolana, who was sitting, resting, nodded. "It is a testament to his strength that the pain from that alone has not driven him mad."

"A strength we would do well to not underestimate," Drake said, rising from his chair at the table where one of Kye's exquisitely detailed maps was spread out.

"He will need it all. The healing of the nerves will be worse even than this, for it will encompass every part of him that those nerves service."

Brander winced. "And he must be awake for this, too?"

"Yes. He must able to speak so that I know that nothing has gotten . . . mis-wired, if you will."

"Of course, we must be certain the leader of our conquerors is able to function perfectly," Kye said dryly. At Drake's glance, she shook her head. "No, I understand, better him than someone without his . . . restraint."

"Have you decided what to do with him?" Eirlys asked, looking at her brother. "When it is done, I mean?"

Drake turned to Iolana. "Does your original estimate still hold?"

"It will take time for him to recover from the stress of what we've done. And he must be kept still during that time, so I believe keeping him under would be best. I will sense when he is ready. Normally I would say a week, but . . ."

Her voice trailed off, but she saw she did not need to explain. Drake nodded. "Agreed, if he is that strong it could be sooner. We will mount a guard from the moment you have completed the process."

"Speaking of which, who is with him now? Grim?" Eirlys asked.

Iolana nodded. "I doubt he will stir for some hours, and I think it best to let him recoup as much as he can in that time, in preparation."

"I don't envy the man," Brander said, looking again at the shard of planium, "if it's going to be worse than getting that out of him."

A scramble of noise came from the doorway, and then two small whirl-winds whipped into the room.

"Is it—"

"True? You have—"

"The major—"

"Here?"

"We do," Drake answered the twins. Iolana never tired of watching this interaction. She'd taken to trying to guess which one would begin the rapid fire bounce of half-sentences, but she was wrong as often as she was right. This time she had guessed Lux and it was Nyx.

"He is—"

"Hurt?"

They sounded concerned, she thought with interest. They hated the Coalition and all it stood for with the passion of any Sentinel, but this one man . . . . She knew they had had more contact with Paledan—even though she'd spoken the name, she still could not think of him as Caze in her mind, or perhaps dared not, she amended ruefully—than just about anyone other than Brander. So was it simply familiarity, that they saw him as just that, a man, while the other Coalition troops were merely the enemy? Or was there more to it? Was it in some remarkable way connected to what she had discerned during her connection with him?

"Your mother is working to heal him," Drake was saying.

The twins flicked a glance at her. She supposed she should be thankful they at least acknowledged she was the person Drake was referring to.

"And then—"

"What will—"

"You do—"

"With him?" they finished together.

She watched as Drake studied the pair for a moment. Then, softly and quite seriously, he asked, "What do you think I should do?"

She saw the flash of brightness in both sets of Ziem-blue eyes, saw the adoration for their big brother gleam as he waited for an answer to what was obviously a genuine wish to know. He had worked miracles with them, Iolana thought, not for the first time.

"We think—"

"You should—"

"Keep him."

Iolana was so startled she almost forgot to breathe. She saw Drake blink, draw back slightly. She was trying to formulate her first question in a way the still-recalcitrant twins might answer when Drake simply asked it.

"Why?"

It was Lux this time. "Because he—"

"Is not—"

"Like those—"

"Others. He is—"

"Not evil—"

"Or stupid—"

"Or cruel—"

"And also because—"

"We like him—"

"And he—"

"Likes us," they chorused.

"He does, does he?" Drake said thoughtfully.

"Yes," Lux said confidently. "He did not want to, but he does."

"You believe us, don't you?" Nyx asked.

"I have seen no evidence that disputes what you say," Drake said.

Both twins smiled widely.

"Can we—"

"See him?"

Drake glanced at her, then back to the duo. "I will have to consider that. I will tell you when I have decided."

They looked disappointed, but didn't argue.

"Don't you have classes with Matta today?" Eirlys asked.

Nyx grimaced. "Yes."

Their sister arched a brow at them. They sighed in unison.

"All right—"

"We're going."

When they'd gone, Iolana looked at Eirlys. "Matta is teaching again?"

"Yes. She was too disheartened at first, after the Coalition destroyed her school. Drake convinced her."

Iolana looked at her eldest. He shrugged. "The children with us needed a teacher. She had no desire to remain in Zelos."

"Hardly surprising," Brander said dryly, "given they were hunting her."

Iolana frowned. "Hunting her?"

"They want no one who knows the whole of our true history," Eirlys said, her tone sour.

"For they want it replaced with their own version," Iolana said in understanding.

"Yes," Drake said, and his tone was harsh. "They want every succeeding generation to believe the story they tell is real. That they were not our conquerors but our saviors."

Iolana muttered an oath she hadn't spoken in a very long time. Both of her children in the room gave her a startled look. Kye and Brander merely grinned.

Drake, meanwhile, was looking at the chunk of metal that had resulted in their having the leader of the Coalition on Ziem in their hands. Brander watched him for a moment before looking at Iolana and saying, "Too bad you can't do . . . what you did with that on a major scale. It would be a lot easier than mining the stuff."

"The difficulty of mining it is the only reason we're still alive," Drake reminded him. But then he looked at her. "You cannot, can you?"

"No," she said. "Nor can I do it when the planium is still in the stone. I believe the ability is connected to the healing only."

"We'd best make sure the major knows that before . . . we do whatever we're going to do with him. Last thing we need is the Coalition thinking it can be pulled out of the mine without equipment," Kye said.

"And we're back to my original question," Eirlys said.

"I do not yet know," Drake said with a grimace.

"What's that old saying?" Brander asked. "About having a blazer by the tail?"

Drake gave him a sour look.

"And your only job," Eirlys said to her mate, "is to stay away from him when he's awake."

"Lucky, aren't I?" Brander teased.

"Indeed you are," Iolana said softly.

Brander's expression changed in an instant. He looked at Eirlys. "Yes," he agreed, and even from here Iolana could see the pure, fierce love in his eyes. And when they left Drake's quarters a moment later, she had more than an inkling of where they were going.

"I am glad you are happy for them," Drake said.

Iolana turned back to him. "I am. Most happy."

"Brander was afraid he was not good enough for her," Kye said.

"Which, in part, is what makes him so," Iolana said.

Drake smiled at that. Then he asked, "When will you start the final phase of the healing?"

"As soon as he is recovered enough. And from what I have seen, I suspect I'll be able to move that timetable forward. In fact, I believe I will check on him now."

Drake nodded. His mouth tightened slightly.

"Second thoughts?" she asked.

"And several beyond that," he said.

"You are likely forestalling something worse," Iolana reminded him.

"And," Kye put in, "it cannot hurt to have him in your debt."

"I'm not sure a debt of that sort would stop him from doing what he sees as his duty," Drake said. "Not as long as he does not experience that kind of personal connection, as we do."

Iolana considered that. "I am not certain I could isolate that kind of emotion, but I could try."

Kye looked at her curiously. "You mean give him the capacity to feel that kind of connection? Or empathy?"

She nodded. "It will only work if it is innate and has been crippled or smothered. I cannot give what someone does not already have."

"Sounds to me like that's exactly what the Coalition does, crushes it out of them," Kye said.

"So you would not be forcing it upon him?" Drake asked.

"No." She found it telling that this was what her son asked, and added, "It is a rare warrior who will allow his opponent to live by the rules he himself lives by. That you would not like to see him forced says much."

"It says," Kye said, with a smile at her mate's obvious disconcertment, "that he is the best kind of warrior. The kind who was a good, noble man before he became a hero."

"I'm not—"

Kye stopped his refutation. "Do not even try to sell that here, in front of two who know your heart."

The look Drake gave his mate then had Iolana quickly rising. "I will go make preparations while you . . . make good use of this respite." Drake flushed slightly, but Kye laughed. Iolana gave her a sideways look and made sure she was smiling as she added, "I do wish for that grandchild, you know."

She left them staring after her, and with the warmth of their love filling even her solitary heart.

Chapter 24

HE SENSED HER presence the moment she came in, although his eyes were closed. It seemed his hearing, always good, had sharpened even more, as if his brain had sensed what still worked was more critical now.

"I will not ask how you feel," she said, apparently knowing somehow that he was awake. "That you are conscious is amazing enough."

He didn't deny it. "I was contemplating what it might feel like to move again."

"I would imagine a man of your fitness expected the cooperation of your body in most cases."

The thought that stabbed through his mind at her words made him glad he had kept his eyes closed. That he'd thought himself long past needing the kind of physical connection a male and female could have made it even more ironic that he was thinking of it now, when his body was totally and utterly incapable of that cooperation.

He supposed it was inevitable, given the hours he'd spent staring at the portrait of this woman, that it was she who gave rise to those thoughts now. That she was everything that portrait had implied, and more, was more unsettling. He had wondered, as he'd lain here helplessly, if perhaps his brain had been damaged as much as his body, to even consider that the things that had happened were real. His mind had ever been grounded in reality, and what had happened since he had awakened here had been anything but.

They were impossible.

What she had done was impossible.

She was impossible.

And yet . . .

He opened his eyes at last. She was seated beside him, on a chair that looked like the one in his office. The office that was also impossible. But then she, alive, had seemed impossible. And if he had to believe this luminous, compelling woman long thought dead was real, why not the rest?

"You look . . . perplexed," she said, and there was an understanding in her tone that he wanted to reject.

"I do not understand. Any of this. It makes no sense."

"And you do not like things you do not understand," she said, as if she were reciting a known. "And if you do not understand something, what do you do?"

His brow furrowed. "Analyze, experiment, learn until I do."

Her expression changed slightly, as if she had just understood something. "Is that how you came to design the air rover?"

His mouth tightened. But he could see no harm in answering, although he was certain she had a motive for asking that he could not yet see, because it seemed she always did.

"Yes. I am not a pilot, but often flew. I needed to understand the principles of flight."

"And so you learned them, well enough to design the rover. Which, my son says, is a most remarkable craft."

He was startled at the feeling her words caused in him. He could only describe it as pride. He was equally startled at the need to acknowledge how his design had been advanced. "He has taken what was intended as a basic transport with some minimal defense capabilities and turned it into an attack weapon. A bomber, and a fighter more agile than I ever would have thought possible."

"He had help to carry out those ideas. We have a clever mind or two among us," she said. "Which I'm certain your masters find hard to believe."

She put the very slightest emphasis on the word "masters," and he guessed he was supposed to react to it. Even knowing that, he could not resist. "You say that as if they are not your masters."

"Your Coalition? I cannot deny that most Ziemites must do as they order. But obedience by force does not make them their masters. A true master is one you choose to serve. Who earns your obedience. And I can promise you . . . Caze, there are very few Ziemites who would not die rather than accept the Coalition. It is true that we grew soft, in our ways and our thinking, but our hearts beat true. We will stand. And die, if so it must be."

He stared at her. "And yet I am told individual life is valued above all else on this world."

"Then I suppose the conflict is in the interpretation of what life consists of. Enslavement, to us, is a direct contradiction."

"I find your world . . . contradictory in many things."

"Do you?" she said with a laugh. He suddenly remembered a place he had seen, on Zenox, a small waterfall over hollowed rocks, where the scattered streams made the rocks ring with an impossible sound that was almost like singing. Her laugh sounded like that.

He caught himself, wondered if there was any one word he had used more since he'd awakened here than "impossible."

He did not like impossible.

"The passage of time is still a factor here," she said. "Do you feel strong enough to begin this?"

"If it is to be, as you said, worse than the last, I am not certain I will ever be," he said frankly.

"I can ease the pain to some extent, but this is a long, difficult process, and any haste is ill-advised."

"Because?"

"You might end up with misconnections, and I imagine it would not do if you involuntarily replaced a Coalition salute with some other, less respectful gesture."

He laughed. He was unprepared for his own response, and suspected he looked startled as well.

"I had heard," she said softly, "that you could laugh. But I was not told what a wonderful sound it was."

He stared at her, the laughter fading as he remembered his own whimsical, ridiculous thoughts about her laughter. Perhaps he truly was losing his grip on his faculties. Perhaps this was some side effect of her treatment, or some aftereffect of his injury. Perhaps these odd feelings were triggered by some nerve that had been damaged. Did that mean if she healed those nerves, as she was about to attempt, that he would no longer feel such things?

He felt a sudden urge to tell her not to do it. To give him time to explore this new oddity. To understand what these were, these strange, new sensations.

Impossible. That's what they were.

"Do it," he said, his befuddled thoughts making his voice sharp.

"As you wish," she said serenely, as if he had not snapped.

And thus began the worst hours of his life.

Chapter 25

"ARE YOU ALL RIGHT?"

Iolana couldn't divert her energy enough to look at Grim so she merely nodded.

"If it is too much—"

She shook her head sharply, trying to keep her mind focused on that crucial strand of intricate, miraculous tissue that sent the impulses to the muscles that then obeyed in this marvel that was the body. This one was damaged badly, and was taking a full effort. She knew she was hurting him as she tried to delicately guide the severed cells back together, but there was no other way.

There. She had it. One more down.

"Save your sympathy for him," she told her tall, hovering friend. "It is he who is in agony."

"He bears it well."

"He does."

"He is aware," her patient said, and she marveled that he was able to attain that dry tone.

They had been at it for . . . she did not know exactly how long, only that it was approaching nightfall. And she was weary, beyond weary. Even calling Drake back from death had been less wearying than this. The meticulous precision required for this was draining. Not to mention that Drake had thankfully been unconscious for most of it, and she'd been able to keep him so through most of it.

This man had to be conscious, and even the echo of the pain he was feeling was nearly debilitating.

"Grim, I will need extra now."

The man nodded and left. She knew that he understood she would need Eirlys for the extra healing power, and Drake to help keep her patient going; they had discussed it before she'd begun.

She had told the major—Caze—that if she and Eirlys coupled their efforts, the worst part would go more quickly. He did not know about Drake, or rather the Raider, for she wanted the full distraction of the man she knew he considered a most worthy opponent.

She turned back to her task, trying to isolate the next pathway to reestablish, to heal. He was breathing rapidly, and she paused to wipe his damp forehead, knowing the pain was nearly unendurable.

"Caze?"

His answer came out rather truncated. ". . . lana."

"Lana will do nicely." She even, she realized, liked the sound of it.

"Shorter," he ground out.

"You are doing well," she told him.

His words came out from behind teeth clenched against the pain. "You have . . . an odd . . . perception of . . . well."

"Then think of it as relative to being dead," she suggested.

For an instant, a mere flash, he smiled. That he could do so despite his current state left her in no small amount of awe. "Contention . . . valid."

The next one was particularly bad, and she was afraid for a moment she had left calling for Eirlys one strand of nerve too long. He let out a groan of pain, and a sharp gasp. Her name again, or at least the shortened version. It rattled her in a way her healing never had before. She hated hurting him, even knowing it was necessary.

And then Drake was there, in full Raider garb, leaning nonchalantly against the wall, striking the perfect note by saying, "How goes it, Major?"

She felt Caze's breathing stop for an instant. Then, with a remarkable steadiness, he said, "I regret even more leaving Jakel alive."

She'd been right; in the Raider's presence he would fight even harder.

Then she had it, the torn nerve endings seeming to seek each other once they were close enough. She sealed the mend, and the wave of black, engulfing agony receded slightly.

And she thought, if she had sensed it properly, that there might now be a bit more encouragement for him.

She reached out and ran a finger lightly across the back of his right hand. His gaze shot to her face, and she could see in his eyes—even the pain could not fully dull the vivid green of them—that he'd felt it. She smiled.

"Lana," he whispered, the wonder of it in his voice. And something warm and thrilling welled up inside her, and she renewed her resolve to heal him completely, no matter what it took.

And then Eirlys was there. She said nothing, merely knelt beside her. Iolana knew she was still uncertain about doing this, but like her brother, once she had given her word she would keep it.

"We must begin the worst now," she said.

"Still better than dead," he said. Then, with a glance at Drake, added, "Depending on what you intend to do after."

Iolana also looked at Drake for a moment, willing him to understand what a tremendous effort it was taking this man to speak so evenly. But she saw by her son's expression he already knew.

"That is something I will only discuss with an opponent at full strength," he said.

The green eyes closed once more. She looked at Eirlys. "Hands over, I believe."

Her daughter nodded. And when she placed her hands once more over the most damaged part of the spine, Eirlys laid her own on top, her palms already warm and ready, as if she had been thinking about the task long before she'd arrived. For a brief moment she let her gaze lock onto her daughter's, let every ounce of the pride in her she was feeling show. Eirlys still said nothing, but her cheeks pinkened slightly, and Iolana knew she'd understood.

"And so we begin," she said quietly.

It was both worse than she'd feared and better than she'd hoped. The pain, she knew, was incredible, but with Eirlys's added strength she could almost feel the spinal cord mending, rewiring itself, could almost feel the body that had been senseless come back to life.

After a few minutes that must have seemed an eon to the man beneath their hands, Eirlys whispered, so softly no one else could hear, "He knows."

"Yes."

She had sensed it a moment before, that the signals now being sent along repaired paths were reaching his brain, signals he had not felt since that moment when the jagged piece of planium had shifted. She felt his body tense.

"Still, Caze. I understand, but you must be still."

He made an unintelligible sound, but he did go still.

She closed her eyes. Reached, deeper than she ever had before. Searched. And finally found.

"Yes or no," she said without opening her eyes. "Right hand."

A moment of silence, then a half-hissed, "Yes."

Sealed. Next. "Shoulder."

Again the pause, but again the yes. She probed again. "Upper arm."

"Left," he said suddenly.

She backed off. "And that is why you have had to endure this."

She changed the path, until he said, "Yes," again.

She went on, connecting, mending, sealing. Then, opening her eyes, she said, "Try a fist."

Slowly, agonizingly slowly, his fingers curled. She felt the blast of hope as it shot through him. Felt him try to tamp it down, as if it were something forbidden. She heard Eirlys suck in a breath and knew she'd felt it too, both the hope and the instant crushing of it.

And driven by some whim or instinct she didn't really understand, she sent him a blast of that emotion, the hope she carried within her. He would not see that it was her hope for Ziem, for her children, and for their children whom she wished to see someday. She held that back and gave him only the pure sensation that some said was the most powerful of all, for it could keep people going when all seemed lost.

"It's real, Caze," she said. "Trust it."

She heard him suck in a breath, and knew it was not from pain but from the impact of what she'd given him.

And because she'd again used his name.

She had no time to spend on it. And could ill afford the energy, given there was still much work ahead.

And this was the most critical, the healing of the main nerves that had been damaged in his spine. Whether she succeeded would determine whether he would ever walk again, ever function at all normally again.

In all the ways a man normally functioned.

She swiftly blocked off the burst of feeling, of wild imagination, that thought caused in her. She knew she'd done it quickly enough to mask it from Caze, for quick as he was, he was still in a great deal of pain.

Eirlys, she was not so certain about.

She put that out of her mind as well as they began the most crucial, final stage.

"Take as deep a breath as you can," she instructed him.

He did so, slowly, and with a hitch or two in the sound of it.

"Let it out slowly," she said. And again he did so, smoothly this time. "How does it feel?"

He gave her a sideways look and said wryly, "Almost as if I were doing it myself."

Again no gasps in the words, no betrayal of the pain. It was Drake's presence—or rather the Raider's—that was doing that, she thought.

"You are," she said. "You have been for a while."

The wryness faded, replaced by surprise, and then growing realization. And through the connection she felt the hope she'd given him spark, grow. Fed from within this time.

She heard Eirlys make a small sound, and knew she'd felt it, too. The emotion she'd given this man who had been starved of them, had them brutalized out of him since childhood, had called to what remnants were left within him. And they had responded, whatever tiny fragments had survived, buried under the crushing weight of Coalition demands.

"We have reached that point I warned you of, Caze," she said softly, and again felt the spark of . . . something when she spoke his name. "This will require everything in you. And even if you feel you must recoil from the pain you must not. You must, must stay still."

"Easier said," he muttered.

"Yes. But you must. And you will."

"Want me to sit on him?"

Drake's drawl came from behind her, and she felt the spark of pride— that was a Coalition-allowed emotion, it seemed—that drove Caze to say, "I'll manage."

And she knew she'd been right to have Drake here. With him here, Caze would hang on until he no longer could, and in those moments it would be up to her. Or rather, the Spirit.

She leaned in, pressing her hands down firmly. She felt Eirlys shift as well, adding her own pressure.

"All of it now," she said softly to her daughter.

She felt the power of the link increase, felt the flow become a rush. She guided it to the goal, that damaged cord of nerve tissue that fed them all. She felt the moment when it hit him, when the pain shot out in all directions as the severed connections reformed. She heard him gasp, but he made no other sound. And he lay still, when she thought any other man would have been writhing in agony.

It went on and on, until the moment when, with one last, main strand to reconnect, she felt him break. Felt that amazingly valiant spirit silently cry out in surrender.

She called up everything she'd learned as the Spirit, as she had one day not long ago on a Ziem mountainside. She let out what she thought of as the power of her world itself, into a glowing blast of power and light. Everything under her hands froze, as if time had stopped.

His surrender hovered, as if waiting. She felt something, shifted her gaze, saw he was staring at her. She could see the flare of light reflected in his eyes, for the first time was able to see what others saw when Ziem gave her this gift. But she never stopped sending the healing waves, holding him in the heat and light for these last critical seconds. And in the moment when she could no longer hold onto that light, she felt the last rejoining seal, and it was done.

Chapter 26

"THEY'RE GETTING restless," Brander said.

"Of course. They want to strike back." Drake tapped a finger idly on the map on the table before him. He wasn't really planning anything, but he enjoyed looking at Kye's amazing work. And it had kept his mind off his second once more venturing down into Zelos, putting himself in the literal jaws of the enemy.

"They're angry that they can't find us."

Drake couldn't help smiling at that. "While we are perfectly happy to let them squander manpower and fuel and time in fruitless searching." And in the process give his Sentinels time to rest, recuperate, and enjoy the respite.

Brander grinned. "I overheard a couple of troopers even questioning the power of the Coalition, if they are unable to even find a 'tiny band of miscreants,' as they called us."

Drake smiled again at that. But it faded as he asked, "Did you hear anything about their . . . missing commander?"

"Not a chirp. His aide is doing a great job in suppressing any questioning, if indeed there is any. Although I doubt there is much. No one would dare question Major Paledan's comings and goings. Speaking of which, how is our . . . guest?"

"Still asleep," Drake answered. "With some help from my mother. She will keep him so, for now."

"Your mother is . . ."

Brander's words trailed away, and Drake gave him a wry smile. "Amazing? Impossible? Sometimes frightening?"

"All of those," Brander agreed.

"And who knows that better than the two of us?" Drake asked.

"You seem much better with her."

"She has proven her worth many times."

"So she has earned your forgiveness. But what about love?"

Drake met Brander's eyes, a little surprised that it seemed to matter to him. "I understand now what I did not before, how it would seem impossible to go on without the one who holds your life in their hands." Brander lowered his gaze. And then Drake understood. "It is not I, but Eirlys you are concerned about."

"Only insofar as it hurts her to hold ill will in her heart."

"She has forgiven, and come a long way toward loving. Given that heart of hers, I would say she will reach it." Drake's mouth quirked. "They have much in common, she and our mother."

"So much that she worked with her to heal Paledan."

"Yes." Drake gave a small shake of his head. Knowing Brander had risked a glance in at times during the process, when the patient was focused only on surviving, he said only, "I've never seen anything like what they did."

"I've never seen anyone endure that much pain without cracking, except you."

Drake shook his head. "This was much worse. She was able to mute the pain for me, for it was but muscle and bone. This was every nerve in him, likely feeling on fire."

"And now that she has healed him," Brander said, "the biggest question remains. What will you do with him? Just send him back?"

Drake sighed. "I do not know."

"There's always the twins' suggestion," Brander said, with another flashing grin.

"Keep him? And what, give him free rein, to learn where we are so he can finally annihilate us? Or keep him imprisoned, until the High Command itself comes hunting for him, and us?"

"Or . . . turn him."

Drake went still. "The man is the most decorated and honored active commander in the Coalition. He was born to it, has known nothing else his entire life. He has conquered more worlds then you or I will ever see. He has the ear of all at High Command, and could likely call in a strike to destroy us on a moment's notice, planium or no. Why in hades would you think he would turn?"

"What I think," Brander said quietly, "is that you having all those reasons immediately at hand means you've been thinking about it yourself."

For a moment Drake just stared at him. Finally he grimaced. "You started this, you know. You were saying he didn't fit the Coalition mold long before my mother reappeared and agreed with you."

"Mine was just an impression. Hers is . . ."

Brander waved a hand as if unable to explain. But he didn't have to. Drake knew what he meant. He did not understand why his mother could do what she did, but he could no longer deny that she could. He'd known, in childhood, that she could see in ways no one else could, but he had never known she was capable of what she'd shown them since she'd first come back to them as the Spirit.

Including discerning the very depths of a person with merely a touch. Who knows what she had learned of their guest, as Brander put it, during the healing?

"Some of what I think is from the man's actions, however," Brander said. "He has shown more restraint with our people than I ever would have expected from a Coalition commander. And I will say I agree with your mother about his frequent referring to the Coalition as something apart from himself. And there is his protecting the twins. And do not forget, he shot Jakel when he came at you."

"And so you counter every one of my reasons with an opposing one, which leaves us . . . where?"

"With all our coin on the table and no idea who has the better hand."

"Indeed," Drake said dryly.

But it was more than just coin at stake here.

It was all of Ziem.

"DO YOU ALWAYS do things with such high drama?"

He half expected her to jab him somehow, perhaps unmute the pain he could sense still hovering. But she merely looked at him serenely.

"Not intentionally. For the most part, it is my history that makes it drama."

"And that bit of . . . whatever it was, at the end, with the light?"

"You remember that?"

"It was . . . unforgettable."

"You were in the worst pain at that moment, and unconscious in the next second. I thought perhaps you did not recall."

"It's what you did on that mountain, isn't it."

She gave him that smile he'd come to know, that almost irked him with its amused understanding. "That," she said, "did not sound like an actual question." She rose to her feet, saying, "You must rest."

"I believe I was?"

"You need more. And you must remain still. It will be some time before we can even test to see how we did."

He studied her before asking, carefully, "But you have . . . a feeling?"

"I do."

With anyone else he would have snapped at the evasiveness. But it did not seem the thing to do with the woman who had, quite possibly, saved him. That he thought it possible was a measure of how far he had come down this road of insanity since the moment he'd awakened in this place.

Then, belatedly, he realized he was judging her as he would someone of the Coalition. Someone practiced in feeling nothing, or presenting whatever image they thought their inquisitor desired. She was not that—far from it. And on the heels of that realization came another: the smile was genuine. She was pleased.

And she was not the type to be pleased unless it had gone well.

A strange, powerful feeling welled up in him. He'd felt it before, in the midst of the pain, although he had been unable to spare the energy to analyze it at the time. But he did so now, and after some puzzlement realized, with a jolt of shock, that it was . . . hope.

Hope.

It had been trampled out of him ages ago, and he had long assumed the capacity for it had gone, too. And yet, strange and unaccustomed as it was, he could not deny that was what he was feeling.

Strange and unaccustomed described this entire interlude. In fact, it described every moment spent in her presence.

Along with other descriptors he didn't wish to think about just now.

Then, before he could form another word to speak, a great sleepiness overtook him. She wasn't touching him, so he suspected it was natural. Then again, if she could render him senseless by her mere thoughts, he would not be surprised.

His concept of impossible was in tatters.

IOLANA KNEW WHEN she came in that she'd interrupted something. Drake and Brander had both gone quiet, and both of them looked extremely grim.

"What is it? Eirlys? Kye?"

"No," Drake said quickly. "We were just . . . discussing something."

"Something very dark, by the look of you both."

The two men exchanged a look. "Brander?" Drake asked.

Brander let out a long breath. "She is the Spirit of Ziem in more ways than one."

Drake looked thoughtful, and nodded slowly. Then he looked at her. "Perhaps your vision would help."

"You know I cannot See in that way on command," Iolana cautioned.

"Not the vision I meant," Drake said evenly.

She felt a warming inside her at the words. It was one thing to be called upon for that unusual talent, something else to be asked simply for her opinion, because it was valued.

"Thank you," she said. Then, with a look at them both, asked, "What is it?"

"Brander has . . . discovered something. The reason behind one of our most basic pieces of knowledge."

"That he has done so is no surprise," she said, looking at her daughter's mate, "so it must be the knowledge itself that is grim?"

Brander smiled fleetingly, as if pleased by her implied compliment. As she had intended. But immediately his expression became dark again.

"More what's to be done with it," Drake said.

"Or not," Brander muttered, staring at something Iolana suspected was not even in this room. This time she simply waited silently. After a moment Brander looked up at her. "I discovered why quisalt must be kept away from the planium."

Startled, she glanced from him to Drake and back. And tried to remember if she had ever known the reason for this unbreakable rule of the foundation of Ziem's former prosperity. She did not think so, and those who might have known were long dead now, and any written knowledge lost with the Coalition's destruction of the annals.

"So you did not know, either?" Drake asked.

"No," she said, looking back at Brander. "It's always just been something I've taken for granted, like 'Don't put your hand in fire.' What have you learned?"

The man who was the clever brains behind so many of their successes let out a long breath, then said, "Some time ago I obtained a sample of each, and began to run some tests."

"Of course you did," Iolana said, trying to tease him into a smile. When the effort failed, she began to realize just how serious this must be. "What happened?"

"The first sample of planium I had combined with a small amount of quisalt seemed unchanged, so I set it aside. But when I went to dispose of it some time later . . . it crumbled."

Iolana stared at him. Planium was the strongest metal known in the entire sector, perhaps the galaxy, given the Coalition's demand for it. It withstood heat, cold, and direct hits from other weapons.

"You tested this again, of course?" she asked.

He nodded. "Same result. At somewhere between two and six weeks, a small amount of quisalt makes planium unstable."

Possibilities swirled through her mind. And one look at Drake's face told her he'd thought of them all as well. She looked back at Brander. "Have you determined a ratio of quisalt to planium?"

"More than a quarter and it will happen within days, but the difference in the metal is obvious. At a quarter quisalt, the process gets slower, a month perhaps, and the planium looks almost normal but it is weakened."

"How weakened?"

It was Drake who answered her, in a tone that told her he understood all the ramifications of what he was saying. "Enough that were a weapon made of it, it would self-destruct on its first firing. And a ship with any significant amount would collapse at its first speed jump."

Iolana sank down into a chair beside the table. "Dear Eos," she whispered.

She didn't look up again until she heard a sound from the back of the room, and Kye came in from their private quarters. She took one look at Iolana's face and said softly, "They told you?" She nodded. Kye grimaced. "And I assume you got to the big picture faster than I did. I wanted to start immediately, since this is the key to the Coalition's destruction."

"And to ours," Iolana said softly.

"Yes," Kye said, sounding as grim as the two men had sounded. "Drake had to slow me down, until I saw what they would inevitably do once they realized we'd sabotaged their weapons and ships."

"We would be condemning Ziem and all her people," Brander said, his tone matching the grim look she'd seen when she'd come in.

"Probably immediately, once they figure it out," Kye said, equally grimly.

"Even as fast as they produce, it would take time for the altered planium to work its way into their equipment. And then time for them to figure out what happened. And where it originated," Drake said.

"But not enough time for us to figure out how to stop the certainty of Coalition destruction," Brander said. "If it could even be done."

Slowly, Iolana got to her feet. "So the decision is . . . to continue to supply the Coalition with the means to conquer and destroy other worlds, or to sacrifice ourselves to stop them."

"And even then it might not stop them permanently," Brander said wearily. "We could do great damage, eventually, but take them out completely? I don't know. Most of their ships and equipment would still be intact."

"It would depend upon how carefully we could balance it." Drake was pacing now. "If we could find a way to slow the weakening to where the sabotaged planium would be well into their supply chain before it fails . . ."

Brander's brow furrowed. "Delay the reaction? And keep the planium looking and reacting as it should, to fool them?"

"I don't ask for much, do I, my brother?" Drake said, with a wry grin at his second. Brander's chuckle and Kye's laugh lightened the mood, while Iolana's mind was racing through possibilities.

"It is not a decision that must be made today, thank Eos," Kye said.

"No," Drake agreed. "And when it comes to it, it is not one I can make alone. This is for all of Ziem to decide."

"Which in itself will be a challenge, getting that decision without giving away the game to the Coalition," Brander said. "If that is the course, it is going to take some time."

"Whereas the decision of what to do with our Coalition guest is one that must be made sooner," Kye said.

Iolana's thoughts were disrupted by the sudden attention shift to her. "But again, not today," she said. "He will still be recovering for some time yet."

"He will have to check in with his aide by morning," Drake said.

"I can ensure he will be awake and coherent long enough for that," she said.

"In a way," Kye said thoughtfully, "it's the same sort of decision, isn't it? Accepting, *helping* the demon we know or risking annihilation by one we don't?"

It startled her to hear him spoken of that way, although she knew many, if not most, of the Sentinels thought of him as such. But she understood Kye's comparison.

And it wasn't until she was alone again that she made herself face the fact that Caze Paledan was not a demon to her. Far from it.

Perhaps too far.

Chapter 27

THIS TIME WHEN he awoke, Paledan was certain of it. He'd thought he had, several times before, but he could not be sure they were not merely dreams, for they seemed so blurred to him. Once the young woman, Eirlys, was there. She spoke only of his condition, and how he felt, which was still peculiarly exhausted, given he had yet to actually move. Assuming, of course, he could.

But this time he was certain it was real. He felt fully awake for the first time since those agonizing hours.

Or perhaps the first time since he'd collapsed on that hillside.

Yet this place still appeared as his office. So the impossible remained.

"Back with us?"

The man who spoke was sitting in the chair opposite, his feet up on a small stool, ankles crossed negligently, as if there were no threat at all in this room. But then, despite that he was not in fighting garb now, this was the Raider, and a man as weak as he felt was no more threat to that warrior than a newborn barkhound.

"Somehow," he said dryly, "I am never sure."

The man smiled. "She has that effect."

Indeed.

He studied Davorin for a moment. "You stand watch yourself?"

"I ask nothing of others I am not willing to do myself."

Words, spoken in that warm, proud voice, echoed in his mind. *My son . . . would go himself, and let them decide whether to follow.*

A direct opposite of Coalition teaching and training. Underlings were there for a reason, and to be used to do those tasks that were beneath their superiors. But if it came to such, he had serious doubts about how many of those underlings would follow orders unto death.

With the Raider, he had no such doubts; they all would.

Davorin told him, since he could not see the outside and had no idea how much time had passed, that it was time to check in with Brakely. When the man used his aide's name, he was once more reminded of the breadth of this man's reach.

"You bother yourself with the name of my aide?"

"It is a well-known name to those who have had the misfortune to deal with the Coalition."

"You speak of his uncle."

Davorin gave a one-shouldered shrug. "Brayton Brakely's rise—and demise—are often used as an example of Coalition whim and injustice."

Paledan's mouth twisted wryly. "Since I have often thought the same, I can hardly deny that."

Davorin said nothing to that, but Paledan had the strangest feeling that he had somehow answered a question the man had not spoken.

He made the necessary contact without demurral. He was not quite able to handle the comm link himself yet, but he dared to think that soon he might, as feeling returned to his extremities.

He heard the undertone of concern in his aide's voice as he relayed the unease and confusion of the troops at the lack of action.

"I've told them you're out hunting the rebels personally, and that has allayed it somewhat, but—"

"Understood. Any inquiries from High Command?"

"No, sir. General Fidez appears to be keeping his promise."

"Amazing," he muttered, with a sideways glance at Davorin.

"Yes, sir," Brakely said, and there was complete understanding in his voice. "Next check, sir?"

"Double, again. I have further possibilities to investigate."

"Yes, sir." His aide sounded cheered at that.

Paledan almost signed off, but in the last instant he said, "Sorry to leave you to deal with everything for so long."

"My job, sir." His aide sounded pleased, but puzzled. Apologies of any kind were non-existent in Coalition policy. "And if you find those brigands, it will be well worth it."

He did sign off then. Davorin took the comm link back, and for a moment Paledan thought he was going to speak. But he did not, merely put the device back on the shelf. Or whatever it really was, underneath the mirage.

"Tell me," he said neutrally, "does this place appear to you as my office, or is it only me who sees this illusion?"

"Afraid she has entranced you?"

In more ways than I dare admit.

"Merely curious."

"Ah. That very un-Coalition trait again. No, Major, it appears this way to all who enter." With a slight smile he added, "Except the living things of supposed lesser intelligence, but perhaps stronger instincts."

"Like the various creatures that come and go seemingly at will?"

"Or at my sister's will, yes."

"Are these . . . abilities inherent in Ziemites?"

"Are they not on Lustros?" Davorin countered.

"If I am supposed to be surprised that you know my origins, I am not." He held the man's gaze. "But in answer, no. I have never seen anything like your sister's talent with animals."

"Or my mother's with people?"

"Or," he agreed. "Tell me, do you share them?"

Davorin laughed, and it was not scornful but genuinely amused. "I would be foolish to tell you one way or the other, would I not?"

To his own shock, Paledan found himself smiling. Again. "Indeed you would. And you are not." For a moment, he studied the man who should be his enemy. "I would ask you something else it would likely be foolish for you to tell me."

"Ask," Davorin said lightly. "Then it will be up to you to decide if my answer is true."

His own smiled widened as the man turned it neatly back on him. "The . . . accident at the mine. The survivor among my men seems to believe it was intentional. That one of the miners actually set off the explosion."

"And you find that hard to believe?"

"I find it impossible to believe. For he died himself in the process."

"And how is that different from being ordered to your death by the Coalition?"

"Are you saying you ordered him to do it?"

"I did not. And I would not. It is not the way of Ziem to demand self-sacrifice."

"Is that not what you did, when Jakel took your sister?"

"That is different. That was . . . family."

Paledan's brow furrowed. These concepts were difficult to understand, so foreign were they to him. "So the miner . . . are you saying he did it on his own?"

"I am not saying he did it at all," Davorin said easily. But Paledan thought he saw a touch of sadness in the man's eyes when he added, "But if he did, it would be a noble deed, and worthy of the highest honors of Ziem."

He had his answer, Paledan thought. It made no more sense to him, but he was certain now that that was exactly what had happened in that mine. Davorin's words about the Coalition rang in his head, and he contrasted this to the truth that death in the Coalition cause was touted as noble as well, but all knew that if you did not comply you would likely be terminated anyway. But to voluntarily sacrifice yourself for the tiniest of gains . . .

"He did not stop the mining, only slowed it for a brief time. He had to know that."

"So you can think of no other reason for such an act?"

Paledan considered that for a moment. He thought of all he had learned of these people since his posting here, in that time that seemed both short and yet the longest of his life.

The life that should have ended here.

And then the idea came to him. "It made the Coalition believe they had not yet the skills to mine the planium. Kept them from wiping out the miners and taking over."

"Them, Major?"

Caught in that way of thinking once more, he winced inwardly. And realized somewhat belatedly that Davorin hadn't directly answered anything. And yet Paledan was as certain as he could be that he was right.

Davorin smiled as if he understood, but only said, "I'm told you've regained some feeling."

"I believe so." He gave the man a pointed look. "But I am still far too weak to do anything."

"Which you would likely say were it true or not," Davorin said, with that same unconcerned smile. Was he so convinced he was harmless?

Is he not right?

With a grimace he acknowledged the truth. "Yes. But in this case, it happens to be true just now."

"Then in that case . . . you have visitors."

Startled, his gaze narrowed. Davorin stood, and made a motion toward the door—or whatever was really in the place where the imagined door stood. Two small figures darted in. He stared in shock as the two youngest Davorins came to a halt next to the cot—or whatever it was—he lay on.

"You are—" the girl began.

"Awake."

"I am," he said, flicking a glance at their brother, who remained silent, but Paledan sensed he was ready to move at the slightest sign they might be in danger.

"We are glad you—"

"Did not die."

"I am not so certain of that yet," he said dryly.

The boy's brow furrowed. "But is not—"

"Life always—"

"Better?"

"I'm told it depends on what life consists of."

The girl gave a short laugh. It was a good sound. And she, he thought yet again, would have been the one destroyed on his world.

"That sounds like—" she began.

"The Spirit," the boy finished.

He raised a brow at them. "You mean your mother?"

"She is—"

"We suppose, but—"

"She has been—"

"Gone a very—"

"Long time."

"We were—"

"Just children."

He laughed, he couldn't seem to help it. He wondered for a moment if this odd loss of his control of such emotions was part of his injury, but only for a moment, for if he had learned anything when dealing with these two it was that they required full attention.

"And what are you now?"

They both drew themselves up.

"We are—"

"Sentinels. And we—"

"Fight with—"

"The others."

"It is just our way—"

"Is a little—"

"Different."

"I'm certain that it is," he said, smothering another laugh. And he realized with a little jolt that he had truly missed talking to these two. Or perhaps listening to them talk. "And effective, too, I'm sure."

The two exchanged a glance and a grin, which made him wonder just what problems could be attributed to them. Probably more than the Coalition would ever realize or believe. But he would.

Their brother cleared his throat. They glanced quickly at him and nodded. In unison. Then turned back to him.

"We have—"

"To go—"

"Drake said—"

"We could not—"

"Stay long—"

"Because you need—"

"Rest. We just—"

"Wanted to—"

"Say we are glad—"

"You're not dead."

"Thank you." He didn't know what else to say. As the duo scampered out, he shifted his gaze to Davorin. "You let them come."

With a shrug, he said, "They very much wanted to see you, that you were truly alive still. They have been denied too much in this life, and this seemed a small enough wish to grant. Although I suppose," he said, looking thoughtful, "I should have asked you first."

Paledan stared at him, then shook his head slowly. "I am at your mercy. Why would you care what I wished?"

"Were you, say, Jakel, or the governor, or some other Coalition boot-licker, I would not." He held his gaze steadily. "Besides, there were many times when you had the opportunity to harm the twins, and a few when anyone else in your uniform would likely have executed them."

He knew this was true. And he could not really explain why he had not.

"They . . . interest me. They are clever. Bright. And utterly fearless."

"They are. Sometimes to my dismay."

"It is . . . a credit to your raising of them."

Davorin looked at him quizzically. "You show an understanding of something you never experienced. As adult, or child."

"I have never flown, either."

The man smiled widely at that. "And yet you designed a near flawless and very adaptable aircraft."

He could not understand why the words so pleased him. He'd received approval from the highest ranking flight officers in the Coalition, and it had never caused this kind of reaction in him.

"I would give much to meet the person responsible for those adaptations."

"Perhaps you already have."

"If you're going to tell me your mother is also an aircraft designer—"

He broke off as Davorin laughed. "She is many, many things, but not that."

"The twins . . . they do not accept her?"

"They have not yet decided, I think. She was, as they said, gone for a very long time. And they were very young when she left us."

He noted how evenly the man spoke of this, tried to reconcile this with what he knew of the closeness of family ties on this world.

"But you have . . ."

"Reached an understanding," Davorin said. "And now I must leave you, Major, to someone else's care." He turned to go, likely to signal another guard to enter.

"Attack plans to make?" Paledan asked.

Davorin turned back. "It would seem a wise thing, would it not? To attack while their commander is absent?"

Paledan shrugged, not even trying to deny it. "It is what I would do."

"Given your record, then, I suppose I must seriously consider it. Rest well, Major."

And then he was gone, leaving Paledan to ponder the rather amazing turn his life had taken.

Chapter 28

"HE WILL BE MOBILE very soon, I think," Drake said. "I've told the watch to be aware."

Iolana nodded. "I am not surprised, but have you some particular reason for thinking it is imminent?"

"He shrugged. And didn't seem to realize. And twice I saw his legs move. I do not think it was conscious, though. He was distracted by the twins."

"That will do it," Eirlys said dryly as she walked up beside them as her brother finished speaking. She'd clearly come from the cooking area of the main cavern, for she held a mug of steaming liquid Iolana guessed was the rich, sweet brew Mahko had a knack for.

"Indeed," Brander added from where he was sitting while industriously putting away a piece of brollet Mahko had seasoned with a new plant he'd found growing in the cracks of the rocks of their mountain.

"How did he react to them?" Iolana asked.

Drake gave a bemused shake of his head. "It was intriguing to watch. They clearly have little fear of him, and he is clearly fascinated by them."

"You're certain he means them no harm?" Eirlys asked.

"He, personally, yes. If those orders came down for mass destruction . . . I don't know."

"I'm not certain he knows," Iolana said quietly, and then thought of the knowledge she had gained, the secret even Caze himself did not know.

"He suggested I should be planning an attack. Or rather, said that was what he would do in my place."

"The families are happy for the stand-down, but the troops are getting restless," Brander said, licking his fingers as he finished; it would seem the new sauce was a success.

"And nervous about our guest," Eirlys added.

"Yes," Brander agreed, then, to Drake, he added, "They trust your judgment unreservedly." He shifted his gaze to Iolana. "And yours. But it still has them on edge to have the Coalition commander among us."

"And rightfully so," Eirlys said.

"I would expect nothing less." Drake grimaced. "And I also expect that, no matter what decision is made about his eventual fate, there will be some unhappy with it."

"That's a given," Brander said with a grin. "We're an unruly bunch."

"What choices do you have?" Eirlys asked. "You either let him go, or execute him."

Iolana saw Drake and Brander exchange a glance that was a bit too pointed to be casual.

"He's Coalition, so he deserves the execution," Eirlys went on. "But in that case it might have been better to save the effort of healing him and simply let him die on that hill."

"It does not occur to you," Iolana said softly to her daughter, "that to heal him and then execute him would be the most exquisitely horrible punishment?"

Eirlys's eyes widened, and she drew in an audible, shocked breath. "No!"

Iolana smiled. "I thought not. Your mind, thankfully, does not run in such hideous ways."

"But yours does?" her daughter said, still staring at her.

"No. But his does, in that it has occurred to him to wonder if that is our plan. And sadder still, he accepts it as a valid choice. Such is his experience with the Coalition."

"Stop," Eirlys said with a small shudder. "You will have me feeling sorry for him."

"And that is your greatest grace, my daughter," she said with a smile.

"Speaking of grace," Kye said, coming up to them with her own mug of Mahko's specialty in one hand, "have you decided yet what's to be done with that slimehog we hold?"

"Jakel?" Drake asked.

"Now there's one who deserves such a fate as you described," Eirlys said with a glance at Iolana.

"He does," Iolana said without qualm. "Interesting, is it not? We hold two men—using the term in one case loosely—and by logic there could be little doubt which we would be better rid of, given his rank in the Coalition and the power he has over Ziem. And yet . . ."

"Jakel grew up here, he was, for most of his life, one of us," Brander said sourly. "His betrayal is worse than a man doing what he sees as his duty, however repugnant that duty might be."

"Just like Barkhound," Eirlys said, using the nickname the twins had attached to their dead but not mourned governor, the turncoat who had handed over his world to the Coalition without even a token protest.

"Who met his just fate," Drake said.

"By the hand of the very beast Kye asked about," Brander said. "That interlude must have been like throwing two rabid muckrats in a pit and seeing which one kills the other."

"Charming, my love," Eirlys said, but her tone was teasing. Brander shrugged, but he was grinning.

Iolana looked at her eldest. "We could remain here for a very long time. It will be only by accident or some new device that the Coalition finds us. We have heat, thanks to Brander power, and Ziem herself provides us food. Most of the Sentinels have their families here and safe now."

"Yes, we could. But then one must wonder if we are still worthy of the Sentinel name," Drake said quietly.

She had expected no less from him. "So you see this as the calm before the storm begins again?"

"You would wish it otherwise? That we stay hidden, and let them have Ziem?"

The others went very still, and silent. They were watching her, and she suddenly realized they were waiting for her answer. As if it mattered, would even decide their course. And she knew she could put an end to the fighting, the dying, by simply presenting it as something she had foreseen, that they would stay here, safe within their mountain. But she had never used her gift falsely, and she would not begin to do so now. She had already made her entire life's quota of bad decisions that night on Halfhead Scarp.

"I only wish that those who fight do so with clear heads and hearts," she said. "I would want no one forced."

"Nor would I. They will be given the choice."

"And that, my son, is why they will follow you into the heart of the enemy, if you lead them."

Drake lowered his gaze, but not before she saw the warmth in his eyes. Kye surreptitiously took his hand in hers, and Iolana saw him smile then.

"We have two more days before Paledan is supposed to check in again?" Brander asked. Drake nodded, and Brander shifted his gaze to Iolana. "Where will he be by then?"

"We should have a good idea how complete the healing is by then. And I suspect he will be beyond ready to push the limits to find out."

"I've ordered the constant guard already," Drake said.

"You took Teal out of the rotation, I assume?" Brander asked. "I think he'd be hard pressed not to kill the man outright, after Gareth's death."

Iolana knew the young man had taken his brother's death in the triumphant ambush very hard, for they had been very close for a long time, being all that was left of their once-large family. She checked with him regularly, trying to do whatever he would allow her to ease his pain, but there were some agonies she could not relieve. She could give temporary respite, and had, but that kind of loss was carried forever.

"I did. He'll be helping to watch Jakel."

"Good. I wouldn't put it past him to gnaw his way out of that cage," Brander said dryly.

"I understand about the major," Eirlys said, "but I'm not certain why Jakel is still breathing."

"Feeling bloodthirsty, little sister?" Drake asked.

"Aren't you? After what he did to you?"

"Extremely," Drake said mildly, but something about his eyes belied the tone. "Although it is not so much what he did as how much he enjoyed doing it."

"He should be put down like the rabid slimehog he is," Kye said sharply.

Iolana smiled for a moment at the woman who had risked her own life to rescue Drake from Jakel's hell. She had become a warrior, had Kye Kalon. Which she was both grateful for and sad about, for it seemed a perversion that an artist of such amazing talent should be forced into such a life.

The artist who had created the portrait that Caze had rescued from the ruins of the taproom. The portrait that had claimed so much of his thought that she had sensed it upon the slightest brush of his arm.

A subject she had yet to get an answer from him on.

She stood up. "I believe it's time I go check on our other guest." She took a few steps, then turned back to look at her son. "If you're not going to do it yourself, for I would say you have first right, you might consider turning that rabid slimehog over to the women who have reason to hate him most. Not only would it do us good, it would be the height of ignominy to that piece of debris to go out at female hands."

"Excellent idea," Eirlys said.

"Indeed," agreed Kye. "I'll even give him a running start."

Drake looked at Brander and lifted a brow. "Ferocious, aren't they?"

Brander grinned. "Undeniably."

"Be glad we're on your side," Iolana said, and both Eirlys and Kye laughed as the two men issued heartfelt agreement.

And then she set off for her own refuge, which had become anything but with the presence of a man she should think of as an enemy, yet could not.

Chapter 29

HE HAD NEVER realized before how the simple act of being upright mattered. True, he was only sitting on the edge of the cot he slept on, not on his feet, but those feet moved, as did the rest of him, and while he was about as strong as a newborn brollet, it seemed miraculous nevertheless.

It *was* miraculous.

And that was where his analysis broke down. Because miracles, along with softening emotions and ties through blood were relegated by the Coalition to the ash heap. In fact, were even more so, for at least the latter two existed and had to be eradicated. Miracles were as unbelievable as the fabled blazers here on Ziem, or the golden horses of Arellia.

And yet . . . here he was, alive, breathing, and even through his current feebleness aware that the sometimes nagging, sometimes breath-stealingly sharp pain in his back, was gone. Completely gone. He'd gone from unbearable pain and the near certainty he was already dead to this.

He could not deny those empirical facts. Impossible as they seemed, they were indeed facts and must be accepted.

It was only the manner of their happening that he could not understand. And it had to simply be that, that he did not yet understand.

He looked at the woman watching him with a smile on her face. The woman who had made it all happen.

"You rested," he said, noting the dark circles under her vivid blue eyes had faded.

"It was necessary," she said. "While it was much worse for you, the healing was a great effort for me as well, and I needed to be ready in case something went wrong, or someone else needed my attention."

Because they are out battling my troops?

The question came and went quickly, for there was nothing he could do about it at the moment, if it were true.

"If you felt even a small fraction of what I felt, I am sorry."

She raised an arched brow at him. "I thought regret was not in the Coalition rule book."

"I long ago made an exception for those who are hurt in an effort to aid," he said.

"You. But not the Coalition."

"I have been too many places, seen too much, to remain completely rigid in my thinking," he finally said.

"And have you found anything of worth in the way of life in those many places?"

"I have found things of interest," he said. Then, before he really thought about it, he added, "Here in particular."

"And what does quiet, peaceful Ziem have to interest Major Caze Paledan, the most awarded officer in the Coalition?"

The way she said it irritated him, and it was in his voice when he said, "I do not control the handing out of those bits of metal and ribbon."

"I should think you would be proud."

"I am good at what I do. That knowledge is all I require."

"Then you are indeed unique."

"Not a goal to be strived for."

"Perhaps in the Coalition," she said. "In other places, it is highly prized."

"Ziem?"

"Only one example of many." Her expression changed, darkened. "At least, that was once the case."

"Until the Coalition arrived," he guessed.

"Yes," she agreed bluntly, heedless that she was prodding an officer of that Coalition. Or perhaps not; she seemed fearless enough to know the risk and do it anyway.

Or perhaps she just knew there wasn't a thing he could do just now.

But would he, even if he could? After what she had done for him, bringing him back from the verge of death, or a life even worse than death?

Coalition teaching on the matter was simple; if the one who aided you was of further use, they were allowed to live. If they were of no harm, it was left to the judgment of the recipient of the aid. But if they were a danger, or had the potential to be, the response was made quite clear; they must be removed, permanently.

And this woman was part of the most contentious, stubborn, trouble-some—and innovative—rebellion he'd ever encountered in his career. She held a position of obvious reverence here, bound by those blood ties the Coalition scoffed at, and some other, strange, uncanny connection to this mist-shrouded world.

"But you avoided my question. What is there on my misty Ziem that interests you?"

He considered his answer carefully. He had the oddest feeling she would know if he lied. It seemed a small enough talent, when laid against her others.

"That very mist," he said. "The way your people have adapted to it. The society that developed here, on such weak precepts as blood ties and personal independence, that was yet able to mount such a rebellion."

"That," she said coolly, "is Coalition blindness."

"Perhaps," he admitted, something he would never have done before he'd seen the accomplishments of that society. He held her gaze. "Then perhaps simply that such a remote, quiet place produced a warrior such as your son."

She was silent for a moment before she said quietly, "If you think to flatter me by complimenting my son, do not bother. I could be no prouder of him than I already am."

"Rightfully," he said. "I may believe such ties are . . . unnecessary, but—"

"They are," she said, almost imperiously, and for a moment he saw the Iolana Davorin who had been the partner of the man who had stirred this peaceful, remote place to battle, "the very glue that holds Ziem together. We are of this world, and this world is of us. Neither would be the same without the other."

Her words rang in the room—whatever sort of place it really was—as if she'd been giving a speech. As perhaps she had, when she had stood beside her mate. Yet another connection he did not believe in. And yet he could understand it. Any man who had such a woman at his side, would be—

"Tell me," she asked, "do you never long for a personal connection, to another living soul rather than the machine of the Coalition? Do you never wish to feel such pride in someone that is part of you?"

"I . . . do not require it."

"That is not what I asked, Caze," she said, her voice softer now, so soft that when she spoke his name a shiver went through him.

"It is the only answer I can give . . . Lana." *Because I am afraid I am learning to want more.*

It was an instant before she spoke, and he wondered if it was his use of that name. "Now," she said, and he wasn't certain if she was referring to his answer or what she intended now, since she had gotten to her feet and crossed the short—very short—distance between them. "I need to assess your condition, which requires that I touch you."

He instantly quashed unwanted images that came to mind on those last three words. "You are the healer," he said stiffly. "You hardly need permission."

"Perhaps in your world, but not in mine. When someone is too weak to protect themselves, we do it for them. Once they have regained that strength and sense of self, it is theirs to give permission. No one else has the right."

"The Coalition—"

"—takes that right. Steals it. It is not given to them, except by those who wish no responsibility for themselves." Her voice changed suddenly, and she tilted her head as she looked at him. "And I cannot believe you yourself are one of those who abdicates personal choice. You accept the Coalition's control only because it is all you have ever known."

"You speak treason so easily," he said, an edge coming into his voice.

"The only treason I speak of is committed by those who welcome the Coalition to a free world and stand by while it is enslaved." Again that intent look. "And I think, in your heart of hearts, you know it is true. They have taken so much from you—"

"They have given me everything."

She gave him a scornful look that stung. "They have given you almost nothing, Major."

Impossibly—that word again—he found himself stung that she had reverted to using his rank.

"They have given you nothing. What you have you have earned. Whether it is of true worth, only you can decide. And they have taken more from you than you realize, more than you even know. But time enough for that. Now I need to make that assessment."

He had little patience for such vagary and gave a sharp nod. She stepped forward that last short distance. Reached out, and he found himself bracing for her impending touch. She put one hand on his shoulder, the other on his back, over the scar, which he had discovered had been intact, undisturbed by the removal of the very projectile that had caused it. He felt something odd, some kind of energy flowing through him, as if there were a connection between her hands. Why it seemed strange, after everything else she'd done, he didn't know.

After what seemed like a breathless age, she straightened. "You are doing very well," she said, while he denied inwardly that the removal of her hands had sent a sensation of loss through him. "Perhaps you would like to try and walk a few steps?" The thought of actually being mobile sent a jolt of anticipation through him. "I see it appeals." The teasing tone was back, and he realized with another jolt that he had missed it.

"Yes. Yes, it does."

"I do not think it wise for you to try this without support on both sides. I will get Grim."

"Your tall guardian," he said. "He is very . . . dedicated to you."

"Grim would die for me, if need be. And so I am more careful than perhaps I would be without him."

"Would you die for him?" He did not even know why he had asked. Surely the mist of this place truly had scrambled his brain. Or perhaps—

"Without hesitation," she answered, cutting off his speculation. "He is my oldest friend."

"But . . . only a friend?"

She gave him a rather strange smile. "He is a closer friend than I imagine the Coalition allows its own."

"Friendship can bring weakness."

"And yet I am told young Brakely would likely die for you."

"I hope not."

"Why not? You are, after all, much more important than he."

"He has had enough undeserved grief in his life."

Her eyes widened. And when she laughed this time, it was a delighted, exultant sound. "Oh, you are much closer than I dared hope! I will get Grim, and we will get you on your feet."

He stared after her as she stepped to the doorway to summon Grim. If he were himself, this would be a moment for escape. Normally it would be nothing at all to overpower a woman her size. But he was not himself, and she was not an ordinary woman.

And those were the only reasons he did not, he told himself. It had nothing to do with that wretched curiosity he'd never quite been able to smother despite the intensive Coalition efforts to force him to it. That curiosity that had done nothing but grow since he'd first set foot on this quiet, remote planet.

And it absolutely had nothing to do with any intense need to know completely who—and what—this woman of the portrait was.

Chapter 30

"HE IS—"

"Doing better?"

Iolana finished the last spoonful of Mahko's tasty brollet stew as she looked at the twins and nodded. "Much. We will be working on getting his strength back now."

The two exchanged a glance, then seemed to mutually decide something.

Lux began it. "We want to—"

"Ask you something," Nyx finished.

Her heart nearly stopped. They had never done this, approached her of their own accord. She set her spoon down in the bowl and gave them her full attention.

"Ask," she said. "Anything."

"It is about—"

"The major."

"We like him but—"

"He is Coalition and—"

"We hate them—"

"And Drake said—"

"He does too—"

"But he could not—"

"Explain why—"

"But he said—"

"Maybe you could."

She didn't know whether to thank Drake for sending them to her, or scold him for sending them to her with a question she couldn't answer. She drew in a breath.

"I will try," she said. "But I need you to imagine something first."

"We are—"

"Good at that."

She laughed; she couldn't help herself. "Indeed you are." The twins waited silently, and she gathered her thoughts to go on. For a moment she considered these two she had birthed, their fearlessness, their wildness, and the connection they shared.

"I want you to imagine if your lives had been different. If you were caged, prevented from being who you are."

"Drake never—"

"Did that—"

"Even if sometimes—"

"He wanted to."

"I know," she said softly. "And that is ever to his credit. But imagine if you had been taken away from him and given over to someone else, who did not know or care, or even automatons, who felt nothing for you. And their job was not just to cage you but to crush that wildness in you that leads you on such adventures. To make you behave exactly as everyone else did, to march in step, never to explore on your own, or learn anything they did not wish you to know."

"We would not like—"

"To live like that."

They were frowning now. And finally Lux began it.

"But what has this—"

"To do with the major?"

"That is the world he grew up in. Alone, tended by machines or people who might as well be. No family, no ties, caged, and every bit of spirit or mind that did not conform with their rules crushed."

"He grew up—"

"Like that?"

She nodded. They were finally horrified, but it was at the right thing. "That is what the Coalition is. And what they did to him."

"But he is—"

"Not crushed."

"Yes. Just . . . hindered in some ways. Which shows you just how strong he is, to grow up like that yet be the man he is."

The twins exchanged a look.

"He has never had—"

"Adventures like—"

"Ours?"

She smiled at their tone, a combination of amazement and sadness. "Adventures for the sake of adventure? No, I doubt he has."

"We would—"

"Like to—"

"Teach him."

She bit back a sudden welling of unexpected emotion. "I think," she said, reaching out to put a hand on one shoulder of them both, "he would be amazed. And delighted."

"We will—"

"Go plan."

They scampered off, leaving her blinking away tears. "You can come out now," she said to the shadows behind her.

Drake stepped through the doorway of his quarters. "You knew I was there."

"Yes." She turned to look at him then. "And it made no difference to my answer."

He nodded as he walked over to her.

She drew in a deep breath. "I know I have said as much before, but . . . thank you. Those two are . . . everything they could possibly be. And that is because of you."

"I merely tried to keep them unscathed."

"You did much more than that. And I could not be prouder of you. Or," she added sadly, "more ashamed of myself. For no one took care of you."

"I was an adult."

"You were still my child."

He sat down in a chair opposite her at the map table. "I think," he said, "we need to put this behind us, for all time."

"I can never forget or forgive myself."

"Kye has taught me much. I have only to imagine how I would feel if I lost her, and I have an understanding I never had before, of why you did what you did. And so . . . I can forgive. As can Eirlys, for a similar reason."

She wished she dared hug him, but knew he was not yet ready. Then, after a moment, she asked, "So it is only those two sprites I need worry about?"

"If there is one thing I am certain of about them, it is that they will do what they will do, and in their own time." She sighed, but nodded. "And now," Drake said, "I have a question of my own."

She braced herself, ready to answer whatever he might ask. After this, she could deny him no truth he sought.

"When you were speaking to them of the major, I had the feeling there was more to it than you focused on for them."

She sucked in a breath; she had not expected that to be his question.

"Yes," she said. "There is more."

"What?"

And just that quickly he asked for the one answer she could not give him. "I promise you Drake, I will share it. But I cannot yet."

"Is it of . . . tactical significance?"

"No. It is personal. Although I think it will change him immensely."

He tilted his head slightly as he looked at her, and her heart skipped a beat. Just so had his father done, when pondering deeply. And she realized with a little shock that that thought no longer brought the sharp, bloodying pain it once had. It was still there, and she knew it always would be, but it was . . . muted somehow.

"Then that brings me to another question, that perhaps only you can accurately answer."

"Which is?"

"Brander thinks that we might be able to . . . turn him." She said nothing for a moment. Then her son said softly, "I see this is not a surprising thought to you."

"It is not."

"So you've thought it possible as well?"

"I've thought about it," she corrected. "And while I will agree it may be possible that he would turn on the Coalition, he will never be coerced or persuaded to it. He is a man who would have to make that decision himself. It would have to rise from within him."

"But you think it could happen?"

"I think it would take a great deal to turn him from the life he has, the only life he's ever known. And words alone could not do it."

"Meaning?"

"He would have to be shown. And then he would make his own decision. He is a man who takes life as he finds it and acts according to his own code. Which is, as I'm sure you've noticed, not the typical Coalition code."

Drake's mouth quirked upward. "I've noticed. It is one reason I've thought it might be possible. They may think they've crushed and remolded him, because he has thus far succeeded so extraordinarily at their aims, but even under the Coalition yoke he has done it his own way."

"Exactly that. It is not by chance that he speaks of the Coalition as 'they,' and not 'we.' And there is what I sensed on the hillside that day."

"But I am afraid it would take more time than we have," Drake said. "We cannot hold him here by force very long."

"Using force on him would slow the process."

"You said you sensed it might not be a new thought to him."

"Yes."

"So it may actually already be underway." She nodded slowly, hesitatingly, and he said, "Your instincts have yet to fail us. What is your feeling?"

"I think our people have made him curious about another way to live. I think their determination not to bow to their conquerors has sparked that curiosity of his." She held his gaze with her own, and put every ounce of pride she felt in him into her voice. "Most of all, I think your example, you yourself and the way you lead, has spoken to him. Something within him, something perhaps not totally destroyed by the Coalition."

"I thank you . . . mother." Her throat tightened in response. "But I am still afraid changing a lifetime's indoctrination and cruelty will take longer than we have."

"I do not think it is a process that will end when—if—he leaves here. As long as Ziem and her people exist, as long as we continue to fight, and succeed so far beyond the scope of Coalition predictions, he will question, search, and—"

"May well get those orders to destroy," Drake ended it sourly.

"Then the real question is," she said, "what will he do then?"

And that she had no answer for.

Chapter 31

"IT IS," PALEDAN said through clenched teeth as he struggled to walk an embarrassingly short distance across . . . whatever this room was, "as if my muscles have completely forgotten their jobs."

"And you have no patience with anyone or anything that has the temerity to do so," the woman at his side said cheerfully.

He glanced at her, and that simple action threw off his precarious balance and he staggered. She caught him, steadied him, and held his arm for a moment until he'd recovered his balance.

"I do not need your—" He stopped himself in the middle of the denial, for in fact he did need everything he was denying he did.

"It is very difficult," she said, in that same cheerful tone that had prodded him into that ill-advised move, "for a person of such strong will to accept that they in fact do need help."

"Was it for you?" He wasn't sure why he'd asked that.

"Me? Oh, no. But I am not as strong of will as you are."

This time he moved much more carefully as he turned his head to look at her. "That," he said flatly, "is the first time I believe you've lied to me."

She looked surprised, and for some reason he did not understand, that pleased him. He was not pleased by the quickly growing pile of things he didn't understand, mostly his own reactions since the healing.

He refocused on her and not the bewildering changes. "You did what they said impossible and removed that shard. I am alive and upright, in direct contradiction of the prognoses of the best Coalition physicians. That was not done without a powerful will."

"Perhaps they underestimated you."

For a long moment he just looked at her. "I promise you, Lana," he said slowly, "I will never again underestimate you."

She held his gaze. "And I have not underestimated you since that moment on the bridge."

. . . what was that moment on the bridge focused on?

The measure of a man.

For the first time he wondered just how deeply she had probed. He could no longer deny that she had this gift, for he had seen too much of it. It had no place in his—and the Coalition's—logical, ordered universe, but neither had much he had seen since he'd come to this misty place.

Just as he had the thought he could not stay on his feet another moment, she turned. "You must not push too hard too soon. Sit."

He would have shot her another glance, half certain she was reading his mind, but he caught himself this time. For he was also half certain he would go down this time, from the sudden weakness that had flooded him. And so he let her guide him to sit on the edge of the cot. But he refused to lie down, not yet. He needed too many answers.

"Ah. You have more questions."

"Do you read my mind?" he asked bluntly.

"No," she said, "although I'm interested that you even consider the possibility. But in truth, after a healing I have a connection to the one healed, until it is no longer necessary."

"A . . . connection?" He was not at all certain what he thought of this.

"I can sense changes connected to the healing. Such as when you had reached the limit of your strength just now. Which, I might add, is impressive. I did not expect you to improve so quickly."

"It does not feel impressive."

"Compared to what you were before the injury, I'm certain it does not. Compared to the moment you went down on that hillside, unable to move at all, it is remarkable."

It occurred to him how his words could have been taken. "I did not mean that as insult."

"I did not think you did, Caze." And every newly reawakened nerve in his body seemed to respond to the sound of his name on her lips. Was this part of it as well? Did that connection she spoke of somehow go both ways? "You are hardly fool enough to insult the one who holds your life in their hands. Unless, of course, you wanted them to end it." He did not reply to this, but it seemed she needed no reply. "I understand," she said.

"Do you?"

Her voice was suddenly that soft, soothing thing again. "Oh, yes, Caze, I do." Why in hades had he ever given her leave to use his name? She went on. "You know my story. You know that I know what it is like to look at the life left to you and deem it not worth living."

"That is . . . different."

"Is it? I suppose you must think so, given what the Coalition has done to you, what they have taken from you."

"The Coalition gives all."

Those Ziem-blue eyes rolled. "Spare me the Coalition mantras, please. They take and destroy more than they could ever give back." It was heresy, worth a death sentence. And yet she said it fearlessly. "They take even the most basic and important of human capacities. To love, fully and completely. You cannot even comprehend that losing the person that made you whole, half of your soul, would be as bad or in some ways worse than losing the function of your body."

He stared at her. The echo of a long-ago agony tinged her voice, and he could not deny it was real. And he felt an odd, unaccustomed hollowness inside him, something that might even be called pain were it not impossible. He struggled to make sense of her words, although the concept may as well have been uttered in Zenoxian for all that he understood it.

"What I cannot comprehend," he said slowly, "is allowing another, single individual to wield so much power over you."

"It is not a matter of allowing," she said. "It is a matter of freely, happily giving. And the treasure of being given the same in return."

He felt exhaustion starting to creep over his brain. How was he supposed to deal with this, these ideas that were not only incomprehensible but antithetical to everything he'd been trained to believe?

"You should rest now," she said. "You've been given a great deal to process in a short time."

"Stop it," he snapped.

"That," she retorted calmly, "was nothing to do with mind reading or the connection between us. That was simply logic applied to your situation."

That, at least, he could understand. But the reference to the connection between them was still unsettling. "Tell me," he said, "who decides when this connection is no longer necessary?"

She looked thoughtful. "I do not think it is a decision. The connection simply fades away. It is not a conscious thing, on my part."

"Then you could not break it before it fades?"

"I do not know. I have, of course, never tried, for it only dissolves when the patient is safe. Before that, there is still the chance more intervention could be needed."

He drew in a deep breath, and closed his eyes for a moment. It was a mistake, for he could feel the wave of exhaustion beginning to take over.

"I understand," he heard her say, again in that soft voice. "You are not a man who would welcome another having that kind of deep, personal control over you. Yet you allow it to the Coalition."

"The Coalition—"

"Gives all. Yes. I know. But while you rest, perhaps you might ask yourself if it is worth the price they demand."

Chapter 32

"WHAT IS YOUR best estimate?"

Iolana looked at Drake. "Much sooner than I had expected." Her mouth quirked. "Which tells me I should stop expecting the expected with him."

Drake lifted a brow at her. "Should I be concerned that this makes sense to me?"

Iolana smiled, widely. But before she could respond, she heard the now-familiar footsteps as the twins raced into Drake's quarters, forgoing knocking. They skidded to a halt just inside. Iolana hoped it was not because of her presence, and was relieved when Lux began it, rather apologetically, glancing back at the door they'd thrown open heedlessly.

"We are not—"

"On alert again—"

"Are we?"

"Not yet," Drake said easily. She gathered that when the Sentinels were on alert, knocking was required even of these two. And wondered when they would be back on alert, how long Drake could stand the quiet. "I thought you were pestering Brander."

"We were but—"

"Eirlys came and—"

"They started—"

"Kissing and—"

"We know—"

"What that means."

It was all Iolana could do not to laugh, so pleased was she. "So what mischief are you up to instead?" she asked. They glanced at her, but only a glance before turning their attention back to their brother.

"Can we—"

"See the major—"

"Again? We have—"

"Something for him."

"And what might that be?" Drake asked.

Nyx held out his hand. Drake looked at the small, green, round thing the boy held, then shifted his gaze to her.

"What do you think?"

Iolana considered. "I think it will interest him."

For a moment the twins were silent, looking at her, but then Lux began with, "Are you—"

"The one who—"

"Decides now?"

She could not read whether there was objection in their words; her skills often failed with these two.

"Only whether he is well enough to see what you bring. Whether he should see whatever you have in mind is up to your brother."

They shifted their gaze back to Drake. "I can't see any harm in it," he said. "But not alone."

"Will you—"

"Go with us?"

"I cannot." He did not sound in the least regretful. "I have a promise to keep."

Something in the way he said it made Iolana think that his plans were much like Brander's; Kye had arrived back from a security flight within the last hour. She smiled inwardly.

She almost offered to accompany the twins herself, but decided to wait and see if they would ask her. It would tell her if they were feeling any more warmly—or at least more comfortable—toward her, and also just how much they wanted to see Caze.

And she was still a bit uneasy herself, mostly about how she reacted when using his name, even merely in her thoughts. She was feeling as she sometimes did after a vivid vision; unsettled, off balance, and disturbed to the point of a physical reaction.

Silence spun out between them, but before it became uncomfortably blatant, they broke.

"Will you—"

"Go with us?"

"I will." She kept her delight masked; it would not do to give these two imps any more leverage than they already had. "You should get something to put it in, after you show him what it is and what it does. I will meet you in the cavern in a moment."

The two dashed out without a word, no doubt headed to beg a plate or cup from Mahko.

"Congratulations," Drake said. "You have made progress."

"And I will gladly take their willingness to ask me as a sign of that."

"Be cautious."

"He would not intentionally hurt the twins."

"Agreed, yet he is still Coalition." Drake studied her for a moment. "And there is still what you are not telling me."

"Because it is his to know first."

"Must I remind you who we are speaking of? The commander of our conquerors?"

"Firstly, we are not conquered, and secondly, who was it who said that if we discard our first tenets—such as individual sovereignty—what are we fighting for?"

Drake sighed. "I believe that was me."

"I believe it was."

"As you see fit, then," he said.

"And you have . . . an appointment, do you not?"

The rakish grin that curved his mouth then gladdened her heart. "That I do. Keep those two occupied, will you?"

"For as long as I can," she promised.

She went out into the cavern and found the twins waiting, as patiently as was possible for them, near the entrance. On the way to her home she watched as they ran ahead of her, but then got distracted by something of interest along the way, giving her time to catch up without altering her stride.

When they arrived, she halted them before they ran inside. "If he is asleep, I must ask you to wait quietly until I check on him. If he is, you may have to wait until he wakes."

They considered this.

"He was—"

"Hurt very—"

"Badly—"

"Wasn't he?"

"Yes," she said. *And he lived with the knowledge this could happen for a very long time.*

"We are—"

"Glad he—"

"Did not—"

"Die," they finished together.

"I know," she said.

"Are you?" Lux asked.

That surprised her, both the question and that the child had asked at all.

"Right now, I am. I hope I do not come to regret the decision to save him."

"You mean if—"

"He turns—"

"Coalition."

That gave her pause. "Is he not Coalition now?"

"He wears—"

"The suit but—"

"His mind—"

"Does not."

She stared at these two marvels she had produced. "A more concise summation I have never heard," she murmured. Then, in normal tones, she added, "Your father would be very impressed with you both."

They looked very pleased at that, and she smiled inwardly. And realized she had smiled more with these two in the last ten minutes than she had since she had come back.

"Let us go in then, and introduce the major to one of the small wonders of Ziem," she said.

Chapter 33

"IT IS—"

"A special plant—"

"Only of Ziem."

Paledan stared down at the small, green ball the boy held out. He could see that it was indeed plant matter, but what was special about it escaped him. Was it edible? Did it have some medicinal value?

Maybe poisonous . . .

Even as he thought it he didn't believe it. These two would not do that. He was not sure of why he knew this, only that he did. But as with anything that presented itself to his mind as a given when he did not have evidence to substantiate the conclusion, or when he could not trace each step of the thought process that brought him to it, he was mistrustful. Hence the thought occurring in the first place, he assumed.

"You must—"

"Hold it."

"She said—" The boy's eyes flicked to his mother.

"You could now," the girl finished.

He shifted his own gaze to the woman who sat on the chair opposite the cot he sat on the edge of. He had tried to keep his focus on the duo that so intrigued him, since he had learned it was best to keep up with them. But this woman was ever unsettling to him, his every sense working at a tangible hum any time she was in this room with him. And she made him work at something that should have come easily, the simple process of logic.

But surely she would not go through what she had in order to heal him, and then simply allow these two to undo it all with some strange, deadly plant of this world. He felt a sense of satisfaction as soon as the thought occurred; this must be what his mind had processed on a subconscious level. He hadn't made some unfounded leap, he had merely realized this before he actually put it into words in his mind.

He turned back to the twins. "And what else must I do?"

"Just hold it—"

"Warm it—"

"With your hand and—"

"It will—"

"Do the rest."

Nyx extended his hand. Paledan did the same, flicking another glance at Iolana as he was able to do so with relative steadiness. The boy dropped the small green thing, which closer up looked like a handful of leaves tightly compressed, into his palm.

"Now close—"

"Your fingers—"

"Around it."

He did so. Without hesitation. And yet it was not long ago it had taken him great concentration to get his fingers to properly respond. But he did not look at Iolana this time; he was certain she would note the improvement. She missed little, if anything.

For a long moment nothing happened. "How will I know when what is supposed to happen happens?" he asked the twins.

"You will—"

"Know," Lux finished, with a smile that inexplicably made him feel an odd, inward tug.

"Is it—"

He stopped as he felt a slight but undeniable movement in his hand, the slightest of tickles against his skin. The twins grinned.

"Hold it—"

"Just a little—"

"Longer."

He did. And with each passing second the movement grew stronger, a brushing, expanding sort of sensation that felt as if the tiny ball were unfurling.

"Now!" they chorused.

He opened his fingers.

The small green ball was indeed unfurling, and the moment it was free of his grasp the thing burst outward and upward into a graceful spray of fronds, which also, impossibly, turned from green to a bright, flaming red before his eyes.

He stared at the thing. He had heard of life forms on various worlds who were able to change their own coloration to blend into the background, to hide from predators, but he'd never heard of a plant that could change like this, so quickly. As if it were a sentient creature, or one with a nervous system to react with.

"It is—"

"A fireplant."

"Appropriate name," he said, shifting his gaze to the twins.

"If you—"

"Stroke one—"

"From the bottom—"

"To the top—"

"It will—"

"Hug you."

He blinked. Now, surely, they were making up stories. He felt the urge to glance at their mother—ah, perhaps that was the way he should think of her, it put her a step further away—but immediately had the thought that if he did it would lessen him in the twins' eyes to look to someone else for assistance with them. And oddly, he did not wish that to happen.

Slowly, he lifted his other hand and ran a finger along one of the fronds, as instructed. And when he had nearly reached the top, it actually did curl downward, wrapping around his finger.

He stared at it for a moment, both startled and bemused. What bizarre things this misty world held. Then he looked up at the twins, who were both grinning at him.

He felt such an odd sensation, unfurling inside him much as this frond had, a warmth and . . . softness. He wondered if this was an effect of the plant, not poison but perhaps a drug of some sort.

"Children?"

Her voice was soft, and in it he heard that undertone he'd often heard when Ziemites spoke to those connected to them by blood ties. Love, he supposed they would call it on this world where they clung to such things.

The twins glanced at her, then at the plant he held.

"We must—"

"Put it—"

"On something—"

"Now that it is—"

"Starting to turn—"

"Green again."

He hadn't noticed that the red at the very tips of the fronds, including the one still wrapped around him, was indeed fading. For an instant he wondered wryly if it would surrender his finger, but he retracted it easily. And the ability to do even this much was still a wonder to him, and he felt another rush of that same warm sensation. This time he did look at Lana, for he could no longer deny that he owed this, and much more, to her.

Lux held out the small, carved wooden cup she carried. He deduced from that he was supposed to deposit the plant in it. He slid it off his palm so that it landed upright in the cup. The green was spreading now as the brilliant red faded.

"You cannot—"

"Touch it now because—"

"It will burn."

He blinked anew and stared at the rather benign-looking plant. "Burn?" he asked.

"Your skin." It was Lana who answered this time. "After it opens and the red fades, it begins to produce a secretion that will blister painfully if touched."

"Effective defense," he said.

"Yet some of our creatures feed on it. They know that in the sphere stage it is safe."

He had just enough time to wonder at that when the twins asked her the very question he would have.

"How do—"

"They know?" They looked as if this had only now occurred to them.

"That," their mother said, "is a very good question. Can you think of a way?"

Nyx frowned, but Lux looked merely thoughtful. Then they exchanged a glance that had him again wondering if they somehow communicated without spoken words, especially when they started again.

"I think that—"

"Maybe one tried—"

"To eat it at—"

"The wrong time—"

"And they learned."

Iolana smiled at her amazing, bewildering offspring. "Excellent deduction. And then?"

The two looked puzzled. Then they looked at him, as if checking to see if he understood what she meant.

"I think," he said to them, "that she means that then the one who learned somehow conveyed this to the others."

Their expressions brightened. "Oh. You mean—"

"Their mother—"

"Won't let them—"

"Eat it."

"Something like that," he agreed.

"That is what mothers should do."

There was a trace of sadness in her voice, and he supposed she was thinking of how she had not been there for these two. It was, he gathered, among the strongest of bonds on this world.

The twins looked at her for a moment. Then Lux said, "Drake says you had to choose between what you wanted and what was best for Ziem."

For the first time he saw her utterly disconcerted. Her eyes, those amazing ice-blue eyes, widened as she stared down at them. He wondered if part of it at least was because it had been a full sentence from only one of them.

"Yes," she whispered.

It was Nyx this time. "And Eirlys says you will probably feel bad about it forever."

"Yes," she repeated. "Forever."

The two exchanged glances, then nodded at each other.

"That is—"

"Enough then."

He heard her take in a quick, audible breath as they shifted their attention back to him. "We will—"

"Go find more—"

"Interesting things—"

"For you."

They darted out. Iolana stared after them. She looked stunned.

He was feeling a bit the same. Not at the twins, but at himself, and his reaction to them. He felt no longer just intrigued. He had long ago admitted he looked forward to their interactions, but until this moment he had not realized that it mattered to him that they trusted him. Even, perhaps, liked him.

And the liking of other people had not mattered to him in a very, very long time. If it ever had.

"Are you . . . all right?" he asked as she continued to stare after the two who had scampered out the exit he could not see but obviously they knew was there. He also knew where it had to be, and were he stronger he might attempt an exit himself. But even as he thought it, he knew it was not true. Not yet.

"Lana?" he said when she didn't respond.

At last she turned back to face him. "My relationship with them has been . . . difficult."

I promised to look after my children by the simple act of bringing them into the world. I did not keep that promise.

He might not understand the concept behind those words she had spoken, but he did understand the value of a person's word.

"They seemed . . . accepting, just now," he said; it required thought to come up with words for these intricate relationships he knew nothing of except descriptions in Coalition research.

"Yes," she said, glancing the way they had gone. "Yes, they did. A first."

When she looked back her smile was as bright as the sun of Lustros. And when that thought formed, it took him a moment to recognize the jab of aversion he felt was to the linking of this woman in any way to the place he'd come from. She was too brilliantly, flamingly alive for that regimented, controlled world. She would never be allowed.

"They are . . . unique." *Just as you are. Another bane to the Coalition.*

"They are very special." She just looked at him for a long moment, as if she were considering something. "And yet twins are not treasured, on your home world," she finally said.

He nearly laughed. "Treasured? On Lustros they are considered a mistake, to be rectified immediately."

"By slaughtering the smaller of the two."

"Yes."

"And what if the smaller one is—or would have been—the smarter one?"

"Then it's for the best." He sucked in a breath, startled at his own words.

"So it is more difficult for an intelligent child to smother that intelligence to fit into the Coalition mold? That must have made it very difficult for you, then."

It was, he supposed, a measure of his current weakness that the compliment pleased him more than the insult to the Coalition bothered him. Perhaps his condition explained all the strange thoughts and feelings he'd been having since he'd awakened in this impossible mirage.

When he didn't speak, she went on cheerfully, as if she hadn't noticed. "Tell me, Caze, can you imagine Nyx without Lux?"

It took him a moment to suppress the odd combination of shiver and heat that went through him every time she used his name. It was ridiculous; it meant nothing. No one used his given name, so naturally it sounded . . . odd to him when someone did. Except "odd" was not the word for it.

But he wondered if perhaps she had inadvertently revealed the crux of Coalition thinking on the matter of twins. Perhaps it was not only that they thought of them as defective, but that such inseparableness, such loyalty between two people could not be allowed, not when all loyalty must be toward the Coalition.

"No," he admitted finally. "I cannot. They are at times like one being."

"Especially when it seems they do not require the mundane methods of communication we do."

The short laugh broke from him before he could stop it. But she had said exactly what he had thought, more than once.

"So it would seem," she went on, as if laughter was not unexpected from him, which in itself seemed important somehow, "that they have progressed beyond we lesser beings, does it not?"

He saw where she was going, now. "You are saying Lustros is making a sizeable mistake."

"You disagree?"

He let out a slow breath. "I never questioned the policy. Until I met them."

She studied him for a moment before saying, "You have shown you can change your mind. When not doing so becomes the impossibility."

"Yes. But as I said, they are unique."

"Are they? How can you know that?"

She had, he had to admit, a very valid point. And he didn't know how to refute it. So instead he said, "From what I understand of maternal ties on this world, every mother thinks her children unique. You do not?"

She shook her head, almost sadly. "Evading again?" He didn't bother to deny it, for she was correct, but he also wanted an answer. And after a moment she gave him one. "I, perhaps more than any mother on Ziem, have the gift of children who are unique."

"A warrior the likes of which I have never encountered before, a woman who has all creatures at her command, twins who communicate without speaking and have an unerring knack for trouble, and all of them utterly fearless? Yes, I would agree."

As he'd spoken, her eyes had taken on that brilliant gleam, lit as if from within. "I thank you for that, Caze. For there is no better way to compliment a mother than to compliment her children."

He could not doubt that she meant it. And yet it somehow wearied him. "I do not understand the . . . treasuring of these kinds of bonds. How do you think, make decisions, without their needs interfering?"

"We do not," she answered simply. "And often their needs obscure all else. It takes a great deal to eclipse them."

"Such as overwhelming grief?" he asked, thinking of her death plunge. "Does that not prove my point about blood ties? How can it be worth it when the loss of one destroys you?"

She leaned back in the chair, tilting her head slightly as she looked at him. A loose strand of that fiery hair slid to one side, and he felt an odd tingling in his fingers that he belatedly realized was a desire to touch that hair, to tangle it with his hands as he . . .

Kissed her. Stroked her. Took her.

He was so stunned by both the realization and the need that it was a moment before he could refocus on what she was saying.

"—each of us must decide. I can only say, and only now, when I am some distance along, that the soaring joy and utter rightness of the truest of love is worth any price."

It took him a moment to be certain he could speak normally. "Even when it brings the kind of pain that drove you to make that leap?"

"Yes," she said. "For it also brought me my children, and they yet live."

In control now, he gave her a warning look. "Perhaps not for long, if they continue on this path."

He saw the admonition register. And she asked another of those questions he could not truly answer. "Tell me, Caze, is it better to die for a cause you know in your blood and bone is right, or simply because you are told it is what you should do?"

"The Coalition equals right."

She gave a roll of those dramatic eyes. "Oh, now you're quoting things that are probably etched on Coalition meeting-room walls. That's beneath you, Major. Perhaps you need to rest."

"Perhaps I do," he said without inflection.

"I will send Grim in, should you awake and need anything."

"More likely to prevent me from trying that invisible exit myself."

"That as well," she agreed cheerfully.

And when she was gone, he was face to face with the fact that what bothered him most was that she had again reverted to calling him "Major."

Chapter 34

WHEN SHE WALKED into his quarters she saw that Drake wore an expression that boded no good. Pryl, Kye, Eirlys, and Brander were all in the room, and none of them looked any happier than her son.

"What is it?" she asked.

They all looked at Drake. Leaving it to him to tell her. The only question was, was it her son they ceded the right to, or the Raider? When she met his gaze, she saw both of them in his eyes.

"The Coalition is building new cannon emplacements."

For a moment she was puzzled, for they had expected the fusion cannon to be replaced ever since the Sentinels had taken it out. Then it struck her; the emplacements themselves had not been damaged in the raid.

"New, in addition to the existing two?"

He nodded at Pryl, clearly the source of the information. "Two more."

"Where?" she asked.

"Southeast of the landing zone, and north of Zelos," Pryl said.

"Which means," Kye said grimly, "they have everything from the mines to the Racelock and the low valley to Halfhead covered."

She frowned. "But that also means a lot more frequent moving of the replacement cannon, if it is between four locations."

"That's where the really bad news comes in," Eirlys said, giving her mate a sideways look.

Iolana looked at Brander, who shrugged. "I was passing—"

"Just strolling along," Eirlys said dryly.

"Exactly," Brander returned evenly. "I went past the one they're building north of town, and noticed something."

"Because that's what you do," Iolana said to him, smiling.

His return smile was fleeting, and he went on. "Then I went by the old emplacement to the south. They were working on it, too, even though it had not been damaged."

"Doing what?" she asked.

"Removing the releasable fastenings and replacing them. With permanent ones."

She frowned. Making all four emplacements permanent made no sense, unless. . . . Her gaze snapped to Drake. "Exactly," he said, his voice as grim as Kye's had been.

"Four?" she asked, feeling breathless. "There will be four active fusion cannons?"

"As a measure of your success that's pretty impressive," Brander said sourly to Drake. "As something to look forward to, I'd prefer skalworm eggs."

"With four cannons, all but one within range of Zelos, they could destroy it completely," Kye said.

"What is left of it," Pryl said gruffly.

Iolana had never wished more than at this moment that her vision would work to order. But it never had, and likely never would. The images came when they would.

"Do you suppose he ordered it?" Eirlys asked. "Major Paledan? He had to know of it, of course, but was it his decision? Or High Command's?"

All eyes in the room went to Iolana. She had no answer for them; if he had, it was not in the forefront of his mind.

"More importantly," Drake said, "will he use them?"

"Not unless his hand is forced," she said.

"You sound very certain," Brander said.

"I am."

"You have Seen this?" Drake asked.

"In a way. He carries an image in his mind, of all of Zelos reduced to smoking rubble."

Eirlys sucked in a quick breath, and for a moment Iolana met her daughter's eyes. They held a combination of recognition and realization; she had seen the image as well, when they were healing him, but perhaps hadn't realized what it was.

"So he's thought of it," Kye said.

"Pictured it. And it not only gives him no pleasure, it disturbs him. He would not—strongly would not—wish to do it."

"You know this?" Pryl asked.

"I felt it, too," Eirlys said suddenly. "I did not recognize . . . what the destruction was, but I felt his distaste."

"Is it enough to stop him?" Drake asked softly. "If he is ordered?"

"I do not know," Iolana said.

"It would take a great deal to make a man like that disobey direct orders," Brander said.

She looked at her daughter's beloved mate. "Yes. But has he not now been through a great deal?"

Brander looked thoughtful, then said, "Contention valid."

She looked back at Drake. "This is dreadful news, of course. But I wonder . . ."

"What?"

"I wonder if perhaps this was Ca—Paledan holding back. Perhaps he asked for the cannon to forestall the order to destroy."

She saw the flicker in her son's eyes when she caught herself on the name. But he said only, "Perhaps. I could believe it of him, if all else he said is true."

"Can you not simply read his mind for the truth of it?" Pryl asked. "You've gleaned other things."

"Yes," she said, "but reading someone for something specific is different than what I get by mere contact. It is more direct, more intense, and requires a channel for just that purpose. It is, in a way . . . invasive."

"Some would say it's exactly what a Coalition major deserves," Pryl said.

"Is your concern his . . . sensibilities?" Drake asked her, his tone neutral.

"My concern is and shall ever be Ziem. However, that includes our laws and traditions, which I am bound by. The individual is sovereign."

"Does it matter?" Kye asked. "Whether it was his decision or not? What matters is what Drake has asked. Will he use them?"

"Frall would have," Pryl said, "just to show his power over us."

"We are dealing with a man who has the authority to order up four of the Coalition's most valuable weapons to hold one remote planet," Brander said rather dryly. "I doubt he needs to prove anything to anyone."

"Paledan and Frall are barely the same species," Eirlys said, surprising her mother. On some level, it would seem Eirlys had sensed much of what Iolana had, although perhaps she had not understood it until now.

"He may well be strong enough by tomorrow that a decision about what to do with him must be made," Iolana said. "Give me that time, and I will divine what I can to aid in that decision."

Drake looked at the others, as if checking for any dissent. None came. Whether it was in support of her or the Spirit, Iolana could not tell. And when it came to it, she supposed it did not matter, although she would prefer their support for herself and not Grim's half-mythical creation.

Then Drake looked at her and nodded.

"Have I your leave to use the twins?" she asked.

Drake drew back slightly. "They are your children."

"But you are the Raider. All aspects of this fight are yours to approve. And there could be a price to pay."

"Such as?"

"They already like him. If the end result is his execution . . ."

Drake's eyes darkened. "They will be hurt."

"Yes." *And so will I.*

The admission nearly took her breath away. She had been removed from all others save Grim for so long, and then her heart was so full from the re-union with her children and the expansion of their small family to include the Kalon cousins, she thought she had room for no more. And yet when she thought of the man she had healed, part of her that had been long asleep stirred. And the thought of him dying in a cold, planned execution, after all he'd been through, and she with him—

She cut off her own thoughts before they destroyed her focus. Managed a level tone as she said, "I feel they may be key to determining his true inclination."

"They must know," Drake said. "I would not have them risk more of their hearts than they already have."

"A reminder that he is still the enemy might not be amiss," Pryl said dryly.

"So they do not give away anything critical in their innocence," Kye agreed.

"In case the decision is to let him live?" Eirlys asked, looking at Drake. He nodded.

Iolana felt a stab of relief at this indication Drake truly had not yet decided. And wondered if she was the one who truly needed to be reminded that Caze Paledan was still the enemy.

Chapter 35

HE WAS ASLEEP when she returned.

Grim nodded to her as she entered. "He pushes himself hard."

"I would expect no less."

No less from the representative of the colossal, brutish machine that had consumed Ziem. He might not have been sent here as a warrior but as an administrator, but a mere reassignment did not change who he was at the core. Would a death experience? Was there truly a chance that this man, who had been taken and molded by the Coalition since infancy could fight his way free?

"What do you suppose it would take," she asked Grim softly, "for a man raised as he was, forced into the shape and purpose they required, to break free?"

"From a lifetime of conditioning both physical and mental, reward for doing as demanded and punishment unto death for not?" the tall man said. "The most powerful of wills."

"Yes," she agreed. *And the desire.*

"I believe he—" Grim nodded at Caze's still form "—he has that kind of will. He needs only the motivation. To be shown something better."

"Or more logical."

To her surprise, Grim chuckled. "My lady has learned him well."

Not well enough. Yet. She cut off her thoughts—as she was having to do more and more frequently—and focused on her old friend.

"You are happy here, Grim?"

"Yes," he said simply. "It is good to be among people again."

"And they are good people, one and all."

"Yes." A smile flickered around his lips. "People who do not care that I am too tall or too quiet."

"Not so quiet any longer."

"A relative term, perhaps?"

This time she laughed lightly. Grim nodded respectfully once more, then left. When she turned around, she saw that Caze was awake and watching her.

"He is . . ." he began, slowly sitting up on the edge of her seating ledge.

"If you say he is odd, I shall have to freeze your tongue."

He blinked. "I was going to say changed."

"Oh. Yes, that is true."

"Although odd might apply. As it does to me."

She studied him for a moment before saying, "What you call odd, we would call normal."

"So I have learned."

She smiled widely. "And that is highly prized on Ziem. The ability to learn. And change when necessary."

"And what," he asked slowly, "would necessitate the people of your world to change? To accept the inevitable?"

And that quickly they were into the deep waters she'd foreseen when Drake had first mentioned the possibility Brander had suggested. Turning this man would be a dance more delicate than any she'd ever done.

"Shall we begin while we talk?" she asked.

He stood up, and she assessed the movement. Smooth. Even. No longer a sign of faltering or struggling for balance. If he was, as she suspected, hiding the extent of his regained strength, then he was well beyond where she would have thought he would be by now.

"Walk, if you are up to it," she said, knowing she could say nothing more likely to prod him to pushing his limits. But the glance he gave her told her he knew the tactic well. His next words proved it.

"You asked the Raider to be here, during the worst of it."

That he used that appellation rather than "your son" told her he indeed understood the difference. "Yes," she said simply.

"Why?"

"I knew it would keep you fighting. You would not wish to appear weak before the man you consider a worthy opponent."

He did not deny it. "And he was willing to be used in that way?"

"He sees things in a larger context than many," she said. "In his own way, his vision reaches as far as does mine."

His expression became assessing, as if he were calculating how she might respond to his next words. "I have said he would do well in the Coalition."

She let no reaction show. "And he has said that if you were able to break free of the shackles the Coalition has put upon you, would do well with the Sentinels."

"They are not shackles. No shackled people could accomplish what the Coalition has accomplished."

"There are all kinds of shackles, Major," she said with a dismissive wave of one graceful hand, and his gaze narrowed. At first she thought it was at her gesture, but then was seized with the idea that it was more her return to using his rank. "I submit to you that no one but a shackled people *would* do what the Coalition has done. For only an unfree people would find glory in stealing the freedom of others. And you should be walking."

He let out a sharp breath, but he began the circling of the room as they had done before. And when she was certain he was steady enough on his feet, she recommenced the discussion they had begun before, which just now seemed even more important than rehabilitating his nerves and muscles.

"As for accepting what you say is inevitable," she said lightly, "your first task would be to convince my people it is inevitable. And since they have the heart and beliefs of Ziem at their very core, I would offer that that would be impossible."

"Your people. You say that with such . . ."

"Affection? Certainty? Zeal?" she suggested when he stopped. She held his gaze. "What do you feel when you think of your home planet?"

His brow furrowed. "That is not a phrase we use. It is my place of origin."

"How very Coalition," she said, smiling. "Specific, logical, and utterly cold."

"Merely factual."

"Then what do you think of as your home?"

"That is not—"

"A word you use?"

"No."

"And you have no idea how very sad that is, do you?" she asked softly.

"Sadness is a useless emotion that solves nothing."

"Except to remind you to treasure what you have while you have it." He said nothing to that, so she went on. "So there is no place that calls to you, no place that you feel . . . more comfortable than other places?"

"No. Anyplace the Coalition rules is my place."

It was a bit like trying to speak a language she'd never learned, but she persevered. "I am speaking of you, personally. I know there were places of great beauty you have conquered. Did none of them call to you, make you wish to stay?"

"My job is to assess conditions and locations for battle, calculate resistance and allot forces accordingly. Not wander about like a sightseer."

"And yet you wander Ziem."

He hesitated for an instant before saying, "To accomplish the job. Your mist makes physical reconnaissance necessary."

Conditions and locations for battle? That was all he had been doing? It made sense, and yet she didn't quite believe it. Did not believe that was all of it, anyway. That slight hesitation only confirmed what she already thought;

there was more to his exploration of Ziem than mere calculations and battle planning.

"So there was nothing on any of those many worlds that felt . . . welcoming?"

He gave a harsh laugh at that. "They do not send me to the places that welcome the Coalition's arrival."

"No, your job is to crush those who dare to have the audacity to prefer their own ways and beliefs, isn't it? And when you have done so, you leave without a qualm, without another thought of the place or its people."

Something flashed in those green eyes then, but it was gone so quickly she could not even put a name to it. Still, she held his gaze until, to her surprise, he broke it and spun around to continue his walking.

Spun around without the slightest wobble, she noted.

After another circuit of the room he spoke. "This . . . sadness you say you feel. It happens often?"

"Since the arrival of the Coalition, yes. It is a longing for what is lost, along with many other emotions."

"Such as?"

"Anger, foremost. Resentment unto hatred. Emotions Ziemites have limited experience with."

That stopped him. She saw an almost astonished puzzlement in his expression, and with a sudden certainty knew that these were the very emotions allowed by the Coalition.

"You're saying you do not feel these things?"

"No," she said, "Only that they are—or were—almost always outweighed by the better emotions."

"Better?"

"Hope, and its brother optimism. Happiness. Joy. And of course, love."

He looked wary now. And she chose her words carefully. "You know of hope. You felt it, when you first began to believe that I could heal you. It was as clear as the sky in sun season."

The wariness spiked into something fiercer, and there was accusation in his tone when he responded.

"You have done something else to me. Made me . . . feel these odd things."

"I have done that once," she admitted. "Although not as you think. I did not give you anything you did not already have; that is not within my power."

"Then what did you do?"

"I let you feel what would naturally be there, had not the Coalition crushed it within you. But it was not here, not now."

He frowned. And then she saw him make the connection.

"On the bridge."

"Yes."

He gave a slow shake of his head. "What I felt then, and after . . ."

"Was what . . . normal people feel all the time."

"You mean you all feel the same thing?"

"No, we all feel the same reaction but to different things. The joy that makes the heart soar comes, for some, from doing something they favor; for others, it is merely seeing the face of one they love. For some, happiness is a day's work well done. For others," she added with a smile, "it is a day's work avoided. But the sensation is the same."

He was staring now. "You all feel . . . that sort of chaos, every day?"

She smiled at him. "What I gave you that day on the bridge was a mere fraction. The slightest taste."

The stare became an astonished one. "How in hades do you even function under that onslaught?"

"Ah, Caze, you have so much to learn."

She guessed that was a phrase he rarely, if ever, heard, and she saw by his reaction that she was right. Or perhaps he was reacting to her return to using his given name. Although it was foolish of her to think it might make him feel, as it did her, a sudden, crackling awareness.

"And you . . . will teach me?"

"Only if you wish it."

Something flared in those vivid eyes, something hot and fierce, so fierce she felt for a moment as if it had reached out to sear her. For a moment she forgot how to breathe. All she could think was that if the Coalition's goal was to turn their fighters to automatons, to think and act only as prescribed, to feel nothing, wonder about nothing, merely follow orders without question, then they had utterly failed with Caze Paledan.

Chapter 36

THERE WAS A sudden noise at the entrance to . . . whatever this actually was. Lana turned to look, although Paledan could see by her lack of surprise she had already guessed who it was.

"And what have you brought our guest now?" she asked, smiling at the twins.

"Eirlys had—"

"Enish Eck's—"

"Pet."

"Are you sure it's his?" she asked, and he had the strange impression she was more curious about their thought process than the actual answer. Perhaps she was still learning about them herself.

They looked at her consideringly. Nyx began it. "There could be—"

"Another like him but—"

"This one is his—"

"Because it has the mark—"

"Where a trooper almost—"

"Sliced him."

"I see," she said, looking proud. Because they had a reason, not just assumption?

"The trooper—"

"Was afraid—"

"Of him because—"

"He is—"

They glanced as one to Paledan, who was watching them—and the cloth bag they held—with interest.

"Different," they finished. And he thought he heard a bit of scorn in both their voices.

"I think you will find our guest of stronger mettle," Lana said, and he was foolishly pleased at her words. The realization sparked concern yet again; was this some further offshoot or lingering effect of what she had admitted herself that she had done to him on that bridge?

I did not give you anything you did not already have. . . .

He shook off the thought as the two came toward him with their bag. He sat, to be at their level. The boy held the bag while the girl loosed a drawstring at the top and reached inside. Paledan went still at the first sight of bright-green scales on a ropy, twisting body. He had no particular fear of snakes, and from what he had read there were no venomous ones here on this misty world, but he'd never seen children quite so fearless about it.

Of course, he'd seen little of children at all, before he'd come here where they seemed to run amok.

And then the boy dropped the bag. He could see the snake was no longer than his arm, and was clearly used to being handled. At least, by these two. But it wasn't until Nyx wrapped gentle hands around the front end of the beast and lifted him up that Paledan realized what they had been talking about. For there was no denying the creature was different.

Four glittering eyes in two heads looked at him.

The body of the snake divided a finger length before becoming a pair of sensitive noses and flicking tongues, the heads at each end of the division apparently fully formed and functional.

"Interesting," he murmured, leaning in to take a closer look.

The twins exchanged a glance, and then they were both smiling.

"We knew—"

"You would not—"

"Be afraid."

"It hardly seems anything to be afraid of," he said. "But it is . . . curious."

He glanced at Lana as he used the word, in time to see a smile curve her mouth and her eyes gleam.

"He is harmless," she said.

"Is he the only one of his kind?" he asked.

"He is—" Lux began.

"The only one—"

"We've ever seen, but—"

"We have not seen—"

"All, so there—"

"Could be more."

His gaze shifted from the snake to the twins. "Would that my troopers could be so logical."

"The one who—"

"Tried to—"

"Kill him—"

"Was not."

They looked a bit perturbed. He found himself searching for something to say. "I cannot explain such reactions. They seem to come from a place deeply buried, where fear without conscious cause resides."

The twins did not look appeased. He tried again, even as he was not sure why.

"Is there nothing that makes you wary upon sight?"

"Only things—"

"That we know are—"

"Dangerous or—"

"Will bite, like—"

"Slimehogs and—"

"Zipbugs and—"

"Troopers," they finished in unison.

He drew back slightly at that.

"They know it is only by your grace that they have not been taken by now," Iolana said softly.

She had come to sit on her chair across from him. He had been intent on the twins, but he could never miss the electrical sort of tingling that he felt when she was close. Somewhat like what he'd felt on his arm after the bridge, only less localized.

"I would not call mere curiosity . . . grace," he said.

"Call it what you will; it has kept them safe, and I thank you for that." He glanced at her, and the moment they made eye contact something seemed to expand inside him. She added softly, "And in return I can explain something, if you are . . . curious about why you've done it."

He knew her choice of the word was intentional. What could she know about why he'd given these two his protection, when he was not certain himself? But he had no time to dwell on it for the twins had already had enough of the adult talk.

"Would you like to—"

"Hold him?"

"He will let you because he—"

"Trusts us."

"Just hold out—"

"Your arm."

Paledan held out his left arm, wondering if he was making a mistake. He had just regained full use of it, if not full strength, and now he was about to let some creature he knew little about curl itself around it?

Yet the snake seemed docile enough as it wrapped itself around his forearm. He noticed a hesitation at the end, as if the two heads were set on different directions.

"We call him—"

"Trouble because—"

"He gets into—"

"So much—"

"But mostly because—"

"He has trouble making up—"

"His minds," they finished.

Paledan couldn't stop the laugh that burst from him. And the twins looked inordinately pleased.

He studied the creature, as the twins peppered him with all their knowledge of the thing.

"The tongues are how—"

"They smell—"

"And he likes—"

"To eat muckrats—"

"So that is good because—"

"There are so many."

He shifted his gaze to them. "Do both heads eat?"

Their smiles widened, and he felt ridiculously like a student who had pleased the instructor.

"They do!" they exclaimed together.

"It uses—"

"Both heads—"

"And the teeth—"

"To divide food—"

"To share."

"How . . . equitable."

After they had apparently decided the snake had had enough, they gathered him back into the bag. He went willingly, perhaps happier in the dark.

Which makes him wiser than many.

"We will bring—"

"More things—"

"If you would like it."

"I would," he said, and found he meant it sincerely.

When they had gone, he looked at Lana.

"They have much of their sister's gift for taming wild things," she said, meeting his eyes.

And the way she looked at him made him wonder what she meant beside the two-headed snake.

Chapter 37

"HAVE YOU NOT wondered why they intrigue you so?" Iolana asked as they began walking again after the twins had gone.

Caze—she was becoming more comfortable with using the name, for better or ill—gave a half shrug. "I told you, I have never observed twins before."

"Most who have not, once the novelty of them has passed, simply accept."

"Anyone who is not alert around those two will pay a price, eventually."

He said it dryly, with a lingering trace of the laugh they had startled out of him. And Iolana found it disconcerting, how much she enjoyed hearing that laugh, and wished to hear more of it.

"Contention valid," she said after a moment. "Are you still thinking of the snake at this moment?"

Looking surprised, he answered, "No."

"Because it is not a mystery of any import to you?"

"Yes."

"But they are."

"Much more than a mishap of nature, yes."

She stopped mid-stride. He stopped as well, and looked at her inquiringly. "But," she said softly, "is that not exactly what the Coalition says they are?"

She saw the moment when what he knew of the twins collided with the teachings of an entire lifetime.

So you are open to changing your mind.

When not doing so becomes the impossibility, yes.

She stayed silent, watching the battle play out in his face, in those eyes.

"Mishap," he said finally, slowly, "is not the word I would use for them."

"What is?"

"I do not know. But they are not . . . wrong."

"No. They are not. They are special."

156

There was barely a hesitation before he said, "They are."

"So has the Coalition then made a mistake?"

He studied her for a long moment. "What is it you wish me to say?" he asked softly.

"The twins say you wear the Coalition suit, but your mind does not." He blinked, clearly startled. "So I would wish that you say what you yourself think. Not what the Coalition teaches."

He let out a breath. "Then yes. I think they have made a mistake." One corner of his mouth quirked ruefully. "About the potential of wordless communication, if nothing else."

"And will you tell them so?"

"No." The answer was instantaneous. Which she found interesting in itself.

"Why?"

"It is not wise to even think High Command could be wrong, let alone speak it."

"And you always act wisely?"

He let out a weary sigh that she guessed had little to do with physical tiredness. "No. No, I do not." He gave her a sideways look then. "I would not be here, like this, if I did."

"Contention valid," she agreed, with a wide smile.

He just stared at her for a moment. And then, as if the words were tearing themselves out of him against his will, he said, "If I told them, and if they believed me, they would doubtless want your twins to study."

Iolana's breath shuddered out of her, all humor vanquished. "They would order you to take them?"

"And send them to some laboratory to be studied, analyzed, tested, and in the end probably dissected."

The repulsion in his voice was the only thing that enabled her to keep her head about her at all at the horrific images his words brought into her mind.

"But you would not do it," she whispered.

Again a hesitation, longer this time. She sensed he was wondering at her certainty, suspected he was worrying just how much she had gathered through that connection between them.

And then he closed his eyes. "No. Eos help me, no. I could not."

"YOU BELIEVE HIM?" Eirlys asked.

"I do," Iolana said to the group standing on the trail outside her home. "He fought saying it, every word. I believe it is truth."

Her daughter looked at her mate. "Then perhaps you are right."

"It has occurred, occasionally," Brander said lightly.

Drake, who had been listening silently, now turned to face her. "This thing that you have yet to tell him . . . could it be enough to turn him?"

She studied her son for a moment. More than anything she wished to tell him yes, for she sensed it would win her the time to make the effort. Yet she would not lie to him, not after what she'd already done. And more, he held the fate of Ziem in his strong hands; she could do nothing that would hamper him.

"Not in itself, no. But I believe it would give a strong start to the process. And I believe he is ready to hear it."

"I am not sure that is enough," Kye said, although she said it kindly. "Those cannons will arrive any day, and that will make our fight . . ."

Hopeless? Pointless? Futile? All of those could apply, Iolana thought wearily. But then there were many who would say it had been that from the beginning, and yet the Raider had bedeviled the Coalition for nearly four years now.

"We can only wait a short time before we must strike to delay the installation of those weapons," Drake agreed with his mate. "But with that stipulation, I leave it to you to decide on your timing."

She watched her son, daughter, and their pledged mates walk up the mountain path and back to the main cavern of the stronghold. Each pair was touching in some way, Drake and Kye shoulder to shoulder and arms entwined, Eirlys and Brander openly clasping hands. They moved like people treasuring each moment of contact. Which they were, for they all knew these might be the only moments they would ever have.

Eos give them more. Give them all the time they deserve. And someday children, for they deserve them as well, and will be strong enough for them.

She bent to pick up the pot of Mahko's stew that Eirlys had brought, and turned back toward her cave. She could feel that it was still quite warm, so she would scoop some up for him now. And wait for the right moment.

When she stepped inside, both Grim and Caze looked up at her. She nodded at Grim, who rose, nodded in turn, and left.

"I have brought you a meal," she said, placing the pot on the grate over her small fire.

"Another variation of brollet?"

"Missing your Coalition menu?"

"No. Just . . . amazed at how one meat can be prepared to taste so differently—and good—so many times."

She smiled at that as she handed him a bowl and one of the carved wooden spoons Brander made when he needed to distract his agile mind. "It is a good thing they reproduce like . . . brollets."

He smiled slightly at that. Then he took a mouthful, and nodded at the savory taste. "And how does whoever does your excellent cooking feel about feeding the enemy?"

"He is a gentle soul."

"And he trusts you." She lifted an eyebrow at him. "Do not think," he said softly, "that I don't know that you are likely the reason I am still alive, in more ways than that you healed me."

"Do not be so certain," she retorted. "My son is a very wise leader. And," she added, deciding that he was too intelligent not to have guessed, "he is very much aware of what executing a Coalition officer would cost us."

He didn't even blink at the enunciation of his own potential death sentence. He simply continued to eat as if it were a fueling process to be finished as soon as possible. Brander had told her that Drake had once said that the only way he could continue this fight was to consider himself already dead. She had the feeling that was a sentiment this man would understand perfectly.

Finally he spoke again. "They would wreak havoc. For the insult," he added, as if he felt he needed to clarify that it would not be he himself they would avenge, but the status he held as an emblem of their total rule.

She nodded, wondering at herself that she found even this sad, that a man such as he had no more significance to the Coalition than the rank and honors he had achieved.

"He is also aware," she went on, "that your replacement could be much worse."

He set down his spoon in the now empty bowl. "Worse?"

"It would seem the next step. Frall was incompetent, so they send the paragon of competence. If you fall, would they not send destruction?"

He did not deny it. "Yes. In one manner or another."

In the same instant she heard the racing footsteps, he turned his head. He'd heard them too. But she kept her gaze on his face, and caught the slight smile that played over his lips for a brief moment.

Yes. This is the key. The beginning.

The twins skidded to a halt and called out, asking for permission to enter. She knew only Drake's sternest of orders slowed them even that much. When she bid them enter, they darted inside. They stopped before Caze, their gaze pausing on the empty bowl he had set down.

"Good, you are—"

"Finished. Because—"

"We brought you—"

"A kwill."

Caze blinked. "A what?"

Lux held out the fist-sized thing that looked prickly enough to be dangerous.

"I have seen these about," he said. Iolana knew he could hardly avoid it, for the trees were nearly as ubiquitous as mistbreakers.

"You must be—"

"Careful or—"

"It will—"

"Stick you." Lux tipped it gently onto his outstretched palm.

"So I see."

"But it is—"

"Worth the risk—"

"For they are—"

"Very sweet."

He looked from them to the brown, oval-shaped thing. "You're saying this is edible?"

The twins grinned at him. "Look right there—" Nyx began, pointing.

"There is—"

"A seam and—"

"If you press it—"

"It will split open—"

"If it is ripe enough."

"And if it is not?" he asked. "Does it spit the spines at you?"

The twins laughed. "No," said Lux.

"But that would be fun." Nyx grinned.

She saw him barely stop a smile. Then he did as they'd instructed, and the brown, prickly fruit indeed split open along that seam, revealing its bright-red interior.

"Just push—"

"One side and—"

"It will—"

"Pop out."

Again he did as instructed. And when he at last tasted the offering, the smile broke through. "It is sweet indeed."

The twins grinned again. "We have many—"

"Such treasures—"

"On Ziem. We will—"

"Go find more—"

"To bring you."

She watched him watch them go, saw the moment when his thoughts turned inward, as if he were wondering at himself as much as them.

Now.

"Would you like to know why they fascinate you so?" she asked quietly.

He looked at her. Didn't speak, only waited. As if he believed she truly had an explanation. So his trust had come that far. This was no small thing, and she hoped what she said next did not destroy it.

"You are—rather were—a twin, Caze Paledan."

Chapter 38

PALEDAN STARED AT her, this woman who had so disrupted his pur-
poseful life, rendered speechless by the unexpectedness and absurdity of her
claim. As much as he had been forced to accept since he had awakened here,
as many inexplicable things as he had seen, this was the most ridiculous. The
reasons why piled up like the useless Coalition documents he immediately
consigned to the waste bin.

This notion of his being a twin was not true. Of course. It could not be
true. And even if it had been, she could not know. No matter her uncanny
skills or her bafflingly accurate guesses, she could not know something like
that.

But of course it was not true, so it did not exist to be known, even by
her.

Perhaps it had all been part of some plan. To present him with all these
things that were nearly impossible to accept, to condition him for the most
impossible of all. But why? What did she or these rebels, have to gain by such
a claim? Did they hope to convince him of the Coalition's ruthlessness? He
already knew that; only he saw it as mere efficiency.

*. . . send them to some laboratory to be studied, analyzed, tested, and in the end
probably dissected.*

His own words rang in his head. And visions of the twins, her twins,
subjected—no, sacrificed—to that kind of Coalition efficiency came with
them, and he had to suppress a shudder.

"Do they tell the survivors? Do the ones chosen to live know? Do they
know the other that grew beside them in the womb has been slaughtered?"
Her voice was low, husky, and annoyingly insistent. "Do they?"

"No." He knew this was true, for he had asked once, when he'd been on
Lustros and seen several newborns loaded onto a cart in a hallway, where they
were being taken.

*They are the mistakes. Lessers of two, who should never have been born and so will
now be disposed of.*

Twins? What of the other?

*They have no need to know. They were Coalition chosen because they were stronger.
That is all that matters.*

He had nodded, as if it were of no import to him. Which it should not
have been. And yet . . . he had felt an odd tug somewhere deep inside him,
and a faint touch of a queasiness he did not recognize.

"You have said the . . . contributors of twins were forbidden thereafter to reproduce. Did yours have any more after you?"

"I don't know." How strange, that he had never thought of this in that way. But those who had combined to produce children had nothing to do with them after their birth. It was not their duty, and he would not have known if they had been forbidden. He knew of them only what had been put in his file, for medical reasons.

"You feel it, don't you?" Her voice had taken on that note he'd only heard before when she'd been healing him, that soothing voice that had helped him hang on and fight the pain as much as the presence of the Raider had. "Somewhere, deep inside, you have always known something was missing."

"I am Coalition. I want for nothing."

The words came out automatically, and he had the odd thought that he'd heard them spoken with more feeling by machines.

"That is not what I mean and you know that, Caze." That same tingling that came over him every time she used his name recurred. "Do you think either Lux or Nyx could lose the other and not forever feel the absence?"

"They are aware; they have always lived as two."

"Yes, but think of what twins are, Caze." And again the tingle. "They are tied to each other as no others. And some begin as one being, then divided into two. The connection is beyond anything a single child or ordinary siblings can imagine."

"You speak of those that are duplicates."

"I speak," she said, her voice going even lower now, "of the kind of twin you were. One being, divided. Had your brother survived, he would be the image of you, and you of him. He would have your green eyes, your strong jaw, and likely your brilliant mind."

And now she had tipped over into insanity. This wasn't just impossible, it was preposterous. Why would she even begin to think that he would believe such a tale? He would sooner believe in the blazers old Ziem legends said had once lived here.

"Is this, perhaps, the reason you have worked so hard to fit into the Coalition mold? Because from the beginning you knew you were . . . different? Would he be as magnificent, do you think?"

She caught him off guard, a rare thing, with that assessment. But his brain only allowed him a split second of wondering just how she meant it before it jabbed at him, letting him know how wrong it was, the way she spoke of this non-existent entity as if it—he—were real. Or had been real. Had lived, for some few minutes of time before he was tossed onto a cart like the one he'd seen—

"Stop." It broke from him harshly.

"This is impossible for you to believe."

"Exactly."

"So was that healing, if you will recall."

He could not argue that. Right at the moment, he wasn't certain he could argue anything. If this was some kind of twisted Sentinel torture, it was effective. But he kept coming back to the obvious question: What did she hope to gain? Did she think he would do anything to get her to stop speaking of this? And what if he did? He could tell her the entire Coalition plan for this world and it would change nothing, since they could never hope to withstand Coalition might.

"So you are saying you have never felt . . . a wrongness, an emptiness, a sense of something absent, lost?"

"No." He said it firmly. But slowly, a tiny cry within him was growing in volume. "No," he repeated, even knowing that if he was truly certain, repetition would not be necessary.

"Yes," she countered, in that luring, soothing voice. "I suspected this from that day on the bridge. I sensed it even then, just from that brief contact."

"Mind reading?" He tried to say it scoffingly, but to his ears it sounded more fearful. It was not a sound he cared for.

"It was only during the healing that I was certain. For that process takes a certain connection. Your injuries involved the nerves leading directly to the brain, and there is inevitably some . . . bleed over, I believe it is called? And somewhere, deep within your mind, some instinctual part of your brain knows I speak the truth."

"Stop," he said again, hating the urgency he heard in his own voice.

"You separate yourself from your feelings," she said. "You wall them off, and declare them vanquished, as the Coalition requires. But there is something else behind that wall. A void that you have no name for, for you have never known what should be there. But now you know, Caze."

"Stop," he said for a third time, but this time it sounded like a plea. He felt as if he were crumbling, as if he were once more lying there helpless, unable to move.

"I swear to you, upon my skill as a healer and a seer, that I tell you this not as torture or to crush your will." It was so close to his earlier thoughts his gaze shot to her face. Something glowed in those incredible eyes, and he found himself unable to look away. "I tell you this," she said, holding his gaze, "because you have the right to know. And the Coalition be damned."

She stood up and walked out. And left him there, staring into nothing.

"STAND SENTRY OUTSIDE," she told Maxon, the Sentinel assigned as guard. "I wish him to have to grapple with what I have told him alone."

Maxon nodded respectfully. "The Raider sent a request that you join him when you were through."

"Thank you. I will go now."

As she walked up toward the cavern, she wondered if it had been enough.

Wondered if she should have established a connection with him and planted the knowledge she had gleaned. By the time she arrived she had decided not, for she was certain the fact that it was truth would not ameliorate that kind of trespass into his mind.

And then she walked into bedlam.

"Why is this even a question?" came a shout from someone she could not see among the gathering. It was followed by more.

"We have the Coalition commander in our hands!"

"How can we just let him go?"

"Better him than Frall."

"I don't know, at least Frall was easy to fool."

Iolana kept silent and hung back as the others discussed the matter. Drake knew her feelings on it, as he knew Brander's and Eirlys's and Kye's. It was the others he'd approached now, as he'd said he would, looking for a valid, compelling reason to do other than what his instincts told him.

As she could have predicted, Teal and Kade were the most adamant for his execution, and she understood. They had both lost all that was left of their families on Paledan's watch. Pryl, Mahko, Tuari, and according to Drake, Maxon as well, all saw the benefit of having Paledan in control rather than some unknown quantity.

Drake, leaning on the edge of the table in the large cavern, his ankles and arms loosely crossed, let them argue the point. His presence alone kept the anger somewhat in check for the most part; no one wanted to completely lose their temper in the Raider's company. Young Kade came the closest to shouting, while Teal merely glowered; he was nowhere near accepting the loss of his steady, calming older brother.

"So they send some administrator who's worse," Kade growled out. "Maybe we'll capture him, too. I still say he deserves to die."

"If anyone deserves punishment for what was done to you, Kade," Eirlys said with a gentle hand on the boy's shoulder, "it is Jakel. What he did, he did without the major's knowledge, permission, or order."

"You're defending him?" Teal snapped.

Eirlys met the other Sentinel's gaze steadily. "No. I am saying he deserves blame only for what he himself has done. It is their way to execute people that had no hand in something, not ours."

Teal opened his mouth, and Iolana sensed he was going to protest, but Eirlys's words seemed to register and he stayed silent. But the argument went on. She could not deny the pain of those who had suffered such losses, nor blame them for wanting retribution. Still, the thought of Drake—for he would do it himself, because that's the kind of leader he was—coldly executing Caze Paledan sent a shiver through her.

And she belatedly realized the true reason she was keeping silent during this discussion; she was very much afraid she would end up pleading for his life, and for reasons that were far too much her own and deeply personal.

Reasons she had not even thought through herself, for she had not had enough time away from his unsettling presence.

In the moment she realized this, Teal turned to her.

"I would hear what the Spirit has to say."

There were nods from others. It took everything she had learned about controlling her own mind so as to keep it from interfering with what she received from others to control it now, and keep herself only to those things that would matter to this gathering.

She went through what she had sensed about him and could say with assurance, to what was more in the realm of speculation, careful about where she drew the line because she knew they were listening to the Spirit and thus might accept what she said simply because she was saying it.

When she told them of his reasons for requesting a meeting with the Raider, that he feared if they did not stand down he would receive orders to destroy them, and he did not want to do that, she felt their attention shift to her son.

"It is true," he said, answering the question they had not asked. "And I believe he was sincere in that wish. I believe all she said to be true. I also believe he is a man of his word. Twice he has personally had an excellent chance to take out the Raider, yet he did not. He has also had multiple chances and reasons to take the twins, and he has not. He has handed us Jakel, but not until he had given that traitor Ordam to him for his just punishment. And perhaps most telling, he suggested that if he died during the healing process, that we make it look like an accident."

There were still mutterings, but they were no longer angry.

"But above all I would have you think of one thing," Drake added. "If we execute him, there is a great possibility the Coalition will not send another administrator to replace him."

They were all looking at him now. And it was the Raider who answered their questioning looks.

"They will simply wipe us out, to the last Ziemite."

Chapter 39

"YOU ARE THE woman from the mountain."

Iolana ignored Jakel and didn't take her eyes off of Eirlys and Kye. "The Raider grows weary of guarding it," she said.

"So we must decide what we will do with it?" Kye asked, as brightly as if she were commenting on the first brilliant day of sun season.

They were having this discussion, purposefully, in front of the "it" they spoke of. Kye had been the one to suggest that the brutal enforcer be referred to only as "it" from his moment of capture, since that was how he treated his many victims.

"I vote we do to it what it did to Kade's mother," said Eirlys.

"Better yet, we do to it what it did to Barkhound," Kye suggested.

"Best of all," Iolana said, "we do to it what it did to Drake."

Jakel scrambled to the back of the small cell Brander had rigged a barred, metal gate for. The movement on his injured leg made him groan in pain. Eirlys glanced over instinctively, but covered the move with a shrug.

"How long would it take you to heal its wound?" she asked Iolana.

"Mere moments," Iolana answered. "But there is no reason to waste the effort on one who is already dead."

"Which brings us back to deciding the method," Kye said.

"I promised he would soon be a eunuch," Eirlys said. "And I hate to break a promise."

"Then you must not," Iolana said.

"Absolutely," Kye agreed. "So we start there."

"I'll need a duller knife," Eirlys said cheerfully.

Jakel howled in fear as they left the small cave.

When they were far enough away that he could no longer hear them, Kye sighed. "Do you know what our trouble is?"

"Yes." Eirlys echoed her sigh. "We take no pleasure in torture."

The two other women nodded.

"I would say hand him over to Kade," Kye said, "but . . ."

"He is angry enough he would likely do it," Eirlys said, "but I fear what it would do to him, in his heart."

"It is not the way of Ziem," Iolana agreed.

"We cannot keep him forever, yet slaughtering him like the animal he is is not nearly as pleasant an idea in reality as I thought it would be," Eirlys said glumly.

"When I think of what he did to my mate, I should want to carve him into pieces," Kye said. "And yet . . ."

"Your happiness has had an effect on both of you," Iolana said. "As has this respite from the fight."

"I suppose you're right," Kye said. "I do not dwell on the painful memory of Drake in that torture chamber, not when I have him alive and vividly well in front of me every day."

"It is as well you do not look back," Eirlys said to her sister by covenant. Then, shifting her gaze to Iolana she added with a small smile, "I have sworn it off."

"And I," Iolana said, letting all she was feeling into her voice, "am blessed far more than I ever imagined." Then, more briskly, "We are agreed then?"

"I think we are agreed we do not wish to be like him," Kye said.

"Yet I hate to leave it to Drake to end him because it is distasteful to us," Eirlys fretted.

"Perhaps your major could do it," Kye suggested with a wry grimace. "He said he had been about to anyway."

Iolana did not think this the time to admit she would hate to leave it to Caze as well, although she had little doubt he would do it. In payment for what she had done for him, if nothing else; she had sensed early on he believed in balanced accounts. And that, she thought, is how he would look at it. Clinically, mathematically, without emotion.

And how she wished to see him as he would have been, had the Coalition not bound him. He had the capacity for great emotion—she could feel that—but it had been so stunted, so locked away she didn't know if even her skills could free it.

Or if he could deal with the result.

Her skills. . . . Iolana studied both women for a moment, her daughters. "He has earned death, has he not?"

"After what he's done? Yes," Kye said.

"Except," Eirlys said with a grimace, "death is a bit too merciful for him."

Iolana smiled, but it was not a happy one. "Exactly my thought. I must speak with Drake."

"YOU CAN DO THIS?"

"I have always known I could damage as well as heal, but it is something I am scrupulous to avoid, normally."

"Of course," Drake said. "But . . . you are certain? You could put him in such a state of constant fear?"

"Yes." Her mouth thinned. "I have never done so intentionally however, so I cannot speak to how . . . exact the results would be."

"A fate worse than death," Drake mused. "But would it be, for one such as Jakel's limited mind?"

"If you give me leave, I would like to discuss this with our guest. He might have a better sense of it, since he's dealt with Jakel more recently."

"And he was ready to end him himself."

"Yes."

"Speak to him. I would be curious to know his opinion."

She pondered how to make the approach as she walked back down the mountain path. He would likely still be in turmoil over what she had told him, unless he had decided not to believe it. And it would be a decision with him. He had the power of mind and will to ignore what she'd told him, for was that not what all his Coalition conditioning as a child had taught him? Ignore what you think, what you feel, anything that does not fit the Coalition mold.

Grim stood sentinel now. She gave him a questioning look as she paused outside.

"He has been very restless."

"Pacing?"

"And more," Grim said.

Curious now, she stepped into her home, although she had grown used to seeing it disguised as an office in the Council building. And she realized that for some time now she had not thought of Torstan's office every time she walked in. She did not know if she liked that, but had no time to dwell on it now.

He was on the floor. Her heart skipped for an instant, until she realized he had been doing some sort of exercise, holding himself above and parallel to the ground on just his hands, his muscled arms tight with the strain.

When he saw her, he tucked his knees up as he pushed off with his hands and brought himself neatly to his feet in one, smooth movement. It would not do, she thought, to forget how powerful this man was. He was rapidly nearing his full strength, and when he did, they would have that blazer by the tail.

"Testing your limits?" she asked mildly.

"That," he said in a wry tone, "seems to be your expertise."

She smiled at that. "I will say only to be cautious of your balance for a while yet."

"My balance?"

"It is always a concern when dealing with severe nerve injuries."

"But not my back?"

She waved a hand rather airily, intentionally. "No. That is healed. You should have no further difficulties with it."

Caze stared at her. "That simply, you wave away the pain and apprehension I have lived with for over a year."

She wondered if he regretted no longer having those things to occupy his mind. Wondered if he had turned to what was clearly a routine of exertion to keep other things out of his mind. Such as the revelation she had made to him.

And perhaps he might even welcome something else to think about, for a short time at least.

"I have something I would like to ask you," she said.

He didn't speak, merely lifted a brow at her. Yes, he was rapidly coming back to himself, for she could easily see him looking just like this at one of his troopers.

"Sit," she said.

"Is that an order?"

She thought she saw the faintest gleam of humor in those green depths. "Or a request. Whichever you will accede to."

He sat, but in the chair she had usually occupied when watching over him as he recovered. She smiled at him. "Reclaiming your dominance, Major?"

"In what small way is left to me."

She liked that he admitted to it. But she liked even more that he frowned when she used his rank. She walked over to the table next to the chair and lifted herself to sit on the edge, within easy reach. She saw him note the proximity.

"You seem certain I will not try to overpower you and escape."

"What I am certain of is that at this moment you know where your best interests lay. And," she added with an even wider smile, "that were you to try, you would not succeed."

"Confidence," he said, sounding almost approving.

"I have not shown you my entire array of weapons."

He just looked at her for a moment. A moment that suddenly seemed fraught. With what, she was not certain. Or did not wish to think about.

"That, I do not doubt," he finally said. "You wished to ask me something?"

"Yes. About your . . . gift to us."

Given what he'd been through since, she wasn't surprised it took him a second of thought to recall. "Jakel?"

"Yes."

"We do not wish his body back, if that's what you wished to ask." He said it so acerbically she nearly laughed.

"That would be difficult in any case, for he is not dead."

His eyes widened with obvious surprise. "He yet lives? I would have thought him long dead by now. Why?"

"It is not our way to capriciously end a life. Nor something we undertake lightly or quickly."

His expression changed, and she saw a trace of something she did not care for. Pity? Superiority? Scorn? "Capriciously? After what he has done to your own? Perhaps those blood ties you treasure are not as strong as I assumed."

"They are stronger than you, thanks to the Coalition, can imagine."

"You will not survive long, if you cannot even execute your enemies."

For a long moment she let his words hang in the air, for the parallel to his own situation was too obvious to ignore. And she knew he realized it in the instant the words left his lips. She wondered why both Drake and Brander thought him hard to read. Perhaps it was only since he had come so near to death that he had betrayed himself so easily. Or perhaps it was only to her, because there was still that slight connection between them, although she could already feel it weakening the more strength he regained.

Or, perhaps he had simply not yet rebuilt those particular mental walls. Whatever the reason, she now knew he still expected that end for himself. Because it was what he would do, were the situation reversed? He would execute any one of them who was classed as an enemy? Drake, whom he admired, or Brander, whose wit he enjoyed?

Or her?

When she spoke again, it was as if the moment had never happened.

"Do not mistake me. We do not say he does not deserve death. And you know too well we have killed in battle, without qualm. But nor do we believe in torture, for that would lower us to Jakel's level."

"Nobility does not win battles."

Interesting, she thought. He classed that as noble? Hardly Coalition of him. But she put that aside and went on. "Still, we find ourselves wondering if death might be too great a mercy for such as Jakel. So my question to you is, is there indeed a fate worse than death?"

"Yes." The reply came instantly.

"Without hesitation or thought," she murmured.

His mouth twisted slightly at one corner. She found the expression . . . attractive somehow. Which was not a word she should be thinking when it came to this man. Yet she could not seem to help it. And he was the first man she had thought it about since the day her pledged mate had been blasted out of this life by the guns of the malevolent machine this man represented. She must be wary.

"Because I have had a great deal of time to ponder exactly that," he retorted dryly.

She smiled again, despite her warning to herself. Even this he approached with that wry humor. They had not stamped that out of him. Perhaps they had not tried, presuming it harmless. She thought in his case, that had been a mistake.

"Yes, I suppose you have. But would what seems the worst possible fate to you be the worst for our caged beast?"

Now he thought. She waited silently, watching him, wondering if he was tackling this so seriously because it interested him, or because it kept his mind off of that thing he did not wish to think about. For he was acting as if she had never told him the truth of his origin.

After a few moments of that deep thought, he shook his head. "I think the worst for Jakel would be to live in the kind of fear he inspired in others."

Now he'd surprised her in turn by landing exactly on her proposed solution. "I have often thought those of his ilk were driven by fear."

"A valid contention, I think."

"Have you ever been afraid, Caze?"

A brief flicker in his steady gaze as she reverted to using his name. But he said only, "Yes. On that hillside."

"That Drake would order you killed?"

"No." For an instant his eyes went unfocused, as if he were back on that hillside in his mind. "That he would not."

Chapter 40

"AND THAT ANSWER," Lana said, "is a good marker of the immeasurable distance between Caze Paledan and the likes of Jakel."

He should be grateful for that much at least. She did not smear him with the same brush as the brutish enforcer. But he was too distracted by his continuing response to the way she said his name to dwell on it.

He tried to shake it off by focusing on those moments on the hillside when he had known he was dead. The only question had been whether it would be mercifully by the Raider's blade or a long, agonizing helpless eon lying paralyzed, perhaps until some strange beast of Ziem came along and delighted in the discovery of still-living meat.

"At the time," Paledan said wryly, "I was not aware there was another option than the two I saw before me."

She smiled, but she was looking at him rather oddly. And for an instant he thought he glimpsed an echo of his own response to her presence. As if she, like he, had never expected to find such enjoyment in their conversations. As if she, too, felt the odd spark he did whenever he looked at her. He had never spent much time analyzing if women found anything in him to admire, nor had he ever thought of any kind of future with a woman permanently in it. Such a thing was not in the Coalition precepts.

But he had never before met a woman like Iolana Davorin.

"And do you now regret that he did not?" she asked.

"That remains to be seen," he said, with that same dry humor. And then, to his own surprise, he retracted it. "No. I do not mean that. I do not regret it. This time of being myself again, physically . . . I cannot regret it, no matter how short it may be."

She simply looked at him for a moment before saying softly, "You are badly served by the Coalition, Caze. You always have been. What you could become if you could shake free of those enslaving bonds . . ."

He understood that she was discussing this with him because in some way it told her as much about him as the object of the question. Whether for the sake of the rebels or out of her own interest he did not know, but how much he would prefer the latter rattled him into giving a rote answer.

"It is the Coalition who does the enslaving."

"Is it truly?"

"You can doubt this? Have you never seen a collared Coalition slave?"

"And what does the Coalition's infamous collaring do that is different from what they do to their children? Isolate them, destroy any sense of self, force them into Coalition thinking whether they wish it or not, assign them to a task that is not of their choice, make them live forever in fear of displeasing their masters . . . it sounds very much the same."

He stared at her. He had never thought about it in exactly that way. And yet the logic of what she'd said jabbed at him. In his time in Coalition service he had encountered many of the collared slaves, from those who did menial tasks on almost every base, to those kept on Clarion and the rowdier Alpha 2 to service visiting officers in any way required.

And he'd heard, of course, of the most famous of them, Prince Darian of Trios.

And look how that turned out for them. Us. For us. Now King Darian, the man had led the only rebellion to ever defeat the Coalition and drive them from his world and that of his mate.

Drive us. *Us.*

That he was more and more frequently having to correct his thinking was an annoyance. He abruptly returned to the original question. "Why did you wish to ask me about a fate worse than death?"

"Because you know Jakel."

His brow furrowed. "But he is from here; surely your people know—"

"He is not one of us. He never wished to be. He resented being here from the day he was born."

"Why has he not left if he hates it so much?"

She met his gaze levelly. "I believe he thought he would have a place in the Coalition. That they would be more to his liking, more suited to his nature. And he was right, was he not?"

"Frall had use for him."

"But you did not?"

"Once I realized he was out of control, I did not." He looked at her curiously yet again. "What will you do with him? I believe your daughter mentioned a little . . . surgery with her blade?"

She laughed again, and again he felt that odd, tingling response. But when she spoke, her tone was serious. "She feels responsible for what he did to her brother."

His brow furrowed. "But why? Surely she realizes she had no choice?"

"Logic does not enter into it when you are angry with yourself for not finding another way."

"Another good reason to eliminate such emotions," he couldn't resist pointing out. "So what will you do with him?"

"Do you care?"

"Only as a matter of curiosity."

"I will do my best to deliver the punishment you suggested."

He drew back. What he'd said played back in his head. . . . *The worst for Jakel would be to live in the kind of fear he inspired in others.*

"And how, exactly, will you manage that?"

"I will plant the equivalent of your planium shard in his mind. To ever be there, to jab and prod and tell him he is afraid. Of everyone and everything."

He stared at her. "You can . . . do this?" He nearly laughed at his own words. After what she had done, what he had seen, how could he doubt she could do this? "Cancel that," he muttered. His mind was already turning the idea over and over, analyzing. "It will mean little if he does not remember the time when he was the one who was feared."

He had, she thought, a very good point. After a moment, she nodded. "I will leave him that."

He drew in a long breath. "Then you will achieve that fate worse than death. And a most fitting one."

"That was my assessment."

He gave her a sideways look. "I think I should begin to fear my own fate, if it is left in your hands. You have such powers, I can but wonder what you would choose for me."

She looked at him for a long moment, the faintest of smiles playing at the corners of her mouth. Something fierce kicked to life within him, catching him off guard—something that happened all too often around her—and he was certain it showed in his face.

"What I envision when I think of your fate in my hands," she said softly, "might surprise you, Caze."

A string of hot, erotic images suddenly flashed through his mind, as if some long-locked door in his brain had burst open. They stunned him with their force, for he thought he had walled off such things completely. The Coalition had slaves aplenty, from any world an officer had a thirst for, but he had given up that pursuit long ago.

Many found the ability to program the slaves to do exactly their bidding, to fulfill any and every desire, and to make them believe it was their desire as well, no matter how degrading or brutal or unnatural to them, arousing. He had stopped availing himself of that privilege long ago, after the second time, when the collar had malfunctioned and he'd seen the real fear in the mind of the slave even as she serviced him. It had destroyed completely the illusion that had already been questionable in his mind.

He fought the wave of images, but when he at last succeeded in beating back the unexpected flood, she was gone. And he was left with a single question at the forefront of his mind. Could she do such a thing as the collars did? Forcibly plant such desire in him? Had she been doing so? Was that the explanation for his obsession—for he had come to admit that is what it was—with her?

But it could not be, for he had been captured by her portrait long before he'd encountered the still-living woman herself. And no matter how suspicious his training made him, he could not quite bring himself to believe she would do so. Logic argued it would be a fine tool to use against him, but something else within him, something he had no name for, was insisting she would not do it. For she believed in that Ziemite mandate about the sovereignty of each individual. Only in just punishment would that be waived.

And the illogic of confidence in her care for him—for was he not Coalition, their sworn and mortal enemy?—nearly swamped him. And for once the power of logic, which he placed above all else, was no match for this strange certainty rising within him. A certainty he had no name, no explanation for.

Except, perhaps insanity.

Chapter 41

IOLANA SENSED A difference in the atmosphere in the cavern the moment she entered. She saw Kade standing to one side, his gaze fastened on her son. She walked over to him.

"They are discussing a raid," Kade said without looking at her. "This time of idleness may be ending."

The boy said it eagerly, clearly weary of the lack of action. Curious, she asked him, "Why do you think it has been so long?"

Kade did glance at her then.

"We are safe here. The Coalition searches, but cannot find us." His mouth quirked. "And I think he wished to spend as much time with Kye as possible. And give Brander more time with Eirlys."

She smiled at the boy who was rapidly becoming a young man. "And do you approve?"

He shrugged. "It is the way of things, isn't it? When people are in love, they wish to spend all their time together. That is what my mother used to say."

For a moment she studied the young man, knowing his pain upon the brutal death of his mother at the hands of Jakel was still raw.

"Yes. Yes, it is."

A few minutes later, she hastened over as the Sentinels scattered and Drake headed for his quarters. When he saw her, he paused and gestured her into the room that served as his planning room. Then he turned to face her. "You have spoken with the major of Jakel?"

"I have. He had a very valid . . . suggestion."

Drake lifted a brow at her. When she explained, his other brow shot up to meet the first. She could see him turning it over in his mind. "I think," he said slowly, "that were it me in Jakel's place, I would not wish that man to decide my fate."

"I think that were you his prisoner, your fate would be quite different."

"Why?"

"In part, for the same reason he is not yet dead by your hand."

"Which part?" Drake asked, his mouth quirking.

"Mutual admiration."

"I cannot deny I would rather he was at my side than against me."

"He has said as much of you." She sensed someone approaching from behind her. Kye, judging by the look that came into Drake's eyes.

"Pryl and Eirlys have gone to check the emplacement locations," she said, with a nod at Iolana.

Drake nodded at his mate, then he looked back at Iolana, who had to suppress a shiver at the thought of her daughter undertaking yet another dangerous mission.

"You can do with Jakel what he suggested?" Drake asked.

"I believe so. Is that the decision?"

He nodded. "He deserves the worst we can give him. But I must ask . . . what will it cost you to do this?"

She was beyond moved that despite everything, he both cared enough and thought to ask.

"I will not deny it goes against my nature. But I have not forgotten your condition when Kye brought you out of that beast's lair. Or how he forced you to give yourself up to him, to save Eirlys. And I see everyday the pain in young Kade's eyes, knowing what Jakel did to his mother. And I have, glowing as if in fire in my mind, a list of those of my people he has slaughtered. What I will feel will be brief, and easily forgotten."

Drake nodded in understanding. "Then you have leave to undertake this whenever you feel it is time."

She nodded in turn. She stood there silently after they'd gone, so lost in thought she was barely aware of someone's approach until he was almost upon her. She turned to look at Mahko, who, now that he had been relieved of most of his healing duties, had turned his talent for cooking with minimal ingredients into an art.

He held out a plate to her with a thick slice from a freshly baked loaf, something he had rarely been able to manage back in the cellars. Beside it was a scoop of stew, rich, thick, and smelling delightfully unlike brollet.

"You have eaten too little of late," the man said.

She took the plate and had to admit that although she had not thought herself hungry, her stomach responded to the aroma. "You are kind to think of me."

"I am grateful," Mahko said with a smile. "I ever felt lacking as a healer, and you have saved me from that."

"You were not lacking, my friend. It was just not the calling of your heart." He smiled at her. She thanked him again and walked to one of the long tables where she sat to eat, thinking it would be churlish of her not to. And foolish, for the stew did indeed smell delicious. She began to eat, but slowed when she realized she was eating much as Caze had at first, as if the food were simply fuel. But lately she'd noticed he'd slowed a little, and she put that down to Mahko's ever-growing skill.

But it did little to keep her mind off her children heading once more into peril. And hovering was the knowledge that soon the battle would begin again.

"IT MUST BE SOON," Drake said. "Brander says the cannons are due by the next full moons."

Iolana did not ask how Brander had managed to obtain that information. He had no doubt risked himself yet again, going into Zelos. A glance at Eirlys confirmed this; her face showed no emotion at all, which for her daughter meant she was hiding all of what she was feeling.

"Have you decided?"

Drake drew in a deep breath and nodded. "And I pray to Eos I do not come to regret it."

That sentiment could apply to either decision. She waited, silently. Just as her daughter held back her emotions about her mate risking himself repeatedly, she held back her own. She was not certain how she would feel if Drake's decision was execution; she only knew it would scar her deeply. And yet she could hardly plead with him, not when Ziem's future—or lack of one—was at stake.

And when she herself wasn't even sure of what she would be pleading for.

"I will escort him myself."

The instant protest broke from all gathered except Iolana. She was feeling too much relief. A warning, she thought, of how far she had fallen under the spell of the green-eyed officer of the Coalition. And yet she could not regret having come to know him as she had, only that it would end here.

But she wasn't so overset that she didn't notice that the protests were about Drake doing it himself, not that it was to be done. Apparently they had all accepted his reasons . . . and hers. And she felt a qualm of the same feeling Drake had professed. She hoped she did not come to regret it.

Drake held up a hand, and they quieted. "We will undertake the mission tonight."

"Tonight?" Teal yelped, startled. "At night?"

All heads swiveled to look at Brander. For they all knew he'd been working on adapting the scopes on the rovers to night vision. He shrugged, but he was grinning, which from him was tantamount to a declaration that he'd succeeded.

"Your explosions will be even prettier," Brander told Teal, who actually smiled for the first time since his brother's death.

"That's why you've all been flying so much," Pryl said in realization. "You've been testing."

"And training," Kye said. "It's a different sort of flying."

"We will go over the plan as soon as I return." It was the Raider speaking now. "Have any problems you foresee ready to present."

"The usual problems of being massively outnumbered and outgunned aside," Brander said jovially. They all laughed. Even Drake.

And more than ever Iolana was proud of her people and their indomitable spirit.

"If there is anything you wish to say to him, you will have a few minutes while I prepare," Drake said to her after the others had gone.

Iolana would have thanked him, were she not wondering if somehow her son had sensed her inner turmoil. And more, the reason for it. But how could he, when she was not entirely certain herself?

She pondered this as she walked back to her residence. She had gradually come to accept that Caze had an unexpected and fierce effect upon her. But the impossibility of it had made her quash the feelings and sensations he roused. But every time she thought them thoroughly vanquished, she would glimpse something in him that set it all loose again. She fairly ached for the man he could have been.

And could yet still be?

Could he? She could do her part, she could break through the barriers the Coalition had built in him, she could set free what feelings he had. But what would it do to him? Would he be able to see that cool, rational logic was only part of the equation? That without the heart, it was a cold, lifeless thing, a pointless existence, just as emotion without rationality was a straight course to insanity? It took the balance to make life work as it should. He should see that, should he not? For balance was a logical, explicable thing. It would appeal to his nature.

But in the end, it was not her decision. It was not something she would do without his assent; he was not Jakel.

When she walked back in, he was standing near the shelf where his comm link had been, before he'd gotten strong enough to rise on his own. He was touching the shelf, as if testing to see if the illusion would hold, if it would feel different than it looked. She knew the illusion, both visual and tactile, would hold; as strong as his mind was, Ziem was stronger.

He turned as she stepped through the illusory doorway. She did not waste time with niceties.

"You will be leaving shortly. And this—" she gestured at the façade of his office "—will be real."

His brows lowered. "I am to live?"

He didn't sound surprised. She wondered if it was because were the positions reversed, he would wish to do the same. And she longed to touch him, just long enough to see if that was truth. Not that it mattered, for she knew the Coalition would not allow it. If he failed to execute the Raider if he had the chance, it would certainly guarantee his own demise.

"You are. Drake has decided."

For a moment she thought, by the way he was looking at her, that he might ask what she had had to do with that decision. But after a moment he only lowered his gaze.

She crossed to the shelf above the cot where he'd slept and picked up his neatly folded jacket. The shirt she'd had to cut through when he had stopped breathing had been mended, rather nicely, by Grim who had an unexpected talent for it.

"I am sorry about the slice," she said as she held it out to him.

He took it and looked at the open slash in the back. "You cannot heal it?"

Her gaze shot to his face. The corners of his mouth twitched.

She smiled widely. He was teasing her. The tough, strong, unflinching Caze Paledan was teasing her. And her earlier thoughts came back to her; surely if they had not managed to completely crush this wry humor out of him, there must be other things left? She knew there was restraint, for the twins still lived. She knew there was the capacity for surprise, for he had shown it here. But more?

"What are you thinking?" he asked, staring as if he'd never seen a smile before.

Her smile wobbled a little. "Wondering if you would survive the return of what should be natural to you."

"That internal chaos?"

"What you call chaos, we call living. With all its joy, and pain, and vitality. The ability to fully experience the ecstasy because we have fully felt the agony."

"I do not know that I would. Survive it, I mean. Is it your intention?"

"It is not my decision. It is yours. You need only ask."

Slowly, he shook his head. "I . . . cannot."

"I know," she said quietly. "Is there anything else you wish to ask of me, now that your time here is over?"

"I will not ask where 'here' is, for I know you would not tell me. But I will ask one question."

"I will answer, if I can."

"Your portrait," he began, and her pulse kicked up. "Does the artist still live?"

She smiled widely. "Oh yes, the artist is alive and well." The smile faltered a little. "Unable to pursue that calling, as things stand, but very much alive."

"That is . . . good to know."

"I thought art of no use to the Coalition was forbidden?"

"It is."

"And yet that piece resides in your office."

She didn't think she mistook the trace of unease that came into his eyes. Something she very much doubted happened often to this man. But he said only, simply, "Yes."

"Why?" She was determined to get her answer, finally.

He looked at her for a moment, his steady gaze both unsettling and calculating. "You meant what you said? I am leaving?"

"Yes," she answered. "Does that change your answer?"

"It changes whether I will answer."

"I see." Oh, she would miss playing these games with words and meanings with him. And she wondered if that thought had shown in her face, for again something flashed in those green depths.

"What spoke to me was not the portrait itself, despite the amazing skill and perception of the artist. It is one of my failings that I can appreciate that kind of genius even in works of no aid at all to the Coalition."

"Some would call that itself great perception."

"No one in my world."

"Contention, sadly, valid."

"I did in fact keep that portrait because it spoke to me. But not of the artist."

For an instant Iolana wondered if this man had some heretofore unknown power, for she felt as if she were about to be consumed by the vivid green of those eyes. And when he spoke again, his voice held a low, rough note that made her welcome it.

"I kept it because it spoke to me of you."

Chapter 42

PALEDAN STARED at Drake, who had entered immediately after he'd utterly betrayed himself to Lana. It took him a moment to realize why the Raider had arrived. "You?"

"Why not?"

"Do you not have . . . other things to do?"

"You mean such as planning our next raid? That is already done." Paledan would have sworn the man looked regretful. And with his next words he confirmed it. "I'm afraid . . . hostilities must resume soon."

"I assumed," Paledan answered. "In fact I am surprised you waited."

"It did my people good to have respite, now that we are safe in a place you—and your satellite—will never find."

So they knew of the satellite. He was not surprised at that, only that Drake was so certain they were beyond the scope of the best Coalition technology.

And he realized with a start that he had thought of the man as Drake, not the Raider.

"Are you ready?" Drake asked.

"Are you not afraid of what I will see?"

"No." He looked at Iolana.

"I'm afraid that this, unlike the other things we discussed, is not up to your volition," she said softly. "I'm sorry, Caze."

He frowned as she gave him a look that held sadness, resignation, and, he would swear, longing. She reached up and cupped his cheek. It was a soft, gentle, yet surprisingly heated touch, and his pulse sped up furiously before he realized. It was almost a caress, and it awakened sensations in him he did not even know how to fight.

Did not want to fight.

And then he felt an odd sort of dizziness, something different than what he'd felt when she'd touched him before.

He came back to himself in a familiar, yet unfamiliar place. The right seat of an air rover. At the controls sat the Raider—for that is who he was now—and there was no one else aboard. And outside was nothing but that bedamned Ziem mist, and he nearly laughed at his own question; of course they weren't worried about him realizing where they were, for who could see beyond the reach of their arm in this?

Questions flooded his reawakened mind. He noted almost without surprise that he did not wonder how Lana had somehow rendered him insensate for a finite period. Given what else he had seen, it seemed a minor enough accomplishment for the phenomenon she was.

Finally he settled on the one of immediate interest.

"No guards?"

The Raider smiled, but did not look at him. "I thought you were no pilot."

"I am not."

"But I suspect you could learn quickly, given you know enough to design this craft. But," he added with obvious amusement, "I think you might find this one a bit . . . different than your original design."

He already knew that; had he not seen the stolen rovers do things that should have been impossible?

"For example," the Raider said, and suddenly they were shooting upward, Paledan feeling the pressure pushing his back into the seat as they climbed at an angle that indeed should have been impossible. And suddenly they burst through the mist and out into clear sky, and he saw the dual moons shining beyond. They held him spellbound for a moment before he looked around and was able to orient himself. They were deep into the badlands, deeper even than he had guessed they might be, for only in the far distance could he see the back side of Highridge.

Then his breath caught as he realized they were rolling, over and over, and for an instant he thought they'd been hit, that somehow Coalition fighters had been in the area, spotted them and been able to fire.

But a split second later he realized that the craft was under the Raider's complete and exceptional control. The craft snapped back upright, then soared upward again. Higher than should be possible. And then, even more impossibly, it hung there at the peak, motionless, apparently immune to the pull of the planet beneath in a way that made him feel weightless, as he only ever had in much bigger, space-ranging craft designed to pull free of such bonds.

And then the rover's nose went over, and it dived back down into the mist as sharply as it had risen.

None of which the craft he'd designed had been capable of doing.

"Bragging?" Paledan asked mildly. "That was quite a demonstration."

"It is different, from inside."

"Yes." He looked at the man at the controls. "You are an excellent pilot."

"It is an excellent craft."

"It was," Paledan said dryly. "Now it is . . . superlatives fail me. I truly would give much to meet your engineer."

The Raider glanced at him and grinned, and Paledan saw in that moment the full strength and depth of the man who had so bedeviled the Coalition since he had risen to fight for his world.

And again, he was thinking of the Coalition as "other," a habit he must rid himself of, especially now when he was apparently returning to its confines. And even thinking of it that way, as confining, was an abomination in their eyes.

He felt a sudden tightness behind his eyes, a throb that made it difficult to think. He rubbed at his forehead as he felt it begin, the start of the tension that would overtake him once he was back in uniform, once he was again Coalition to the bone.

But would he be? Would he ever be again? He had seen another way, had seen people who lived with those blood ties the Coalition decried, had seen that they were, in some ways, the better for them. The braver. The more determined.

And to his shock, he admired them. To have done so much with so little had already been impressive, but to see how they interacted, to see the fire in their hearts glow in their eyes, to see that they were alive and vivid in a way he'd never known before, had never even seen, seared him to the core.

How could he go back to that uniform knowing that his single, most important goal would be to destroy them? Destroy this man, who were he in the same uniform he would be honored to call a brother in arms. And the boy who had guarded him so fearlessly, despite his youth. And the twins . . .

His mind careened away from that which he had still not come to accept. It was impossible. It could not be. And yet . . . what she had told him had rung true in a place so deep inside him he did not know what to call it. And Lana had no reason to lie, not about such as that.

Lana.

He would be called upon to destroy her as well. Perhaps foremost, for if the man beside him was the heart of this fight, she was the soul.

He could not.

"We could turn around," the Raider said quietly.

Paledan's head snapped up, and he turned to stare at the man who was now looking directly at him. "What?"

"I know it is not in your makeup to betray, but my mother has told me you are capable of changing your mind, when the evidence forces it."

"What," Paledan enunciated carefully, "are you saying?"

"Simply that when what you are loyal to is proven false, then it is no longer a betrayal to turn away."

Paledan stared at him. Some part of his mind noted that the man seemed to be flying through this bedamned mist without even looking.

"The Coalition has not been proven false." If his words lacked certainty, it was because that nagging feeling inside him that had been in the background until the moment Lana had made that incredible claim, was getting stronger by the moment.

"So you agree, then, that twins are an . . . abnormality that should not be allowed? That Lux should have been slaughtered at birth?" Paledan felt an odd clutching in his stomach, as if he had eaten something foul. And then the Raider added quietly, "As your own twin, your other half, was?"

He drew up sharply. "She told you this. This . . . idea of hers."

"She has a gift. Many gifts. It is more than an idea. It is a fact. And I think deep down you know it to be."

"It is . . . impossible."

"As with many things involving my mother," the Raider said, so wryly Paledan wanted to smile, "it is only impossible until she proves it otherwise." And at last he turned back to the front, although what he could be looking at—or navigating by—Paledan had no idea. All he saw were varying shades of gray.

"This is," Paledan said honestly, "the strangest world I have ever seen."

The Raider smiled then. It was an expression both loving and reckless at the same time. "Ziem is that. She is also the most amazing. And the most worth dying for."

"I think Triotians might argue that," he said, knowing that the man already knew that tale of Coalition defeat.

"And theirs," the Raider answered, "might be the only challenge I would accept as valid."

Paledan's mouth twisted. "You and their king seem to have much in common."

"I'm flattered." He glanced at Paledan again. "I would think it would be easy enough to verify the Spirit's claim. Does not the Coalition keep meticulous records of everything?"

"Of course."

"Then if they feel twins abnormal, would they not record and track the survivor?"

He blinked. Record and track.

You must report to the Tracking Division regularly, cadet.

The others do not.

They are not . . . special. You are, and must be recorded and tracked.

He had always been told that his specialness was his knack for battle tactics, but had there been other reasons that he alone in his class had been required to go for scheduled assessments by both the medical staff and the brain mappers? Had they in fact been checking for—perhaps even expecting?—some sign that he, too, was abnormal?

"Think, Major. You have an incredible capacity for logic and reason. Reason it out. You know, on some level, that there is more to life and living than what the Coalition allows you."

"The Coalition is my life."

"And that," the Raider said, "is the biggest injustice done to you. They have taken from you the very meaning of what it is to be truly alive. The right to find and follow your own path, to seek what gives you joy."

"You sound so certain," Paledan said, not wanting to admit that it was an effort to keep his voice level. For the Raider's words were echoing in his head, hammering at him. He had the wild thought that this had all been planned out, that Lana had done her part, softening him, and now her son was finishing the job.

"As someone who was spared leaving this life by a handsbreadth, yes, I am certain."

A handsbreadth. His mother's hand. Lana's hand. Just as she had healed him, she had healed her son when it should have been impossible.

. . . it is only impossible until she proves it otherwise.

And she had. Time and again she had. Were he to set aside the implausibility of all she had done and look only at the facts, the results, he would have no doubts. For there was no way to discount what he had witnessed first hand. And there was no way to push it aside, to forget, when every move he made free of the pain that had been his constant companion was a reminder.

"And what, in your certainty, would you have me do?" he asked.

"Come to us," the Raider said. "Break free of the bonds forced upon you. Find the man you were truly meant to be."

"That is not . . . possible."

He felt the irony of his own words bite even as the Raider laughed. "I think we've already addressed the issue of possibility, Major."

The rover suddenly banked right, and they were skimming the side of . . .

something. Something huge. The Raider reached into a pocket and pulled out his comm link. He handed it over.

"It's reactivated. I suggest you order your lookouts to stand down. I'd hate to have gone through all this only to have them blast us now."

He hesitated, but then gave the orders. A few moments later they dropped down out of the mist. He recognized the spot immediately; it was where this had begun, on the hillside where they had met. Where he had lain helpless, asking this man to kill him. And now he was back. Healed, and free of the knowledge that any solid blow or even a wrong step could end his life.

The impossible made possible.

The impossible demonstrated.

The Coalition proven wrong.

He gave a sharp shake of his head as the rover came to a stable hover barely inches above the ground. Another modification; his original design had required at least three feet to hold like this. There was a hiss, and the clear canopy lifted. He glanced back at the pilot.

"I'd appreciate two minutes to get clear," the Raider said, with that grin touched with recklessness again. "But if you feel you must, fire away."

It would indeed be, Paledan thought, an honor to serve with this man.

And for the first time he did not follow that up with any thought of converting him to the Coalition. And not solely because he knew it would be impossible—that word again, but in this case fact—but because . . . he did not want to.

He climbed out of the rover and dropped easily to the ground. Without even a hint of pain from his back. He turned back. The Raider touched his right hand to the silver helm.

"You would be welcomed, Caze."

And then the canopy closed and the rover wheeled back the way they'd come. It vanished into the mist at a speed that startled him anew. He stood there looking after it.

It was a long time before he started the trek back to the compound.

And he never gave the order to blast the Raider out of the sky.

Chapter 43

DRAKE STOOD LOOKING down at Jakel. The brutish creature sneered at him. "I should have made certain you were dead."

"Yes," her son answered mildly, "you should have."

"And now you will pay for that mistake, forever!" Kade declared. Iolana put a hand on the boy's shoulder in comfort, willing him what she could against the tide of his anger. It was enough to calm him slightly.

Drake looked down at the man who had tortured him so nearly to death. Then he looked over his shoulder at her questioningly. She nodded. He nodded in turn.

"In the name of Ziem," he said, and stepped back.

Iolana steeled herself by recalling all the Ziemites Jakel had turned upon, tortured, and murdered. She reinforced it with what Brander had told her of the brutal death of Kade's mother, who had died at Jakel's hands without giving away anything that might have betrayed the Sentinels. And then she summoned up the vivid memories of Drake, beaten, bloodied, broken, hovering on the wrong side of the doorway of death, intensified by the fact that he had subjected himself to it knowingly, to save Eirlys.

It was more than enough.

They were gathered, those who had had the most personal reason to be. Drake had questioned Kade's presence, but she had told him she thought he was the most important of all to be there; he needed to see the fittingness of the punishment, or he might be driven to take further action himself.

It was clear, as he sat restrained in a chair, that Jakel himself did not believe in what was about to happen. The sneer on his brutal face, the glint in his reddish eyes said so. The images of Drake, the effort it had taken to coax him back when his pain-wracked body had wanted to surrender, made her want him to believe. She wanted him to know, to understand, before she altered his mind, his memories. And so she reached out, drew from this world she loved the power, and let loose the flare of brilliant light.

"It is the Spirit of the mountain, the Seer of Ziem who will punish you now, Jakel."

Her voice reverberated with all the force she could give it, and she saw those small, reddish eyes widen. Saw the fear growing as he realized the tales were true, and that he was face to face with the legend, and with his fate.

"For all those you have murdered, and the more you have harmed, those who never earned your animus, who would have welcomed you as one of us had you only asked, I render their judgment."

She reached out. He tried to pull back, but she held him now, and no amount of strength would avail him. She put her hands on his temples.

The jolt of pure evil rippled through her. It swelled, grew, twisted until she felt nauseous with it. The ugliness of the mind she touched was nearly overwhelming, would have been had it been coupled to a soul full of the same, but Jakel had surrendered that long ago.

It took her a moment to isolate and scour out the impulse center that drove him, yet leave the memories. And then she carefully implanted the awareness that everyone he encountered was to be feared, that he had no power to hurt them or even intimidate them. That they now held the power he used to wield, that of life and death.

It was a delicate, intricate process, and it drained her in a way healing did not, but at last it was done.

When she released him and he stared around at those gathered around him, he cowered back. Terror glowed in his eyes.

"Don't hurt me," he cried out.

Jakel the enforcer was no more.

"ARE YOU ALL RIGHT?" Eirlys asked.

She looked at her daughter, grateful beyond measure for her concern. "I will be. But it will require some rest and thinking of other things to recover from that wellspring of evil."

"I am not surprised."

There was a murmuring from the other end of the cavern. Iolana stood still, watching, for a moment, feeling both pride and fear as she watched her son again don the silver helm of the Raider. They were, Kade had told her with no little excitement, going after the new cannon emplacements before they were completed.

"The Raider says we can no longer wait, staying safely hidden."

"I am surprised he waited this long," she murmured.

She watched as he gave instructions to those Sentinels gathered around him. Including, she noted, his mate. Since they were down to four rovers—Paledan-designed rovers—after the crash during the ambush, they would split up, one to emplacement. Ground teams would strike first, followed by the rovers to finish the job and allow the fighters on the ground to escape.

Drake thought they could succeed, and set the Coalition timetable back. Teal Harkin had built some interesting explosives, something he'd always had a knack for. But he was deadly intent now, all the joking that had always been part of him vanished in the crash that had claimed his brother. But the recklessness remained, and not even Drake could restrain it now.

And in the back of her mind hovered the knowledge that the man who had just this morning been in this place, with them, would again be in charge of stopping them. Would he hesitate at all, now? Or would the Coalition own him anew once he put their uniform back on?

They were yet safe enough here, and would be until the Coalition came up with a way to read past the fierce, fiery heart of this mountain, but the Sentinels who went out to fight . . . would he crush them wherever he had the chance? It was what the Coalition would expect of him, but . . .

She shook off the thoughts. They had to go out assuming the Coalition would be as they ever were, ready to kill.

When they began to walk toward the cavern entrance, she stepped over to Drake and Kye. "Be safe, my children."

Drake reached out and clasped her hand before they moved on. It was a small gesture in the larger picture, but it meant more to Iolana than she could express.

And yet still she thought of the man below, back in the office she had replicated by now. And wondered. Perhaps even hoped that the seeds they had planted might bear fruit.

"THE CANNON emplacements are almost ready," Brakely said.

"Mmm."

"The cannon themselves will be arriving by midweek next."

Paledan nodded, still staring at his steepled fingers.

"The logs of activity while you were gone are on your console."

"Fine."

Brakely seemed to hesitate, then said, "I spoke to General Fidez's aide yesterday."

That got his attention. Paledan lifted his gaze to his own aide's face. "Who contacted whom?"

"He contacted us, sir. For a progress report." His aide looked uncomfortable for a moment.

"And you told him?"

"That you were out hunting the rebels yourself. They seemed . . . pleased with that."

Paledan nodded his thanks, but his thoughts were rebellious. *And if they knew the truth? That I was in their hands and their leader within my reach, yet everyone left alive?*

He nearly laughed at the thought; it would be beyond their ability to comprehend.

"There is more?" he asked, looking at Brakely's edgy expression.

"He believes that the High Command will soon order that Zelos be leveled."

He had expected as much. "I presume they are excluding our compound from the destruction?"

He said it so sourly Brakely's brows rose. "I . . . of course, sir. All Coalition infrastructure is to be maintained."

He went back to his contemplation of his fingers. "And the miners?"

"He did not know. Apparently that is still under discussion."

"Mmm."

Silence spun out, until Brakely asked, a touch of concern in his voice, "Are you all right, sir?"

He looked up once more. "You think I am not?"

"I . . . don't know. Sir."

The hesitation before the honorific told him Brakely was uncertain whether to pursue this. "Out with it," he said.

"It's merely that . . . you seem different since you returned. You are not usually gone that long, so I wondered if . . . something happened."

Something? Yes, something. Many things. Things that are hard to credit now that I'm back here.

"In truth," he said slowly, "I feel much my old self." *Physically.*

Brakely smiled, and it was genuine. "That is good news, sir."

When his aide had gone, he made himself turn to the drudgery, going over the numerous logs of post activity while he'd been gone. The routine had continued: drills, repairs, and other work he'd assigned before he'd gone, and more he guessed Brakely had assigned to lessen the appearance of his absence. He had chosen well when he'd pulled the man from that death cage.

Without thought, he turned in his chair to reach for his handheld log to double check the numbers on the weapons inventory. Three things slammed through his mind in succession: that he was able to make that move without pain, a vivid image of the woman who had made that possible, and finally the Raider's regretful statement that hostilities must resume soon.

It was a moment before he could force his mind back to work. He finished the logs and reached out to turn off his console, already weary of staring at a screen. His finger hovered over the shutdown button. And then, slowly, he picked up the input device. He switched over to his private records. At least, they were as private as the Coalition allowed anything to be, which only meant those below him in rank could not access them; those above, as always, had free rein with their underlings.

He called up his own records, opened his medical file, stared for a moment at the image of the shard that had nearly ended him. Then, leaving that file open, he went backward in his history. His excuse would be his aware-ness—former awareness—that he could die at any moment; even the Coalition should understand the need to look back at your existence in such circumstances. Existence. Not a life, but existence.

They have taken from you the very meaning of what it is to be truly alive.

The Raider's words rang in his mind. And then other words, in that voice that taunted, teased, tortured him. *Ah, Caze, you have so much to learn.*

He looked around his office, the place where, in his mind, he had been all along. He had given up trying to figure out how she'd done it for it did not matter. It mattered only that she had.

And that he still had no idea where in the badlands they were. He didn't believe they were near where they had burst through the mist in that modified rover the Raider flew, for he knew the man was too clever to give away any real clue. They could be somewhere else entirely, but he would never know.

He did not know how long he sat there, lost in the swirl of memory and thought, of logic battling a longing he tried not to admit, when Brakely burst into his office without announcement. He was on his feet before his aide came to a halt before his desk.

"The rebels have attacked the new emplacements! Both ground and air assaults."

For a moment he went very still. "And?"

"One destroyed, the others seriously damaged."

I'm afraid hostilities must resume soon.

"Sir?"

It was all he could do not to laugh.

Chapter 44

"IT WENT WELL?" Iolana asked Kye, who was the first one she'd seen back from the mission. She had followed her into Drake's planning room.

"It did," she answered with a wide smile. "Mara was slightly injured by a fragment of Teal's explosive, but it is minor."

Iolana turned, ready to go to the woman. "Does she need me?"

"It would not be amiss, but there is no hurry." Kye looked at her as if she were considering saying something else. Then, "You knew Eirlys was with them?"

"Yes." She thought she managed to speak rather evenly, considering.

"It was Eirlys who healed Mara enough for her to get home safely."

Pride burst within her. "She has learned so much!"

"Once she opened her mind and heart to it, yes," Kye said.

"All of my children have heart beyond imagining," Iolana said, rather fervently. "And I include you, and Brander, in that number."

"And we both feel the welcome and are thankful," Kye said.

Once more she seemed to hesitate. "Surely since we are then family, you can speak your mind?"

"It was only a thought, and perhaps a wrong one."

"Out with it, m'girl," Iolana teased.

"You . . . when the major was here . . . you reminded me of . . . me."

"You?"

"Before I knew Drake was the Raider. I was so torn. I loved Drake, I always had, but . . ."

"You thought him a coward," Iolana said softly.

Kye nodded. "As he intended, in my defense."

"Yes. And it nearly ate him alive inside." But then what she'd said truly registered. "And I . . . remind you of this?"

"You are torn about him, aren't you? In a different way than Drake is. Or my cousin."

"I see . . . what has been done to him, and what he could otherwise be, and it is . . . difficult."

Kye studied her for a moment, with the wise eyes of someone who had walked a very difficult path. "You came to care for him."

Iolana sighed. But she could not lie to her son's mate. "I neither expected or wanted that. But he is the most intriguing man I have ever met."

Kye gave her a wry smile of understanding. "And if he intrigues the Spirit, that says much of the depths of the man."

"Yes." She sighed. "Torstan was open, his heart in full view, all knew where it lay, with his family and with Ziem. Caze . . . I don't believe he has ever truly known what he feels in his heart. It was never allowed."

"I cannot imagine living like that. Although," Kye added wryly, "I can see where it might sometimes be less painful."

"But is it still living?" Iolana asked.

Kye smiled. "Contention valid." Again she studied Iolana for a moment before saying, "That thing you thought might . . . change his thinking. You told him?"

"I did. I am not certain he yet believes, however."

"Will he?"

"I think he will try to verify it. And if he is able to find some bit of proof—his kind of proof—that it is true, then . . . I don't know, but I will say it could shake his perception of his entire life. And now," she added, "I will go check on Mara. And express my pride in my daughter."

"Do that. It will gladden Eirlys. But . . . if I may?"

"You have as free a rein as your mate. Speak what you will."

"Be aware when you speak of him, it shows. Especially when you use his given name."

Iolana's cheeks were still warm when she reached the infirmary, where Eirlys and Mara were both inspecting the gash on her left leg. It was nearly healed already; only a reddened line remained.

"You did well," she said approvingly.

"Thank you," Eirlys answered, smiling. "But it is good you are here to finish the job."

"I think you can manage," Iolana said. "I will just give you a little boost."

And for the first time it was Eirlys who did the healing, while her mother channeled her just a little extra through the pathway. And when it was done and her daughter turned to her with sparkling eyes, her heart filled anew.

Yes, life might be less painful cut off from all blood ties.

But it would be a cold, joyless thing.

PALEDAN OPENED his eyes, looked into the darkness, and was for a moment disoriented. Reality snapped back. He was in his quarters, not his office. Or rather, that illusion of his office. A flame-haired, vividly alive woman would not be momentarily appearing. The woman who fascinated him, in part because she felt so much, while he felt nothing at all.

Or at least, he once had felt nothing at all. Now he'd had a taste of what she called "normal," and he wasn't sure he could handle any more. He thought if it were true, that what she'd given him was but a trace of what Ziemites felt every day, that it was a miracle they weren't all insane. But weren't they? Wasn't it insanity to go against the Coalition in such small numbers, with such minimal weapons?

Perhaps not, if I measure it by their relative success.

He sat up, then went still, still savoring the novelty of the absence of pain. And thinking. Thinking of things he would never have dared consider before. Questions that had no answers tumbled through his mind.

He thought of the dead end he had reached in his search of his own records. His birth document showed the names of the contributors—what Ziem called parents—and the date and time of his birth, and statistics on his size. The only other things of note were the label "special attention" at the top, which he had been told meant he'd already been headed for officer training thanks to the status of his contributors, and the check mark in the box labeled "Acceptable." He had always assumed that to mean he had been born without visible defects. But now he wondered if the placement of that box next to his birth length and weight meant something else.

Meant that he was the larger, stronger of two.

He picked up his handheld unit from the table beside the bed. He didn't think about the ramifications; he'd been through all that in his mind repeatedly. If he used this, he could then destroy it, report it stolen, and while they would still have the record of inquiries they would not be able to prove he had made them, although his personal inquiry would cast suspicion.

This path of thought was always followed by an inward jab of a strange sort of amusement; since when had the Coalition required actual proof? In which case his original inquiry was likely already being questioned, in some dimly lit room full of monitoring equipment. A second round might set off an alarm he might find it hard to quell.

Oddly, he was having difficulty caring.

He sat there in the dark for a while, pondering not for the first time the possibility she had done something to him, something that made it difficult for him to think about the things he once had, and all too easy for him to think about things he should not. If that small blast of normal Ziemite feeling had permanently altered him. He had not thought to ask if she could remove what she had so easily given.

He did not use her name in his thoughts, did not have to, for there was only one *she* in his mind. If he were as honest as he tried to be when the Coalition allowed it, he would admit at least to himself that she occupied far too much of his mind.

When he first realized some small part of him was wishing he had not left them, those insane rebels, he was almost certain she had done something, planted something in his brain that was corrupting his thinking. And yet . . .

He pulled himself out of the fruitless thinking and snapped on the handheld unit. He would do this, and it would resolve both problems. He would prove her wrong about this, and then his life could proceed. Of course if he did, it would make her a manipulative liar, and he could not make his mind accept that.

Because you do not wish to.

The words formed harshly in his head, with an almost angry ferocity. He who had always been honest with himself wanted to deny this, but he could not. He did not want to think of her in that way. And it was only now that he was away from her that he could even entertain the idea; when he'd been in her presence, when he'd looked into those vivid, almost glowing blue eyes, he could not even question the truth of what she was. Had he not felt the very miracle of her? Had she not done what the very best Coalition doctors had claimed impossible?

He realized he was twisting his body, as if driven to test yet again that she had indeed accomplished the impossible. There was no pain, not even the faintest trace of a lingering ache at the site where that shard of planium had once hovered. She had given him back his life. Not only had she saved him when he should have died on that hillside, she had removed the ever-present threat he'd lived with for over a year.

And then, unbelievably, they had freed him. The highest representative of their mortal enemy on their world, and they had freed him.

He remembered when he had wondered if this was some exquisitely chosen torture, to give him back the strength and body that had been irretrievably damaged, only to execute him. For in truth, had the Raider done what he would likely have done on that hillside, Paledan would have welcomed it. And not simply because his death would have been long, slow, and horrible had they left him there, but because he had begun to wonder how long he could tolerate living with that ever-present threat.

It struck him then that even that had changed. That if she had merely— merely?—saved his life and left the shard, then they had freed him, he would still have wanted to live, if only to solve the mystery that was this planet and its people.

The mystery that was the woman known as the Spirit, a mystical legend he had scoffed at, only to be confronted with the absolute truth of both her existence and her capabilities.

They truly believe in her. They trek up to that barren edge to seek her, in the full faith she can heal them.

Brakely's words, forgotten until now, came back to him. Issued in the first days of their time here, when at Paledan's behest he had been venturing out amid the people to learn what he could of them, his aide had delivered them with a laugh of disbelief. He himself had shaken his head at the preposterousness of it.

And now he found himself wondering if perhaps this strange world made up to its inhabitants for its inhospitable nature by providing them with strength and endurance and other powers unknown elsewhere. Which led him to wonder if there were other planets like this, perhaps ones he had even been to, where he had never known or questioned, only followed orders to destroy if they would not capitulate. Which led him further, to wonder if those planets they had destroyed had held things of great worth they had not known about; after all, the properties of planium had only been discovered in the last century although it had always existed.

When he realized his idle thoughts were, in essence, questioning the entire Coalition mission and protocols, he knew he was out of control. He turned the handheld back off and stood up. That he did so without the familiar pain unsettled him even more.

He ordered the lights to full, pulled out fresh clothing. And then reached for his civilian jacket before he remembered. He held it before him, staring at the back, thinking of that moment when he had asked if she could not heal it. He did not joke, he never joked, and yet he had made a joke with her. And she had seen it, immediately. It had made her smile.

It had made her smile, and he felt as much sense of accomplishment as after a successful battle.

He felt an odd sort of hollowness inside, as he'd never felt before. When he realized he'd pulled out this jacket because on some level he wished to be back there, wherever there was, he tossed it into his travel locker and slammed it shut.

And spent the rest of the day weighing the logic that Iolana had done something to him to scramble his mind against the instinctive disbelief she would do so. He knew which one he should believe.

He just couldn't seem to do it.

Chapter 45

"WELCOME BACK, MAJOR. For a while there, I thought you'd escaped this dreariness permanently."

Paledan looked at Brander Kalon, whom he'd encountered on his circuit of the compound. The man was sitting under one of the larger trees near the wall—one Paledan had once found the twins sitting in, peering into the compound. The twins. He pushed them out of his mind by staring at Kalon, who appeared to be blithely carving something out of a long piece of wood with a small knife.

"I very nearly did." *Not quite how you mean, but nevertheless true.*

The man raised a brow. "They recall you?"

"No." *Not yet.*

"Word is you've been out hunting rebels personally."

"Is it?" he said in a tone of mild curiosity.

"Find any?"

The most amazing of them all. "Would I be back here alive if I had?"

Kalon held his gaze for a moment, almost pointedly. He had often wondered how this man could not be one of those rebels; he was far from beaten down. Yet he seemed to care so little, about the fate of not only his friends but his entire world.

"Tell me, Kalon, how do you stay so . . ." Oddly, a description failed him.

"Indescribably me?" Kalon said with a grin.

Paledan couldn't help the way his mouth twitched upward at the corners slightly. It was strange; never had he ever had trouble maintaining an impassive visage before coming here. And he wondered how many times he had prefaced thoughts about this place with the phrase "It was strange."

Or perhaps he should be wondering more about why he was having such troubles now.

"That will do," he said.

"What use is being downcast all the time? What does it change?" Kalon asked. He made what appeared to be a final long sweep with his small knife, then folded the blade back into the handle and slipped it into a pocket. No doubt troopers had let him keep the thing, as it was much too small to be used as a serious weapon.

Or perhaps he had simply charmed them into it.

"Contention valid," Paledan agreed. "But what does your world have left to inspire such cheer?"

Kalon stood to meet his gaze steadily in a way no one except Brakely had since his return. The way those with the Raider did. "It is true, the Coalition has not left us much."

"It is their way." *Their. Yet again he had done it.*

"And when you have all of our planium, what then?"

"If the people of Ziem cooperate, cease this useless rebellion and accede to Coalition rule, 'they will be allowed into the Coalition on a probationary basis. If they do not, they and their planet will be destroyed.'"

Kalon arched that brow again. "Well, that was straight out of the Coalition rulebook."

"Quoted exactly," Paledan said, realizing he'd said it by long practice, not belief.

"Tell me, Major, don't you ever feel smothered by their rules and demands?"

Again he fell back on one of the mantras. "The Coalition has given me everything I have."

"No doubt," Kalon said softly. "But what have they taken away from you?"

With that the man handed him what he'd been carving, nodded, and walked away. Paledan stood staring in the direction his one-time chaser opponent had gone long after the man had sauntered out of sight, by all appearances carefree.

But what have they taken away from you?

The words, spoken now by both the woman who bedeviled him and this scapegrace gambler, echoed in his head. And when he looked down at what he now held, saw what it was, they echoed even louder.

A small but near perfect replica of a Ziem saber.

IOLANA SAW DRAKE draw in a deep breath before he spoke. "It is a fine line we walk. While I agree we might, given enough time, see him break free of those bonds, I am certain that the Coalition will only allow even Paledan so much of that time without sending that order to annihilate us all."

"Including Ziem itself," Brander said grimly. "I've heard they have a way to cut up a planet and leave pieces big enough to extract what they need."

"Planium mining on an asteroid?" Kye asked.

"Only if their destructive process doesn't push the planium and quisalt together," Iolana said.

The three looked at each other rather as the knowledge Brander had gained in his experiments hung over them like a grim, particular dark bank of mist.

"Fine choice, is it not?" Drake muttered. "Suicide soon, if we continue to fight and push them to destroy, or suicide later, but perhaps striking a crippling blow first."

"One that none of us would live to see," Brander said, "and which would end the same way, in Ziem's destruction."

Kye let out an audible breath. "There is no true Ziemite who would not die to save her. But die to save other worlds, populated by people we do not and will never know? That is a mighty sacrifice to ask."

Drake looked almost pale, and Iolana sensed it was from the dread of having to ask for that sacrifice from the people he had risked his life time and again to save.

"This," she said firmly, "like all else on Ziem, must be a free choice for her people. If it comes to this, you must present the situation as you just did, and let them decide."

After a moment, Drake nodded. For thus had it always been on Ziem.

And what, she wondered as she made her way back to her home, would Caze think of such a method? She knew what the Coalition would call it; primitive, ridiculous, born of ignorance of the simple fact that only the elite should be allowed to rule.

Yet had been the way of Trios, even with her king, for it was a title earned, not inherited, and could be revoked at any time by the Triotian people. And the Triotian people had beaten the mighty Coalition on two different worlds.

She walked through the masked entrance of the cave without much awareness, and around the inner wall to her quarters, but came to an abrupt halt there. It was a surprisingly strong jolt to see it as it always was, and not disguised as an office in the Council Building. Caze's office. Although deep down she knew the strength of the jolt was not because of that, but because of the man who was no longer here.

And she felt an echo of the odd sensation that had overtaken her when Brander had returned from Zelos and reported he'd both seen and spoken to Caze. It was somewhere between an ache and a hollowness she couldn't quite describe. That he was up and around and functioning as if nothing had ever happened gladdened the healer in her, but at the same time it squeezed at her heart in a way she didn't like feeling, for the only explanation she could see for it was one beyond foolishness.

You have been worse than a fool in your time, but that does not mean you must do so again.

She gave herself the warning in the sternest internal voice she could muster. But almost instantly another voice, one she had not heard for a very long time, seemed to answer.

Perhaps the foolishness is in denying what you feel.

She sank down onto the cushions someone—likely Grim—had replaced on the stone protrusion that served her as a settee. She was shaken to her core. For she had not heard that voice since the seconds before she had hurled herself to what she hoped would be death, when it had screamed out this was wrong.

She sat in silence. She did not know for how long. But then Grim was there, seated opposite her and gazing at her with some concern. When she looked up and met his eyes, understanding dawned in them almost immediately.

"You feel his absence," Grim said, and it was not a question.

"How could I not?"

"Contention valid. Even damaged, he had such a presence even I mark it. But you feel it . . . differently."

He hesitated, and she sighed inwardly. Just the fact that he was uncertain told her what was coming.

"We are still us, Grim, who have shared the worst," she said quietly.

He nodded. Then, still looking a bit wary, which for him was tantamount to an expression of total trepidation, he said, "You miss him as . . . a woman misses a man."

She looked at this tall, gaunt man who had saved her so that she could save others, who had been her loyal companion for all these years, asking nothing for himself except to serve her.

You have long paid me back, Grimbald Thrace. You needn't take care of me any longer.

Do you wish me to leave?

Of course not. I merely ask why you would wish to stay.

You alone of all people do not think less of me because of . . . what I am. And am not.

I think you underestimate Ziemites.

"You have never felt this, Grim?" she asked. "Or have you simply never allowed it because you cannot carry it to the natural conclusion?"

"I do not know any longer," he said simply. "And it does not matter. I am not a man in the sense other men are, and that is how I must live."

"I wish I could heal you, my friend."

"You cannot replace what was taken." He did not flinch as he said it. And he continued to look at her steadily. "And you have in essence answered my question."

She sighed. "If I cannot give the truth to you, then who?"

"Perhaps the man it concerns most?" Grim suggested.

"Would that not be foolish?" she asked, beyond curious as to how he would answer.

"Not if he feels the same."

She suddenly could not take a breath. For Grim had a knack for recognizing other's feelings. "Are you saying . . . you believe he does?"

"I have never seen a man fight so hard against it, which speaks to the power of it."

She felt a shiver go through her. Was it possible? Was all the strangeness she had felt around Caze Paledan attributable to such a simple, basic cause?

"But . . . he is Coalition and I am of Ziem. Would it not be . . . hopeless?"

"As things stand . . . yes. But they may not always be so."

"You think things—or he himself—might change?"

"I think one or the other is inevitable. Perhaps both. The only question is in what direction."

She laughed, and felt lighter. "Ah, Grim, what would I do without your wisdom?"

But as she later lay in the empty darkness, that was not what she thought about. Because what she really didn't know was what she would do without Caze's compelling, room-filling presence.

Chapter 46

PALEDAN STARED AT the screen of the handheld. He'd gone through the records, searching the troops for those who originated on Lustros. One triggered recognition; it was Stron, the lieutenant he had marked for possible promotion up the ranks. It was the perfect excuse, and he called up the man's records. There would be nothing strange about him checking into the background of a man he was considering for higher rank. In fact it would seem amiss if he did not.

It took a few minutes to work his way back to the birth papers, and once there he did not linger, not wishing to raise suspicion. It didn't matter; he'd seen what he'd wanted to see, and that his suspicion had been proven right gave him no pleasure.

There was no check box, labeled acceptable or otherwise, on the birth form. And the form also lacked the odd symbol that had been in the corner of his own form. He went back to his own to verify the differences.

"Sir?"

He did not react, although he was surprised that he had been so intent Brakely had been able to get so close without him realizing. Or perhaps he had realized and had known there was no threat.

"Yes, Brakely?"

"The damage assessments are ready."

"Estimated delay?"

"Three to six weeks, sir."

Well done, Raider. "Next?"

"The landing zone repairs are ready for inspection."

Paledan nodded.

"And," Brakely continued, "there is word from several troopers that they have seen Jakel skulking about. And that he is . . . not himself."

Paledan drew back slightly. Had they done it? Had *she* done it?

"In what way?"

"He is no longer menacing everyone in sight. In fact, he appears to be afraid himself."

"Of?"

Brakely gave a shrug and a shake of his head. "Everyone. Everything."

And once more he had undeniable proof that the woman this world called the Spirit could do exactly what she said she could do. As if he needed it, after what she had done for—and to—him.

"I would consider that an improvement," Paledan said.

"As would I," Brakely said, his tone dry, Paledan suspected to keep from laughing. But his aide's tone shifted back to serious when he asked, "Are you all right, sir?"

He leaned back in his chair. "Never better." *Physically.*

"It's just . . . I noticed you've been looking at your medical records."

"I'm fine, Brakely." Then, noticing the man's disquiet, gave him a nod. Brakely, after all, had not come from Lustros, and so had not had the capacity for emotion quashed. It struck him to think about this later, how his aide functioned so well if he carried a full load of these tangling feelings. "It's all right. I . . . appreciate your concern."

He would grant that to no one else, that freedom to worry about him. *At least, no one else on this base.*

An image came back to him with jolting clarity, a pair of blue eyes lit with the cool fire of concern. She had worried about him. And while logic told him it was the worry of a healer about her patient, something else, something deep inside that had been stirring since he'd arrived on this planet but had roared to life in her presence, told him it was more. Much more.

"What was it you were looking for?" Brakely asked, snapping him out of the reverie he'd been battling since the Raider had left him on the hillside where, by all reason, he should have died. For a moment he wished that he could tell Brakely the truth, that he was healed, but he knew he could not. For the truth of how that had happened might stretch even Brakely's considerable boundaries, and he did not want to put the man in the position of having to decide whether or not to report what would clearly be a reportable offense to High Command.

Realizing somewhat belatedly that Brakely dealt with these records much more than he did, he pointed to the symbol on the screen.

"Do you know what this means?"

Brakely leaned in. "I've seen it before." He frowned. "I've always thought it indicated some . . . irregularity. But if this is your record, that cannot be true."

Paledan was not certain what he had done to earn such blind faith. "Is there no guide to such things?"

"There is, sir. Shall I look it up?"

"Please. And search for anyone assigned here who also has the symbol on the birth record." He looked up at his aide who was already turning to go do as he was bidden. "Door is closed, Marl."

Understanding flashed in the man's dark-brown eyes. "Yes, sir." And he was gone, to set about fulfilling the request.

I think you would be proud of him, Commander.

He went very still. That thought, even the concept of that thought, was forbidden in Coalition practice. Blood ties were nothing; the Coalition was the connective unit. And so pride in a genetic offspring was non-existent. And yet . . .

The pride in Lana Davorin's voice when she spoke of her children was beyond denying. Even when she spoke of the twins it was there, despite that they were defects of nature.

Defects of nature.

We are glad you did not die.

"And I you," he said under his breath, as if saying it aloud in this place, in the face of all the Coalition trappings, made it somehow fiercer. For he was glad. His life would be the lesser had he not met those two. They had opened his mind to so many possibilities. . . .

Including that you are one of their kind?

No, it was their mother who had done that. But it was Lux and Nyx who made proving—or disproving—the idea essential.

It was on his way to inspect the repaired landing zone that he unexpectedly encountered the other Kalon, the woman, near the wreckage of what had once been Davorin's taproom. Even had he not known who she was, he could have guessed the connection by the color of her eyes, that bright turquoise that stood out even amongst Ziem blue.

"First your cousin, now you," he said when the woman met his gaze.

"We like to keep track of what of Zelos has been destroyed," she said flatly.

"But this," he said, gesturing back over his shoulder at the ruin, "was destroyed long ago."

"Yes. The moment the Coalition discovered Drake was the Raider."

"And yet neither you nor your cousin have joined him."

She lifted one shoulder. "I am no fighter by nature. And I have long ago accepted what my cousin is, and is not." She said it calmly, almost wearily. Then she shifted her gaze to the flattened space, where the citizens of Zelos persisted in leaving tokens to their hero despite the fact that a troop crawler rolled in and flattened it all again every week. "I miss it."

That surprised him. "I did not think you ever frequented the place."

"It was not my favored place to linger." She shifted her gaze back to him. "I miss, rather, something that was in it. Something I was very proud of."

His brow furrowed. "And that would be?"

"The painting."

He blinked. Drew back, staring at her. *Proud of?*

"It was," she went on, "the first piece in which the feeling, the inspiration perhaps, really took hold. To where I could not work as quickly as my mind provided the way, the details."

His breath caught. He could not deny what she was saying, yet. . . . It took him a moment to get out the question.

"You? You are the artist?"

"I am." Her mouth twisted. "Or I was."

He realized she must think it destroyed along with the building. "I was told it was painted by a student."

"Yes. At the time, I was."

His brow furrowed in doubt. "How old were you?"

"Fifteen."

"Impossible." It broke from him almost unwillingly, he who had never said anything he didn't mean to say. Or had not, until Ziem.

To his surprise, the woman smiled at him, and there was a glint of . . . something in those eyes. "I will take that as a compliment, Major."

And whether it was the way she said it or that glint he did not know, but he suddenly knew she spoke the truth. She had created the portrait that had so seized him. Haunted him. Enchanted him. "It is . . . deserved."

"I thought there was no place for useless bits of art in Coalition thinking."

"That portrait is many things, but useless is not one of them."

She glanced around at the ruin. "You speak as if it still exists."

Of course. She wouldn't know. Driven by an impulse he didn't understand, he answered, "It does." He did not speak of the subject, for he could think of no way that did not sound insane.

Her brows rose. Then lowered. "You have it?"

"I do." She simply looked at him, waiting. She had, he realized, a great deal of her cousin's unshakeable composure. "I cannot give it back to you." He was a little stunned at the amount of regret he felt.

"What use could the Coalition possibly have for it?"

"None."

"And yet it is now theirs."

"No. It is mine." What was it about these Ziemites that had him speaking of things in ways he never did? Or should? She looked surprised, perhaps at the utter possessiveness in his tone. But then she smiled, as if she had taken that as a compliment also.

As she should.

"I understood the Coalition did not believe in personal possessions."

"They do not."

He let the words lie there between them. After a moment she said quietly, "In that case, you have quite a dilemma, Major. I wish you luck in resolving it."

When she was gone he stood there for a long time, not really seeing the ruins around him. For he was wrestling with another much, much larger dilemma.

The simple fact that he liked these Ziemites much more than he liked almost anyone in the Coalition.

Chapter 47

IT WAS IMPOSSIBLE. He was well now, healed, there was no reason for the connection to linger. And yet . . .

Iolana paced her quarters restlessly, unable to shut down her equally restless mind. Which in itself was odd, for she usually had much better control over her thoughts. But ever since the rover had lifted off carrying her son and the man she should by rights loathe, the boundaries seemed not just breached but destroyed. For all she could think about was Caze.

"Iolana?"

She turned at the call from the cave entrance. "Come in, Kye."

"I don't want to disturb—"

"Please. I welcome the distraction." Kye stepped in. She smiled, but still seemed hesitant. "My daughters do not need to stand on ceremony," Iolana said, and Kye's smile widened. But in her way, she dispensed with the niceties and went straight to her purpose.

"I've just come back from Zelos."

"And my son breathes again," Iolana teased.

Kye finally relaxed. "Yes. I know he does not like it, but I needed to test whether my concealment still holds. And he agreed—finally—as long as I did nothing more than that."

"The people of Ziem hold you as their rightful leader's mate, those who might know would not give you away."

"I was afraid Jakel might. I heard talk of him, and he saw me here."

Iolana waved a hand. "He no longer has knowledge of any of us." She looked Kye up and down. "You do not look as if you trekked down on foot."

"I did not." Kye grinned then. "Kade flew me to the old ruin and I went from there."

Iolana smiled herself. "That should hold him for a while."

Kye nodded, then went on. "I thought you might wish to know I saw him."

Iolana knew the subject had abruptly changed, even though Kye did not specify it was no longer Kade they spoke of. "He seems well?" she asked, surprised at how hard she had to work to keep her voice even.

"Yes. He moves well, and the lines of pain have faded already." Iolana nodded, but sensed there was more. And after a moment Kye spoke again. "He told me he has the painting."

"If he does not know you know that already, then your secret holds."

"Yes, it seems. As does Brander's."

"You have told him you are the artist?"

Kye nodded. "I believed it would dissuade him from believing my true life." Iolana thought sadly that the artist should have been her true life, but said nothing. "But it was what else he said I thought might interest you."

And now Kye was sidling around the subject, enough unlike herself that Iolana wondered what was coming. She waited silently. Kye took a breath and said, "Once he learned I had painted it, he told me he could not give it back. He said it was his, rather... vehemently, even though he admitted the Coalition allowed neither art nor personal possessions."

"He is ... fascinated with your work."

Kye studied her for a moment, and Iolana suddenly knew what she was going to say before she actually spoke the words. "I think he is fascinated with the subject. And not simply because you healed him when he thought it impossible. I think you have made him question ... everything." Kye's steady gaze softened. "And as I've told you, I know you feel more for him than healer to healed."

"He is Coalition." She said it almost desperately, clinging to it as if it were a shield.

"And I thought my own dilemma, loving Drake while also loving the Raider, was complicated." Only Kye's sudden shift to a very wry tone allowed her to hold her composure. "It is . . . understandable. He is a very different sort of man. In addition to being very . . . eye-catching."

Iolana felt her cheeks heat. Dear Eos, was she blushing? For one of the few times in her life she had to look away from another pair of eyes. "You are being very . . . kind."

"It is easier for me," Kye said quietly. "While I revered him, Torstan was not my father."

Iolana looked back at her daughter by covenant. "And Torstan is why it cannot be. Ca—the major represents the malignancy that killed him."

"Then that must be resolved," Kye said, waving a hand much as she herself had over her concern about Jakel.

"So you, too, think he might be turned?"

"I think he would be much happier if he were free to become the man he could be."

"On that," Iolana said sadly, "we agree."

"I FOUND ONLY two on base with the symbol, and one of those with the check box."

Paledan looked across his desk at Brakely. "Both from Lustros?"

His aide nodded. "One had the check box and symbol from the beginning. On the other, the symbol had been added sometime after the document was created."

"And the symbol, you found its meaning?"

For the first time since their earliest days, after Paledan had pulled him from the death line, Brakely looked fearful. And, in an odd counterpoint, concerned.

"It is . . . from the birth regulation ministry."

Paledan had to prompt him to go on. "And it means?"

His aide took a deep breath, then answered. "It is the symbol indicating the two contributors are banned from further participation."

There suddenly seemed to be a lack of air in the room. For there was only one reason contributors to the population program were banned from further production. Defects in the child they produced. Defects such as deformities, mental incapacities—some of which did not manifest until later, hence the later application of the symbol—or other abnormalities.

"I would speak to the trooper with both the symbol and the check box," he said abruptly.

"I will summon her, sir."

When the trooper arrived in his office, she saluted instantly and stood stiffly, but Paledan saw the tremor go through her. The young woman was clearly terrified. His first instinct was to reassure her but he did not, for he thought fear might get him the answer he wanted. So instead he studied the woman as she stood there, searching for any sign of a mark or deviation from proper physical or mental condition. There was none.

At last he released her from the salute. He bade her sit, then walked around to the front of his desk, standing so that he not quite loomed over her.

"Tell me of your birth, trooper."

She looked astonished. On top of the fear, which lingered. "Sir?"

"Do you know your contributors?"

She looked aghast. "I . . . no, sir. I never met them."

"Have you seen their records?"

"Only in passing, during medical assessments."

"Are they still alive?"

"The male, yes. The female . . . no."

"How did she die?"

The trooper lowered her gaze. After a moment she said, her voice unsteady, "She self-terminated, sir."

"Was she ill?"

"No."

"Insane?"

The trooper shuddered. "I . . . don't know, sir." He understood the fear better now, for insanity in a contributor would merit a permanent mark on your record, for constant monitoring. But he also heard something else in her tone.

"What do you know, or suspect about the reason, trooper?" he asked softly.

With an effort that was visible the woman drew herself up. "I overheard two from the ministry talking, saying there was some . . . defect in my production."

"And yet you are whole and functional."

"Yes." Her head came up then. "And I have passed every assessment, sir. There are no defects. Even my birth record deems me acceptable."

The record that bore the same marks as his own.

"Tell me, Trooper Brun," he said, using her name for the first time, and the same soft tone, "have you ever felt that there was something . . . missing in you? Not physically, but a hollow sort of place that you did not understand?"

The woman stared at him now, as if stunned. "I . . . how did you know? Is there something written on my record that—"

She stopped when he shook his head. He was only vaguely aware of dismissing her, and of the woman leaving his office and quietly shutting the door behind her.

Paledan turned back to his screen, where his own birth record was still open. He stared at the symbol at the top of the page.

. . . the two contributors are banned from further participation.

Defects. And yet the box labeled "acceptable" was checked. So he had been acceptable, but the contributors who had produced him were banned from any further production.

Because of defects in their combination.

Then there was that hollow, empty place he'd always felt, had thought normal.

Defects.

Twins.

Chapter 48

IOLANA FELT THE moment when he believed.

The connection with one she had healed had never lasted so long, nor at such distance. Was this particular connection so strong because the healing had been so complex? Because it had taken so long? Had so many stages?

Or was it something else?

She was pacing her living area restlessly. He had such presence, filled a room with his own kind of power, that this place where he had been, even helpless, seemed empty now.

No, this was more than feeling restless. She had the odd feeling that if she didn't expend some kind of energy, it was going to overwhelm her. But simply walking the floor was not going to suffice, for it was more than physical energy she needed to offload. It was a kind of internal, mental—no, emotional energy that she didn't quite know how to get free of.

And when did you start lying to yourself?

As the words echoed in her head, she found herself face to face with the truth of it. This was not the connection she felt with someone she'd healed, for it felt entirely different. This was a much more elemental thing, something she had not felt in over a decade.

This was the connection of woman to man, and no amount of telling herself fascination with a portrait did not equate to his desire for the subject would tamp down the feeling of connection. Nor did the sense of longing she got from him necessarily have to do with her, for he was thinking much of the twins. As she had expected he would, once he came to believe. She wondered what had convinced him. Knowing the immense logic of his mind, he had probably searched for proof.

And there it was, the wall between them that was nearly as immense as the uniform he wore; Caze was a man of logic, while she inhabited a mystical sort of realm that was utterly foreign to him.

And yet he had come to believe more than she would ever have expected. The truth of his healing had opened his mind until the impossible had become the possible. And once he had taken that final step of acceptance—which she sensed had occurred when he'd taken that first physical step without the pain he'd lived with for so long—he had proven he truly lived by his own words. Once not changing his mind became the impossibility, he changed it.

She wished she could have been there with him when the truth had cut through to his heart. She could feel his turmoil, wished she could soothe it. She—

The sound around the corner of the stone wall that separated her living area from the entrance to her sanctuary was slight, but unmistakable. Footsteps. Light, quick . . . and a pair. It was the only warning she had before the twins darted around the wall and came to a halt.

She halted herself and turned to look at them. They were no small miracle, these two, and she was amazed she had produced them. She was amazed at all her children, and what they had become helped fill the empty space within her that came from the simple fact that they had done it without her because she had not been strong enough.

Lux held out what she had been carrying, and Iolana saw that it was a large spray of mistflowers.

"We brought these—"

"Because you—"

"Like them and—"

"We are glad—"

"You healed the major."

She took the offered bouquet, smiling. "I thank you both. This was a very nice gesture."

"We can—"

"Be nice—"

"Sometimes."

Her smile widened. "When you're not being mischievous, devious, and utterly brilliant?"

Iolana felt another slam to her heart when they both smiled at her, for they were not the glib or knowing smiles she had seen before. These smiles were the ones they gave Drake and Kye, Eirlys and Brander.

Family smiles.

"We have been—"

"Thinking."

"And when are you not?" It was an effort to keep her tone light and teasing, so full was her heart just now.

"Never," Lux admitted.

"But we have not—"

"Liked to think—"

"About this."

She lifted the spray of mistflowers to her face, inhaled the sweet scent, and waited. After a moment, starting with Nyx, it came in a rush.

"We have been—"

"Very angry—"

"With you—"

"Because you—"

"Left us. But then—"

"We started thinking—"

"About what Drake said—"

"That if he had—"

"Stayed mad at us—"

"Every time we—"

"Got in trouble—"

"He would—"

"Hate us by now."

Drake had said that? He had told her more than once that her relationship—or the lack of one—with the twins was her problem to handle. Yet it seemed he had done a bit to help her along.

"We do not—" Lux began.

"Want to—"

"Hate you. You have—"

"Done good things—"

"For the Sentinels and—"

"The major—"

"And you have—"

"Not gotten mad—"

"At us."

"No, I haven't. For I find you too wonderful to be angry."

They exchanged startled looks, and then those smiles returned. Lux looked around the room, now free of the illusion the Stone of Ziem had helped her maintain.

"It seems—"

"Different now."

"It is," she agreed, for she had felt the emptiness since he had gone.

Lux gave her a sideways look. "Do you miss him?"

They were both watching her, and she had the feeling her answer was important to them. So, honestly, she nodded. "I do."

They seemed relieved. "So do we," they said simultaneously.

"I know," she said softly.

They studied her for a moment. "Do you—" Nyx began.

"Know if he—"

"Is all right?"

She smiled at them again. "He is. Although he is wrestling with some new knowledge just now."

They exchanged those glances again, and she wondered anew if they were able to communicate directly.

Then Nyx turned his gaze back to her. "You told him?"

She blinked.

"We heard—"

"That you knew—"

"Something about him—"

"That could change—"

"Everything."

"It seems," Iolana said with a smile and a laugh, "that your four ears are better than any observation network."

They smiled at that, so clearly pleased that that warmth in her heart expanded another notch.

"We would—"

"Like to—"

"See him," they finished together.

She opened her mouth to remind them he was back in Zelos, amidst his forces, then stopped. They knew this perfectly well. And underestimating these two would, she feared, set her back greatly with them. Not to mention the twins always found a way to what they wanted.

That they had come to her with this, rather than just going on that way they always seemed to find, meant everything to her. And yet, she could not let them run amok, not even for her own gain, not when it would put them at risk. She chose her words carefully.

"I can understand that," she said. For had she not just admitted she missed him as well? "So do you have a plan?"

Again they exchanged glances, and when they looked back at her she saw in their faces that she had done the right thing, at least for her relationship with these two youngest of her children.

"We thought—"

"You could—"

"Hide us—"

"Like you did—"

"This room and—"

"We could—"

"Go to him."

She looked at them consideringly. It was a clever idea, but then she would have expected nothing less.

"You mean me to go with you?"

"You want—"

"To see him too—"

"Don't you?"

Yes, these two did not miss much. It took her a moment to control the leap her heart took at the idea. And it was still strange enough to her that she did not yet wish to admit it aloud. So she focused instead on their proposal.

"It is an interesting plan. I have never tried to mask others, although I have fogged people's perceptions of them. But perhaps, if I carried the Stone of Ziem, it might work. We shall have to experiment."

Delight fairly burst from them.

"You will—"

"Do it?"

"I think we must see if it would work first, don't you?" They nodded enthusiastically. "And I'm afraid this is where I must be responsible. We cannot do this unless Drake approves it."

"We could—"

"Convince him."

"I have no doubt you could. But perhaps the Raider might have to say no."

They went quiet, but after a moment nodded.

"If the Raider—"

"Says no—"

"It is no."

She felt a burst of sadness, that these two, so young, so well understood the necessities of war. But underneath it was a vivid awareness that her pulse had picked up, and her nervous tension increased.

All at the prospect of seeing Caze again.

Chapter 49

HE HAD, PALEDAN thought, lost his mind. Left a piece of it trapped in that illusion.

Or with the woman who had created it.

When Jakel had slunk into his office he had been surprised. That had turned to near amusement as he assessed the change in the creature who had once been the most brutal enforcer. She had indeed done as promised. Cowering, clearly terrified, the man barely managed to set the small object on the desk before he scuttled out. For a moment Paledan thought of those the man had tortured, murdered, for no better reason than he enjoyed it. True, he had done some of it at the behest of the Coalition, but that he had taken such pleasure in it made Paledan's skin crawl.

He deserved what she had done. And that she had been able to do it unsettled him, not because of her power, but because she had not used it on him. For surely there would have been great pleasure in destroying the mind of the leader of their enemy? Or in taking his free will on the choices before him? But then, Ziemites had ever acted contrary to their best interests. Hadn't that been in one of his first reports to High Command after his arrival here?

With her forbearance safely categorized out of the realm of the personal, he at last had unwrapped the small object. The page around it was one of those bedamned calling cards from the Raider, left at the scene of all his raids. But the object was one of those prickly fruits the twins had given him. And at the bottom of the page were written two words.

The hillside.

His mind had taken a leap. And he'd known it was right.

So here he was now, approaching the hillside where he had, in essence, died. And been brought back to life by someone he'd thought also dead, someone who was an impossibility in herself, the legend he'd put no credence in, the woman they called the Spirit.

But she was alive, vibrantly, undeniably alive. And he of all people could not deny her powers were real. Every step he took without pain reminded him. But it was what else she had done to him that was uppermost in his mind and had been since he'd left their stronghold, wherever it truly was. Even in the three days since he'd been back, he'd felt the difference strongly. Everything seemed . . . not just different but more intense. His reactions to the simplest of things seemed . . . out of proportion. Even what color there was in this gray world seemed brighter. A snappy salute earned a return with a nod; a sloppy job got stern but not angry instruction. And Brakely's concern for his well-being got a smile and his thanks. Which only seemed to stoke his aide's worry.

When he had found himself staring at his office wall, appreciating the curve of the Ziem sabers, he knew it was time to move. Realized there had never been any doubt that he would go to meet them.

But every step he took without that pain reminded him of what he was trying not to think about. And when he found himself almost admiring the way that bedamned mist swirled, he knew something deep within him had changed. He would have thought it was merely the relief from the pain, except that he had never felt such things even before he'd been injured.

What he didn't know was if the change was permanent, or just an effect of this place.

Or perhaps the knowledge that his entire life had been a lie.

A twin.

He'd had another, as close as any two beings could be, until they were expelled into the world. A duplicate, she had said. A mirror image of himself.

He wondered what it would have been like, to have had another being so close, so in tune you could communicate without words as the Davorin twins seemed to. What potential had the Coalition missed in their arrogance?

Their. Not our.

It was consistent now. He thought of them as something apart from himself. And the distance between seemed to have grown geometrically since he'd spent those days with Lana. Even now his report on the damage done in the raid on the cannon emplacements sat unsent, for he knew reporting what had happened would put the blackest mark ever on his record. Oddly, he did not care overmuch, except that if his reputation slid, his ability to stave off the destruction of Ziem would also lessen. But eventually he would run out of time; the cannons were to be delivered next week, and he would have to send the report before then or he would end up with four fusion cannons and no place to install them. Such was the damage the Raider had done. And he had noted without surprise that all he felt about that was admiration.

He looked around as he reached the hill and started up, retracing the path he had taken that day. The mistbreaker trees seemed wreathed in strands of the mist, which swirled with his passage. The gray got thinner, more transparent as the path climbed, until he could see a good way around him.

And then he heard a whisper. Her voice. Her voice, as low and gentle as he remembered. It sent a shiver up his newly healed spine.

"It is safe. He is alone."

He stopped. And as if they had materialized out of the mist, the twins were there, running toward him. To his surprise they flung themselves at him, throwing their arms around him. To his even greater surprise he returned the action, almost reflexively, as if such a greeting from children had been the norm instead of this being the first time in his life.

When they released him and looked up, it was Lux who started it.

"We have—"

"Missed you."

"You are—"

"Well?"

He had no words for the sensation that filled him. He only knew that it seemed to grow, expand, until he could no longer contain it. It was a warmth unlike any he'd ever felt, but it was also tinged with a horrible sense of loss. Had he truly had the chance for the kind of connection these two had, and it had been destroyed before it began?

"I am fine," he said to them. "Thanks to your mother."

"She is—"

"A very good—"

"Healer."

Among the many other things she was, Paledan thought. And on the thought, she emerged from the mist. His memory, however vivid, had failed to capture her accurately. She was more beautiful, more graceful, more vibrantly alive than seemed possible. But hadn't he learned much about possibilities from her?

She smiled at him as she approached. He did not know what made him say it, but he could not seem to resist. He gestured at the twins and said, "No such greeting from you?"

"Would you wish it?"

That voice was like a physical thing, brushing over him, until he thought it must be some lingering effect of her healing of him.

"I believe I would," he said, sounding oddly hoarse even to himself.

"Then by all means," she said, still smiling as she closed the gap between them. And then she was there, and her arms came around him, much more slowly, almost like a caress compared to the careening embrace of the twins.

He felt as if he was back under the sun of Clarion, with the brilliant heat flowing over him. His own arms moved instinctively again, pulling her tight against him. The feel of her, so close, slender yet wonderfully curved, set off a new kind of heat in him, so fierce it blasted the breath out of him. This was not the stream of connection he'd felt when she'd been healing him, this was something much more elemental, much more . . . necessary.

She tilted her head back to look up at him. Something in those vivid eyes stabbed at him at the same time it lured him in. It was a trap. His every instinct knew it. But he plunged ahead anyway, and his mouth came down on hers.

The warmth he'd been feeling exploded. He'd read of this, this monumental sort of need between male and female. But he had never experienced it. Had assumed himself apart from such things, assuaging the occasional need in the Coalition-approved manner at the various Legion Clubs scattered throughout the galaxy, and otherwise feeling nothing.

But the feel of her mouth beneath his, her lips soft and warm against his own, seared him more deeply than that planium shard. His head was reeling, as if the mist were indeed that poisonous thing they'd first thought it. He wanted more. No, he must have more, if he was to keep living. He tasted her, deeply, and the sweetness of it eclipsed even that surprising fruit the twins had given him.

The twins.

Even as he thought it, he heard them.

"Are you—"

"Finished yet?"

Reluctantly he pulled back. Found himself sucking in quick breaths as if he'd forgotten to breathe. And the only thing that saved his sanity was the fact that she was looking rather dazed herself. As if she was as surprised as he at what had happened, the way . . . something had erupted between them. And surprising this woman was, he somehow knew, no small accomplishment.

It took all his considerable will to look away from her. He found the twins watching them rather impatiently. But, he noted, with no surprise at all.

That seemed important, although he was not certain why.

"If you are—"

"Through kissing—"

"We have—"

"Brought you—"

"More things—"

"Of Ziem."

He risked a glance at Lana. She looked less dazed, but no less surprised. And when her arms slipped away he felt a sense of loss he could not describe.

He turned back to the twins, who were industriously emptying the small pack Nyx had set upon the ground. Towering over them seemed wrong, so he sat down on the ground beside them. They grinned at him, and he felt an odd sort of pleasure that he'd chosen the right course.

Still, he glanced around, then looked at the woman who had both ended his torture and added to it. "You came alone?"

She gave an elegant, one-shouldered shrug. And he had the sudden thought that he would give much to see her in the flowing white dress of the portrait. Not that he didn't appreciate the sight of her slender form in the rough, close-fitting Sentinel gear she wore now. Appreciated too much.

But no weapon, he noted, quite belatedly.

As if she needed one.

He made himself look away from her. The collection the twins had brought was fascinating, not only because it contained many things he did not know about, but because of what it told them of how their minds worked. And also, he admitted to himself, it told him a bit about what they thought of him, because of what they thought would interest him.

He picked up what looked like a huge curved shell of some kind.

"That is—"

"The horn from—"

"A ramhorn."

"They live in—"

"The mountains."

He hefted the weight, gauged the size.

"They are—"

"That big," the twins assured him before he asked.

He glanced at Lana, then looked back at them. "Learning your mother's gift for reading minds?"

The twins exchanged a glance.

"We hope so—"

"That would be—"

"Fun. Except sometimes—"

"With grown people—"

"Like when—"

"You were kissing—"

"We would not—"

"Want to—"

"Read that."

"Too bad," he said, in a wry tone he wasn't sure he'd ever used before. "If you could, perhaps you could explain it all to me."

They looked startled. Then they looked from him to Lana and back again. Then at each other, then back to him. And he marveled at how anyone could miss the fact that they were communicating.

"We are not—"

"Old enough—"

"Yet. You will—"

"Have to ask—"

There was a split-second longer break in the cadence, and they both looked at Lana as they finished with, "Our mother."

He did not know how to describe the look that came over her face then. It was a sort of radiance, a kind of utter joy he'd only heard about, never seen. He thought he would carry the memory of it until he died. As if it were overpowering, she sank to the ground, completing their little group of four.

And he had the crazed, unallowable thought that this must be somewhat what it was like to be a part of what Ziemites called family.

Chapter 50

"YOU MUST—"

"Break it—"

"In the—"

"Middle."

Paledan looked at the hammer Nyx held out and the heavy blade Lux was offering to him. Both were clearly planium. Which was technically a violation of regulations, since no one outside the Coalition was permitted to own the stuff, even—or perhaps especially—Ziemites.

But it was a measure, he supposed, of how far he'd pulled back from them that he never even half-seriously considered enforcing that regulation. He simply took the offered tools and did as instructed. The first blow cracked the fist-sized gray rock almost on a center line; the second split it open.

He stared down at another impossibility; the glint of color and crystal within the plain, stone shell was not just unexpected, it was . . . beautiful. He held it up to look closer. The crystal seemed to magnify what light there was, sparkling in contrasting shades of green and purple, when there did not seem to be enough to make that happen.

"Amazing," he murmured.

"Secret stones, Ziemite children call them," Lana said. "They are among my favorite things of our world."

He glanced at her. She looked as if she were truly enjoying this. And the moment he formed that thought, he realized he was as well. And that he had never felt this kind of simple, easy contentment before.

Nyx, already eager to move on, handed him something wrapped in a cloth. It appeared to be an oddly regular pattern of some solid material, but dripping with a thick, golden fluid.

"And this is?" he asked.

"Sweet," the twins chorused.

"You must—"

"Taste it."

He looked at them doubtfully, for the stuff looked more like the lubricant used on machinery than anything.

"Here," Lana said, in that husky voice that made him suck in a breath. She reached out and touched a slender finger to the viscous fluid and held it up to his lips.

He hesitated, but the temptation was too much. He licked up the bead of gold. And he could not say if the blast of sweetness was from the proffered treat or simply the taste of her skin. All he knew for sure was that he wanted more. He wanted to do what he had just done to every inch of her. He felt the blast of a kind of hunger he had never known, a hunger to touch, taste, savor. He even wanted to stroke the line of the scar on her arm with his tongue, for he knew a bit about pain survived.

For a moment they simply sat, gazes locked, until a slight cough reminded him the twins were waiting expectantly.

"It is . . . as promised," he said. "Very sweet."

They grinned. "The buzzers—"

"Make it."

"Buzzers?"

Their eyes widened. "You do not—"

"Know of the—"

"Buzzers?"

"I do not," he answered. "At least not in this sense."

"You should because—"

"They can sting you—"

"If they—"

"Are afraid."

"As many things can," he said, again wryly.

"We will—"

"Find you one!"

With the exclamation they scrambled to their feet. They glanced at Lana, and added, "We will—"

"Be careful and not—"

"Get stung."

She smiled. "I assumed you would be."

The smiles they gave her then put that glowing joy back in her expression again. Then they darted off, disappearing into the mist. He stared after them. And the realization he'd come to suddenly overwhelmed him.

"What you told me," he said, half whispering, "is the truth."

"I know," she said gently.

"How? How did you know I was . . . half of two?"

"It is there, Caze. The knowledge, the connection, is buried deep, far below conscious knowledge, perhaps below knowledge at all, but there."

"Do you know anything of . . . the other?"

"No," she said, sounding sad. He turned to look at there then, and saw that the emotion was real, for it showed in those vivid eyes. "There was only a trace. Only enough to know he was a duplicate. And that he lived to be born. Which," she added as she glanced back at where the twins had vanished, "is what I think you wished to know?"

He nodded slowly. Tried to imagine Nyx without Lux, or the opposite, and failed completely. It was impossible. "They slaughtered him, this other half of me," he said, his voice low and harsh.

"And thought it right," she agreed.

It is not right!

The exclamation echoed in his mind so loudly he almost shouted it aloud. And when he looked at her again and she nodded, he thought she had somehow heard it anyway.

"I must thank you," she said softly after a long, silent moment.

"Thank me?" he asked, startled, the only thing coming to his mind the kiss he still hadn't quite processed himself.

"That is the first time they have referred to me as their mother."

He studied her for a moment. "That is very important on your world."

"Yes." She turned her gaze back to him. "And for now at least, your world, too."

He didn't want it for now. He wanted it . . . forever. And that realization stunned him more than anything ever had. Except that kiss.

Perhaps it had been a fluke, an accident of timing. Perhaps it had just been building; perhaps he had ignored the need for too long. Perhaps if he took the break he was due and visited the nearest Legion Club—assuming he could overcome his dislike for the usage of collared slaves—this would be sated and go quiet again for another year or two.

"Are you wondering if it would be the same again?" she asked softly. He drew back sharply. She read the motion correctly. "I'm not reading your mind. Merely wondering the same myself."

"Then . . . we need proof."

"Of course we do," she said, and this time it was she who leaned forward and pressed her lips to his. And in the first instant, he had his proof. Heat billowed through him until he thought he must be shaking with the force of it.

He was lost in the surging sea of rippling sensation when a sound from above finally bored through it. A moment later his comm link crackled to life announcing the arrival of a ship from High Command.

Brakely's question was clear in his voice.

"No," he answered. "I am on my way." He snapped off the link.

"You did not expect this?" she asked.

"Using your powers again?" he asked.

"No," she said, sounding a bit surprised herself. Which left him with the even more unsettling thought that she read him so well without any inexplicable power necessary. But the most unsettling of all was the strange notion that that idea pleased him.

"I must go." He said it with regret. He got to his feet, sensed her watching him as he moved. "Your miracle holds," he said.

"I was not watching for that, although I am pleased." At his lifted brow she colored slightly. And he found that pleased him as well. "You move with such grace."

Something hot and urgent slammed through him. And he knew by the answering heat in her gaze that she felt it too. And he wished, he who had long ago discarded wishes as useless, ridiculous things, that they had time and privacy here and now to pursue what had sparked between them.

"Give me more," he said before he thought.

Her color deepened, and he realized his words could be interpreted more than one way. And then it hit him that he meant it in all ways.

But he had no time, not now.

"You said I need only ask."

He saw it register, knew she realized what he meant. And she nodded. He had expected her to touch his arm, as before, but instead she reached up and cupped his cheek, then slid a slender finger along his jaw line. For an instant he froze, remembering when she had rendered him unconscious for transport. But this was . . . was . . .

He felt as if he'd been hit by a blaster. Heat and chill, tightness and expansion, all impossibly gripped him at once. It was all he could do to breathe, and even that was coming raggedly. He stared down into those bottomless blue eyes, the eyes that had haunted him for so long, realizing that as vivid, as captivating as the painted version was, they were nothing to the original. The real woman of the painting was so, so much more. And he wanted nothing more than to spend the rest of his life—the life she had given back to him—searching out all the facets of her.

He had to look away. He could not function, could not deal with the reality of her at the same time as what she had given him. If this was truly what Ziemites felt all the time, he wondered that any still walked. And yet . . . he had never felt more alive. More now than when he'd first regained his feet, more even than when he'd first realized she truly had healed him completely.

He realized the twins were gathering the things they had brought. Except that as Lux picked up the pack, Nyx held out the stone to him. He took it and slipped it into a pocket. They had, he realized, known instinctively what he would wish to keep.

For a long moment the two just looked at him. Then Lux began it.

"You are not—"

"Like them—"

"You are—"

"Like us—"

"And you—"

"Should be—"

"With us."

His glance flicked to Iolana. "I bow to the wisdom of my children," she said quietly.

"You believe I should . . . turn traitor?"

"It is only treason if you would be betraying what you truly believe. Not what they have forced you to think."

He quoted the mantra almost instinctively. "*We brook neither rebellion nor failure. There is no way but the Coalition way, all else is treason. The penalty for treason is death, be it an individual or an entire planet.*"

"Is this truly what you believe?" she asked softly.

"It is . . . all I have," he said, hating the way that sounded, hating more that it was true.

"Not any longer. You have us."

He sucked in a deep, harsh breath. Held her gaze as he asked, "Does that 'us' include . . . you?"

She didn't flinch or look away. "I am as surprised—and fascinated—as you are at . . . what happened here today. So yes, Caze, it does."

And then they were gone, fading into the mist just as they had seemingly materialized out of it. He stood there for a long time, stunned all over again at how hard he had to fight not to follow.

Chapter 51

"SHE SAID—"

"We should—"

"Thank you for—"

"Letting us—"

"Go. So—"

"Thank you."

The twins chorused the last, and Iolana saw Drake's mouth twitch. Then her son looked at her. "It went well?"

"Yes. I think . . . he is closer than I dared hope."

Drake lifted a brow at her. "You know how impossible that seems."

"But have you not always sensed he is different?"

"Yes." He looked back at the twins. "As did they."

They both smiled proudly as she said, "And so they told him," she said, and explained what they'd said.

Drake's gaze shot back to her face. "And what was his reaction?"

She couldn't find the words for a moment, but it didn't matter because the twins stepped in.

"He wanted to know—"

"If being with us—"

"Would include—"

"Our mother."

And again she felt that joy flood her at the simple acknowledgment of her status with them. And she saw in her son's eyes that he'd recognized the huge step the twins had taken.

"We think—"

"He wants—"

"To kiss her—"

"Again."

They said it lightly, casually, but she flushed anyway. *And such is the price for their acknowledgment.*

She was embarrassed enough that it took her a moment to realize that Drake was looking at her not with surprise, but with the expression of one who has had a suspicion confirmed. Kye, she supposed. She was not one to hide things from her mate, nor would Iolana ask her to. And in fact it made this easier.

"I believe Eirlys could use your help in the sanctuary," he said to the twins. "Enish Eck's snake is acting rather sickly."

They darted out without another word. And Iolana braced herself for an explanation she was not sure she could give, for she was not sure she understood it all herself.

"Leave it to you," Drake said dryly, "to choose the most complicated man in the quadrant."

"It seems to be my wont," she said with a sigh. She hesitated, for this was her—and Torstan's—son. "You know no one will ever hold the part of my heart I gave to your father."

"I know that you loved him so much that you very nearly followed him into death." He reached out, put a hand on her shoulder. "I am glad you did not. But it was long ago, in both time and . . . history."

"Indeed."

"What you feel for him . . . does he feel it for you?"

"I think he is yet too stunned to fully realize what he feels. For feeling anything at all is a new experience for him."

"And so he leaps into the most complicated feeling of all," Drake said in that same wry tone. "With the most complicated woman on Ziem."

She had not thought of it in quite that way—she was still a little stunned herself—and her embarrassment faded and she smiled.

"It seems very like him, does it not?"

"Yes," Drake said. But then he became very serious, and she knew it was the Raider who spoke next. "Do you truly believe he will turn? Will this unbalance the scales enough?"

She knew he did not mean to be callous. It was simply that the Raider had no choice but to look at things, even things like this, in a tactical manner. So she considered her words carefully before she spoke.

"I would not be so vain as to think I alone could change a lifetime of conditioning. But he was already well upon this path, I think, before we ever actually met." She looked steadily at this man she had borne. "And I think the Raider began the process years ago."

Drake smiled, clearly pleased at her words, but said only, "He has never had to walk among the people he conquered before. I think he only needed that to see the truth about his masters."

"And I would not call them his masters any longer. I sensed today that in his mind, he is almost completely separated from them." She smiled widely. "And I think we must thank the twins for that in large part."

"They have ever fascinated him." Drake gave her a questioning look. "Does he now believe what you told him?"

"Yes. He found enough of his kind of proof to believe."

"Then he knows you did not lie."

"Yes."

Drake was silent for a moment before saying, his voice quiet, "If he does not make the decision we hope for, and this ends badly for him . . . what will you do?"

"I do not know," she said, holding her son's gaze, "but I do know what I will not do. The top of Halfhead will not be seeing me again, unless it is to fight."

Drake let out a clearly relieved breath. And Iolana Davorin marveled again at the nature of her people—and her children—that even her most foolish of actions could be forgiven.

PALEDAN CALCULATED the time in his mind as he went, decided he would be better served to return directly to his office than try to make it to the landing zone; whatever official contingent had been sent—for whatever unexpected reason—would have gone before he arrived.

He would have to come up with some reason he had not yet sent the report on the damaged cannon emplacements, for if they had taken the normal flight path they would have passed right over the one in the worst shape. Then again, the mist was thicker there, and they might not have been able to see at all.

Or might have been so consumed by their own glory they didn't notice.

He grimaced at his thought as he hurried—glorying with every step he took without pain—back to the compound. Which itself looked much better than it had; most of the debris had been cleared away, and the fragments of wall knocked down so that it almost looked like a whole building again, albeit a smaller one.

When he reached the back door he'd left through, the sentry snapped to attention and saluted. Paledan threw him one back but kept going. It wasn't until he reached the hallway where his office was situated that things changed. The two sentries normally stationed at each end of the hall passed him at a run, casting rather wild, terrified glances at him as they ran.

An unaccustomed jab of . . . something went through him. He quickly decided he would deal with that later; right now the High Command troops lined up outside his door were of more concern. Well-trained—or conditioned by Coalition harshness—those troopers never even looked at him as he passed, just stood with weapons at the ready, as if they were expecting an attack.

Another strange jab. He realized he should have asked Lana to explain what all these . . . emotions were before he had so blithely asked her for them.

He reached the doorway to his office. He felt the lingering crackle in the air that told him a blaster had been fired. He turned into the anteroom outside his door. Brakely was not at his desk, but next to it stood General Fidez and two flanking troopers. Fidez was holstering his own sidearm.

The general turned to look at him. There was an expression on his face Paledan could not put a name to, but it turned his stomach.

"Paledan," Fidez said flatly.

No rank. Not a hint of a salute, or even a nod. "General," he said neutrally.

"You will be returning to High Command with me."

Paledan managed not to react, but it was an effort. Much more than it would have taken before. Because now he was rebelling inside. He did not want to leave this mist-shrouded place. Which told him just how far he'd fallen under the spell of Ziem.

And her Spirit.

He waited, the general's expression telling him he would not be adding a new medal to the collection.

Fidez broke first. "You have obviously lost control here, Paledan. I see that you were correct when you said you were not suited to an administrative post. Or perhaps it is this accursed place, and this bedamned mist has adversely affected you. Either way, you have much to answer for."

So. It was to be execution. His gut roiled. Less than a moon's cycle ago he would have almost welcomed that. But now . . .

"Not the least of which," Fidez said, "is the blatant audacity of your aide. Were you aware he actually had the impudence to search Coalition records? To call up files outside his purview? And had no excuse for it? Refused to speak of it, even when given a direct order? From *me!*"

Paledan felt a sudden chill ripple down his spine. Remembered that unmistakable tingle he'd felt before he'd even stepped through the doorway. And the image of Fidez holstering his weapon played back in his head.

"What have you done?" he asked, his voice harsh.

Even as he asked it, he took a stride forward. To where he could see behind Brakely's desk. Could see the sprawled, lifeless figure on the floor.

The man who had been his right hand had proven his loyalty.

Unto death.

Chapter 52

IOLANA FELT THE burst of sensation as if it had originated within herself. She gave a little gasp, and both Eirlys and Brander turned to look at her. They were in the sanctuary for the animals which was, to Eirlys's great satisfaction, nearly empty at the moment.

"What is it?" Eirlys asked.

"Something has happened," she said, barely aware of how tremulous her voice sounded.

"What?" Brander asked.

"I do not know, I—" She put fingers to her head, trying to sort it out.

"Have they done something?" Eirlys asked anxiously. "That ship with the High Command symbol that arrived?"

Iolana shook her head in negation. "I only know he . . . Caze . . . is enraged."

Brander looked at her curiously. "He has seemed ever controlled."

She lifted her gaze to them then. "When we parted, he . . . asked for more. Of the emotions I had given him before."

"So," Eirlys said slowly, "what would not have enraged him before could now?"

"I think it is beyond even that. This is so . . . fierce, I think he would have felt a form of it even without."

"Drake will want to know of this," Brander said. "And I think a trek to Zelos would be wise, to see what I can find out."

Iolana sensed Eirlys's tension as they went to the main cavern and Drake's quarters, but her daughter said nothing. She knew Brander had the most freedom to move about the city, but that didn't mean she had to like it when he ventured there.

They had just explained when Kade burst into the room. This alone was unusual enough that they all fell silent, looking at the usually diffident boy. Young man, Iolana corrected her own thought, for no one stayed young long when locked in a battle for the life of your very world.

"They're everywhere! Coalition troopers, a hundred of them must have come in on that High Command ship!"

Drake, who had been leaning against the map table, straightened. Kade had been on watch at the high lookout. "Everywhere?"

"They're at the compound, and the landing zone, of course, but they must have brought a fleet of rovers with them. They're at the old ruins, and some are going beyond that up the Sentinel, others up the Brother, and I saw some headed for Highridge."

"What could have happened?" Eirlys said, looking from her mate to her brother.

Drake looked at Iolana. "I think it too coincidental to believe this has nothing to do with what you sensed from Paledan."

"Agreed," she said. "And his anger is growing, not abating."

"I did not see him," Kade said. "But there is more. The river, they have boats, and they're going both directions from the port."

Drake went impossibly still. "Both directions?"

Kade nodded. "I hope they go all the way and go over the falls."

"I pray they do not," Drake said grimly, "for the twins are there."

Iolana gasped. "At the falls?"

Her son nodded. "They wished to see if they could find a bigger secret stone." And then, his voice softer, he added, "For you."

Emotion roiled within her. That this gesture of acceptance from her two youngest should put them in danger . . .

"They have Runner," Brander said, referring to the graybird messenger who adored him and would fly to him no matter where he was. "It was the only way we would allow them to range so far, even if the Coalition never ventures there."

"But they might not have had a chance to free her, if the Coalition came upon them unexpectedly," Eirlys said, sounding beyond troubled.

"I'll go get them," Brander said, turning to go at once.

"Then I'm with you," Eirlys said instantly.

Drake started to protest, but Brander cut him off. "You cannot, Drake. I know it is your instinct, but we need a quiet reconnaissance first, and you can hardly do that. You would be shot on sight."

"He is right," Iolana said. "I will go with them." The ache in her heart was growing. That the twins had gone to get something for her, after she had merely mentioned the secret stones were one of her favorite things, tore at her.

"If we have to go after them in force, I may need you," Drake said to her reluctantly.

She was silent for a long moment as a battle of sorts waged within her, the need to go to the twins, who had at last accepted her as their own, with the bigger knowledge that her particular skills might in fact help save them were the worst to happen. She saw in her son's Ziem-blue eyes that this was the kind of battle he had been waging for years.

And, she thought in sudden realization, it was a variation on the inner battle Caze was fighting now.

"I may be able to help avoid that need," she said. "I will take the Stone of Ziem with me."

They all knew how the legendary stone magnified her powers. Drake let out a long breath, but finally nodded. "Eirlys, take one of your other birds."

She nodded. "We'll send word if we can."

"You have flares, in case you cannot?" Drake asked. Brander nodded. Drake looked at his second for a long moment. "You may not be able to hold your façade through this."

"So be it," Brander said. "I won't miss it."

Drake nodded, and Iolana knew no one understood better than Drake the cost of maintaining a false front in a dangerous world.

"I will ready a force, then," Drake said. "In case it is needed."

Iolana felt compelled to say then, "The major is as close as he has ever been to breaking. He may have already. That may be what I sensed."

Drake glanced at Brander, who nodded. But it was Eirlys who said softly, "We will not hurt him, unless he gives us no choice."

As they left, Iolana wondered if all the Sentinels knew what the foolish Spirit had done, that she had fallen for the enemy.

THE HIGH COUNCIL wishes to hear your explanation.

Fidez's words echoed in Paledan's head, and caused a sour, inward laugh that echoed the sour feeling in his stomach.

He had, he realized, chosen the worst possible time to ask Lana to gift him—or curse him—with more of those emotions she'd said he already had the capacity for. Emotions that men, like the four escorting him, had had stomped out of them. For he had never felt such fury, and every thought of Marl Brakely's fate prodded it higher.

He violated strict Coalition regulations.

He did so on my order!

Then why did he not say so? It would have saved him.

Because he was loyal to me, not the Coalition. And it cost him his life. Just as being loyal to his commander had cost his uncle. Which made it even more incredible that Marl had trusted him at all.

The knowledge was a piercing, throbbing ache within him. The image of his aide's lifeless body, his life terminated because he had refused to betray him, would torture him forever.

He saw knots of his own men watching curiously as he and his escorts passed. Word of his arrest—for that's what it was, despite all Fidez's fine words to the contrary—had not yet spread, then. And an idea began to take root.

Sedition, treason, betrayal . . .

And yet . . .

The streets of Zelos were deserted. He couldn't keep from looking toward the ruin of the old taproom as they neared it. And found himself wondering what the Raider would do right now.

He would not go tamely. Of that I am certain. It was only Jakel's hold on his sister that had forced his hand that day.

And he had no one to be used as leverage.

An image flashed into his mind, of a flame-haired woman with a gentle touch yet a fierce mind.

They would never be able to hold her, and they would never understand why.

It was a moment before he realized what he had just admitted, that there truly was someone who could be leverage to be used against him. It was an odd feeling, yet a good one, bolstered by the fact that they did not know.

They. Ever and always they. She is right; you no longer think of yourself as one of them.

Then what was he? His identity, his very self, had been tied up with the Coalition his entire life. If that was taken away—no, if he was to be honest, if he threw that away—what would be left? What would he be? Adrift? Lost? Purposeless?

If you were able to break free of the shackles . . .

Her voice—that lovely, deep, husky voice—echoed in his mind.

So you are open to changing your mind.

When not doing so becomes the impossibility, yes.

They came up to the barren spot where the taproom had once stood.

Where he had first seen the painting that had changed his life, changed him. He had the odd thought that the last time he had been here, he had still carried that shard of planium in his back. The crippling piece of metal that had constrained him on all levels, limited his very thoughts. And now it was gone, now he was himself again, but he was likely on his way to his death anyway.

He realized his pace had slowed as his mind wrestled with tangled thoughts. The four troopers automatically slowed with him, but the leader turned to look at him.

And in that moment he realized his decision was already made.

And what better place than here?

He dropped into a crouch. Grabbed the leader's weapon and pulled. The blaster fired as the man's hand contracted automatically. The blast caught one of the rear guards. In the same instant Paledan spun and caught the other front man in the gut with a powerful kick. He went him sprawling. He sent his elbow sharply into the leader's throat as the man grabbed at him. He reeled back. Paledan wrenched the blaster free and turned it on him. Fired. The man went down hard. The second front guard was getting up, raising his weapon. The other rear guard was staring at his fallen comrade. Paledan fired at the bigger threat, then spun back and put the last one down.

He stood there for a moment, glorying in the fact that he had been able to do it without a twinge of pain. In fact, in being able to do it at all, he'd wondered if the year of living so carefully had erased the advantage of intense training and fitness he'd always had before.

He glanced down at the blaster, saw it had been set to stunning force only. So they had not wanted to risk killing him before Fidez dragged him back before High Command.

Marl had not even been given that formality.

Fury boiled up in him again. The fury that had made him forget one very basic thing.

Now what?

He glanced at the sprawled troopers, realized he'd best be long gone before they roused. He gathered their weapons then moved through the ruin toward the narrow lane that had run behind the taproom. He needed to assess first, then decide. He worked his way toward the river, knowing he would be able to see across to the landing zone from there.

When he cleared the last pile of rubble that had once been a riverfront building, he could see the hulk of the High Command ship. It was one of the largest, designed to ferry equipment as well as troops. Rovers, fighters, it had the capacity for a sizeable number of each.

He kept going, although he was still not certain what he was going to do. He reached the bridge across the Racelock, on the road to the landing zone. The bridge where he had encountered Lana for the first time, where she had merely brushed him and set up such chaos within him that he thought he'd been ill. He realized now, now that she had unleashed these things within him, now that he felt what she had sworn Ziemites felt every day, that she had not lied. What she had given him that day here on this bridge had been merely a faint touch of the totality of emotions.

He glanced down at the fast-flowing river as he crossed. Fidez had come prepared, for there was a small Coalition vessel just arriving on the landing zone side of the river. They had apparently already begun patrolling the banks of the Racelock. He wished them luck; this river was nothing to take lightly. And the Raider and his band had rather thoroughly destroyed the docks in one of their raids, so they were working with temporary structures that were questionable at best.

He shifted his gaze back to the High Command ship. And then he heard something that snapped his head around. Voices, loud ones, protesting. He stared back at the river, at the troopers now wrestling with something on the boat.

His breath jammed up in his throat.

Not something. Someone.

Two someones.

The twins.

Chapter 53

IOLANA STARED AT Pryl. "You're certain?"

The old man looked at her grimly and nodded. "The boat beached there," he gestured toward the river, then pointed at the shallows they stood beside, "and they struggled there."

She could see the marks in the mud at the edge of the water. In these last few yards before the falls, the river split around a large boulder, and the smaller stream slowed in a bend and created this place where it was possible to find all sorts of things washed down from above. Including the secret stones the twins had been looking for.

For her.

She forced down the horror, the pain. She would do her children no good by falling apart now.

"But who would do this?" Eirlys asked.

"No Ziemite would lay a hand on them," Brander said grimly.

"Truth," Pryl said, sounding equally grim.

Iolana closed her eyes, reached out. Caze came to her first, his anger still high, but now different somehow. As if something had greatly changed within him. She couldn't take the time to dwell on it long enough to read further; she was reaching for her children, for the two who had finally accepted her after resisting for so long.

Her eyes snapped open. "They are afraid."

All eyes turned to her, for all of them knew what it would take to put fear into two who were known for being fearless.

"They have them," Eirlys whispered.

IT WAS THE ONLY thing he could think of. But it depended on so much that was outside his control he felt beyond edgy. This was a tactic more suited to the Raider.

So think like him. He carried on an impossible charade for years; surely you can do it for a few minutes.

He strode over the last few feet to the dock. "Halt."

The two troopers turned. He glanced at the twins, enough to see the fear in their eyes. The sight did strange things to him, but then, as the fear was replaced with a trace of their old daring and he realized it was because of him, the strangest feeling of all flooded him. They would not be hurt. He would not allow it. He gave a barely perceptible shake of his head, hoping they would understand they needed to stay quiet and still.

"Major?" one of the troopers said, sounding both puzzled and nervous.

"Release them."

"But we found them outside the perimeter, which is not allowed."

He looked at the two coolly, thinking as he did that if the Raider managed this while under such an onslaught of emotion, he was an even stronger man than he'd realized. "You question me?"

The two in uniform exchanged glances. The one who had not yet spoken then did, saying carefully, "We heard rumors that you were being recalled, sir."

"And why do you think?" He gestured at the twins. "The general has sent me for them. I am to escort them to High Command where they will be turned over for examination and testing." The two troopers looked at the children, then at him, blankly. "They are twins," Paledan said.

The two men jumped back, releasing the two as if burned. As if the defect were contagious. Paledan saw Nyx straighten the small pack that slid from his shoulder, the same pack they had filled with the carefully chosen gifts they had brought him. Paledan turned his gaze from their guards as if they no longer mattered. As he once would have.

"You two will come with me," he ordered. "And you will stay close." He saw them go still, perhaps at his tone of command. He held their gaze, trying to communicate the truth behind the words. "We'll soon have you exactly where you belong."

He knew how the guards would interpret what he said, for they were from Lustros. He knew this because all of the High Command troops hailed from the planet of origin. Others were allowed elsewhere, but not at the center of power.

For a moment they simply looked up at him. Then they glanced at each other for merely an instant. When they looked back at him, the trust in their eyes nearly put him on his knees.

"You'd best have your blaster at the ready, sir," one of the guards said. "They're a troublesome pair."

"Of that I am sure," Paledan said, and it was a struggle to keep from grinning at them. As Lana had once told him, he obviously had a great deal to learn.

He did keep his hand on the blaster as he guided the twins away, but what he watched for was not any antics from them.

"We do not have long," he said to them under his breath. "They will be searching soon." As soon as his escorts regained consciousness. And it would not take them long to couple that with his appearance at the landing zone. "We dare not stay in Zelos."

"We can—"

"Go back—"

"To where—"

"We were at—"

"The falls."

He blinked. "The falls?"

"Where the—"

"River goes—"

"Over the edge."

"I can't think of a more appropriate place," he muttered dryly. "And how do you suggest we get there? I don't think going back and stealing their motored boat wise."

"We won't—"

"Have to. We are—"

"Going the—"

"Other way."

"We will—"

"Borrow one and—"

"The river will—"

"Do the rest."

He lifted a brow at them. "Including sending us over the edge?"

"That would—"

"Be silly. We will—"

"Stop before—"

"We get there."

He barely stifled a smile. They looked back at him, grinning.

"You were—"

"Joking!"

The duo led the way out of Zelos along the bank of the Racelock. As they went, Nyx looked back at him.

"Is it true?"

"What?" Paledan asked.

"You have been—"

"Recalled?" Lux finished.

"Not exactly," he said with a grimace.

"Then what?"

"They are . . . not happy with me."

"But you are a hero."

He shook his head. "Not to them. Not anymore."

The twins exchanged a glance, and when they looked back at him there was utter delight in their expressions. "What?" he asked, his brow furrowing at their obvious glee.

"You have—"

"Done it!"

"You are—"

"You, and they—"

"Are they."

He wondered if it was a sign of how far down this careening path of emotion and feeling he'd already gone that this made complete sense to him.

By the time they were clambering aboard a small wooden boat that seemed to him more raft than vessel, the two were chattering quite like themselves, their narrow escape apparently no longer of concern. He only half listened, for he was still trying to deal with the newness of all these tangled feelings, uppermost at the moment the complete and utter trust of these two who on his world would not have been allowed to exist.

As his own twin had not been allowed to exist.

He shook off the thought, knowing it could well overwhelm him, so unused was he to these feelings. And this was not the time to become lost in a maelstrom of thoughts, not when they could easily become lost in an actual maelstrom upon this river.

But the twins seemed to handle the questionable vessel easily enough, as if they had done this before. He wondered who, here in this place where individuals still claimed property despite the edict that all belonged to the Coalition, claimed this shaky craft.

"Whose . . . boat is this?"

"Enish Eck's," Lux said.

"The man of the two-headed snake?"

They looked pleased that he'd remembered. "Yes. He will—"

"Not mind."

"Or rather—"

"He will, but—"

"He will—"

"Get over it."

This time he couldn't stop the smile. And the smile they gave him back only widened his own.

He became aware that the flow of the river had quickened in the same moment a distant roar registered. And he felt a qualm; he'd only observed the falls from the air, on a flyover inspection, but they had seemed fierce enough that he understood why High Command had classified the river as unnavigable beyond the bend east of the landing zone. If you got caught in this rush and went over . . .

But in the moment he thought it, the twins moved, using the wooden paddles to steer the boat to the side opposite the port. For a moment he thought they were headed straight for a large boulder that jutted up out of the water, but then he saw that a thread of the river veered around the other side. They slowed the moment they were out of the main force of the flow, and the twins beached the little craft with surprising efficiency. Although why anything about these two yet surprised him he did not know.

"This is where they picked you up?" Two synchronous nods. "We should get out of sight. In case they come back."

They. Always they. The twins were right; he had completely separated himself from the entity that had once been his entire life.

They reached the trees that ringed the curved shore where the calmer, separate stream slowed lazily, with the fierce flow of the river visible beyond. Nyx set down the pack, and Lux immediately reached into it. When the girl drew out a small cage containing a bird the likes of which he had seen frequently on his reconnaissance walks, he frowned in puzzlement. He glanced at Nyx, who had pulled out of a side pocket of the pack what appeared to be a tiny fragment of paper and a writing instrument of some kind. The boy wrote something on the paper, then rolled it up into a tiny tube. His frown deepened, until his sister held up the bird she'd freed from the cage, and the boy slid the paper into a small tube fastened to the bird's right leg.

It hit him abruptly. He stared, almost unbelieving as Lux held the bird to her cheek and whispered something that sounded like "Go to him, little one." Then she opened her fingers and lifted; in the same moment the little bird's wings unfurled, and it took flight.

"That's how?" he whispered incredulously. "That's how you communicate, why we could never figure that out, no matter that we monitored every possible airwave?"

If they noticed he'd slipped back into "we," for he did take this one failure a bit personally, they did not react. Nyx shrugged and began it. "Except the—"

"Simplest."

"Our sister says—"

"The simple creatures—"

"Are beneath—"

"Their notice."

"And she is right. Once again Coalition arrogance has cost them."

Lux nodded, but Nyx was already on to something else, and darted away into the trees. Were it anyone else he would have questioned it, but he knew the boy would not desert his sister, and so he simply waited. And the boy was back in just a few moments, a wrapped package in his hands.

"I knew they did not find it!" he said triumphantly.

"Good. I am hungry," Lux said.

The package turned out to be an array of foods, some he recognized, some he did not. The twins looked at him.

"We will—"

"Share. You are—"

"One of us—"

"Now."

What he felt at the simple declaration outweighed even what he'd felt when they'd pinned the Legion Cross, the highest award the Coalition could bestow, on him.

And he supposed it was yet another measure of how much he'd changed in such a short time that this mattered more.

Chapter 54

"THEY WOULDN'T HAVE sent the message if they weren't safe, you know that."

Iolana nodded but didn't look at Brander when he spoke.

"They would have passed Runner off as merely a pet," Eirlys said. "They have always known to do this."

Again she nodded, but kept staring at the small curl of paper.

At falls. Caze saved.

Caze. He had done it yet again.

"They call him Caze," she said, almost to herself. "He has ever been the major to them."

She heard someone take a quick breath. Eirlys. She looked up as her daughter pushed her heavy, golden braid back over her shoulder. "You think . . . he has turned?"

"I think they believe he has," she said, not daring to agree even though she felt it in every beat of her pulse. "And it explains what I've sensed."

Runner, perched on her beloved Brander's shoulder, let out a quiet warble of sound. An instant later a second, lighter-colored graybird came out of the mist, circled once, then went straight to Eirlys. She gave the bird a welcoming stroke as she freed the message it carried.

"Drake," she said. "There is bedlam in Zelos. He says to avoid it if we can. They are searching madly."

"For the twins?" Brander wondered aloud.

"Or a traitor," Iolana said softly.

"You do believe it, then." Brander's words were not a question.

"Are we going to discuss this until their searching reaches the falls?" Pryl asked pointedly, then turned and started moving through the trees.

"Contention valid," Brander said briskly and started after him.

Eirlys lingered for a moment, and Iolana felt her gaze. She looked up to meet her daughter's eyes.

"I hope it is true," Eirlys said softly. "For your sake."

Iolana's breath caught. "Your father," she began, but stopped when her daughter shook her head.

"I have learned a great deal about what it is to truly love. And more about what it is to love a hero. Both pay a price, and you and my father paid the ultimate one. If you can find comfort now, after all this time, I would never begrudge it."

The way it came out made Iolana think it had been practiced, but there was no doubting the sincerity in Eirlys's voice and eyes.

"I thank you, my daughter, more than you can know."

Eirlys smiled at her, and it brought the brightness of sun season to her. "Let's not let those two get too far ahead of us. You know how they'll mock us."

The small force made their way through the mist and trees quickly, quietly. When they reached the point at which they could see the characteristic swirl of mist rising that told them they were nearing the river, they stopped and let Pryl creep ahead. None of the three remaining beyond spoke, and the long minutes spun out tensely.

When he came back, he was sliding his spotting glass back into his pack. He looked at Iolana. "They're there. The three of them. They did well; they're in the trees in a spot I might have missed if I'd not known of it already. No sign anyone's yet found them."

Iolana let out a long, relieved breath. "They're all right?"

"Like miscreants on a picnic," the old woodsman said with one of his rare smiles. And then, with one of the most direct looks the man had ever given her, he added, "And there's something different about Paledan. I could see it even in the way he held himself. He's still alert, aware, and no less dangerous, I fear, but still . . . different."

"Thank you, Garnon," she said, putting a hand on his arm. The old man flushed, but smiled. Whether at her use of his given name or the tiny rush of genuine gratitude she sent through the touch, she did not know.

They edged forward, slowly, quietly. And then she could see the river, the narrow, slower current closer in, and the curve of the shallows where they had seen the signs of the twins' kidnapping. Pryl led them through the trees, along the edge of the muddy bank, until they reached the side where they could look back up the river. Where they could see anyone approaching from the river. Caze must have chosen the spot.

And then she could see them through the branches, and although they were still too far to hear, she could tell the twins were laughing, delightedly. Caze was looking at them seriously, but even from here she could see what Pryl had meant. He had changed. She could sense he was holding back amusement at them, but overlaying it all was something else, something darker, something . . . painful.

Iolana held up an arm, and the others stopped. She supposed the others thought she was being cautious, making certain this was not a trap—for it would do the twins no good if their rescuers were captured along with them— but she already knew Pryl had been right; there was no one else around. And because of that, she allowed herself this stolen moment just to watch them, these two children who had made her work so hard to earn their trust and acceptance, and the man who, in his own way, had been an even more difficult battle. Difficult because a different part of her heart, a part she never expected to hear from again, had awoken to him.

"You could probably stay back and out of sight," Eirlys said to Brander.

"If your mother is right, it will not matter if he sees me. If she is not, if this is an elaborate trap, his fate is sealed anyway."

"It is not," Iolana said, hoping her certainty sprang from her Ziem senses and not the hopes of that newly reawakened part of her heart.

"In that case, a bit of warning would be in order," Pryl suggested. "He's still armed, and a warrior."

"He will ever be a warrior," Iolana said. But she nodded at Eirlys, who was the best at imitating the long-extinct trill.

"Then may he now be ours," her daughter answered, squeezing Iolana's hand. She thought she might burst from the joy of it, her family regained.

And almost—almost—complete.

She turned her gaze back to the man who watched over her other children. *Caze saved.*

And she wondered if that pain she sensed from him had been the price he had paid to do it.

BOTH TWINS TURNED their head at the odd, up-and-down tremolo of a bird's call, one he had occasionally heard before. They had already been smiling, but now the smiles widened and they started to get to their feet, Nyx stopping only to roll up the cloth the food had been wrapped in.

"They're here," Lux explained at his questioning look.

His gaze flicked in the direction the sound had come from. "That wasn't a bird, was it?" he asked, already knowing the answer.

"No. Trills have been—"

"Gone from Ziem—"

"For an age, but—"

"Their call is—"

"Easy to make."

He couldn't stop the upward curve of one corner of his mouth, or the slight chuckle of wonder. If the Coalition knew the scope of what these people had achieved with such simple tools and ruses, they would . . . refuse to believe it. Just as they had refused to believe that twins were not abnormal, but instead a wealth of potential.

He turned to face the direction the twins were looking, his hand on one of the blasters as a precaution. If by some slim chance those who approached were Coalition, they would likely blast him on sight. If he engaged them, it would give the twins time to run. It was unlikely troopers would have come this way, through the trees, but he had not survived this long on assumptions. They could—

All thought was blasted out of his mind as a woman with flaming-red hair stepped out of the mist. It swirled around her as if it had created her, which at the moment seemed no less fanciful than everything else he'd had to learn to accept on this strange planet. His fingers curled up and away from the weapon, instinctively.

She smiled at him, in a way that reminded him of the day they'd kissed, the day he'd carried, emblazoned in his mind ever since. He was only vaguely aware she wasn't alone. On the edge of his vision he saw another woman. The other daughter, he thought, barely registering the golden hair.

But then someone else strode out of the mist. A tall, rangy man with a small, gray bird perched on his shoulder, rubbing its head against his neck. The bird the twins had released less than an hour ago.

Kalon.

"I should have known," Paledan said as Kalon stopped in front of him, a crooked grin on his face. "It never did make sense that you would not be one of them."

"And yet you let me continue the façade," Kalon said, sounding more relaxed than he'd ever heard him. Only now that it was gone did he see that under all the insouciance had been an undercurrent of tension.

"I did not wish to believe you were with them," he admitted.

Kalon looked puzzled, but Lana said in understanding, "Because then you would be forced to do something about it."

He didn't deny it. Not only was it pointless, he would not lie, not to her.

The twins had apparently been silent as long as they could, and erupted into their half-sentence staccato, telling them what had happened since the troopers had caught them.

"How . . . fortuitous that you were there," the younger woman said, her voice holding a tinge of suspicion.

"What is it, Caze?" Iolana asked softly. "Something has changed."

"Many things have changed," he said, not caring that his tone betrayed his bitterness.

"But something . . . awful has happened. I can feel it."

He hadn't thought about sharing this, but now realized that they would need to understand. "My . . . aide searched some Coalition files, to confirm what you had told me." His gaze flicked to the twins, then back to her. "About . . . what I am. Or was."

"I knew you must have found some material proof," she said, not looking at all offended that he had been unable to simply take her word.

"They . . ." His jaw tightened as he fought a welling up of a sensation he neither recognized nor could put a name to. He tried again. "They slaughtered him for it."

Lana paled slightly, and he heard a quick intake of breath from someone else. The daughter, he thought.

"Brakely?" Kalon asked, his voice sounding tight.

"Yes."

"What happened to 'I was following orders?' Isn't that the usual out for the lower ranks?" Kalon asked, in that same tone.

Paledan shifted his gaze to his one-time chaser opponent. "He refused to tell them that I had asked him to do it."

"Then I had his measure right," Kalon said. "Loyal to you, not them."

"And it cost him his life." He didn't even try to mask the bitterness this time. "They blasted him for merely accessing files above his level."

"I am sorry, Major. He seemed like a good man, despite the uniform he wore."

"He was." His mouth twisted. "And you can drop the rank, Kalon. It no longer applies. I had no desire to return to High Command for a trial whose outcome is already set."

"Caze . . . it is you they look so desperately for," Lana said.

It amazed him how much that simple use of his name, and the touch of anxiety in her voice, eased the billowing inside him. He looked back at her, every newly granted emotion she'd given him shifting now, focusing. And he could not help the upward quirk of one side of his mouth.

"I'm certain they are. I left four of them lying in the dust of your son's former taproom."

A sharp bark of laughter made him glance at the older man who had remained silent until now. "Only four?"

Paledan shrugged. "I believe since they had disarmed me, they thought me helpless."

"Deserved what they got, then," the old man said.

From Lana's smile and Kalon's lifted brow, he gathered that this was the highest of praise from the old man.

"We had best beware, then," the golden-haired woman said rather dryly, "for there are only four of us."

He shifted his gaze to her. And again had trouble suppressing a smile. "But I understand you have all the creatures of this place at your command. I'm sure a swarm of—" he glanced at the twins, who were watching raptly "—buzzers would do the job."

They grinned at him. And he smiled back. Then he looked back at Lana.

"Those four guards had no chance of holding me. You do."

"With Ziem's help, I could hold you," she agreed, and there was an undertone in her voice that made him think of all the ways those words could be taken. And a fire as fierce as the flame of her hair licked to life anew inside him. "But caging a wild thing is no mercy," she said. "It must stay by its own choice. Have you made that choice, Caze?"

He held her gaze, that uncanny, bottomless blue gaze. And at last said what he knew had been hovering since the first time he'd set eyes upon a portrait hanging on a taproom wall.

"I have."

Chapter 55

IOLANA FELT HER heart leap, for she read in those two simple words everything behind them. She sensed rather than saw Pryl turn, lift a hand to hold them all in place, then head down toward the water. But she spared it only an instant, for what she saw in Caze's green eyes was overwhelming her.

"Drake will be glad," she whispered, "for he did not wish to fight you."

"Will you?"

She didn't speak, in fact could not, her throat was so tight. So instead she reached out and touched his hand, sent him what she could not say. His eyes widened, and she saw him draw in a deep breath. For an instant his eyes closed, and she wondered if she had sent too much. But then they opened again, and everything she could ever have wished to see in the green depths was there.

"I see you were right." It was Eirlys, speaking rather bemusedly. Iolana glanced at her daughter, saw her looking up at Brander, who only shrugged. But he was grinning.

"Can we—"

"Talk now?"

Iolana looked at the twins. "You have been remarkably quiet."

"This is—"

"Because this—"

"Was important."

"But now that—"

"He is—"

"One of us—"

"We can—"

"See him—"

"Anytime—"

"Can't we?"

"More importantly," Brander said dryly, "you won't have to sneak down to the compound to do it."

Iolana saw Caze's eyes flick to Brander. "You knew that they did this?"

"We knew."

v"And yet . . . you let them?"

"We trusted you," Iolana said quietly.

"Why?" he asked, sounding bewildered. She wondered how he was doing with what had to be never-before-experienced feelings. "I am—I was—a Coalition officer."

"But now—" Lux began, clearly impatient to get their question answered.

"You are not." Nyx finished it, but his brow furrowed. "But," he began, glancing at his sister. It took only a moment for her eyes to widen. And then she looked at Caze.

"You are—"

"Not the—"

"Major anymore."

"So what are—"

"We to call you?"

She thought her heart would overflow when the one-time most celebrated hero of the mighty Coalition dropped down to crouch before two children.

"I think," he said, "I would like it very much if you would use my name, as your mother does."

They grinned happily. "We already—"

"Did in—"

"Our note."

"Then we are agreed," Caze said, and straightened.

"Drake will want to speak to you," Brander said, almost warningly. "Probably at great length."

Caze looked at the man who had faced him across a chaser table so often. "He would not be the leader I think him if he did not."

"What would you do, if the situation were reversed?" Eirlys asked, with genuine curiosity in her voice.

"What I would do now, I find is vastly different than what I would have done when I first arrived here. Perhaps even different than what I would have done this morning." His countenance darkened, and Iolana knew he was thinking of the man who had died simply for fulfilling a request. A request for information Caze had every right—more than anyone—to know. "But in your brother's place, I would make very sure of both my certainty and intent. Whatever and however long that took."

"But you," Iolana said softly, "went with your instincts with the twins."

He looked startled, as if he'd never thought of it in quite that way before. "That was . . . different."

"Because some part of you already sensed the truth," she said.

He shook his head. "No." Then he met her gaze. "Yes." He let out a breath that sounded weary, almost broken. "I do not know any longer."

Iolana saw Eirlys move slightly. "Then you need time to think it all through," her daughter said, and for the first time her tone was gentle, kind. A glance at her face told Iolana that Eirlys was responding as she ever did to a creature in distress, and in that moment she was as proud of her daughter as she had ever been.

"Not going to have that time right now." Pryl's voice came in the instant before the man stepped out of the mist. He looked at Caze. "They're coming."

PALEDAN'S GAZE shot to the old man. The deference the others showed the man told him much of the esteem they held him in. And he knew enough of the Sentinels to know this would not be granted without cause. So in an instant he accepted the assessment.

"How many?"

"As many as those two little boats of theirs will hold."

"Thirty, then," he said grimly. Against the five of them, with the twins to protect? He didn't even stumble over the "them" this time, for he had cast his lot, and he would not change now. "How far out?"

"They're going slow, afraid of the falls I'd guess. But they'll be here before we finish arguing about it if we don't get moving."

"You must go," he said.

"*We* must go," Lana corrected.

Slowly, reluctantly, he shook his head. "If they find me, they will not continue to look for the twins. They do not see them as that important." He glanced at the two, who were wide-eyed now. "Which makes them the fools," he added, and it was worth it to see them draw themselves up straight, strong.

"But a traitor to the Coalition," Brander said, with a nonchalance that reminded Paledan of those games, when this man had been playing a much more reckless game than that on the table, "would be the real prize. You figure they'll execute you on the spot?"

I know they will. I would have. But he said nothing.

"No," Lana said, so fiercely it eased some of the chill that had overtaken him. He shifted his gaze to her face, trying to memorize it, then nearly laughed at himself for thinking he needed to look at her for that. He would hold this image in his mind to his last breath. Which was likely to be in the next few minutes.

"You must know I did not come to you simply because they turned on me," he said, the words hard to get out; he would not have chosen this time or place or company, but all choices had been taken from him.

"I already know this, for I know what is in your mind and heart, Caze Paledan."

"Do you?" he whispered.

She met his gaze steadily, and he saw in her eyes a reflection of what she saw in his. "Yes, for it is in mine as well."

"Time," Pryl said, rather sharply this time.

"Yes," Lana said. And suddenly she was giving orders with all the command presence of any Coalition general. "Pryl, you must report to Drake. Brander, Eirlys, take the twins to safety." The two children protested, but she hushed them. "Caze has risked his life for you. Do not make it for nothing."

That succeeded in silencing them, but the duo looked at him worriedly. "Go," he said. "And know that you helped me break free."

And in that moment, as he watched the others go, his only regret was that he would know that freedom for such a short time. Then he realized Lana was making no move to follow the others.

"You must go, too," he said, wondering that the words made it out as all, given the tightness of his throat.

Her head came up, and she looked at him regally. "Do you think I, the Spirit of the mountains, will let you sacrifice yourself? When you have only just discovered that self?"

"Lana—"

"And when I am learning to love that name only you use?"

"But—"

"Before," she added, with a heat that nearly swamped him, "we have discovered what we can learn from each other?"

He nearly gasped aloud at the images that flooded his mind. It took him a long moment to right himself, and he wondered if he would have ever gotten used to this constant poking and prodding of feelings and sensations. And felt a sense of profound sadness that he would never know.

When she spoke again it was with that same crispness of command. "Will they have sent the same men who were here before and found the twins?"

His brow furrowed, and it took him an instant to drag his befuddled mind back to a Coalition mindset. "No. They were merely patrollers. They will send fighters."

She gave him an arch look. "Thirty of them, for one man and two small children? That says much of the man." Before he could react to that, for he did not know how, she spoke again. "And what are the chances those men will have been to this spot before?"

"Zero. Fidez would only trust his own, who just arrived with him."

"Ideal," she said with a smile he'd seen before.

Then, to his shock, she walked out of the trees and into the clearing along the edge of the separated stream of the river. In plain sight she stood, and all he could think was that at any moment two boatloads of Coalition troopers sent to kill would be here. He went after her; he would drag her to shelter if he had to, somehow keep here there, while he surrendered himself to them to keep them from her.

"Be still, Caze," she said as he reached for her arm. She had turned back to face the trees. She reached into a small pouch tied to the belt of her Sentinel gear. She came out with a palm-sized, polished, oval stone. He felt a strange, hair-raising sort of vibration, that seemed to be coming from the stone itself. But then a sound drew his attention, and he turned to look at the river, expecting to see the boats whose motors he'd just heard to appear at any second.

"They are closing," he said, urgently. "You must go."

"Hush." She closed her eyes, wrapped her long, slender fingers around the stone she held. The strange vibration increased, but he could not tear his gaze away from the river. He was on the verge of breaking, of grabbing her and throwing her over his shoulder and making a run for it, when she said, "That should do it."

She said it with such satisfaction he turned back to her. And gaped. For where a thick forest of trees had once stood, there was now nothing but a towering wall of rock. A soaring cliff, unclimbable and impenetrable.

With absolutely no place to hide.

Chapter 56

CAZE STARED AT HER, then toward the forest he could no longer see. Lana smiled back serenely.

"Shall we?" she asked, and took a step toward the image of a towering cliff. He didn't move. "I understand, but they are getting close and I really must ask you to trust me."

"I . . . do trust you."

But he sounded so cautious she knew stronger measures were needed. If they had time, she would let him fight through it in his own way, but they did not. So she reached out, took his hand, and tugged.

"Close your eyes if you must, it helps some the first time." Still he resisted, and she sighed. It was directed at herself, for underestimating the tenacity of his mind. "The choices are these. You come with me, and we both survive. Or you insist this is impossible and we stay here. You know what will happen then."

She felt the tension through his hand, felt the battle going on within him. She curled her fingers slightly, knowing they were down to mere moments.

"I . . ."

"Have I not led you through worse, Caze?" she asked softly, putting all she was feeling into his name.

She felt the moment he changed. The moment he gave in. And barely in time, for they were so close now she could hear the shouts of the leader of the troops, directing them into the branch of the river that would bring them to the beach just a stone's throw away. She moved quickly then, and he was no longer following; he was beside her. When Caze Paledan made up his mind, he did so completely, she thought with an inward smile as they stepped through what to her was a shimmering fall light and energy.

She saw him stop dead and stare when they were through and the forest surrounded them once more. He looked back toward the river. The boats had come into view, and she felt him tense.

"They will see only what you saw," she said.

His gaze came back to her. "As with my office," he murmured.

She smiled. "Yes. This is the same sort of illusion, on a grander scale."

"The stone," he said.

"It magnifies the power," she answered, although it hadn't really been a question.

The Coalition boats had beached now, and she felt him tense as he heard the shouted orders to search. He moved, she thought instinctively, behind one of the larger trees. She went with him; although she knew it was unnecessary, he did not.

"They will not see us," she whispered, "but they could hear us, so we must stay silent."

They watched as the Coalition troopers scattered along the beach, searching. Behind the boulders that genuinely lay strewn there, beneath the shrubs that clung to edge of the clearing. They barely glanced in their direction.

When their search proved fruitless, one of the men took out a set of distance goggles, donned them and scanned the cliff he saw. Iolana felt Caze tense again, but again she squeezed his hand to let him know the illusion would hold.

"No way in hades they climbed that thing, and there's no way around it," the scanner announced to the troop's leader.

"If they didn't come back here, then where did they go?" the leader said in frustration.

"I've heard from a couple of the troopers posted here that Paledan knows this wretched planet. That he's spent hours on reconnaissance."

"Sounds like him," the leader muttered. "But if we don't find him we'll face his fate. The general will drop us on the spot."

"Or leave us here," one of the others said, sounding as if he thought that a worse fate.

As they watched, the troopers made one last sweep of the area they thought was all there was to search, and then they got back in the boats and began the fight upstream, away from the falls. Caze and Iolana stayed silent, watching, until the troopers were well out of sight.

"Will they come back?" she asked.

"Possible," he answered, still staring after them. "How long can you hold the illusion?"

"As long as I am here," she said. "Or at least relatively close. The stone, and Ziem herself, is doing most of the work."

"We should move to the farthest extent, then."

"So when I release it and it fades, we will be as far away as possible? Agreed. I know a place we can shelter unseen."

They had walked through the trees to the faint path she and the others had followed to come after the twins before she said, "I thank you for trusting me."

"It is as you said. You have led me through much worse."

"I know it is not in your nature to . . . follow."

"I have done many things I thought not in my nature since coming here."

She laughed. "I am glad to hear it."

He stopped in his tracks. For a moment he did not speak, but when he did he said only one word. But he said it with everything in him; she could feel it. "Why?"

"It is the real Caze, the one the Coalition tried so hard to crush, that I wish to know."

Again it was a moment before he spoke, and she sensed this usually articulate man was having to search for words to express things entirely new to him.

"I believe you . . . already know more of him than even I do."

She had not thought of it quite like that. And that pleased her in a way even she did not understand, which contrarily pleased her as well. He would ever be a challenge to understand completely, and that was a prospect she looked forward to with joy.

She heard him make a sound, take a choking sort of breath, and she realized her thoughts must have shown in her face. Or perhaps shone, for she was feeling as if she were glowing.

"Lana."

That name only he used echoed in her ears, and the sheer urgency in his voice fired her every nerve. She saw what glowed in turn, and how fiercely, in those impossibly green eyes. And when she spoke, she knew what she was answering, just as she had known this was inevitable, probably from the first time she had seen the image that went with the reputation of this man.

"Yes," she whispered.

IMPOSSIBLE.

He had applied the word too often since he had come to Ziem, yet it was the only one that fit. For surely it was impossible, this rushing, swelling torrent of sensation, both inward and outward.

Mating was a need, but only slightly more than an itch to be scratched. At least, he had ever thought it so, for that was as high as it had ever measured on his scale of needs. The Coalition had made certain of that.

It had never been like this, a craving so deep and so powerful, it was more important than his next breath.

It had never been imperative.

Yet with every taste of her, that imperative grew. He savored the warm, soft feel of her lips, the taste of her mouth, more intoxicating than the finest of lingberry liquor, sweeter and smoother than the clingfruit juice he had once bought in Drake Davorin's taproom. The taproom which had held the image of the reality he now had in his arms—the woman who had haunted him, captivated him, entranced him from the first time he'd seen her portrait.

She made a tiny sound, and it was as a blaster to his control. This, too, was impossible; it had never mattered overmuch to him if his companion in mating was taking pleasure from it, for they were merely doing their Coalition-prescribed job. As he had ever looked upon that mating merely as something he needed to get out of his system so he could get back to his own Coalition-prescribed job.

But this . . . this was consuming, overwhelming. And uncontrollable. Another word he had rarely used before he had come here.

He felt a sudden swipe of fire across his ribs, and his breath jammed in his throat. For a split second, he wondered if they had been found. In the next, he realized it had only been her fingers on his skin; she had tugged his shirt free and slipped her hands beneath, while he had been drowning in the depths of her luscious mouth.

"Lana." It was nearly a gasp as it broke from him. She lifted her head, and the expression on her face drove what little air he had left out of him. Slowly, like a dazed animal, he shook his head. Some small, still-functioning part of his brain reminded him of what mating meant to the people of this world. What it meant to her. And for the first time in his life that mattered more than his own need. "You . . . want this?"

It was all he could do to focus on her answer, because she was still touching him, stroking the skin of his chest now.

"Caze."

He realized as her voice caressed that one syllable that he'd even begun to think of himself with that name. Changing even that, since her. And there was no doubting, no questioning the husky promise in her voice. And it struck him that she knew so much more of this than he, this kind of connection, of need, of one person being essential. And even though the thought itself was heresy, he could not deny the truth of it. Not now with her in his arms, with his body, mind, and heart for the first time in his life utterly in tune.

He felt like a starship bursting free of gravity, no longer held back, free of constraint. And he stared at her in wonder.

"This is, and has been for some time, inevitable," she said softly. "Why are you surprised?"

He struggled to find the words. "Because it has never mattered to me before. Nothing has mattered to me . . . as this does. As you do."

She merely looked at him, with those blue eyes that both saw and Saw, and suddenly he had to kiss her again. And again and again.

He had thought this kind of compulsion, this fierce, driving urgency a thing of legend, or a sign of more primitive beings, and his usual control of the urge a sign that he had succeeded in conquering it, as the Coalition required. But now, as with so many things the Coalition required, he was on the verge of letting it slip away.

No. You are casting it away, consciously, with full awareness and willingness. Because nothing, not your career, not your reputation, not the Coalition itself is more important than this woman, and this moment.

He hovered on the edge, some small part of him amazed at how clear it was and how easy it seemed to shed the trappings—the shackles, as she had so correctly called them—of a lifetime. Incredibly, although he supposed he should not be surprised, she seemed to sense the moment when the light burst through, and she laughed, that silvery laugh that was so full of joy it seemed to well up and wash over him.

They went down to the mossy floor of the misty glade, shedding clothing as they went, for she seemed as eager to have him naked as he was her. Yet another sharp, fiery difference, and a realization that eagerness in return was more arousing than he could have ever imagined. She made him feel perfect, whole, in a way he'd never known.

She was more beautiful even than he'd pictured. Her scars were as nothing to him, for he had enough of his own. And one, which marked the place where she had not only saved his life but changed it forever, was even precious to him.

He stroked, caressed here, kissed there, feeling like a man newly born into a world full of color, sound, taste, and the sweet smell of mistflowers. He nuzzled her lovely breasts, teasing the tips with his lips and tongue, amazed at how her arching response sent a renewed jolt of hot, fiery need through him.

And when she touched him in turn in the same way, as if he were something she had long coveted but only now had in her grasp, the blaze grew to a firestorm. Her hands touched every place, every nerve that was tingling and raised the sensation to a fever pitch.

"Eos, Caze," she moaned, "please, I have waited so long. Do not make me wait any longer."

He wanted to savor, but he could not. He wanted to go slowly, to be sure she was with him, but he could not. He wanted to linger over every inch of her, but his control wavered, and he could not. And when her fingers curled around rigid flesh that had never in his life been so demanding, his control snapped.

He shifted, and her legs parted to welcome him. He could not hold back; he drove his body into hers in one fierce stroke. She cried out, but it was full of that joy that washed over him anew. He heard an echo of it, realized it was his own voice, and that it held that same joy.

Again and again he moved, able to stand being out of her warmth for only a fraction of a second before he had to sheath himself again. She clung to him as if he were a lifeline, urging him on, saying his name in that way only she ever had. And then he felt her body clench around him, low and deep and hot, heard her cry of that name, and felt as if he were spinning off into space.

And the never-rattled, rarely moved, icily cool Caze Paledan shattered, shouting her name in a triumph he had never felt even on the wildest of battlefields as he poured himself, body, heart, and soul into her.

And when he sank down atop her, trembling, he knew that however he might put the pieces back together, he would never be the same again.

Chapter 57

"THE ILLUSION IS gone. I'm afraid I lost my focus," Lana said, sounding not at all concerned. In fact, she sounded rather pleased.

Paledan was not at all certain how he felt, other than utterly, completely drained. At this moment, when it should be least likely, for they lay naked and exposed in this quiet glade, he felt . . . he felt . . .

"It's called peace, Caze," she whispered to him.

No longer surprised that she knew what he'd been feeling, his brain automatically called up the meanings of the word. Not the meanings from his world, such as lack of hostilities, but from hers. Like a checklist he went through them. Calm. Quiet. Stillness. Tranquility.

Yes. They all fit. Which left him feeling something else. Something he'd seen in her, despite what should have been a dangerous, precarious existence.

Serenity.

"Is this . . . what it is always like for . . . normal people?"

"Yes, and no." Despite himself he laughed. It was such a Lana answer.

And she smiled back at him. "That," she said, "is a sound I would like to hear often."

"And that is not an answer."

"No, it was not. For I'm afraid I cannot answer that. I have never been . . . normal, even for my people."

"Because of your powers." She nodded. He frowned. "You did not . . . use them, here, now?"

She sat up abruptly. Reached out and grabbed his hands. "I would never. Not like this, not between us. That is a time that is sacred to all Ziemites, when all façades are cast away, when the sharing is of your true self, sometimes only revealed in those moments."

He was staring at her. "It is . . ."

"Exhilarating? Breathtaking?" *Oh, yes, all of that.* The memory of the heat they'd kindled together swept him. She was watching him, and he somehow knew she was trying to put herself in the place of someone who had never experienced what they just had. "Frightening?" she added softly.

He couldn't deny it. Wouldn't, because it seemed it would lessen the power of what they had found. "Yes. And . . . explosive."

Her smile widened into a joyous thing. "Indeed. Rather more than I have ever experienced."

And her words gave him nearly as much pleasure as her body had.

LANA WATCHED AS a very male smile curved his mouth. That mouth that both tenderly tasted her and voraciously demanded her fullest response. That smile sent a rippling wave of need through her, and she nearly gasped with the power of it. What she had known with Torstan was not less than this, it was merely different. She had loved her children's father since she had been old enough to understand, but he was a very different sort of man, solid, attentive, and reserved by nature until stirred beyond passion by the invasion of his beloved world.

She suspected Caze Paledan was reserved only by dint of a lifetime of brutal Coalition restraint, not by his nature. And she could feel him breaking free on all fronts with a speed and power that astonished her, although upon reflection she supposed it should not. He was a powerful man in so many ways; it should not have surprised her he would take down the walls he'd lived inside with the same fierce energy that he unleashed on everything.

Including her.

"If you keep looking at me like that, we shall end up starting all over again." His voice held the mildest of warnings.

"Then you had best begin, for I have no intention of looking away from the most beautiful sight I have encountered in an age."

She was secretly delighted to see the flare of pleasure in his eyes, as much because he allowed it as that she had caused it. He was not simply scaling those walls, he was ripping them down. But when he spoke, it was in obviously genuine curiosity.

"You are not in a hurry to rejoin your people?"

"I am in a hurry," she said frankly, "to rejoin with you. Although I would also hazard to say you are one of those people, now."

He looked momentarily distracted. "I doubt they will feel the same."

"Some already do." She settled back against him, taking private joy in him putting his arm around her to cradle her against his chest, for she knew that for this man, the gesture was anything but small. "But I do not deny it will take longer for those who have lost everything to the Coalition."

"Young Kade, for instance?" he suggested.

"Yes. And others. But there are a few even of them who understand. Brander and Kye, for example, lost everyone and everything. And yet Brander was the first to determine you were not like most others of the Coalition we'd encountered."

"I think he only looked twice because he was not used to being defeated at the chaser table," he said dryly.

She laughed, and was pleased to see him smile in return. "Contention valid," she agreed. "And I'm sure he is looking forward to renewing that competition."

"As am I," he said, and now he looked surprised, perhaps at his own realization.

"It will be a long journey to get all to trust you," she warned.

"I assumed nothing less." He hesitated, then said, "I have done things, many things, to deserve their mistrust. Not here, perhaps, for this was all new to me, but still . . ."

"One thing you will find true of Ziemites. They believe in second chances. They will not easily tolerate being taken for fools, but redemption is a cornerstone of our culture. Which is," she added, "a very good thing for me, for I had much to be forgiven."

"But you are one of them."

"As were, until they abused the privilege, Ordam and Jakel."

She felt him go still beneath her cheek. "I am not certain I like the analogy."

She lifted her head so she could meet his gaze straight on as she said, "I made it only to show you the extent of our tolerance. If we can accept the likes of those two, then a courageous, honest, just man such as you should have no problem, in the end."

He stared at her. "You give me too much praise."

"I do not," she said simply. And then, unable to wait any longer, she reached for him. "Although if you do not ease this ache soon, I might have to reconsider," she teased, and was delighted that he knew it instantly. And she thought his smile then, a quiet, almost shy smile, the most wonderful thing she'd ever seen.

And then he slid her on top of him, giving her the freedom of his body. And she took it, and him, with a fierce pleasure she had never expected to find, doing everything she had wanted to do for so long, touching everywhere, urging him to touch in turn, learning as quickly as he did how to stoke this fire that threatened to consume them both.

And when she could wait no longer she changed the angle, leaning closer to him as his hips drove upward. It was the final stroke she needed, and her body clenched, launched on that spiraling upward flight. She heard him groan out her name, that name, and he clutched at her like a man clinging to the only thing that mattered in his life.

And she knew no matter what else happened, she would treasure this to the end of her days.

"YOU'RE CERTAIN?"

"As I can be," Iolana said, not really wishing to tell her son how she knew, but knowing this was crucial. "I have . . . seen his mind, Drake. Specifically, the portion still occupied with Coalition concerns. Which, I might add, is much, much smaller already than it used to be. I'm afraid normal emotions have overtaken much of it."

"And how is he dealing with that?" her son asked, rather warily.

"Better than I expected. He is very quick to learn."

"We have ever known that."

"What overlays all of his thoughts of them is loathing, and a certain sadness that I think is both for what was taken from him and the needless execution of a good man." She lowered her gaze, for this had bothered her. "I feel in part responsible. Had I not told Caze what I had sensed, he would not have had Brakely investigate those records."

"You are not responsible," Drake said, sharply. "Rather blame the monstrosity that would both create a need for such records and then execute a good man for merely looking at them."

She knew he was right, but she also knew how much pain Brakely's death had caused Caze. And how much guilt for it he himself carried. She knew everything, for whether knowingly or not, when he had opened himself to her physically, the mental walls had fallen as well. And being Caze, he had done it completely, sparking her own opening to him, and together it had nearly consumed them.

"I . . . see."

She snapped out of a luscious haze of images, highlighted by the memory of that strong, beautiful man driving into her body with his, his skin dappled by the shadows of the glade, and the moment when one look at the open, honest amazement and wonder in his green eyes had sent her flying.

Cheeks flaming, she looked at Drake, who was studying her intently. "I . . ." She could think of no words. Not for this man who was the son of the only man she had thought she would ever love.

"I will say only that neither I, nor I think Eirlys—and certainly not the twins, since they clearly adore him—begrudge you what happiness you can find in what is left to us." His mouth quirked. "Even if it is with the former commander of our enemy."

"You believe me, then?" she asked with some urgency. "That it is indeed former?"

"You have yet to be wrong." He gave her another considering look. "But your emotions have not been entangled in this way, either. It would be very difficult for you if he is not truly changed."

"He is. Brander was right from the beginning; he was only one of them by circumstances of birth and by force."

Drake nodded. "I believe it. That he would so easily give himself up to save the twins . . ."

"Remind you of anyone?" she asked, smiling at him, knowing she didn't need to truly remind him that he had done the same for his sister.

"But he is not theirs by blood."

"But he is theirs by their choice."

"And yours?" Drake asked softly.

She drew in a deep breath. "Yes."

"And he feels the same?"

Her mouth quirked wryly. "Yes. Although I am not certain he has sorted it all out yet. He's a bit . . . bewildered by it all at the moment."

"I can imagine. Falling in love with the Spirit would be daunting enough, but to do so when all such feeling has been beaten down in you your entire life? You will have to tread carefully."

"I intend to handle it with great care," she said, the color that rose to her cheeks defeating her effort to sound merely practical.

"If it has so stripped even the Spirit of her power to hide her thoughts, then it must be both real and immense," Drake said dryly. "And now, if you don't mind, we'll end this discussion of my mother's mating intentions. Although," he added, "I suspect you're well past intent."

Something struck her suddenly. "And you," she said accusingly, "are enjoying this."

Her son grinned then, widely. "I am. And I am looking forward to jabbing at the major—rather, the former major, the same way."

"I think you will find him . . . more relaxed than before," she said, rather archly.

Drake groaned. "Mother . . ."

"Perhaps it is being . . . out of uniform," she added.

"Enough," Drake exclaimed.

Iolana laughed, more delighted at teasing her eldest son, who had exceeded even her dreams for him, than at anything except what she had found so unexpectedly with Caze.

And it was with some reluctance that she let him go, knowing that this encounter would and should be between two warriors who needed to take each other's measure in a very different way than they had before.

Chapter 58

CAZE WAS STILL contemplating the latest impossibility, that this warm, spacious cave, turned into a welcoming, comfortable place by various cushions and weavings, was the same place he had been during those long, agonizing hours. Although after what he had seen down by the river, the illusion of his office seemed rather simple. And he still did not know for certain where he was, for understandably he had been masked for the journey back to this place. All he knew was that it was one of their bedamned mountains. And he was beginning to suspect, from the surprising warmth of it, that it was—insanely—the mountain that still lived.

The only thing he was sure of, because he could practically feel her presence, was that this was Lana's home. And that she had brought him here had set off a new war inside him; here because she wanted him in her home, or here because it did not matter if he saw it because she had the power to erase his memories?

A small shudder went through him as he caromed off of that thought to another battle; should the Raider decide to oust him but let him live, would his life be easier with or without the memories of their time in that sheltered glade?

And when did you begin searching for an easier way? Besides, it would not be letting you live; the Coalition is after your head now.

He spun around at a sound from the entrance. When Drake entered, it did not surprise him. That it was indeed Drake, not the Raider, did. And suddenly, belatedly, it struck him anew that the woman who had so completely undone him was this man's mother.

"Yes," Drake said with a wry smile, "things have gotten rather complicated, haven't they."

It wasn't a question, and Caze realized he knew. The idea that Lana had told her son about what had happened between them was both gratifying and terrifying. For he had not even had time to process the enormity of it, the shock of realizing everything he'd been taught about relations between men and women, that it was a need akin to scratching an itch, far from essential and with no lasting connection formed, had been a lie.

"I hear you have met our clever engineer, as you wished to," Drake said. The man who had done so much with so little leaned against the table at one side of the room in a casual, relaxed posture. Belatedly—as everything seemed to be at the moment—he registered what the man had said.

"I have?" And then the inevitable hit him. "Kalon?"

Drake nodded. "He is much like you. He is not our best pilot, but his modifications make him worth more than a squadron of them. I would wager he can turn one of your rovers into a fighter-bomber faster than the Coalition can build one."

"He would have to be very fast, since they have production for even the larger craft down to mere weeks."

"I shall have to toss that challenge to my engineer."

"Whose acting skills rival your own," Paledan said dryly.

Drake grinned. "Now you've hurt my feelings. His façade was much closer to his real self than mine."

For a moment Caze could only stare at the man. He'd never seen this side of him before. He'd never seen a side like this in any commander before. Such banter was not present in the Coalition, and the only laughter he ever heard from their leaders was in mockery. Of course, none of them would have had feelings in the first place. And now he himself had so many he could not even sort them out. He didn't even have names for some of them.

But Drake's words made him slowly smile.

"I think I am relieved, but I am not certain."

"I imagine you're not certain of much right now. Having spent your life with emotions hammered out of you, and now . . ." Drake gave him an empathetic shake of his head.

"You are not . . . angry?"

Drake lifted a brow at him. "Now? No. As long as you do no harm, you will have a place here. If you damage our cause—or my mother's heart—that will be another matter."

Caze felt uncomfortable in a way he'd never known before. Again. He asked the first thing that came into his whirling mind. "She no longer masks this place from me." Drake smiled, almost serenely. And Paledan realized the foolishness of his comment. "For if you will it, she will turn me into another Jakel, with no memory of any of this. Or of myself."

"I would not do that to such as you. Better a commander's death, don't you think?"

"Yes," he said rather fervently.

For a moment Drake studied him in silence. Then, quietly, he said, "Do not think I underestimate the enormity of what you have done. I have only to imagine turning my back on Ziem to fathom it."

"There is a difference. You have ever been certain of the rightness of your way, have you not?"

Drake smiled then. "And you, deep down, have ever doubted the Coalition."

"Not ever," Caze said, feeling a need to be utterly honest with this man.

"But you have always felt something missing."

"Yes. But I did not truly doubt the rightness of the Coalition until—"

He broke off suddenly as a now-familiar pain stabbed at him.

"Until?"

He finished it in a harsh voice. "Until I saw Marl Brakely awaiting execution for the mere fact of being connected to his uncle, who was executed for his own commander's mistakes and failures although he was blameless." *And he ended up dead anyway, because of me.*

"Odd, isn't it? That an entity that utterly devalues blood ties will yet use them as a reason for such actions?"

"Exactly the contradiction I could not process."

"I am sorry about your aide. My second speaks well of him."

"Your second . . ." Drake smiled again, and it hit him. "Kalon is also your second in command?"

"He is." It suddenly occurred to Caze that the man was revealing, and allowing to be revealed, a great deal about his Sentinels. "Something bothers you about that?" Drake asked.

"Only that you are letting me learn far too much," Caze said warily.

"Figuring that means I plan to execute you after all?"

"It is what I would do."

"I don't think so. Not anymore."

Caze realized the man was right. He'd lost the stomach for such Coalition actions. *Perhaps I handed it over when I handed everything else to that flame-haired enchantress.*

"You are right," he said, sounding much like he felt.

"I realize you have a great deal of learning and adjusting to do," Drake said. "But I'm afraid just now I cannot afford to give you time to do it before I must ask you something."

"Will I completely turn and help you and your Sentinels?" Drake nodded, clearly unsurprised he had guessed. "I . . ."

"I understand what it must feel like, to a man of your honor."

"I have been 'feeling' for mere hours, and I have no understanding at all," Caze said wryly.

"Yet you are here. Voluntarily."

"Apparently there is more than one kind of compulsion," he said with a grimace. And to his surprise Drake burst out laughing.

"Welcome to my world, and all its joys and complications," he said after a moment. And to his further surprise, Caze found himself smiling.

"I do not . . . regret my decision," he said, finding yet more surprise in the fact that this was true.

"They will keep looking for you, will they not?"

"Yes."

"What will their orders be if they find you?"

"I think you know that."

"Kill you on sight? No returning you to their headquarters for some grand, show trial to further stomp down anyone who dares to have a thought of their own? For if the great hero Major Paledan can be condemned, they all will know their lives depend utterly on pleasing their masters."

"That was their wish, initially."

Drake studied him for a moment. Then a slow smile curved his mouth. "They're afraid of you." Caze blinked. He had not thought about it in such a way. Drake's smile grew wider. "They are no doubt exchanging tales of your exploits even now, building an already formidable reputation even higher."

"Into the realm of myth?" Paledan suggested dryly.

"If it gives them second thoughts, if it forestalls them at all, I am fully in support of any myth."

Caze studied the man who had bedeviled the Coalition for so long. "I am not so certain that the myths of this world are truly that."

"The Spirit, for example?" Drake said, almost blandly.

"Contention valid," Caze said. "I can hardly deny what she is when she has proven it to me time and again."

Drake smiled. Then asked, "How intensely will they search for you?"

"Very. Unless more important Coalition business arises."

"Well, then, we must be certain they are kept too busy to devote much effort to it."

Caze found his throat oddly tight, enough so that it was difficult to speak. "It would be much wiser of you to simply hand me over to them."

"No doubt," Drake said easily, clearly dismissing the idea.

And with those simple words the man who was the Raider told him he still did not fully understand these unexpected people. And on the heels of that thought came one he should have had long ago, would have had had he not been so distracted, so consumed by what he'd found in Iolana's arms.

"If they hunt too hard for me, they will find you if I stay." It wrenched him in a way that he would never have expected to say it. "So I cannot."

"Someday soon," Drake said, "we must discuss this urge you've developed to sacrifice yourself. It is not something we normally allow."

Caze didn't miss the implication that he would yet be with them to have that discussion. But that only tangled these wretched emotions further, so he focused on something else. "Normally?"

"On rare occasions, when death is already closing in . . ." A shadow darkened Drake's eyes for a moment, and when he went on, it was the Raider speaking. "I believe you know of one occasion."

It took him a moment. Everything seemed to be slowed by the mass of newfound feelings, and he wondered that the Raider was able to function at all. But then it struck him.

"The mine explosion . . . he was dying? The man who set off the explosion?"

"Yes. It was his plan and his choice."

"So you did not order him to his death?"

"I would not. We value life too highly."

"But sometimes it is necessary, is it not?" he asked, struggling to understand. "Fighters are killed in battle."

"Yes. But I will have no one fight who does not choose it. I want only those who believe enough to risk it at my back." His eyes narrowed. "And I do not accept self-sacrifice when there are other ways."

"Such as fighting an endless holding action?"

"If that is the only course." The Raider held his gaze. "Is it?"

Caze knew they were, in essence, back to the original question. If he would turn against a lifetime owned by the Coalition and help these rebels.

"They will never leave as long as there is planium to be had here," he said honestly.

"I assumed as much. And what will they do when the supply is, at last, exhausted? Blow us out of the sky?"

Caze considered this thoughtfully. "I am," he admitted, "having trouble putting myself back in those boots."

"Glad to hear it," the Raider said. "I would also be glad of your best assessment."

"Frankly, as out of the way as this world is, and as much destruction as they've wrought already, I'm not certain they would bother, or expend the effort and resources to maneuver the necessary weapon to obliterate an entire planet." He gave a sharp shake of his head. "But I cannot promise they would not, if they were angry enough."

"Always a given," the Raider said in the tone of a man who knew exactly what he was up against.

"If you continue to fight them," he began, and then stopped.

"What?"

Caze shook his head. "It is pointless. I know you will continue to fight them."

"Yes. The more resources they have to devote to that fight, the slower the path to our potential destruction."

"Contention valid," he said. "But also the angrier it makes them."

"We will just have to hope continuing the supply of planium will restrain them long enough."

"Long enough . . . for what?"

"For us to find another way," the Raider said easily. So easily Caze had the strangest feeling that, perhaps, they already had.

Chapter 59

IOLANA HAD SPENT each night wrapped in Caze's arms, feeling warmer and safer than she had in years. Even if he awoke before her, he did not leave, but stayed, holding her as if she were as necessary to him as breathing.

You are the only thing I am certain of in my life now.

She knew him well enough now to know what a tribute that was. These past days had been a struggle for him as he tried to deal both with his new life and his new self, and free himself of the teachings of a lifetime. But she could almost see him rise, grow, testing the freedom of being out from under the Coalition bootheel at last.

Although a few of the Sentinels were yet wary of him, most had accepted him. Some because they had such faith in her, some because they saw the Davorins and Kalons had, many because of the twins. Drake had made sure the story of how he would have sacrificed himself to save the twins and give them all time to escape had gotten around.

She knew how much Drake had risked when he'd allowed him not only to stay, but allowed her to abandon all illusion. "The reasons for them not to destroy this place even if they found it still stand," he'd said.

He'd also told Caze, almost conversationally, that were they discovered now, he would assume it was his doing and his fate would be sealed. This was the first time he'd allowed Caze to leave her quarters and see the rest of the stronghold.

"You cannot trust me with this knowledge," he'd said to Drake, more in amazement than anything.

Drake had merely answered, "It is not yet you I am trusting," with a look at her.

Once he had seen, Caze had understood with the quickness she had come to expect. And she sensed he had already figured most of it out. "It's the mountain. It yet lives, and the heat of it masks your presence from the thermal satellite."

She had smiled widely as he shook his head in wonder.

Tonight when she awoke in the darkness, he was not with her. But the moment she got up, pulling on her nightdress, he came back into the sleeping alcove from the main room and put his arms around her.

"I should have stayed, but . . . I heard something. A ship passing overhead."

She went still. They rarely saw ships up here. "We are above the flight pattern for the landing zone. Except for . . ."

"Yes. It sounded like a High Command transport."

"The general leaving, dare I hope?"

"Or making room for more ships," he said, sounding as grim as if he were one of the Sentinels who would have to deal with it. She felt a quiver of hope that it was true, that he was already thinking of himself that way. But it faltered under the memory of the horrible images his words brought.

"I cannot bear it," she whispered. "What they could do, Ziem in ruins, crumbled, her mountains leveled, what few of her people that may survive destined for a life nearly impossible to sustain."

She felt him go very still. "How can you . . . want me? Forgive me? For so long I was a part of it, and I visited what you speak of on so many worlds."

She fought down the rising tide of panic, pushed aside the visions of what might be to cling to the reality of the man holding her.

"I had to forgive myself for what I did when I was mired in despair. Forgiving someone trapped as you were, crippled by the Coalition and with much less choice than I had, is much easier."

It was a moment before he asked, his voice rough, "What do you See, of us?"

That he even believed she could See in that way was a marvel in itself. "I cannot See to our future. But I See that we are right, as right as Drake with Kye, and Brander with Eirlys. Destined, in fact." She heard him suck in a deep breath. "I know it is hard for you to accept."

"It is like touching water and finding it solid," he said. "My mind feels battered."

"Perhaps it had to be. Perhaps the walls the Coalition built in you needed to be battered down."

And then, because she simply had to, perhaps because she was so uncertain of how much time they would ever have, she kissed him. That quickly, the fire reignited, and he swept her up in his arms and carried her back to her bed. *Their bed.*

And later, in the darkness, he spoke. "I never thought there could be such a place in the midst of chaos. A place to rest, despite what goes on outside. To be . . . quiet. To feel warm. Safe. At ease. And . . . and . . ."

"Love, Caze. The word you want is love."

She felt him go very still. Held her breath, waiting. And finally, after an internal battle she could practically feel, he battered down that last wall.

"Yes. Love."

HE LOOKED AT THE fist-sized stone, thinking yet again of that day by the river. When she came up behind him, slipping her arms around him, he put his hands over hers and held them against him.

"The Stone of Ziem fascinates you?"

"What you did with it that day intrigues me."

"I do not know how or why it works, not in a way that would satisfy your logic, I'm afraid," she said.

"But it does work."

"Yes. It amplifies what I call upon Ziem herself to do."

"Your illusions."

"Not only that. It once helped us find Brander and young Kade when they were in trouble, far away from here."

"How?"

"They are of Ziem, and with the help of the stone Eirlys and I were able to send a signal centered around them."

He shook his head slowly, not in denial but in wonder. He was vaguely aware of a small spark firing at the back of his mind, but his life now was such a constant process of untangling that he couldn't quite get to it. He could only hope if it was important it would catch, and push its way through the chaos.

"I believe your afternoon amusement has arrived," she said at a sound from outside.

He turned to face her, not releasing her arms, then leaned in, close to her ear. "I was rather fond of my morning's amusement," he whispered.

"As was I," she said, nipping at his ear in turn.

The two sets of footsteps came to a halt outside the entrance. That much they had learned, he thought with an inward grin.

"Caze," she said suddenly, rather urgently. "You must know I understand that you have so much to grow accustomed to. I would never wish for you to feel trapped all over again, in a new way."

It took him a moment to understand. "By you? By what has grown between us?" He shook his head. "You are so rarely wrong I hardly know what to say except that I have never felt more free. Or whole."

"I—"

"Can we come in yet?"

The impatient query in two voices made him smile despite the interruption. Of all the many things that had happened since he had come to this world, finding himself the center of attention for children . . .

"They are not . . . annoying you?" Iolana asked.

He reached up to cup her face. "I am not sure what it is that I am feeling about those two, but it is definitely not annoyance. It never was."

"And they sensed that, from the beginning. And more, I think."

He stared down at her. What she seemed to be implying was impossible, but he had come to believe in more impossible things than he ever would have thought . . . possible. He nearly laughed at himself, such a convoluted mass had his brain become.

"You think they somehow sensed I was once . . ."

"Like them? Yes, I do."

"Please?" came the chorus from outside.

It was Lana who smiled then. "Ah. They have remembered that lesson at last."

"Proper protocol?"

Her smile widened. "So is it you I have to thank for that? And for them waiting outside?"

"I may have . . . mentioned it would be a good idea to pause before bursting in," he admitted.

And he had done so, after the morning they had interrupted something he wished they had not. But then again, it had been almost worth it to watch Lana rise naked from their bed and slip on that silky white gown to go and greet them. The scars she bore only made her more amazing to him; as she had once whispered in the night, they were both warriors who carried as many scars inside as out.

Later, as their party of three trekked along the flank of the mountain, Caze savored every step, every scramble, every reaching upward that he was able to do without pain. He had no idea where the duo was leading today, he only knew he had never regretted one of their expeditions. It also pushed him, to keep up with his two agile—and younger—companions, who had the habit of running ahead and vanishing in the mist.

When he finally commented on that, the two exchanged a startled glance.

"We are—"

"Sorry, we—"

"Forgot."

"Forgot to slow down for your aged companion?" Caze asked.

Nyx scoffed. "You are—"

"Not aged."

"Thank you," he said dryly. "Then what did you forget?"

"That you—"

"Cannot see—"

"Through the mist—"

"Like a Ziemite. We will—"

"Go slower."

They proceeded to do so, but it was a moment before Caze followed. For he was standing there, staring at the swirling gray as if a shaft of blinding light had just pierced it.

Of course. It only made sense. And in the way of the Coalition, they were too arrogant to even have considered the people of this backwater planet had a skill they lacked.

It all made sense now, how they managed to evade troopers so easily, how they appeared and disappeared so stealthily. They had produced a woman who could bring back the near-dead, heal injuries the best physicians had given up on, who could conjure a towering rock cliff out of thin air; why should this seem amazing?

When he caught up with them he asked, "Should you not have a care about revealing such things to me?"

They turned and looked up at him with earnest expressions that made him feel that strange sensation inside again, a warmth, a closeness, an urge to ever protect that startled him with its strength.

"Why?" Lux began.

"Do you—"

"Intend to—"

"Betray us?"

And he realized in that moment just how complete his conversion was, for he would willingly go back to carrying that death sentence shard of planium before he would betray these two, or their mother.

"Never," he said softly. And the two smiles that earned him made even the mist seem lighter.

"We know—"

"Because you—"

"Are ours now."

As if to prove it, Lux reached out and took his hand, while Nyx nodded solemnly. It took him a moment to breathe again.

"And you are mine," he said, and with a sudden blast of recognition he realized what this feeling was that he had when he was with them. It was simply a variation of what he felt for Lana. Whether it was because they were a part of her, or for their own, unique, troublesome, clever, amazing selves, he was not certain. It did not matter anyway.

"We are—"

"Almost there," they said.

"Will you—"

"Close your eyes—"

"And trust us?"

He did it without hesitation. They led him carefully forward. Nyx directed him to step up and guided his feet. He felt an odd sensation, as if the air had warmed in even those few feet. And then Lux told him to turn to his right.

"Now look!" they chorused.

He opened his eyes. And looked around in wonder. He had not seen the sun of any world in a long time. But he was in sunlight now, and it poured over him as if in welcome. And before him was a long line of jagged peaks, jabbing up through the mist as if reaching for that light and warmth. He had been flown over these mountains before, but seeing it all like this was entirely different. Compelling. Awe-inspiring.

And he suddenly understood what it was like to have a place, a world, and people who mattered to you above all others.

Chapter 60

"WHAT?"

Caze stared at the people gathered in the Raider's map room. He'd felt at home the moment he'd walked in for the first time; this was the room of a commander, a leader, a warrior. His attention had been caught that first time he'd come in by the huge map that adorned one wall. It was not printed but painted, on what appeared to be heavy canvas. Painted in exquisite detail, with a fine and sure hand.

He'd spun around then to look at the woman who had painted the portrait of Iolana Davorin.

"He got there quick," Kalon had said, looking at his cousin with a grin.

But, now, Caze was stunned into immobility by Drake's explanation of his plan. It was the most insane thing he'd ever heard, and given these past weeks, that was amazing in itself. But to purposely, intentionally sabotage the single thing that kept the Coalition from destroying this nuisance of a place?

His gaze shifted from person to person, the artist turned cartographer, to the engineer turned gambler, to the woman who had any creature at her beck and call, to the one-time taproom keeper turned warrior who had waged an impossibly successful battle against a force so much bigger, it defied logic to think he was even still alive.

He gave a sharp shake of his head. He was still wrestling with finding room for all these new, strange sensations and at the same time thinking clearly. Slowly he said, "You intend to mix these two elements that must never be mixed, in the hope that sometime, somewhere, everything built of it will crumble?"

"Not in hope," said Brander. "It will."

And at last he turned to look at the woman who had, in her way, brought them all together here. And when he spoke, he heard the baffled tone in his own voice. "I do not understand. You know what the Coalition does with worlds they have no further use for. You have ever said Ziemites value individual life above all else. And yet you are seriously considering intentionally doing this?"

She looked back at him with a calm that seemed uncanny given the subject.

"Worried about dying here?" Drake asked, as casually as if they were discussing the time of day.

He was surprised they were discussing anything strategic in front of him, but this was so outlandish perhaps it was a feint, a false front put up to test his loyalty. His gaze shifted to the Raider, for he was indeed that once more, in air of command if nothing else. "I spent long enough wishing for death not to fear it," he said. "But I would like to understand why."

"Because," Lana said softly, "they must be stopped."

"And you assume," Brander said, "that they will understand what we've done."

"I certainly do not, for such a thing is outside their ken. It is outside *mine*," Caze said. "You are willing to risk this, in the hopes of a victory that even if it comes, you may never see? How do your beloved people feel about it?"

"They prefer," Lana said, "to go down fighting. And so they voted."

His amazement grew. "They chose this?"

"This is not a decision any one person could make," the Raider said. "And the alternative is to destroy the mines ourselves."

"That is no alternative, for the Coalition would surely destroy Ziem in an instant."

"So we assumed. Which is why we chose this course."

"Which may well end the same. Your people were all willing to die for this?"

"To try and kill the cancer that infects a galaxy," Lana said softly. He felt a knot tightening in his gut. He knew now it was worry, concern, for he had learned of these feelings, and he'd accepted that these people could inspire it in him. But at this moment he could not decide if they were epically heroic, or simply insane.

He had thought he had learned to understand these people. He had come to admire much about them, and as their acceptance, and even kindness, toward him had grown, he had grown to care about them in turn. But now he was no longer certain he understood anything.

For a moment he just stood there, but finally he remembered the Raider had called him here to ask him something.

"What is it you wished to know?" he asked.

"How likely are they to believe the planium was intentionally contaminated?" It was the first time the artist—for he could not truly think of her otherwise—had spoken. He tried to put his mind back in the Coalition shackles, tried to think as they thought, as he once had thought.

"I . . ." He felt Lana's hand on his arm, and suddenly he was steadier. "I'm not certain it will even occur to them as a possibility. I know how foreign the idea seems to me, even after I have come to know the truth about Ziem and her people." Caze thought for a moment. "But there was a hand weapon powered by the two combined," he began again, but stopped when Kalon grinned.

"We know," he said, sounding much like the twins. His one-time chaser opponent reached behind him and picked up what looked like the shell of a weapon from a shelf. "This was on its way to you when it conveniently fell in our path."

He took the large handheld device, studied it for a moment. Saw the insignia that indicated it had come from the laboratory on Lustros. He looked at that for a moment as he searched his mind for reaction to this symbol of his planet of origin. He found only repulsion.

"We call it the obliterator," Brander said. "Because that's what it does."

Caze's head came up. "I know," he said. Then, ruefully, "I had to account for its disappearance."

"So we know they know what mixing the two does, in essence."

"Yes. But High Command found the combination for that weapon was too dangerous to attempt in sufficient quantity to power a larger version. It tended to explode rather than fire the weapon, so they halted that experiment." His mouth twisted. "I think they didn't like the . . . cleanliness of it, either. The Coalition prefers to leave visible rubble in its wake, as a warning of the cost of resisting them."

"And rubble brings me to the real question I have for you," the Raider said. "What is the tipping point? What decides the Coalition on whether to destroy a world, or simply abandon it?"

"Whether they feel it is worth the effort of destruction," Caze answered flatly. "And if they come to believe this was intentional, they will count the insult well worth the effort to avenge."

"And if not?"

"They would still likely bomb the mines, to prevent anyone else from accessing the planium. I would guess that your remoteness might save you. It is no small task to transport the weapon that can destroy a planet. But that is only a guess. And it is still a terrible risk, for if they take it in mind, they will slaughter everyone before they leave."

"Worlds are gained with risk," Iolana said. "Perhaps this one can be saved the same way."

CAZE SAT ON THE rocky outcrop, staring at the mist, wondering yet again what quirk of biology or genetics allowed the Ziemites to see through it. He thought of the pilots who complained unceasingly about being reduced to flying by instrument only, relying on locators and terrain scanners because they could not see to fly normally.

He kept his mind on that small puzzle to avoid the bigger one. The fact that these people they had classified as simple, slow, and soft had turned out to be clever, quick, and tough enough to make an impossible decision. To risk total annihilation for the chance to do some serious damage to the Coalition.

How many other worlds, worlds he had helped conquer, had in truth held similar people? People dismissed by the Coalition establishment, deemed useless, or useful only as slaves? How many brilliant warriors like the Raider had they not found, how many people of ingenious thought like Kalon? He could barely stand to dwell on how many people of what the Coalition would term lesser talents, the artist for example, and lesser still the woman who commanded the lowly creatures, they had wiped out without thought.

And how many of wondrous powers like Lana? And if they had discovered her, had realized her talents—No. That did not bear thinking about at all. For he well knew what would have happened to her, as he knew what would have happened to the twins.

But the most difficult part of all was knowing how he had been an integral part of it all, that he had been the vanguard of Coalition action in so many places. . . .

I had to forgive myself for what I did when I was mired in despair. Forgiving someone trapped as you were, crippled by the Coalition and with much less choice than I had, is much easier.

For a moment he wondered if perhaps that was why he'd been unforgivably good at what he did, for the choices of strategy, of tactics, were the only choices he had ever truly had.

"You are sad."

He'd heard them approaching, although Lux's words were not what he might have expected.

"We don't like—"

"To see you sad."

"Are you not—"

"Happy here?"

He turned to look at two sets of curious and concerned eyes. And he smiled at them. It had become a habit; just the sight of them seemed to make him smile.

"Before I came here," he answered honestly, "I did not even know what happiness was."

That made them smile. And they seemed so relieved, he was, he realized, flattered. For this was not the false unctuousness of the Coalition; this was the honest response of two children affected, but untainted, by that world.

"So you will—"

"Stay? With our—"

"Mother and—"

"Us?"

"As long as I am welcome," he said cautiously. He was ever wary that there were some who still did not trust the change in him, and he did not blame them.

"When you—"

"Pledge with—"

"Our mother—"

"No one—"

"Will doubt you."

He stared at them. Lana had never even mentioned this, at least not to him, and yet these two were speaking as if it were a given. Did she want this? Or was this simply the assumption of someone born into and raised in this culture?

Not long ago the idea of pledging oneself, mind, body, and soul to one person for life would have been laughable to him. But now that the twins had put it into words, with such casual confidence that it would happen, he thought of the other side, what it would be like to have someone pledge the same to him.

What it would be like to have a woman like Iolana Davorin pledge mind, body, and soul to him.

It took his breath away.

"Are you—"

"All right?"

They were still looking at him in concern.

"You have made me feel . . . better," he said, hoping they would leave it at that, for he did not think he could explain further. Thankfully they did, and were soon chattering away about some new project of Brander's. He thought of the clever inventor that way now, the man having insisted upon the familiarity. *If we're going to be connected, the formality is a bit much.*

Abruptly it struck him, in light of the twins' assumption, what Brander had meant. *If we're going to be connected . . .*

Brander was pledged to Lana's daughter. Which would connect them, if . . . he assumed, as the twins did, that he and Lana . . .

He felt an ache welling up inside him that was almost physical. For a moment he thought he was suddenly taken ill, before he identified it as one of those emotions he was still learning to deal with. There were times when he missed the cool, dispassionate man he'd once been, but they were quickly overwhelmed by vast richness of his life now.

It is like an equation, Caze. Cool, rational logic is only part of it. Without the heart, it is a pointless existence. Just as the heart without rationality leads to disaster. It takes both, to make life what it should be.

"—watch it with us."

He blinked, suddenly tuning back in to the twins' chatter.

"What?"

"You should—"

"Watch the stories—"

"With us."

"The stories?" he asked.

"Brander has fixed—"

"The old holoprojector—"

"And projects them—"

"Right onto—"

"The mist."

Was there nothing the man couldn't fix or invent or adapt? Coalition engineers were skilled, but there wasn't an ounce of imagination in any of them. Likely because it had been crushed out of them like everything else. They could repair existing things, or occasionally improve on them, but leaps of intellect such as Brander's were beyond them.

If our locator goes bad, we'll end up bombing our own compound. . . .

He wasn't sure why the old pilot's complaint popped into his head just then. But it set off a cascade of thoughts, wild, disconnected thoughts . . . or were they so disconnected? He wasn't sure he knew any longer. He suspected he had lost the ability to wall off such crazed ideas when he had surrendered to what Lana had given him.

And that, he'd decided long ago, was a tiny price to pay.

Chapter 61

THE THOUGHTS continued to batter at Caze, leaving him restless for days on end. He took to his old habits of walking, marveling at the secrets this mountain held. He had at first, when Lana had explained, been wary of their chosen location, but she had assured him she would know if the mountain was about remind them all it still lived. And he trusted that. For he trusted her, as he had trusted no one in his life.

And they trusted him. Were the positions reversed, he thought he would have been much more hesitant than the Raider to give him such freedom, the freedom to wander at will, provided he kept out of sight from below. But then, the Raider had a weapon no one in the Coalition could even conceive of. Lana, who could wipe his mind, his very self, as she had with Jakel.

It would succeed where Halfhead failed, Caze, were I to ever have to do that to you. It would destroy me.

He shivered at the memory, and vowed anew that she would never face that task. Not that it truly took a vow; he had been seduced, utterly captured by this place and these people. And the joy he found every day in the simplest of things hammered the lesson home until he knew he could never, ever go back, for it would destroy him in turn.

He heard a light, warbling sound that made him smile. He looked around just in time to see the pale-gray bird in the moment before it landed upon his shoulder. He had been surprised when Eirlys had asked him to let her train one of her creatures to come to him, but she had said simply, "It might be necessary some day."

He spoke quietly to the messenger as he removed the curled paper from the tiny tube fastened to its leg. It was an invitation, and one he would not refuse. He sent the bird back with a single word written on the back of the original message. *Yes.*

He thought he was familiar enough with the mountain now to make his way directly rather than go back to his starting point and begin anew. But there were parts that were a scramble, though he did not mind. Instead he took more joy from the fact that he could do it without pain or fear. It took more focus than just meandering, but he found himself enjoying that, too, the calculations of the best approach to a climb. He nearly slipped once, and sent a cascade of rocks downslope. He turned to see where he had misjudged, just as one of the tumbling rocks hit another and exploded into fragments. He—

He stopped dead. As often happened for him, as he was focused on something else, another problem came together. He thought of the weight of that Lustros-born device in his hand, of what it did. How applying a flash of fire to that combination of planium and what he now knew as quisalt had generated a power that was explosive in any larger quantity than the small coils that had powered the hand weapon.

We'll end up bombing our own compound. . . .

The words continued to nag at him as he made the rest of the journey. He was still turning the idea that had come to him over in his mind when he arrived at the unexpectedly beautiful spot near a pool of clear, deep water, the source of the supply that drained down into the main cavern. What he saw there took his breath away, and he stopped before they saw him.

He looked at the tableau for a long, silent moment. Savoring it. He did not think he would ever get used to it, this kind of belonging. He'd always been taught—had had hammered into him—that the Coalition was the only group that mattered. That it was all you needed. That personal connections were not just unnecessary, they were detrimental; they were limitations. Bonds that held you back, and thanks to the glory of the Coalition you didn't need them.

But now he knew the truth. He needed those bonds, the kind these people had offered him. They were not limitations, they were freeing.

You can soar higher and freer if you know where home is, and that you'll always be welcome—and loved—there.

Lana's words rang in his mind, words spoken when he lay drained and content in her arms. She had taught him most of what he now knew about that word scorned by the Coalition. But a different kind of love had been not just demonstrated but given to him, freely, by others. In particular the two who had just spotted him.

The twins leapt to their feet, and he saw another thing he knew he would never get used to, never take for granted: their simple joy at the sight of him. They ran, and he braced himself for the impact. They leaped, hit him simultaneously, and he swept an arm around each of them to hold them steady.

"We have—"

"Been waiting—"

"For you."

It welled up in him anew, that strange feeling Lana had had to name for him. *Love for your children is different. It is consuming, yet more joyous than nearly anything we are capable of.*

He had stared at her, caught by that one word more than any other. And she had laughed, that glorious, silvery sound that stroked that deeply hidden place inside him that only she had ever reached.

Oh, yes, they are yours, Caze. They were the first, after all, to stake their claim on you.

He looked up then, feeling her gaze on him. She was smiling with such pleasure as she watched them that for a moment he doubted he could contain the sensation inside him. In the beginning he had been unable to quite believe this wasn't an illness of some kind; now he knew it was instead a growing, an expansion, an unfurling of things so long crippled.

And more, the others, Eirlys, Brander, Kye, even Drake were looking at him with open welcome, smiling as well as he made his way toward them with his double burden that was not a burden at all. They had more than accepted him, they had welcomed him, and once their decision was made, they did not stint.

Even young Kade, who sat now with Brander and Eirlys, who had taken him into their keeping, seemed to have forgiven him, although he suspected it was as much because Brander had told him he'd designed the rover than anything else. And he and Grim, who stood a few feet away, had reached an accord, once he understood the man's true place in Lana's heart, and hers in his.

You have made my lady whole again. For that alone you would have my gratitude and my service, but you also have my respect, Caze Paledan.

He approached the group of them now, drawing in a deep breath.

"A moment," he murmured to the twins. "I must talk to your brother."

Drake, who was closest, seemed to hear, for he looked up. Their eyes met, and he rose. The twins released him, although they promised they had much to show him today.

"You needed to speak to me?" Drake asked.

He hesitated. He wished he would never have to disrupt this kind of gathering, for it was all new and precious to him. But they were still at war, and sometimes . . .

Reluctantly, he said, "I need to speak to the Raider."

THEY GATHERED IN Brander's workshop, in the corner of the cave they used to house the rovers.

"What exactly are you proposing?" Brander asked.

"The Coalition does nothing quickly," Caze began.

"Except condemn its own," Kye said dryly.

Caze looked at the woman who held both the heart of the Raider and the most incredible skill in her slender hands.

Your work is extraordinary,

It must be, since it brought you to us.

He smiled, as much for the recalled exchange as the truth of her words. "Contention valid." He turned back to the matter at hand. "You already know the planium is shipped out monthly, aboard a cargo vessel."

"Just as we know the cost to the miners if the quota is not reached." Eirlys this time, and he had no counter. For it was true, the standing order was that since they had to keep the miners alive, it was their families who would be punished if they, in the Coalition's opinion, slacked in their production. "However," she added, in a quieter tone, "we also know that since your arrival, that cost has not been collected."

"I merely instituted a different time period for the quota."

"Giving the miners time to make up any shortfall before their mates or children were harmed," Drake said.

He shrugged, but he met Drake's steady gaze. "I often wondered why you never attempted a full-scale liberation of the miners."

Drake lifted an eyebrow. "And now?"

"Now I know why. They were willing to stay in Coalition hands, to keep the rest of their people alive."

He felt rather than saw Lana smile. Drake nodded slowly. "You have learned much. We gave them the choice. We could—and would have—rescued them all, and damn the consequences, but they chose to stay. Until the balance tipped."

"And the Coalition found their own way to work the mines."

"Yes."

"It might please you to know," Caze said with an upward quirk of one corner of his mouth, "that they are not even close, despite all their resources, to finding a way to see through your bedamned mist."

Drake grinned.

"The matter at hand?" Brander suggested, using the very phrase Caze had thought moments ago.

"Yes. The planium is loaded aboard the cargo ship, then scanned for any anomalies or devices with the ship's detectors. Then it is taken directly to a production plant on the quadrant station."

"Where their High Command is stationed?" Drake asked.

"Yes. Currently in the next sector."

"Too bedamned close," Kye muttered.

"Agreed," Caze said.

"Is that production plant big enough to process it all as it arrives?"

Caze turned back to Brander, smiling inwardly as the man arrived at what would have been exactly his own first question. Caze recognized the tone that said his agile mind was already darting through the possibilities.

"No. So it is held in a storeroom until needed, locked and guarded at all times."

"Where is this storeroom?" Brander asked.

Caze looked at the man whose mind was so like his own, and held his gaze steadily. "It is," he said, "precisely seven feet from the power core of the station."

Brander's eyes widened. Caze could almost see his mind racing now. And saw the moment when Brander arrived at the same possibility he had reached.

"That," Brander said in an admiring tone, "is utterly insane. I'm proud of you."

Caze grinned, and heard Lana laugh. She had told him how delighted she was that they had grown to be the friends they always could have been, had Caze's uniform not been between them.

Then the questions came rapid fire.

"How much does the room hold?"

"It varies, but there is always a reserve of ten tons."

"Inspected again?"

"Only visually, after the scan aboard ship."

"Held, or rotated through?"

"Rotated through, replaced with the new shipments."

"How long?"

"Minimum two weeks, maximum three months, average six weeks."

"Who moves it?"

Caze had the wild thought that if his twin had survived, what they could have had might feel like this. And it mattered to him, greatly. Not only Brander's razor-sharp mind, but how all the others fell silent and let him run. They truly knew what they had in this man. This man who would no doubt have been crushed by the Coalition for his out-of-the-ordinary thinking. As they had tried to crush him. And had succeeded, until he was freed by the flame-haired woman who stood silently watching.

And finally he gave the answer that would nail it down. "Troopers who would not know raw planium if it fell upon them."

And suddenly Brander was grinning back at him. "Holy Eos."

"Pardon me for not keeping up, but what are you two thinking?" Drake asked, sounding a little wary.

"You tell him," Brander said. "It's your idea."

"But he trusts you."

"If I did not trust you as well, you would not be here," Drake pointed out.

Caze drew in a deep breath. Then he turned to face the man who had bedeviled the Coalition for so long. "That rather than a long, slow sabotage that is tantamount to suicide, you commit to striking a blow that could change everything. In this quadrant at least. A blow for your freedom."

Something glinted in Drake's eyes, and Caze knew it was the spirit of the

Raider, rising to the idea of not just harrying or annoying, but truly striking back.

"Explain. In detail," the Raider ordered.

And Caze counted it a personal triumph that he felt not the slightest qualm as he committed what would, if it worked, be counted as the worst treason the Coalition had ever seen.

Chapter 62

"IS IT POSSIBLE?" Caze asked.

Brander looked at Iolana with a lifted brow. "I don't know how long I could hold an illusion of such size," she answered. "I am stronger than I was, but this is rather immense in scope."

"Stronger?" Brander asked.

She felt herself color, and flicked a glance at Caze. He glanced at her in the same instant, and she saw a small, intimate smile curve the corners of his mouth.

"Ah," Brander said, as if in complete understanding. They both looked at him and he half shrugged, half grinned. "Eirlys has the same effect on my imagination." Then, with another grin at Caze, he added, "Despite the fact that you have apparently gone insane."

"So it is not—"

"Hold, there, I did not mean it couldn't be done, just that I can't see exactly how."

"Yet?" Caze suggested.

Brander's widening grin showed just how well these two had come to know each other in the weeks Caze had been here. "Exactly."

It was later, as they walked down the path from Brander's workshop to her quarters that she reached up and cupped his face in her hands. "You are as remarkable as I always thought you were, Caze Paledan."

For a moment he was silent. Then she saw him swallow and he said, quietly, "And you are even more remarkable than I knew you were when I first saw your image. And all the times after that when, before I knew what the feeling was, I mourned that you were dead and I had never known you."

They were alone on the path, but she would not have cared if every Sentinel was watching. She leaned up and kissed him. She meant it only as thanks for what he had said but it quickly deepened, and the flame that was ever only banked roared to life.

And then he pulled back, at the same time grasping her shoulders. He looked down at her intently. "I know it is important, this pledging of your people."

"It is the foundation of Ziem life," she said, tilting her head to look at him curiously.

"I have no knowledge of the tradition except from what I have read, and now observed with your son and daughter and their mates. It is . . . enviable. And daunting."

She smiled at him. "Exactly as it should be, and not to be taken lightly."

"Until death never is, is it? And is that not what the pledge is?"

"Yes." When he didn't go on, she said his name softly. "Caze?"

He hesitated, and in this man, that told her much about the import of his next words. "Could you . . . have you forgiven me that much? Enough to trust me with your life?"

Her heart raced in her chest. She didn't doubt he understood what he was asking; he was too intelligent not to know. "You wish to . . . pledge with me? Do not feel that is necessary, Caze."

"I wish you to be certain of . . . me. How I've changed. How my life was nothing before you, and everything now. And this tradition is the best way I can think of to show you. For I know what it means to you."

For a moment she just stared up at him, marveling at how the stern, tough major had become . . . almost a poet. "You have come a very, very long way, my heart."

"How could I not, with such a blazing torch to light my way?"

Yes, his words were poetry to her ears.

THE MAN WAS tireless, Caze thought. Yet again the Sentinels had embarked on a raid. It was part of the plan, and Drake had set the schedule himself, but it was still an exhausting pace. Today there were three groups plus the rovers, hitting four different places, all chosen by himself for maximum effect, distraction, and irritation.

Brander, after several days—plus some singed hair and a few burn blisters that had required Lana's skills—had determined the exact ratio needed of planium to quisalt. And then a week ago he'd left, dressed in rough, miner's garb to join the group that had not hesitated an instant when presented with the plan.

His mind flitted from that to that moment when the twins had turned up with a large bundle that turned out to be two stolen Coalition uniforms, that of a sergeant and an ordinary trooper. He had been torn between amazement and terror at what they had risked.

How have you not locked them up since they could walk?

He had asked Drake that with all sincerity, and been rewarded with a wry smile.

Do not think it did not come to mind. But I have learned they will ever do their part, and so it is best to give them their task.

Rather than have them choose their own? Eos forefend.

I am glad to have you to share that particular worry.

Drake's words had been the spoken acknowledgment of his place with them, and Caze knew he would remember them forever.

But now, now it was all down to timing, Caze thought as he paced the floor of the Raider's map room. He went over it again in his head. They'd prioritized everything, worked down from the maximum they could hope for to the minimum that must be done. They were only at the beginning now. He was wound up to a pitch unlike anything he'd ever known even in the heat of battle. For never had more depended on this working. This was no striving for a tactical victory, with more Coalition glory the by-product. This was for his heart and soul.

For his redemption.

The rest of his life depended on this working. For only if this succeeded would he feel he had atoned, at least somewhat. Only then would he feel he had proven himself worthy of their acceptance. Of the love they'd given him.

The only peace he found was in Lana's arms, in the quiet warmth of the home she'd created in this unlikely place, the shelter of a fiery, living mountain.

"It will work," she told him into the darkness one night nearly a month after they'd set everything in motion.

"You have Seen this?"

She sighed. "I cannot tell if it is Sight, or wishing."

When it began to happen, two days later, it all came quickly. Caze first heard the rumble of the big cargo ship as it made the turn toward the landing zone. With it, he knew, would come the High Command troops to guard the shipment; they no longer trusted the occupying contingent. In fact, Caze wondered if any of the men who had served under him had been left alive, after his betrayal. But he felt badly only for those who had had no choice.

Shortly after the ship had landed, Eirlys came into the map room with one of her birds nestled in her hands. She looked at her brother. "Brander says it is ready."

Drake nodded. "Good, for Kade has just sent word the convoy is on its way." He turned to Caze and his mother. "You are prepared?"

For a split second he could not speak, for there was an aspect to their preparations the Raider did not know, an aspect they had explored in great depth just last night.

I do not know quite how or why, but I take strength from our joining, Caze.

And you must be very strong, when the time comes.

Indeed, I must.

The look she had given him then, teasing, tempting, alluring had driven him mad in an instant.

I must do my duty, then.

As you ever have. Only now your only duty is to yourself.

And us.

"Yes," Lana answered for him, "we are . . . quite ready."

"Then we begin," said the Raider.

He and Lana changed quickly into the stolen uniforms. With her artist's hand, Kye used whatever she had at hand to change how they looked. She concentrated on Caze's face while Lana bound her hair—now, not to his liking, darkened to the muted brown he remembered from the bridge—up tightly.

"It's more likely you would be recognized, so I must be sure you look quite different," Kye said as she worked.

"I have some false scars you could borrow," the Raider said, almost teasingly. Caze glanced at the man who had so bedeviled the Coalition while wearing those scars.

"That," he said as he held the man's gaze, "is an honor I have not yet earned."

And suddenly he was Drake again, looking a bit taken aback. "I might argue that, had we the time."

"But we don't," Eirlys said.

Caze knew she was anxious, for once again her beloved creatures would be pressed into service, causing what disorder they could as the convoy made its way back to the ship with their precious cargo. It still amazed him how they did her bidding, but he and Brander had put it to good use; by the time the convoy arrived back at the landing zone they would be feeling mightily harassed by flocks of pecking birds, uneasy from the unearthly howls of creatures with oddly striped tails, and impatient after waiting for the passage of a herd of huge animals with deadly horns, who could toss a man with a flick of their head and would attack if one of them was hurt. With luck—which these Sentinels seemed to always have at their back—by the time the convoy finally reached its destination they would be off schedule and scrambling to make it up, and just careless enough to allow the next step.

Which would be he and Lana walking boldly up to the convoy, posing as part of the landing zone crew, which Drake and the other Sentinels would be busy distracting. Their disguises need only hold for a minute, long enough for Lana to begin. Her part was the biggest, the most crucial, but he had utter and complete faith in her. Be she the icon of Ziem or the Spirit of the Edge.

Or the woman he loved.

Drake and Kye flew them down to within reach of the zone. In the cover of a stand of mistbreakers, they got out of the rover. Kye gave Lana a swift fierce hug and then, to his surprise, gave him the same.

"You are ours now," she said simply.

He did not have time to pull his words together for a reply. Instead, he looked at the Raider, drew himself up, and gave the most heartfelt salute of his life to a leader who had earned it.

"What she said is true," the man he'd once fought answered. "And I do not care to lose any of my fighters . . . or my family."

And then they were gone. Lana looked at him as if she understood completely the wrenching effect of those simple declarations. As she no doubt did.

They made it to the edge of the landing zone and waited. It was not long before Lana said, "The flare is up!"

He couldn't help glancing, but saw nothing but the usual mist, no trace of the green many Ziemites could see. "Amazing," he muttered.

In the next moment he heard shouts and the rumble of engines as the troopers guarding the zone rushed to respond to the sudden, unexpected Sentinel attack. He heard someone yell, "It's the Raider!" and knew they would redouble their efforts. And at the yell, the last of the troops at the zone spun around, and as he'd hoped, were unable to resist joining this unforeseen chance to take down the man the Coalition wanted most.

"Now," he whispered, and started toward the zone. Lana followed him a half pace behind, like any good trooper behind a superior.

The crew of the ship was coming down the gangway as they reached the bottom of it. The convoy was yet a few yards away. Caze could tell by their slightly broken ranks that they had indeed been harassed on the way down from the mines; he could hear the mutterings even from here.

The ship's crew seemed torn, sensing something amiss with the convoy they'd been awaiting, but curious about the two unfamilars at the bottom of the gangway.

Just a little further.

Caze pulled out his handheld device. It no longer accessed the Coalition system, since it would send a signature they would no doubt be looking for, but the men above didn't know that. He pretended to study the screen as if he were simply the sergeant in charge awaiting an expected delivery.

Almost here . . .

He sensed rather than saw Lana move, her slender hand reaching for the pouch at her belt and removing the stone.

"The second line should do it," she whispered so that only he could hear.

He did not ask if she was certain she could hold it that widely. She knew what was at stake, and she would not attempt what she was not sure of. But he knew also, because she had explained carefully, that for this to work, the men above had to be on the ground. Their feet must be on Ziem herself, for the Stone of Ziem to hold them.

When the advancing convoy was mere steps away from that line that marked the ship's space, he barked out a command to the men above, putting every bit of command presence Major Paledan had ever had into it.

"They're late! Get down here so we can hasten the loading and get back on schedule, or we'll all pay the price!"

The last booted foot hit the ground in the same moment the convoy crossed the line. Lana instantly put her other hand over the stone. He swore he could feel the sudden burst of energy radiating out from it, could almost hear the hum Ziemites could hear.

Every man of the crew and convoy froze in place, with blank expressions. Lana moved slightly, and closed her eyes. Nothing changed to his own eyes except he could now see a slight shimmering in the air around them and the ship. But he knew that if anyone looked from outside the circle she cast they would see only what had been there all morning; a Coalition cargo ship, quietly waiting.

Caze raised his arm and gave the sign. And mere seconds later more Sentinels came out of the trees at the edge of the landing zone. They ran, even Grim, and there was no hesitation in any of them. Even the one he knew as Teal Harkin, whose brother had died in the ambush, simply did as planned, ignoring those representatives of his brother's killers and going for the cargo pallets that held the planium. Before they had even begun their task, Brander was there, still in his miner's garb, he and Kade lugging between them a large box.

He was loathe to leave Lana alone, but it was the plan. He ran up the gangway into the ship. It was one he had flown on before, and nothing had changed. He made the necessary entries; not for nothing had he overseen this process before. He finished just as Teal, Grim, and the others raised the load of planium up to the hold with the lift. They slid it into place as he directed. He set the scanners, directed them at the pallets, and set it to run.

For three full minutes they waited. He tried not to think of Lana having to hold this massive illusion. Told himself if she could hold the image of a towering cliff by the river, she could do this. And when the memory of exactly how she had lost the focus required to hold that image, of that day in the peaceful green glade when he had first learned what could truly be between a man and woman when it was real, swept through his mind he used it to steel himself, to bolster his strength.

It worked, for when the scan was at last done, showing nothing but what was truly there, a load of pure planium, he began to move quickly with the others, shifting with ease the heavy chunks of the softly gleaming metal. Then Brander and Kade were there, with the nearly identical-appearing, yet very different pieces, they slipped into each full crate, and covered back up with the normal product of the mines.

When it was done they secured the pallets as they had been. He signed off on the ship's scan logs, using the ID Lana called up to him, that she had drawn from the crewmaster's still-frozen mind.

They hastened down the gangway.

"Caze, I need you."

Lana's quiet words spun him around. He ran to her. Put his arms around her, as she had told him in their dry runs had helped. He felt a shiver go through her, but then she steadied. He knew what she was doing now, holding the men frozen and simultaneously planting the images in their minds, memories of what had never happened, memories of themselves doing exactly as they always did, loading and scanning their cargo. The stone was glowing now, and he feared she was pushing too hard.

But then she nodded, and they began to move back, toward the trees. He gestured to the others to go, while he stayed with her as she slowly backed up step by step. When they were at the edge of the trees, they stopped. He knew this was the hardest part for her, holding the illusion at this distance, but the timing was critical now. He reached for the flare gun at his waist. Readied it. Watched as the stone she held grew brighter, until he was certain it had to be burning her hands. He wanted to take it from her, but knew he could not.

"Now," she whispered at last.

He fired the flare. Before it had died away the Coalition troopers jolted awake. Within two seconds the Sentinel rovers roared overhead, dangerously low. The troopers looked up, distracted, too startled to fire.

And Lana collapsed. He swept her up into his arms and ran.

It was done.

Chapter 63

CAZE WONDERED which of these new emotions had destroyed his patience. There had been a time when he would have been able to wait with equanimity, no matter how long a certain action took to bear fruit. Now it had been but a short time since their effort at sabotage, but he was as edgy as if he were fighting blind.

But they were fighting. That, at least, helped.

"There," Caze said from their spot in the trees near the compound fence, "the vent above the turbine."

Brander nodded. He glanced at the man beside them. "Teal? Can you do it?"

"Watch me," Harkin said.

"There is a bend," Caze warned, "and the pipe narrows slightly after it, so your device can be no bigger than three units across."

"Might take two, then." He looked at Caze. "Any reason that wouldn't work?"

"Not as long as they are enough apart to clear the bend separately."

For a moment Harkin held his gaze, then nodded. "I can do that."

"Take care, Teal," Brander said. "Remember what happened to me when

I didn't get clear of that superheated glowmist."

The man flashed a smile. "Yes, but I'm better at this than you are at flying."

Speaking thus to a Coalition commander would get a man blasted on the spot, but Brander only laughed. "Contention valid," he said.

Caze watched the man vanish into the trees, headed for the target. They had reached an accord, he and Harkin, somewhat to his surprise.

I am sorry about your brother.

At least I had him for most of my life.

Harkin's gruff response had startled him, and he realized word had apparently spread about his own loss to Coalition cruelty.

Will I need to ever watch my back if you are present?

If your plan works, I will ever have your back, Paledan.

If my plan works I will take the life offered to me. The life I covet more than anything I have ever wanted. For I will feel as if in some small way I have atoned and have earned it.

He reined in his impatience again. Even if his plan did work, he had no control at all over when it would. All they knew for certain was if the maximum time Brander had calculated passed with no results, it had failed. And then . . .

He did not know what would happen, or what he would do then.

The mist was so thick that he—and the troopers casually guarding the power plant—could not see more than twenty feet. But Brander obviously could, and at some signal Caze could not see, he fired the flare from the weapon he drew from his belt.

"Green," he muttered as he tried to envision what those who had the knack could see.

"Very," Pryl, the old woodsman said cheerfully.

You're very accepting.

Because the Spirit wills it. But if you betray us I will slit your throat, and even you will never see me coming.

That I do not doubt, sir.

The old man had smiled at the respectful term. But Caze had said it without hesitation, for he had now seen the man at work often enough to know that much of the Sentinels' success had likely come because of his skills.

He heard the sound of weapons firing at a distance, as two of the Sentinel rovers—flown, he knew, by young Kade and the pilot Tuari—made a strafing run over the western guard tower, drawing attention away from the compound. Less than two minutes later he heard the explosion as Harkin's devices took out the main turbine of the power plant. And less than a minute after that, Harkin came silently out of the trees to rejoin them, looking immensely satisfied.

"That'll have 'em in the dark for a while."

The words were barely out before another, more distant explosion echoed through the mist.

"And out of touch," Brander said with obvious satisfaction, "because the Raider just took out the comm array."

As they drew back through the trees, Caze looked at the man who had made that possible. "You promised you would show me how you managed that, giving rovers that kind of altitude capacity."

"Maybe it's just magic," Brander said with a reckless grin.

Pryl gave a short, amused laugh. "Magic of your brain, maybe," he said, and Brander laughed in turn.

"Contention valid," Caze said.

Brander gave him a startled look. Then he jerked his head back to where they'd secreted their own rover. "Come on. I'll show you now. We've done enough for one day."

"Enough to keep them from looking too close at what they've carted back to their headquarters, anyway," Harkin said with satisfaction.

That they would continue raids had also been part of the plan, for it would not do to act any differently after that load of planium had left for High Command.

"You're risking a bit, coming with us," Harkin to Caze said as they reached the waiting craft he was piloting.

Caze shrugged.

"He's right," Brander put in. "They're hunting for you as hard as they hunt for the Raider."

"Harder," Pryl said. "I'm guessing you've truly hacked them off."

"I'm aiming for the highest price ever put on a Coalition head," he said lightly. Brander burst out laughing, which set the others off as well.

"If your plan works, you'll likely hit that target," Harkin said as he settled into the pilot's seat.

Pryl scrambled nimbly up behind him. Brander held back, and with a hand on his arm held Caze back as well.

"I am very, very glad we did not have to fight you," he said, too quietly for the others to hear.

"As am I," Caze said. Then, with the lighthearted feeling he was still not accustomed to, he added, "We'll keep it to the chaser table, shall we?"

They were both laughing as they boarded the rover and headed for home.

Home.

He had no words for the feeling that simple concept gave him.

"YOU MUST COME! Quickly!"

They turned to look at the twins, who had chorused the words and looked more excited than Iolana had ever seen them. Since they had the lookout tonight, her heart quickened. When the duo turned and raced back outside the cavern, they followed, and gradually the others in the main cavern realized and came as well.

"Look!" Two young hands pointed upward, to the east. "It's happening!"

Iolana's breath caught at the new, unusual star that hung in the heavens. An odd color, more orange than white. And even as they looked, it blossomed into a roiling orange cloud of burning gas. And she knew Caze's idea, and Brander's inventiveness, coming up with the triggers they'd buried in the altered planium, had worked.

If it works, the explosion and fire in the storage room will spread to the core of the station.

A second cloud exploded into the darkness, combined with the first. Together it grew, expanded until it was a small sun in the night sky above the Edge. And then, as Caze had predicted, the oxygen from the station was used up, and the glow vanished in the cold vastness of the space around it.

"It worked," Brander breathed beside her.

"Of course it did," Eirlys said with a grin at her mate.

"Of course," Drake agreed.

And then they all turned to look at Caze, who stood still watching where what had once been the seat of Coalition power in an entire quadrant had gone dead.

"Regrets?" Brander asked him quietly.

Caze snapped around to look at him, and then the others. "Not a bedamned one," he said, and the truth of it rang in his voice. And then he grinned at Brander and clapped him on the shoulder. And they laughed, a triumphant sound that buoyed her heart.

There would be much to do now, but it would all be handled. Right now, for this moment, the Sentinels of Ziem stood above the Edge, the home of the Spirit, and watched a sky that was theirs once more.

Chapter 64

"HOW DOES IT feel, my brother, to have a fleet of Coalition fighters and cargo ships at your command?" Brander asked Drake as they looked out at the landing zone, now empty of Coalition personnel, the last of whom had grabbed at the chance the Raider had given them to evacuate. Except for Sorkost, who had seemingly vanished. Caze suspected he'd been first aboard, likely in disguise to protect himself from any retribution either from the Sentinels or the Coalition.

"A little short of pilots," Drake admitted ruefully.

"We'll fix that," Kye said airily. "Kade's first in line for one of the fighters, and more will soon follow. We've got an expert"—she glanced at Caze with a grin—"charged with building our forces. We'll have a full contingent before long."

Caze looked at the Raider's mate. She was even more beautiful now, and he realized it was the absence of the strain she had lived with for so long, loving a man who led the most dangerous life of them all.

"We can only start where we stand," he said. "But this is enough to hold for now."

"And we'll have an actual fusion cannon!" Kade's excitement took his voice up a notch, to his obvious embarrassment.

"Well, not quite done with that yet," Brander cautioned.

"But you will be," Eirlys said with utter faith.

Brander also looked at Caze. "With help, yes."

"It will be done," Caze said easily. He saw Kade glance at him, and in the boy's gaze and shy smile, he saw acceptance. The success of his plan had changed many minds among the Ziemites. Drake had made it clear to all that they owed their freedom to two people above all, their beloved Spirit and . . . her chosen mate.

He had actually used the words, and Caze had been stunned at the power of them. Somewhere inside him he had made the decision that only success would earn him the right to their acceptance, and more importantly, the right to take that place at Lana's side. And the night that massive explosion had destroyed the Coalition's capabilities in this entire quadrant he had at last felt he could believe in their welcome. Ziemites were a very unusual people.

I feel more than welcomed. I am honored.

They were the only words he'd been able to get out the day they had all voted to offer him citizenship. And they'd been true; all the honors he'd received in his career meant nothing compared to this. It had caught him off guard, and he'd known what he was feeling was showing in his face. He did not care, for they had earned his honest feelings. He was still learning, was still at times startled, and sometimes wearied by the onslaught of the emotion Lana had given him, but in their hours alone he knew the heights they found together were worth any price.

And tomorrow he would take his place beside the woman who had not only changed—and saved—his life, but had changed him at a deep, funda-mental level. He would pledge to her, and it would be a covenant he would keep unto death, for only through her had he learned what it truly meant to live.

They had stripped the equipment left behind of all Coalition connection. Brander had replaced all comms with their own, and removed any Coalition system that could trace them. And they were all now adorned with the new logo Kye had designed, with the curved, crossed sabers of Ziem. And even as he'd admired the design, Caze had suddenly realized she was now free to do what she had been born to do, create things such as the incredible portrait that he would treasure forever. And he had seen by the gleam in her eyes, so like her cousin's, that she could not wait to start.

"Oh, speaking of done, here," that cousin said, reaching into his jacket pocket and holding something out to Caze. He took what the man who had become his fast friend handed him and looked at it. It appeared to be a pair of the wraparound spectacles like those worn on Clarion to shade the eyes from the unforgiving glare. Of what use such would be on a world that saw so little of their sun, he was not sure.

"I . . . thank you?" he said, puzzled.

Brander grinned at him. "It didn't seem fair that we can see through the mist and you can't, so I made those."

Caze's eyes widened, and he slipped them on. They hugged his face closely, and suddenly even the farthest hangar sprang into focus. He nearly gaped. "This is how you see, all the time, through the mist?"

"Welcome to our world." Brander's grin widened.

"In all ways," Lana said from beside him. He instinctively reached out to her, and she took his hand as he thanked Brander.

"Will they—"

"Come back?"

The twins asked it anxiously, looking at the aircraft that had so recently belonged to the enemy. He pulled off the clever glasses to meet their gaze directly. "Perhaps, someday," he said honestly. "Although they will, I think, forever doubt the wisdom of using planium from here. But if they do return, by then we will be ready for them."

The twins immediately relaxed, and scampered off to find some mischief to get into. It forever amazed him that they believed in him so deeply. It made him more determined to never let them down than he'd ever been about anything in his life. Except for holding and loving the woman beside him now.

"With great love comes great responsibility," Lana said softly.

He only smiled. He no longer asked her if she was reading his mind, for he knew she was not. She simply understood him, better than anyone ever had.

"Are we ready?" she asked of the group, but aiming it at her eldest son.

"I just hope it works," Brander said with a grimace.

"It will," Eirlys said. "For has not the Spirit foreseen it?"

"And," Caze added, "it need only work once."

"There is that," Brander said with a steadier expression. "Just that one blast to the satellite, with the code you overwrote to send it on, and who knows, it might just make it."

"Are you all right that we might never know?" Kye asked her cousin.

Brander shrugged, then grinned. "It's a lot better than what we almost did, when we'd never have known if it worked or not."

"Indeed," Drake said, and it was heartfelt.

And so they went inside to the communications section of the former Coalition compound, where Brander and Caze had spent nearly a month rigging, re-rigging, tuning, focusing, and finally coming up with the code that they hoped, just once, in a single, short burst, would take over the entire string of Coalition satellites across the galaxy.

Once there, they had a final discussion on the content they were about to send. Drake seemed nervous, but they all knew it must be the Raider.

"Speak for your father," Caze said to him quietly. "Say what he cannot."

The two men simply looked at each other, the weight of the past a tangible thing in that moment. But Caze held his gaze, and after a moment Drake gave a nod that was as much salute as acknowledgment. Then he turned to step into the spotlight Brander had rigged, and Lana hugged Caze fiercely.

And so the Raider recorded a message to be blasted across the galaxy, in the hope that somehow it would reach those who had sent them precious help, help that had led to the ouster of the Coalition on Ziem.

And anyone else who needed hope as they had needed it.

Epilogue

Trios

THE SUN WAS JUST rising when a clatter outside woke them.

"Sorry!" came the call from the doorway. "But you're going to want to see this."

The man and woman in the bed sat up, smiling at each other, for it had been a glorious night. They each still bore faint marks on their skin, for their passion for each other had never ebbed in all these years.

"Today?" suggested the voice from the doorway.

Laughing, they rose and quickly dressed to follow their son's command.

In the room where he led them, they found others, including their son's bonded mate, next to her her father, the man who had once been the most famous skypirate in the galaxy, and his own mate who had once worn the enemy uniform.

And in the large chair sat a man with wisps of gray hair clinging to his skull, his skin weathered and wrinkled, but his eyes clear and bright.

"You all know of Ziem?" asked a man with a patch over one eye, souvenir of his own encounter with the Coalition.

"Where planium comes from," said Queen Shaylah with a nod.

"Yes." The man nodded at the son who had fetched his parents from their bed. The old man in the chair watched eagerly as the royal prince of Trios hit a button on the communications array before them.

A holoimage snapped to life before them. A man, tall, strong, with dark hair and clear, blue eyes looked into the holorecorder as if he could see whom he was speaking to. There was the ring of power, of presence in his voice when he began to speak, and it grew as he went on.

I am Drake Davorin of Ziem, the world that is the source of the planium used by the Coalition to build their ships and weapons. I am also the leader of the Sentinels, the force of Ziemites who just weeks ago successfully drove that Coalition off of our world and, for now at least, out of the quadrant. No longer will they use our resource against us, or anyone else. We will see to that.

We send this message for two reasons. One, to thank those who sent us hope, via a hologram and a brilliant plan for a device mimicking a fusion cannon that bought us the time to mount both a defense and an offense. To the people of Trios, in particular the inventor of the device, and a former skypirate and his Coalition officer—one of the best of which is now with us, I might add—we send our thanks, for it was your help that changed everything.

The second reason is to say to anyone who might see this while still entrapped by the Coalition evil, there is hope. They are not all powerful; they can be beaten. Fight on, in whatever way you can, for the thinner they are spread, the more vulnerable they become. We began just over four years ago with little more than worn-out hand weapons and ancient blades, and yet the Coalition is gone.

King Darian of Trios, you were right. It was not easy. There were deaths. But we did win. We no longer live under the bootheel of the Coalition, and those who died, died free so that their fellow Ziemites can now live free.

And it was worth it.

The image flickered out.

They all stared, transfixed.

"We picked it up just before dawn," Dax Silverbrake, skypirate turned Defense Minister for Trios said in an awed whisper. "As far as we can tell, it bounced off every Coalition satellite between here and there."

"That's some clever work," his mate, former Coalition major Califa Claxton said.

"As was yours, my old friend," the King of Trios said. He turned to face the old man in the chair, who was still watching the air where the image had been, his cheeks suspiciously wet.

"It's spreading," whispered Queen Shaylah, crouching down and putting her hands over the old man's thin ones. "And it's your doing."

"And in the end," said King Darian, forgoing protocol and kneeling before the old man who had earned even a king's deference, "they will lose, Paraclon. Because such evil cannot stand against good forever. Know that, as I know it. As we know it." He gestured at the spot where the unexpected holoimage had hovered. "As he knows it, and as others will come to know it.

They. Will. Lose."

And when the King of Trios straightened to his full height to look upon them all, it was with great satisfaction.

"I'd like to meet this one, someday," Dax said. "He looks like a true fighter."

"And leader," Califa added.

"I'd stand with him," Tark said, his arm around his mate, Rina.

"I would like to meet his inventor," said Paraclon, his voice stronger than it had been in months.

"Perhaps," Dare said with a slight smile, "that can be arranged, someday soon."

They departed to the great hall, to lift a morning toast to the people of Ziem, half a galaxy away. And the man who had once been a collared Coalition slave and was now a king, dared to believe that everything he'd said to his old friend was true.

The End

About the Author

"Some people call me a writer, some an author, some a novelist. I just say I'm a storyteller."

—Justine Dare Davis

Author of more than 60 books (she sold her first ten in less than two years), JUSTINE DARE DAVIS is a four-time winner of the coveted Romance Writers of America RITA Award, and has been inducted into the RWA Hall of Fame. Her books have appeared on national bestseller lists, including *USA Today*. She has been featured on CNN, as well as taught at several national and international conferences and at the UCLA writer's program.

After years of working in law enforcement, and more years doing both, Justine now writes full-time. She lives near beautiful Puget Sound in Washington State, peacefully coexisting with deer, bears, a tailless raccoon, a pair of bald eagles, and her beloved '67 Corvette roadster. When she's not writing, taking photographs, looking for music to blast in said roadster, or driving said roadster, she tends to her knitting. Literally.

Find out more at:
justinedavis.com
facebook.com/JustineDareDavis
Twitter: @Justine_D_Davis
Pinterest: pinterest.com/justineddavis/